THE CROWN OF NIGHTINGALE

THE CROWNED SERIES | BOOK ONE

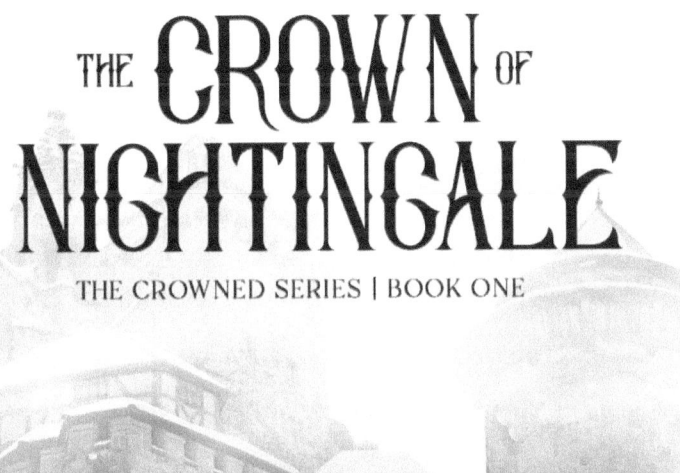

JOSEPH WOLFE

Dedications

To those few who waited a decade for this book to become what it is. And also Tammy, my dentist, who probably didn't believe me when I said I would mention her here.

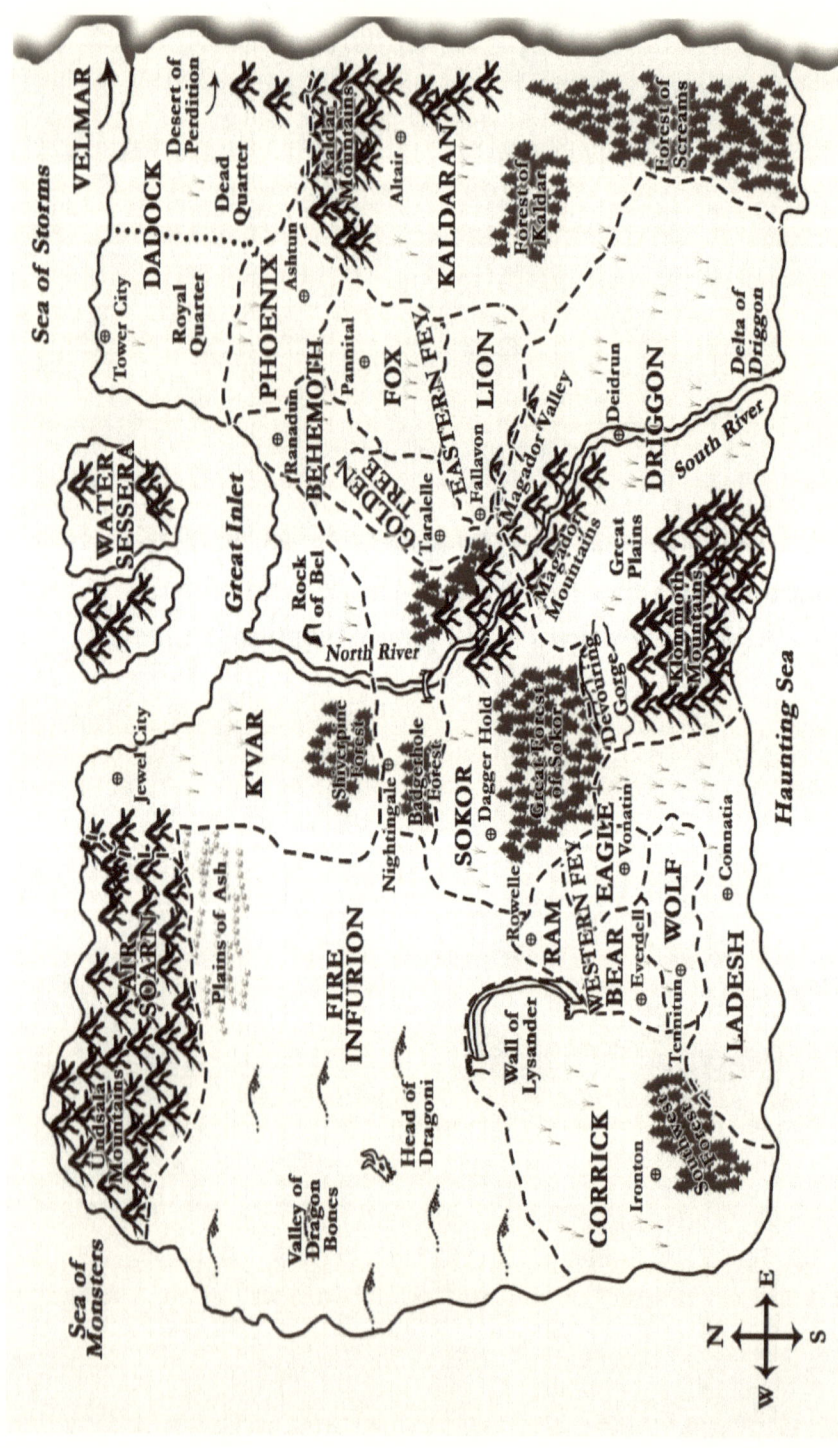

Chapter One

Donovan held back the flap to the fortune teller's tent. *Here goes nothing,* he thought as he stepped inside.

"You come seeking the future, child of Driggon?" the fortune teller asked him.

Donovan examined her head covering of thick purple cloth, patterned with golden colored thread. Each part of the pattern was a different god's symbol. Her fingernails hovered over her crystal ball, as long as arrowheads, and filed down just as sharp.

In the back of the tent, a bottle with burning incense rested on a small table. The smell made his nose itch.

"I'm no child of Driggon." Donovan's long, black hair, pale skin, and green eyes placed his ethnicity in there, but he had no loyalty to any kingdom nor god.

At least, none that he could remember.

The fortune teller's silver and black brows raised slightly, her tan skin wrinkling her forehead into three small lumps. She pointed to the cushion across from her. "Sit." When he was seated, she continued, "what is it that you seek? And what god *do* you answer to?"

Donovan studied her reactions closely. This was always where things went awry with soothsayers, no matter where he found them. This particular one moved into town a week ago, and she did not know him yet. "I want to remember my past and who I am. If any of the gods can do that for me, maybe I'll start believing in one."

The fortune teller suddenly scowled. "Soulburned!" she spat. "Don't waste my time, little rat! Get you gone! The wisdom of Sorsha is not for your kind!"

Donovan sighed then stood. "Thanks for your time."

"It's not free!" she all but screamed at him.

Donovan slowly turned his head to her. "My apologies," he growled as he reached into his cloak and pulled out a worthless wooden coin. "Here, this will help you as much as you've helped me." He dropped the coin into the pot on the way out.

"K'var curse you, son of Driggon! May she always be against you!"

"Add her to the list," Donovan mumbled as he stepped out of her tent.

Outside, the early evening streets of Nightingale were alive with merchant carriages, shopper foot traffic, and the cries of tradesmen and women hawking their wares. It was chaos. It was home. Donovan spotted a few city guardsmen down the road and pulled his hood up. *Bad enough I can't remember my past. One charlatan bullying me is enough for the day.*

Donovan checked the position of the sun, then started walking home at a fast clip. Ramon would probably want help with the shop, and if not, Martha would have something for him to do. It wasn't good for him to be out when they needed him, not since Lionel passed. The man he considered to be a father had left a tear in the fabric of life that could not be mended. The best Donovan could do was mend around the edges a little.

As he rounded a corner, two city guards stumbled out of a tavern, their white tabards with the purple bird in the center stained by the evening meal.

Bag of bones! Donovan cursed to himself as he turned in the other direction.

It didn't work. The guards spotted Donovan and quickly shuffled to block his path.

"Where are you going, soulburned?" one of the two said. He was clean cut as required by the guard, but his voice was rough, his manners rougher. The Guard wasn't all that picky about who they took in. As long as you followed the rules, were not a soulburned, and were not full-blooded fey, you could make a bit of gold there.

And you could push around anyone who wasn't in the Guard.

"Forgive me, but you are in my way," Donovan said in an even tone.

The other guard, shorter but stronger looking, shoved Donovan against the cobblestone wall. "Looks like you aren't going anywhere, so we can't be in your way. Makes sense?"

"Bastard," Donovan grunted.

That earned a punch to the gut, the cobblestone wall being an unwilling participant adding backstop to the blow.

Donovan groaned and braced himself, but the next punch didn't come. A sudden whistle from down the street saved him. He looked that way to see Officer Jillian, one of the leaders in the Guard, standing next to a vegetable cart with a lost wheel that was blocking the street. She waved for the men to help her.

"You lucked out this time, hollow man," the gruff-voiced one said. They took a second to toss him to the ground before moving on.

Donovan stood up slowly and brushed off the dirt the best he could. If it wasn't for Ramon and Martha, he might have left Nightingale after Lionel died, and gone to a place no one knew who he was. But the little past he knew was built in the small city, and that wasn't something he was willing to let go.

And without a past, how can I direct my future?

Donovan's head turned at the sound of a loud thud. Across the street, a stone carver used Technique, human magic. He sliced a large chunk out of a stone with just a small blade. Donovan stopped for a moment and listened closely as the craftsman muttered "*sunder.*" The blade in his hands glowed a bright orange before he ran it through the stone like a knife through lard, another thud following. *Imagine using that for something so mundane. Doesn't he know how powerful it is? How dangerous it is?*

Not all humans could use Technique. Donovan was one of them. He had burned himself out on it, sending his soul into a spell, erasing his memory and severing his connection to magic. In spite of that, he wished he could use it again. A skilled Technique user wasn't someone to be pushed around. *If only...*

"Donovan!" a familiar voice called out. Just a little bit down the road, Farmer Crandell walked next to a horse-drawn cart and waved at him far too enthusiastically. He was a good man, but a little overly optimistic for Donovan's taste.

"Crandell, always a pleasure," Donovan said, stifling a groan. "How's the farm?"

Crandell was short and stocky, nearly bald on the top of his round head, and full in the cheeks. Farming had treated him well. He walked up to Donovan then tugged on the reins for his horse and cart to stop. "Better since your help last week. I couldn't have made those repairs to the barn without you."

"Don't mention it," Donovan said, which was code for "please mention it, a lot; my reputation needs all the help it can get."

"I brought something for you, thought you could make some money off of it." The Farmer turned to his wagon and started working at a knot holding down a blanket and a bundle.

Donovan raised an eyebrow. Farmer Crandell wasn't poor, so to speak, but he had seven children and did not have extra gold to go around. Donovan had volunteered to do the work on the barn because Crandell always put in a good word with other farmers, and when the fur trading business was slow, Donovan worked as a hired hand on the farms. *I can't take his coin. That just wouldn't be right.*

The farmer scattered long sections of rope as he finished undoing the knot, then took the blanket off. There rested the carcass of a female stone lion.

Donovan grimaced and wrinkled his nose as the musky smell wafted over him. "You shouldn't have."

"Nonsense! One of my traps caught her trying to get to my cows. The meat's too gamey and stringy for most—but the fur is good."

The two paused and looked at each other, then the farmer waved his hands to indicate the stone lion. "Well, aren't ya going to take her?"

"Drag it through town?" Donovan asked.

The farmer pulled on a rope he had bundled the animal in and she flopped off the back end of the wagon. "Why not? You don't have far to go, do you?"

Donovan realized he couldn't say no without offending the kind-hearted man. That was bad for business and just felt far too mean. "Alright. Thanks, Crandell."

The farmer smiled and jumped up to the front of the cart. He grabbed hold of the reins and waved. "I know people don't think much of you, Donovan, but you're a good man. That's all that matters to me."

Donovan smiled a little, waved goodbye, and the farmer was off. It was just Donovan and his new, less-lively friend now. He grabbed the rope and dragged the heavy carcass.

It's worth a few coins. And gamey meat is better than starving. Donovan kept telling himself similar things so the load wouldn't feel so heavy, and he wouldn't feel so stupid for taking it.

A few minutes later, he turned onto Half-Street. Now it was a straight shot to his shop. He had only to survive what he called "the gauntlet."

First up, Linda the soap-maker.

"Donovan!" she called out. "You should try one of my specialty creations. It will get you clean for a change, maybe let the ladies see that distinguished jaw of yours free of dirt for once!" Donovan knew that the only difference between her specialties and her normal soaps was a bit of honey—and a much higher cost. Still, it sounded heavenly. Today was one of the days the Nightingale baths were open. *And for another hour or two,* he thought as he guessed the time. But on his last visit, everyone glared at him and his scar, a nasty thing that ran down his neck and toward his heart.

"Another time," he called back and continued on. Round one was over, but the gauntlet had much more to come. Round two: the women of the night. It was only another dozen paces before he saw the first one. She paid him no mind—this time. A strong-looking fellow had her attention. He was putting coins into her hand.

"Blasted mercs," Donovan muttered. "Curse them and their whoring and looting." He looked again and noticed the mercenary's forearm had a tattoo of K'var, who was supposed to be the Righteous Matron of War. K'var did not allow prostitution, nor did she care for men. *They call me the god-hater, but at least I don't claim to serve one and do the opposite. That is the greatest form of hatred I can imagine.* He looked up in the direction of the Chapel of K'var, its tall tower visible from nearly anywhere in the city. The Kingdom of K'var, named after the goddess, owned Nightingale. They routinely took hefty tribute in exchange for "protection." Donovan spat, and immediately realized he was about to enter round three of the gauntlet.

"Eh, you!" a clearly drunk man, Dadockian by the look of his big sailor forearms, lumbered over to Donovan a few paces. "You want to apologize for that?"

Donovan recoiled from his foul breath. "Wasn't directed at you."

"You think I'm some kind of idiot?!"

Yes, Donovan thought. "No," he forced himself to say. He was looking to see where the inevitable punch would come from when the man's eyes caught the lioness he was dragging. He laughed, his mouth opening to reveal teeth the color of old butter.

The foul smell has layers, many, many layers, Donovan thought as he pulled his head back as far as he could go without taking a step.

"That your pet? Not looking so good, is he!" the drunken sailor asked.

"Just taking a little nap."

"You hear that, boys?" the drunkard spun around, and Donovan realized he was not alone. Three more men, also Dadockian, sat outside with their drinks, keeping a careful eye on the situation. They glared at Donovan.

This could actually be bad. I wonder if Ramon is heading this way by chance.

The drunkard spun back around, nearly tripped on himself, and grabbed on to Donovan's shoulder for support. "Your poor pet, he's speaking to me."

"Sounds like a spiritual experience."

"He's saying that you're a wee little man who wets the bed at night. What do you think of that?"

Donovan shrugged. "Well, don't listen to him. He's *lion*."

The drunkard's face turned to stone for a second, then split open in the loudest, smelliest laugh Donovan had ever...experienced. He waved for Donovan to come over and join them at their table.

"I will be right back, gotta make sure my pal here is taken care of," he said, and continued on down the street. None of them pursued.

That was close. The City Guard didn't allow drunken brawling in the streets, but they were pretty slow to respond sometimes, especially when he was involved.

Donovan took one last look to make sure he was safe, then exhaled a sigh of relief. "Gauntlet complete."

"I didn't know you made gauntlets."

Donovan turned to the speaker, then smiled. "Alexis!" he said a little loudly, then immediately felt embarrassed. "I mean, it is good to see you."

She smiled back and gave him a quick hug. Her long brown hair brushed past his nose; the scent of vanilla filled his lungs.

"I hope none of my men are giving you trouble."

"No, of course not; don't be ridiculous."

Alexis raised her chin. "Names, now. I will have them all do a hundred laps around the barracks, in full gear."

"Everything is fine," he said, trying to keep his tone believable. She didn't look convinced. "Just drop it, please. If you get involved, it will only get worse."

She frowned. "We will see about that."

"I'm alright. Just leave it alone."

She sighed and shook her head. "Other than problems with my men, how have you been? What's with the dead animal?"

"Well, I *am* a fur hunter."

"Yes, but usually you have a litter for it, or something besides dragging it along the streets. The guards could technically fine you for that."

"And I'm sure they would, but this wasn't planned. One of the farmers just gave it to me."

"Oh good, I'm glad to hear you're making nice with them. Remember what happened when you first arrived?"

Donovan's lips tightened. "I thought we agreed not to speak of the Thirsty Horse incident."

"You just mentioned it, not me!"

"Alexis, please."

She laughed, the brightness in her smile made his stomach jump. He had no memory of ever loving anyone, but Alexis made him feel happy. He wanted more of that feeling.

"I'm just teasing you, Donovan! How about you come get a drink with me? I'll buy first round."

Donovan felt his face flush. "I can't. I promised Ramon and Martha I would bring them dinner and…well…I think this is it." He indicated the stone lion.

"Ugh, my condolences to your taste. How about tomorrow night?"

Donovan wanted nothing more than to say yes, but he worried what their friendship was doing to her reputation. Rumor had it, she was passed up for being Captain of the Guard because of her "strange connections" in town. Donovan knew that was him.

"Alexis, I don't want to cause you trouble. You know how it is around here for me."

Alexis crossed her arms. "I do. And I don't care. The Thirsty Horse, tomorrow at sundown."

Donovan smiled. "I will be there."

Chapter Two

The aged, stout, wooden sign for "Lion's Paw Furs" hung steady in the windless evening. Donovan dragged the stone lion up the wooden steps, then opened the door with one hand while hanging onto the rope with the other. He held the door open with his foot and made it halfway inside when he could no longer hold the door and it shut, getting the stone lion stuck halfway.

Sitting there at the front desk, faithfully waiting for customers, was Donovan's friend and business partner, Ramon, a strong man with skin the color of brown leather and black hair that marked him as being from Corrick.

"I would say look what the cat dragged in, but…" Ramon eyed the stone lion up and down. "This situation has me all kinds of confused."

"It was a gift from one of the farmers. We can sell it."

"Not as-is."

Donovan tugged at the dead animal a little more, but to no avail. "Obviously. Help me with this damn thing, would you?"

Ramon grinned and ran over, holding the door open and giving the beast a shove with his foot. Once it was clear of the door, he jumped in to help carry it the rest of the way. They set it down on a weathered table in the back room, ready to be worked.

"Where were you today anyway?" Ramon asked.

"Just…you know, out shopping."

"You hate shopping. Must have been something important. What did you buy? I'd like to see it."

Lying was not going to deter Ramon's questions. "Fine, I wasn't shopping. I went to a fortune teller."

"Another one?" Ramon sighed. "I wish you wouldn't waste your coin on those charlatans, Donovan."

"Joke's on her, I gave her a fey coin."

"That's the other thing! You wouldn't make so many enemies around here if you knocked it off with that kind of behavior. You think that fortune teller is just going to keep quiet about you stiffing her?"

Donovan paused. "She said there was nothing she could do," he said in a low voice.

Ramon scratched his black beard. "Sorry to hear that."

Donovan knew how angry he could get when it came to being a soulburned. *Ramon is right. I'm just proving what bad people think about me when I do things like that.* He grabbed his skinning knife from the wall and started in on the lion pelt. "I'll go back and pay her properly tomorrow."

"You don't need to do that, Donovan," Ramon said. "What's done is done, and if there's any consequences to our business, we will deal with it.'

"Any other bad news while we're at it?"

Ramon sighed. "You're going to hear talk about it at some point. Oliver is gone."

Donovan dropped the skinning knife to the floor, the point stuck into the wood a handsbreadth from his foot. "What?"

"You asked if there was any other bad news."

"I was kidding; are you?"

Ramon shook his head. "Wish I was. They found him in a noose he made himself."

Oliver was a mercenary. Pretty run-of-the-mill man, as far as Nightingalens were concerned. But one day he returned and...didn't return. He and a few others were hired to capture or kill bandits causing trouble on the farms. Oliver got trapped by two of them and unleashed a *Sunder* spell that turned a iron rod into a blade sharp enough to cut clean through a thick stone. He sliced through both bandits and survived. It was impressive. It had also soulburned him.

The other mercs saw it and told everyone the tale. Oliver had no idea what happened.

"That's awful," Donovan said, then added, "Can you take care of this thing?"

Ramon seemed to understand Donovan wanted to change the subject. "If you want to watch the shop."

"No one else is coming tonight," Donovan grumbled. "All the taverns are filling up around this hour."

"Then you can start on closing it up if you like. Your call."

Donovan nodded, picked up the skinner from the floor and set it down on the work table for Ramon. Before he could move toward the front desk, Ramon stepped in his way.

"Donovan, I really am sorry about the fortune teller, and for Oliver. But I want you to know that Lionel always supported you, and so will I. And you know Martha will do the same. But…perhaps I could make a suggestion."

"Ramon please just…" Donovan started, but a thought came to mind. *What kind of man am I if I ask strangers like fortune tellers for help and turn away the help of a friend?* "Go ahead."

"It's been over three years since your soulburn. If there is an answer out there, I don't blame you for seeking it. But maybe, just maybe, you should stop focusing on the past and look to the kind of future you can make. And believe me, this same advice can apply to nearly everyone out there. You're not alone."

Donovan nodded slightly and Ramon moved out of his way. *He's right, and I know he's right. But he also doesn't know…how hollow I feel.*

Donovan busied himself with the usual end-of-day routine, but he left the front door unlocked just in case. Now wasn't the time to miss out on any business.

The shop was set up on the first floor of their house. All the skinning and curing were done in the back room, and there was an enclosure behind the attached stable where they kept all their tanning racks. The second floor housed the kitchen, bedrooms, washroom, and dining area. When Lionel the house, he bought the one next door so he could combine the two and have a spacious upstairs and build the stable next door.

Lionel and his now widow, Martha, found Donovan a few years ago, wandering into Nightingale with clothes in tatters and no memory of his life. That's what they told him, anyway. His early memories were foggy at best. They took him in and taught him the fur trade. He picked up on it quickly and their business thrived. Then Lionel passed away, and the shop struggled.

About half an hour later, Donovan was nearly done closing. The floors were swept, the door locked, the furs checked for moths and other bugs. The only thing remaining was a stuck window that sat partially open all day. The nights were getting cold and it was becoming a big problem. He worked it up and down then tried bringing it down closed with a little force. The window sash chose that moment to loosen up and the window slammed down, one of the divided panes of glass shattering with it.

"Are you serious," Donovan muttered.

"Solving one problem means time for the next one," Ramon said. He was standing in the doorway to the back now.

"One of the many Lionel-isms," Donovan said with a groan. "Why did he have to always be right all the blasted time?"

"Don't worry about it; I've got a few spare panes of glass that I picked up from the glass blower last time I went."

"You have spares?" Donovan asked as he walked toward Ramon and the back room.

"We break a lot of glass, and so will the winter weather when it hits. The glassblower gets busy. I'm nearly done with the stone lion, then I'll fix it."

"I owe you one."

"A few, in fact. I'm saving up for something big favor once I think of it."

A knock on the front door interrupted their conversation.

"I'll get this one," Donovan said. Ramon nodded and returned to the back.

Donovan opened the door to the shop and there stood Sebastian, a short, plump merchant from the Southern Kingdoms—Ladesh, Sokor, and Corrick. Sebastian was known for three things: his opulent carriage, the idols of the gods he sold, and being a complete pain in neck to deal with.

"I'm not interested in buying any garbage shaped into different garbage," Donovan said in a level tone.

"My good man, I'm not here to sell, but to buy!" the plump man said as he bumped his way inside. He stood in the center of the shop and tugged at his fine, purple silk coat. It had a fluffy, almost feathery, white lining puffing out along the fringe. "Is this all you have?"

Donovan crossed his arms. He was about to tell him to leave, but remembered what Ramon said about the way he acted towards people. "There's more in the back. What are you looking for?"

"Plain furs are rather barbaric, but they are warm." Sebastian scanned the room for a moment before his eyes locked onto something. "What about that one hanging over there?" He pointed a large index finger. The gold ring on it glittered and the large ruby inset on top sparkled in the candlelight.

Donovan stepped over to the coat Sebastian indicated and smoothed it out with his hands. *Salesman time.* "The hide of a Shiverpine bear, a very healthy adult male. Salt cured within a day after the kill, and tanned for six weeks. I expect it to be sold within the week, but I'll only charge you two gold coins for it."

Sebastian laughed, his belly jiggling with the motion. "I saw one of the same quality in Sokor several weeks ago, and the vendor there would have only charged me *one* gold for it."

Donovan turned up his chin. "I wasn't born yesterday, Sebastian."

"But as far as anyone is concerned, you might *as well* have been born three years ago, correct?"

Donovan's blood boiled. "I gave you my best price to start, so take it or leave it."

Sebastian took a step towards him. "Best price? Seems more like you are desperate for coin and trying to pass the cost on to me--and in my time of need in this bitter cold! If Lionel were here, he would never have done such a thing." Sebastian bounced a purse in his hand. "Lionel knew how to price things right. But I will overlook it if you sell this hide to me for one gold and three silvers."

"First you insult me, then you bring Lionel in to this?" Donovan pointed his finger at the fat man. "You're as hollow as the gods you sell! Go find a beer and a whore to keep yourself warm, but don't come crawling back to me when Madame Silva kicks your fat ass out and you're shivering like a pig locked out of the barn!"

Sebastian snorted and walked back out with what he considered dignity.

Ramon popped out from the back, a pane of glass in hand. "Improving your haggling skills, I see."

Donovan kept his eyes steady on the fat man as his carriage headed in the direction of the nearest whorehouse. "We do need the coin, but not that desperately. I just wish—"

"That Lionel was still here? I know, Donovan, me too. But if he was, I think he would have said the same things you did. We'll get two gold for that bear pelt easy, don't give it another thought."

Donovan sighed. "I just hate ending the day on a non-sale."

Ramon walked over to the broken window and started clearing the glass, then suddenly paused and craned his head. "You might still get that chance."

Donovan was about to ask why when the door to the shop opened. "Toby!" he almost shouted, reining himself in at the last second. Toby was a bit of a friend, not close but the two got along. And he was one of Donovan's best customers. "Good to see you! You need furs?"

Toby nodded. "That's what I was comin' for, if yer still open."

"For you? Of course! Come on in!" It was odd that Donovan got along so well with him, considering he was a mercenary, but Toby ran a tight crew and didn't contribute to the steady, moral decay of Nightingale. He also didn't seem to care that Donovan was soulburned. His short red hair, cut well, and trimmed beard spoke to a cleanliness and pride not found amongst the other mercs. Very ironic considering his Kaldaran lineage, but Donovan didn't judge people that way.

"How are ya this cold autumn day?" Toby asked. His voice was deep, his accent thick but clear.

"I've been better," Donovan replied, catching movement out of one of the windows. He peeked out of it to see Sebastian's carriage coming to a stop at end of the street in front of Madame Silva's. "I just dealt with some fool trying to undercut me on a bear pelt. Would you be interested in a fair price on it?"

"I'll take it, and also seven sets o' warm furs for me and me men."

Donovan's heart raced; this was exactly what the shop needed. "I can get you that at a great price. You came in at the right time, my inventory will shrink in a few weeks with the weather."

Ramon was focused on glazing the new windowpane, but he did look over at Toby with a polite wave.

"Full sets?" Donovan asked as he piled furs into his arms.

"Might as well, better to be prepared," Toby answered. "The bear pelt will be part of my set."

Donovan set a pile on the counter in the front before going to the back to fetch more. "Any reason for the stock-up, besides the coming cold?"

Toby picked up one of the furs and looked it over. "Well, there's somethin' about a large job comin' up that may require a lot o' time in the field, dontcha know? K'var might be puttin' an open contract out."

Now, that's interesting.

"Haven't had one of those in a while," Ramon chimed in.

"I was thinking the same thing," Donovan agreed. "Open contracts usually deal with a specific group. Is K'var declaring war on someone?"

"I've probably told ya more than I should've," Toby said as he set one fur down and picked up another. "Always good work, Donovan. This is why I come to you."

"I can't take all the credit," Donovan said, noting Ramon. As he reached for the last set of furs, an idea came to mind. *What if there's a better way than selling furs? A more bright future that helps the people of Nightingale?* Ramon was right. He had to stop focusing on the past. Or at least he had to try.

Donovan grabbed one final set of furs and set it on the table. Toby began counting them.

"Six...seven...I told ya seven, yes?" Toby looked confused as he held up the eighth set.

"I want you to count me in," Donovan said. "I want the work."

That got Ramon's attention. "Hang on there, Donovan, I need you here at the shop."

"You should listen to Ramon," Toby added. "I always keep my crew the same size. Seven is a good number."

"Keep it that way, then. Drop that Sokorian fellow who gave you a haircut the other day."

Toby reached for a spot on the side of his head. There was a scab there, mostly healed. "I already did get rid of him. Found someone much better with the bow, and a fellow Kaldaran as well."

"Fine, let's go to eight. The number of Corrick, yes? Supposed to be lucky?"

"Donovan," Ramon put in again, but Toby held up a hand to cut him off.

"Donovan, I have somethin' big coming' up. Somethin' no one in Nightingale knows about. I don't like it, but it's what I need to do for me and me people. Me crew is on board with me, and we have a circle of trust I cannot break. So even if I wanted to bring ya on, I couldn't break me oath. Understood?"

Donovan thought that was a little odd. Toby never talked like that before. *Whatever's about to happen must be something like we've never seen.*

"Besides," Toby added, "Yer not a merc. From what ya told me before, ya hate mercs."

"Not you, not your crew, and you know that. You've got the best reputation around here. We need coins now before the cold freezes us out of good hunting, and I'm a sharpshooter with a bow."

Toby shook his head. "I'm sorry, but no. Even if I hadn't made the oath I did, everyone knows ya hate the gods. Me and me men are religious. All of us. It wouldn't be a good fit. Besides, I need ya to hunt the good furs for me and me crew."

"I can deal with religious folk—what do you think I do here all day? And if I'm on your crew, I can get you the best deal on—"

"How much is me total?" Toby said quickly. He was done talking about this.

Donovan suppressed a sigh. *I suppose it wasn't my best idea anyway.* He ran his fingers through his long, black hair. "Seven sets of furs with the bear pelt will run you twelve gold. It's my best offer."

"I wasn't gonna argue with ya," Toby said as he reached for his coin purse.

Donovan felt foolish. Ramon was glaring at him, and for good reason. They had talked about bringing on a third hunter, or at least someone to mind the shop while they were away so Martha wouldn't have to do it. *And here I am talking about leaving Ramon to himself near the start of the busy season.*

Toby paid and left. Ramon said nothing, returning to the glass grazing, but Donovan knew he was still upset.

"Boys, dinner is ready," Martha's voice sounded from upstairs.

"Ramon, I--"

Ramon turned, heading for the stairs. "Food's getting cold."

Donovan's and Ramon's boots thudded on the wooden steps. The smell of freshly cooked meat filled the dining room, and the warmth from Martha's cookstove heated the upstairs in preparation for the temperature to drop in the evening. The dining room was about a third of the second floor, but Martha had taken up plenty of space with all of Lionel's things on the walls and a cabinet full of more. His two short swords were crossed and hung on the far wall, his halberd fixed on the longest wall, several shields hung here and there.

Lionel had a lot of weapons for someone who was a humble fur hunter. That had been the subject of more than one discussion. His answer had always been the same, "I'm a bit of a collector."

Of course, Donovan noted that Lionel's collection of weapons never seemed to grow.

Martha added the final touches to the meal, muttering aloud about her work. Her long, gray hair was tied up in a bun and she wore a gray linen apron, dirty with the evening meal's preparations.

"There you are, Donovan! How did things go with farmer Crandall?" she asked, her voice as warm as the cookstove.

Donovan automatically removed his cloak and hung it on the wall. "How did you know about that?"

"He came by asking about you earlier today. Also, Ramon told me when he brought up the meat from the stone lion."

Donovan looked over at the stew and frowned. "Well, if there's anyone who can make that meat taste good, it's you."

"True, and if there is anyone who shouldn't complain, it would be the person who brought us the meat to begin with."

Donovan smiled. "Fair enough." He walked over to the table and sat down.

Ramon brought a platter of vegetables from the kitchen and joined Donovan at the table. "I met someone claiming to be from Velmar today."

"Really?" Donovan asked. "Did you make sure to ignore him like everyone else who lives in Drannus would?"

Ramon helped himself to some vegetables. "Can't say I blame them. The guy was a horse's rump. He acted like we did everything backward, but when I asked him how he would do it better, he scoffed and said, 'my advice would be a waste on people like you'."

The sound of a wooden bowl clunking lightly on the table brought Donovan's eyes to the soup placed in front of him. "Thanks."

Martha sat down with a bowl of her own and scooped up vegetables to add to it. "I was hearing arguments earlier…"

"Sebastian," Donovan said.

Martha nodded. "Of course, and good job on that one. But after that?"

Ramon and Donovan exchanged a look. Donovan said nothing and took a spoonful of the stew. *Not half bad. Martha's magic works again.*

"If you don't tell her, I will," Ramon said.

"Tell her what?"

Ramon glared at him.

"Oh fine. One of the mercenaries says there's an open contract coming up, and I tried to join his crew."

Martha paused with her spoon in the air, mouth agape. "Donovan, that's not like you at all. What made you think to do that?"

"Ramon made a good point about looking toward the future."

Martha glared at Ramon.

He held out his hands. "I didn't tell him to become a mercenary!"

Marth turned her glare back to Donovan. "I don't understand, Donovan. You've always said you hate mercenaries."

"Sure, but they get respect around here. The good ones do. And nothing says I would have to participate in their…leisure activities."

"Those mercenaries are not as well respected as you think," Martha said. "And you get plenty of respect running an honest business."

"As much respect as a soulburned god-hater can get, right?" Donovan asked.

"That sounds like something the City Guard would say. Did they rough you up again?"

Donovan crossed his arms. "Just a little."

Martha looked concerned. She took a few more bites of stew before asking, "Is there anything else you want to be doing besides the fur trade and mercenary work?"

"How would I know?" Donovan mumbled.

Martha smiled at him, but her brow was wrinkled with sadness.

The rest of the meal was eaten with little more said. Martha cleaned up and Ramon leaned back in his chair.

"What do you plan on doing for the rest of the evening?" he asked. "If you want to go get drinks, the Thirsty Horse isn't too bad around this time. Plus, old man Doll said he owed me a free one for breaking up a fight there the other day."

"That's very kind of you, considering you used to start them."

Ramon grinned. "That's your job now. I have passed on the mantle."

Donovan chuckled. "I think I'll pass. I want to get up early and go hunt tomorrow. It's my turn, and Toby cleared out a good bit of our stock."

"I won't argue with that. Just promise you'll be careful."

Donovan raised an eyebrow. "*Ramon* asking *me* to be careful?"

"You heard what Toby said. Open contract. That means trouble, and we don't know from which direction."

"True, but if anywhere is safe, it's to the north, toward K'var. I will head that way and hunt in Shiverpine to play it safe, and with any luck, I can get us another bear."

Ramon nodded. "That's reasonable. I will let you get to bed then. Good night."

Donovan tossed and turned in his sleep. At least once a month, he would have a strange dream that showed him things he never remembered seeing.

In this dream, he was in a throne room. White light beamed onto a polished marble floor, filling the space with a heavenly brilliance. *Have I died in my sleep, and this is the afterlife?* It was not the first dream that gave him that impression.

He stood at the end of a long, red rug which led up to a throne. There sat a man whose eyes were made of fire, his beard of gold. His skin was like bronze and his tongue a single large ruby set by polished ivory teeth. The room's light emanated from him.

Men and women stood in a crescent formation in front of the king. They were adorned in full-plate armor that shone in his illumination, and on their backs were glowing, ethereal wings, like long ribbons, flowing in a not-felt breeze and swirling all around. They all wore crowns and glared at Donovan with eyes of burning anger. All except one, who had a proud smile. Donovan looked at that one—a man who looked like him. Black hair, green eyes. At his feet was a nameplate that read "Driggon."

Donovan looked at the others, numbering six in total. They all had name plates at their feet. Corrick, Ladesh, Sokor, Kaldaran, Dadock, Driggon…and K'var, whose nameplate had no one standing there.

"Missing one?" The voice from the throne thundered in Donovan's ears and echoed throughout the room.

"Where is K'var's champion?" Donovan asked.

The enthroned king shrugged. "You know the answer to that."

"I don't—I'm soulburned."

The king's bronze brows rose. "Oh. You've slept for a long time. I assumed you were tired, not soulburned."

Donovan took another look around and couldn't shake the feeling that if he took one step in the wrong direction, one of those crowned champions would reach out and kill him.

"They can't get to you here," the king said. "And don't trust Driggon. He's pleased with you but would also kill you if he had the chance."

"That sounds like people from Driggon," Donovan mumbled.

The king laughed, and the halls shook. "My champion! Full of whit and fire!"

"Champion?" Donovan asked. "You're mistaken. The only thing I've ever been champion of was darts at the Thirsty Horse. And Ramon regained his title the following night—the bastard."

The king only smiled now. "This won't do. I need you back soon, and at full strength."

Donovan eyed the king up and down. "I'm not sure I like the sound of that."

"You will, in time."

Donovan nodded slowly. "Assuming you are right, what should I do now?"

The king rose from his throne and reached out a hand toward Donovan. "Awaken!"

The words were still ringing in Donovan's ears when he came out of the dream. His head ached, and it took him a moment to realize he was lying on one of the boards of the bed. *Where the gol is my pillow?* He rubbed his eyes and forced his legs over the side so he would have to get up. He stood up on the pillow and groaned. "Found it."

After a moment to light a candle, he made the bed and changed into warm underclothes. He stepped outside and opened the pantry. Bread and cheese would do for the day. Once downstairs, he grabbed his real gear: furs, bow and quiver, trappings for making a tent if he had to spend the night in the woods, several knives, and plenty of rope.

Going through the side door, he stepped inside the stable. Chomper, Donovan's horse, turned his head and flicked his tail.

"Ready, boy?" Donovan asked. "We're hunting in Shiverpine today." Chomper rubbed his nose gently on Donovan's shoulder. He brought the horse out of the stall and put on the saddle, saddle bags, and bridle. He led Chomper by the reins, out the large stable door, and closed it behind him.

He produced a lock from one of the pouches and attached it with a firm click.

Donovan mounted and raised his head to the sky for just a moment. Cold rain pelted his face. He prodded Chomper onward, passing by Sebastian's carriage. "Well, well, he managed not to get kicked out of Madame Silva's, after all. I guess the two deserve each other."

Donovan rode through Nightingale and considered the dream he had. This one was not like any other, though he had the vague sensation that he had seen the man on the throne before in a different dream. He had always romanticized his past. In every story he read, he imagined himself as the hero, in his heart believing that it might be possible. He was always a little bit eager when a new traveler came to town, not just one of the regular merchantmen. He spent many nights at the Thirsty Horse, trying to get someone to recognize him, but no one ever knew him outside of his time in Nightingale.

Now he had this dream to deal with. Why did all these champions from other nations hate him? Why was K'var's champion missing entirely? Was it all the muddling of dream logic?

Or what if he had done something to deserve their hatred?

Donovan rode toward the northern City Gate, and for the first time in his memory, he wondered if he had once been a wicked man.

Chapter Three

The dream stuck with Donovan enough to sour his mood. It wasn't a bad dream; quite the opposite. He wanted more. *Is this dream a symbol of my past? The champion of a king? Was he a good king?* It bothered him. It bothered him more than a dream he once had, pressing his lips against Alexis's, swearing he could feel it. That one was pleasant at first, but the next time he saw her, he immediately felt guilty.

Donovan had not known Oliver very well, but they had a few conversations several months back. When Donovan asked the other soulburned what his dreams were like, the answer surprised him.

I don't think I dream at all.

Donovan approached the exit to Nightingale with little more than a glance from the City Guard. They didn't care who was leaving, as long they didn't have a cartload of goods. He passed by a fellow who was trying to get in and had what looked like his entire body weight in possessions strapped to his person. That was one of the loopholes in Nightingale—someone could avoid the tariff for anything on his person. People were only charged for what they brought in on beasts of burden and carts. That was the letter of the law, and the way people abused it sometimes ended in hilarious falls into the mud.

"Sir, we're not taxing your goods, but we can't let you in without searching and…" The guard's voice faded as Donovan prodded Chomper to pick up the pace.

"That must be boring," Donovan said to himself, then chuckled. "How does Alexis do it?"

The rolling hills of farmland which surrounded Nightingale stretched on for quite a distance. At the peak of some of the taller hills, Donovan saw the green of Shiverpine in the distance, lined between the brown, rocky, mountain-like hills which wove in and out of the forest. The sun was coming out for a bit, but there were heavier storm clouds moving in fast.

Donovan inhaled deeply and ushered in all the usual smells of the fields into his lungs—cattle, hay, and the pleasant, auspicious scent of corn nearly ready to be harvested. And, of course, some fresh horse dung from a merchant cart. Anyone from Nightingale would tell you that you had to learn to tolerate that smell if you were going to stick around.

For a moment, it felt like everything was right in the world. That's what Donovan loved about hunting most. It took him away from everyone who preached another religion to him, or glared at his scar, or slung Technique around like it was the easiest damn thing in the world.

"Just you and me now, Chomper. I promise carrots when we get back, alright?" Chomper gave a short whinny in response. Donovan grinned. "You're smarter than most men."

The last time Donovan caught glimpse of the sun peeking through the dense trees, he calculated about four or five hours passed since leaving Nightingale, and that meant he had been hunting for half that time. Shiverpine forest could be a cruel mistress at times, but his luck was usually better than this. He took Chomper down one of the deer migration trails and kept an eye out for another bear.

"Early hibernation?" he quietly asked himself. It was too early in the year for that, but it had been a cold autumn.

Donovan heard a noise that sounded like someone talking. He muttered curses as he reined in Chomper and listened. *Another hunter?* He had competition in town, but they rarely hunted Shiverpine. Lionel said he made an agreement with them years ago and they left Shiverpine alone. *But Lionel is gone now…and it could be someone else looking for food.*

Out of the corner of his eye, Donovan saw something move. He fired off an arrow before he even knew what he saw. It missed—that might have been a good thing. If he shot someone on accident…he didn't even want to think about it. He took in a deep breath to calm his nerves. *Greenhorn mistake!* He cursed himself, repeating what Lionel would tell him when he messed up. He dismounted and moved around looking for any sign of animal or hunter.

Nothing.

Blood throbbed in his head and sweat beaded on his brow despite the cold of the rainy day. *Predator, not prey,* was something else Lionel once told him when his nerves were on edge.

A twig snapped; Donovan spun on his heels, but didn't see anything. *Must be an animal. That's the only thing that makes sense.*

Something startled Chomper; Donovan ran back to his horse with an arrow notched. But the horse hadn't gone far. *Nothing too scary, eh Chomper?* He quietly slid underneath a pine with low branches and waited to see if whatever it was would come around again. Half a minute later, a buck slowly crept out of his hiding place about twenty paces away.

Donovan smiled. *Thank the gods. Yes, if you exist, you can have this one.* He was downwind; that was lucky. The deer couldn't smell him yet and he wasn't waiting. He took aim, just like Lionel had taught him. There seemed to be a deathly silence in the air that always preceded a kill.

Donovan moved the bow in slight adjustments. A single bead of sweat trickled down his face and threatened to run into one of his eyes. The bow creaked and the deer looked over at Donovan, but at that moment he loosed the arrow. Straight through the eye—an instant kill.

"Yes!" Donovan breathed out. He jogged over to the deer to examine the kill. Setting down the bow, he grabbed the antlers and took a good look at this prey. "Maybe the best damn shot I've ever made."

"Fancy yerself good with the bow, eh?" a man said.

Donovan turned and watched him step out of the trees. A tall man, with fine leather armor covering his chest, and over that armor a long, green tabard fringed with gold and bearing a serpent's eye in the center. It was the Kingdom of Kaldaran. The only legal tabard in Nightingale was that of the City Guard, so to see someone wearing a different one was a shock.

The man held a long sword in his hands, which left an empty scabbard to swing back and forth at his hips like a pendulum ticking down the seconds until Donovan's doom. Ten paces and a few rocks were all that separated him from Donovan.

"What the gol is a Kaldaran soldier doing so far from home?" Donovan asked.

The man only smirked.

"Don't try anything. I'm a citizen of Nightingale. If you cause me trouble, you'll be dealing with K'var."

The man chuckled. "The goddess or the kingdom? I have no fear of either one."

"You should. The Kingdom of K'var will rout your asses so hard and fast, not a single Kaldaran will sit on a horse for years."

The man eyed Donovan carefully and took a couple of steps closer, his leather boots clapping on the rocky ground. "Ah, ya be a smart man, a smart man with a big mouth, dontcha know? Who are ya, *smart man*? What are ya doin' out here?" He took a few more steps, with a look to kill in his eyes accompanied by an unsettling smile.

Donovan thought about reaching down to the ground for his bow, but the Kaldaran was close. Instead, he slowly pulled one of the knives from his belt. It was balanced for throwing.

The Kaldaran chuckled a low rumble and took another few steps closer. "Ya thinkin' that wee little knife is goin' to kill me?" He moved his sword through the air gently, back and forth, displaying his superior steel.

Donovan put the knife between his fingers for a throw. The Kaldaran man roared and charged forward.

Donovan threw the blade, his wrist snapping in perfect motion, sending the metal whizzing through the air and striking the Kaldaran in the leg. He stumbled to the ground, and Donovan didn't waste a moment. He ran forward and stomped the man's sword hand. The Kaldaran grunted and lost his grip.

Donovan reached down and grabbed the sword, but the Kaldaran grabbed his ankle. He yanked it. Donovan fell and pain rattled him as his knee smacked into stone. He rolled away just in time to avoid getting stabbed by a knife the Kaldaran had drawn. Donovan brought the sword around and cut the knife out of the Kaldaran's hand.

Donovan thought he had him. He pressed the attack and brought the blade around for the kill, but the Kaldaran drew a second knife, and with a flash of bright orange light, he parried and cut clean through the sword. Donovan panicked and brought the stub around, going for the throat, but the Kaldaran lunged at him with the knife.

Donovan stepped to the side, and the Kaldaran tumbled to the ground, missing, but recovering quickly. Donovan took three quick steps back, and on the third, tripped over the corpse of the deer.

The Kaldaran roared again and limped over with much more speed than expected with his wounded thigh. Donovan grabbed his bow and as quick as lightning fired a shot, striking the Kaldaran in the heart. He tumbled to the ground, dead.

Donovan's head swam. He took a few seconds to calm his rapid breathing back to a steady rhythm. He had not killed a person before—as far as he remembered. He knew if he had joined Toby's crew, that's what he would be doing, but this…this felt different. He was alone, and not under contract to kill the man.

It was self-defense. I will load the deer and get the gol out of here, and no one will know one way or another.

Donovan looked around for Chomper, and when he found the horse, he went back to where the deer and the dead Kaldaran were. He grabbed some rope and was about to bind up the body of the deer, but a thought struck him.

Could this Kaldaran be one of many? Is Nightingale or K'var in real danger?

Donovan moved over to the body and grabbed the dead man's knife, slicing the tabard off. He would keep that to prove his story. When he ripped the cloth from the body, he saw a small pouch attached at the man's belt. Inside there were a few silver coins, which were of no immense value. But there was a note.

Patrol Shiverpine, kill all outsiders. Find out who they are first, if possible, so we can have our men inside Nightingale run interference as needed.

Signed,
King Santos, Crowned of Kaldaran.

"Orders from the Kaldaran king himself. This can't be good." Donovan rolled up the note and the tabard and stuffed them into one of Chomper's saddlebags.

He went back to his work with the buck, but a sound rang out. Someone was shouting in the forest, and they had a Kaldaran accent.

"Roden went that way, tell him to get the gol back here!"

"There's more," Donovan breathed out. He mounted Chomper and prodded him back to the migration trail, then dug his heels in deep as soon as they were there. The shouting faded.

"Bloody gol," Donovan said. "Nightingale is under attack."

Chapter Four

It was afternoon by the time Donovan made it back. He was exhausted, panicked, and so soaked, his boots had a finger of water in each one.

He crested the last hill, Nightingale's strong stone walls creeping higher into visibility as Chomper trotted out the last couple hundred paces of the journey. At the top, Donovan pulled on the reins and Chomper slowed to a stop.

"What the gol?" he muttered. *There's a line to get in? A long line?* Donovan had seen this before, but that was on the mornings of feast days. And this was the North Gate. The South Gate got most of the traffic. *Is the Guard taking a long time to get people through?*

Donovan approached the back of the line, stopping about ten paces away. From what he could see, the Guard was carefully searching everything being brought in. Much more thoroughly than their usual rundown. *What a pain. At least I don't have anything that would—*

His eyes went wide. *The tabard and the note.*

He swallowed hard. He could break off and ride to the South. It would take a little while to get there—Nightingale was not small and was on top of a hill, so the ride would be uncomfortable for Chomper riding along the hill slope.

"What do you think, boy?" Donovan asked.

Chomper snorted.

"Sure, that's fair. You've been doing all the walking today."

On top of his animal friend's complaint, Donovan knew the line at the South Gate was probably worse. *North Gate it is.*

Donovan prodded Chomper the rest of the way and took his place in line. "What's the big hold-up?" he called out. One of the men there scoffed in answer.

"Some idiot tried to get an elementium sword through the gate this morning." He turned around to look at Donovan and narrowed his eyes. He had a rough look about him, probably one of the mercs. "I bet the Queen of K'var's happy, they just got one for free."

"What do you mean?"

"That skot ain't cheap. Elementium? Easiest thing to use Technique with, not to mention the blades don't dull easy. But that's contraband here, so they took it. No way in gol they give it back, and K'var has a law sayin' we have to give it to them."

A guard near the front pointed at Donovan and signaled for him to dismount. He would have to wait through the rest of the line on foot.

"Now they are checkin' everyone's bags thoroughly, slowin' everything down. Just my luck. Tech that guy from this morning, right?"

Donovan wasn't so flippant with the stronger language, but he nodded along. *Why today of all days?*

After an hour of waiting, it was Donovan's turn. He approached the heavy iron gate and the guards standing in the way.

"State your business," one City Guardsman asked.

"I'm Donovan, a citizen of Nightingale."

"I know who you are," the guard said, his eyes level. "State your business."

"Fur hunter, coming back from a hunt."

The guard eyed him up and down and leaned to the side to get a better look at Chomper. "No luck today? Or are those saddlebags full of racoons?"

Donovan sniffed. "I wouldn't bother going to Shiverpine to hunt something I can easily get in the city."

"It's illegal to hunt in the city."

"Of course."

The two looked at each other for a moment, but no one said a word. After a few seconds, the guard looked back down at his list. He had a long scroll and was making notes.

"Alright, everything checks out, just need to look through your saddlebags. Anything we should know about?"

Donovan froze. They would find the tabard, but it was just a lump of cloth. Why would they look through it? It wasn't big enough to hide anything like an elementium sword.

"Nope," he answered. The guard started going through the saddlebags while Donovan waited. He pretended not to care and look the other way, and nearly locked eyes with a middle-aged fellow wearing a Guard's uniform. His gray hair was cut short and his face clean shaven. His eyes pierced through the crowd, taking in each detail like reading words from a book. And, most importantly, the bird on his tabard had three stars above its head.

Captain Gerald. What is the leader of the Guard doing here, monitoring searches?

"Alright," the guard said. Donovan jumped a little at that. "Nothing suspicious. You're free to enter."

Relief flooded through Donovan's body from head to toe. "Thank you."

"Hold a moment, Xavier," Captain Gerald's deep voice cut through the air with ease. "The saddlebag on the front left, please remove its contents and show them to me."

Donovan's stomach dropped.

"Right away, Captain," the guard answered. "Only a bit of green cloth in here. Nothing of—" the guard paused when he unfurled the tabard, the note from King Santos falling out of it. "What in gol…"

"I can explain, I found that—"

The captain stepped forward. "Guards, please seize this man and escort him to my chamber immediately, along with the contraband."

The three guards, including the one who had searched, sprang into action, and within seconds, Donovan was forced to his knees, his hands bound by rope. One of the guards pulled out a handkerchief to gag him, but the captain waved him off.

"No need for that. He's soulburned."

Donovan took a deep breath as he was escorted through the double-door entrance to the barracks by the captain and one other guard from the gate. A Nightingale city guardsman stood on either side of the entrance, spears in hand, and chain mail that ran from the coif around their head down to their thighs with an apron.

The two guards eyed Donovan as he was marched forward, and when they saw the captain they both stood straighter and saluted.

Inside, a late-middle-aged clerk sat behind a desk at the end of the room, lit by a small window. Soldiers milled about, but stopped what they were doing to salute.

"Be about your business," Captain Gerald ordered. "And don't tell the Second in Command about this."

The captain turned Donovan down one of the hallways and they passed by a few other halls and doors before coming to a heavy looking wooden door with no window. The captain produced a key from his pocket and shoved it into the lock. The metal clicked as the tumbler shifted. The captain motioned for the guard to prod Donovan through.

Once inside the captain's office, Donovan took notice that the place was generally…very wealthy looking. That was surprising. He did not think the captain's pay would be anything special, but he did more or less run the city, as well.

The captain walked over and took a seat behind his desk. It had intricate carvings on the edge, and Donovan knew if Lionel was there, he would comment on the craftsmanship.

"Not bad for a simple Captain of the Guard, wouldn't you say?"

Donovan blinked. "Is that why you brought me here? To show off?"

The captain shook his head and rubbed at his eyes. "Of course not. You know why you're here. You were bringing in an illegal tabard as well as a…most interesting note. Why don't you take a seat?"

The guard nudged Donovan over to a chair, and he complied. With his hands bound behind him, it wasn't comfortable. That was probably the idea.

The captain looked up at the guard. "Hand them to me."

The guard handed over the saddlebag which contained the tabard and the letter.

The captain opened the bag and pulled out the letter, reading it over one more time before his eyes went back to Donovan. "You didn't strike me a traitor. But everyone in Nightingale knows you don't swear by any god, and you're soulburned. Did Kaldaran offer you a good deal?"

"Neither one of those things are mine. Can I explain myself?"

The captain swirled his hand in a "go ahead" motion.

"I was hunting in Shiverpine. I shot a buck, and while I was inspecting it, a Kaldaran man approached me."

"How did you know he was from Kaldaran?"

"The tabard and the accent. You know the one, dontcha know?" Donovan imitated the accent on that last line; the captain didn't react to that. "The Kaldaran threatened to kill me, and we fought. I lucked out and won. I searched him and he had that note on him."

"Did he have anything else?"

"Some small coins, plus all of his gear."

"Did you take those?"

"Just the coins and the two things you're holding right now. I heard more Kaldarans coming so I got out of there as fast as I could."

The captain took in a deep breath. "Donovan, that's quite the story. Are you telling me that you know more about what's going around my city than I do?"

Donovan tugged on his binds. "Nightingale is my city too!"

"Perhaps, or perhaps it was until you got a better offer. Maybe a few days in the prison will—"

The door to the office suddenly flung open. A woman with long brown hair, soldier's leathers, and a tabard with two stars above the nightingale, came into the room. The guard turned to stand in her way. She raised her brows at him, and his eyes fell as he stood aside.

"What in all of gol is this, Captain?" Alexis asked. "You arrested Donovan?"

"Alexis, a pleasure," the captain said through tight lips. "Now, if you'll please excuse us—"

"Donovan hasn't done anything wrong. Why did you parade him through town in binds?"

The captain rolled his eyes and held up the tabard and the note. "These were in one of his saddlebags."

Alexis stepped over and grabbed them. Her brow furrowed when she saw the Kaldaran tabard, and her eyes went wide at the note. She looked at Donovan and asked, "Where did you get these?"

"Killed a man who tried to kill me, in Shiverpine."

Alexis turned to the captain. "This is serious. A major human kingdom is sending soldiers between us and the Kingdom of K'var. We have to send word to K'var immediately."

The captain stood. "We have no idea what Donovan saw. He doesn't remember a damn thing, how can anything he says be trusted?"

Donovan squeezed his hands into fists, not that he could throw a punch anyway. Alexis moved between him and the captain before he could try anything stupid.

"I trust him, and *I* can be trusted. Therefore, he can be trusted."

"It is well within my right to arrest him and toss him in prison, if I decide to do so. Only the Guard is allowed to handle contraband."

In spite of his anger, an idea was brewing in Donovan's head. *This is the big contract Toby was talking about. There might be another way I can get in on this.*

"If only the Guard can handle contraband," Donovan put in, "then make me a guardsman."

Both the captain and Alexis looked at him, brows raised.

"Donovan," Alexis whispered. "This is just a political game the captain is playing. He wants me to put in a good word for him with K'var."

"Which you will do," the captain said.

Alexis winced. "Alright, you and I both know what's going on here, Captain. I will put in a good word for you with the letter we send to K'var, and you will let Donovan go."

"Let him go? He just said he wants to join the Guard, and recruitment has been down."

Alexis raised a hand, frustrated. "You just said ten seconds ago you don't trust him!"

The captain suppressed a grin. He was enjoying this game, but maybe Donovan could use it.

"I said I would join. Does the captain accept?"

Alexis's mouth moved but with no words.

"Sure," the captain said. "Start tomorrow. I know you have a place in town, but it's standard for new recruits to live in the barracks during training. Dismissed, recruit."

Donovan nodded and stood up. The guardsman at the door looked stunned, and it took him a moment to realize he needed to undo the binds. The Captain nodded at him, and the guard worked the ropes off Donovan's hands. Donovan shook his wrists out then walked away.

"You better give him fair treatment," he heard Alexis say to the captain. He was heading for the exit but was only a dozen paces there when a hand on his shoulder turned him around.

"What was that about?" Alexis asked. "I was about to have that all handled; you didn't need to give anything up!"

"I didn't. I decided I wanted to join. You tried to get me to join for a while."

She crossed her arms again. "I know that, but you said you didn't think the Guard was a good fit. You didn't have to join to stay out of prison; I would have found a way."

"I want in on what's going on."

"What do you mean?"

Donovan looked around to see if anyone was listening. Alexis caught the gesture and took him to her small office. She pointed out a couple chairs near the fireplace, and Donovan took a seat.

"One of the mercs said there's a rumor about big contracts coming up. He bought a lot of furs from me and didn't haggle, so I think he was telling me the truth. I asked to join his crew, but he turned me down."

"Donovan, there's no indication that the two are related. Kaldaran is likely messing with K'var, and we will stay clear and let those two kingdoms deal with it."

Donovan considered that. "Perhaps. But I want a chance to earn some respect around here. The Guard has respect."

Alexis lowered her head. "I respect you."

Donovan paused at that, and took a few moments to find the words. "I don't think fur hunting is for me. I want something greater than that. I think being part of the Guard can help with that."

"I can't protect you at all times. Some of the other Guardsmen don't like you, and they will make it known."

"I can stand up for myself," Donovan snapped. There was a chilly pause, then he added, "If you do respect me, and I believe you do, give me a chance to stand up for myself."

"That would have been a much better first attempt at saying that," she said, her eyes downcast.

Donovan shook his head. "I'm sorry. Sore subject for me. I will buy the first round of drinks tonight."

"I forgive you, but no way are you going drinking. The captain said it's your first day tomorrow, and first days are brutal."

"You're probably right. But...we will get drinks again sometime, won't we?"

Alexis smiled at him, and Donovan sat up a little straighter. "When you finish training. Then I'm buying."

Chapter Five

"I just don't see why you had to get yourself tangled into this mess, Donovan!" Martha stared Donovan down with an intensity that kept him in his seat. He had told her everything that happened.

He lifted his chin. Martha was not getting the gist of what he was saying. "It was either this or possibly prison."

"Maybe you *should* be in prison! You tell me you lie to the Guard, then join them?"

"Does seem odd, I agree—"

"And now, after turning everybody away for months, you leave Ramon with no one to hunt with. You should at least have found a replacement for yourself before going off and joining the Nightingale Guard!"

"True, but Ramon is free to look for whoever he wants now, and I can help at the shop in the evenings until he finds my replacement."

Martha crossed her arms. "What do you have to say for yourself?"

"Well...I didn't die."

Martha uncrossed her arms and took Donovan's hands. "And, of course, I'm glad for that."

"But I did take someone's life."

Martha looked surprised. "It was clearly self-defense."

"I just don't remember doing that before, but in the moment it felt easy. Easier than I wanted it to be."

She paused at that.

"What if I was a criminal in the past? I know Ramon said I did the right thing, but it bothers me. I want to know that, if I'm capable of killing, then at least I'm doing it for the right reasons."

Martha sighed. "I know it hurts not knowing your past. I also know that you have been a wonderful person since Lionel took you in. So, maybe you *are* capable of doing something awful. But I also know you're capable of doing good. And I think that if your past has made you who you are, then you were not such a bad person in it."

Donovan kept his gaze away from her.

"Donovan, no one is asking you to be perfect. Ramon and I are your family, and we want to be one of the things that is right in your life. I just wish you would talk to us." She stood up from her seat and took his hand.

"I'm sorry for being so upset—I worry about you. I want you to know that even though I may not approve of your hasty decision to join the guard, I think you showed great courage and strength against that man from Kaldaran. And now the captain knows what is going on and can send for help."

Donovan nodded again. "I'm sorry I acted rashly. But I think my decision to join the Guard still stands."

Martha smiled and moved her hand to his shoulder. "And a fine Guardsman you will make. I'm sure of it."

"Thanks. Sorry I didn't bring back any food."

"I don't care about that, I'm just glad you are alright, *Sonna*." The term of endearment was of the ancient tongue, and it was where the common tongue got the word *Son*.

Donovan smiled.

Martha smiled back, patted Donovan on the back, then turned to the kitchen to start cooking. "Did you see Alexis today?"

Donovan sighed and put a hand to his forehead. "I may have closed the door on that. She will be a superior officer now, and that means we can't be together."

"You can always quit the Guard later," Martha said. "If you discover something with her. The oaths there are renewed every six months, so just see how she feels about you in spring. It might be good to get to see her every day."

"I suppose. We got into a little bit of an argument. She is always trying to protect me."

"She cares about you."

"I know. I just want to be able to hold my own ground without her having to step in all the time."

Martha didn't respond. Donovan looked around the room at Lionel's collections of weapons. *If there was ever a man who knew how to stand his ground...*

"Did Lionel ever talk about this with you?" Donovan asked. "I know his beliefs made him a little bit of an outcast."

"Lionel definitely did not have a lot of friends who shared his faith in his god. I know that made him feel lonely from time to time, but he was not going to change his mind. He was going to serve Orimin, one way or another."

"Do you think Nightingale would be a better place if people were more like Lionel? I mean, more religious."

"Depends on what god they follow, I suppose," Martha answered with a sigh. "Most have no idea what the idol they have in their home represents. Just the other day, Harvey the Turner was trying to convince me that his bust of Driggon would grant him prosperity and good luck with women. Little does he know, if a true follower of Driggon caught a 'pagan' like him with that idol, he would be dead with a Driggon cross cut across his chest, exposing his rib cage."

Donovan blinked. "And people call me 'god-hater' like it's a bad thing."

Martha laughed, but quickly turned the conversation away. "How about a hearty dinner to celebrate your new profession?"

"I won't turn that down."

Martha nodded and started working up a fire.

"You said Lionel served a god called Orimin?"

"Not one of the gods you would find Sebastian selling idols of, that's for sure," Martha answered from across the room. "The name is similar to our word for *origin*. It is believed that he is the creator of the world."

"He sounds powerful. I would have a hard time imagining serving anyone else if that's who the competition was."

"You seem to have a hard time serving anyone now."

Donovan shrugged. "Come on, though, the creator of the world or the god of…trees or something. If I was forced to choose, that's an easy one."

"Perhaps," Martha said. Donovan knew that meant *you're wrong, but I'm going to let you figure it out.*

"Notice how there are no kingdoms in Drannus that bear his name, like the other gods?" Martha asked.

"You mean for Orimin? I don't think that's as great of a tribute as people think."

Martha chuckled and shook her head. "You have much to learn, Donovan. I think time in the guard will be good for you. Plus, I think you will look handsome in one of those uniforms."

Ramon appeared from downstairs and looked at Martha and Donovan, then asked, "What did I miss?"

"Donovan was asking me questions about Orimin."

"Ah, Lionel's god," Ramon smiled knowingly. "He used to tell me campfire stories about that one. I can say with certainty it was never boring."

Donovan crossed his arms. "You mean to say you two had fun before I came around?"

Ramon laughed. "I've only told you half the stories of Lionel and myself. He was a bit of a troublemaker when he felt like it. Remember when he started a fight at the Safe Haven Inn?"

Martha glared at him. "We agreed some of those stories should remain untold."

Donovan slid a chair all the way across the room and sat on it backwards, his arms resting on the back. "Now, this is getting good. Pray tell, my friend?"

"Donovan joined the Guard today," Martha cut in.

Ramon looked stunned, but after a moment, he said, "So I can finally hire more people? It's about damn time! I have a five-year plan that should expand the business to two shops in Nightingale, and of course, I'm thinking of bringing our brand to Sokor and Ladesh in that time. When I'm done there—"

Donovan's glare stopped Ramon.

Ramon smiled in reply. "I'm hiring someone as soon as possible, and you can't stop me. When is your first day?"

"Tomorrow."

"Bones! That's sudden."

"I can help evenings and on my days off, I promise."

"I don't think recruits get days off for the first month at least," Martha said. "And recruits get the brunt of the chores to fill up their evenings."

Donovan's face froze. "I, um...I didn't know about that."

Ramon laughed, then walked over to give Donovan a firm pat on the shoulder. "Don't worry about the shop. And when you finally get some time off, I will be there. At the Safe Haven Inn, I mean."

"Speaking of..." Donovan started, but received a glare from Martha. He leaned in toward Ramon and whispered, "You will tell me about that bar fight when you get the chance, understood?"

Ramon gave him a conspiratorial nod.

Donovan awoke to the sound of shouting coming from the streets in the middle of the night, "What in all Abaddon," he mumbled as he sat up and looked around the barracks.

It had been two months since Donovan had joined the Guard, and training had been brutal. Alexis worked him harder than any of the others. When Donovan tried to bring it up with her, she told him he was out of line and ended the conversation. If he was late to wake up, she was there with a bucket of cold water on a frigid morning. A few times, she'd worked him until he vomited, though when she witnessed that, she did go a bit easier.

He blinked awake, wondering if this was some new torturous training regimen she'd devised, and looked around. The still half-asleep Nightingale Guards hurried to get themselves dressed. Donovan gathered his wits enough to join the others in getting ready. When his tabard was over his chain mail and his sword strapped to his hip, he joined a few others and ran toward the exit. Chain mail swished and echoed through the halls as the soldiers hurried to find an officer and receive orders.

Alexis stood at the end of the hall, her left hand up, warning them to stop and wait. The way her eyes and right hand moved, it looked like she was counting.

"Alright, you twenty follow me," she said as she broke into a jog and motioned them forward. "Watch your back, we're still not sure of the situation. Kill anyone, I mean *anyone*, who is wearing any tabard but Nightingale's."

"What's going on?" Donovan asked.

"We're being attacked, god-hater," one of the other men said.

"Shove off, bastard," he fired back.

"Enough!" Alexis snapped. "A small band of Kaldaran soldiers are in the city, and we need to kill them. Steven, Brom, Hadrian, Gregory, Benedict, Walter, Thea, Thomas, Autur, and Ellyn, follow me. Donovan, take the other nine with you and go down Broken Street until it loops around to the City Gate. Make sure to clear the alleyways and don't get flanked."

Kaldaran is attacking Nightingale? And Alexis is asking me to lead? Neither one made sense, but then again, Nightingale was an easier target than the Kingdom of K'var. As for his new-found leadership role, that made no sense at all. He was still new, and she had acted like he was the laziest recruit Nightingale had ever seen, but now she was showing faith in him.

"The soulburned is going to lead us?" whined one of the soldiers who was chosen to go with Donovan. His name was Chadwick. He had been the most irritating to deal with. If Alexis wasn't running Donovan ragged enough already, Chadwick was there to make sure he did not get a single good night's rest. The captain repeatedly looked over the harassment as "pranks."

Alexis locked eyes with Chadwick. "You have your orders! Do not make me say them again."

Chadwick's shoulders slumped.

Alexis pulled a torch from the wall and handed it to Donovan. "Go."

"Acknowledged." Donovan saluted Alexis, then moved outside and turned down Broken Street. There was some grumbling, but nine followed him, regardless.

"What's the plan?" one of the soldiers, Arabella, asked Donovan.

"Stick close. We need to go down Broken Street far enough to flush them out. If they are further south into the city already, then it's going to get bad. Come on."

"How can you know that's what Second Alexis meant?" Chadwick asked.

"Because it's the only thing that makes sense," Donovan barked back in a low voice.

The night was pitch black, and the town only lit a little here and there by torches hung for the night watch. Sounds rang out, alternating between screams and battle cries followed by metal clashing and silence. Donovan readied his sword and his nine did the same.

"Clear," Donovan said as he looked down a side street.

"This is pointless," Arabella said. She was a recruit of one year, still young, and probably not happy that Donovan was chosen to lead a squad at two months. "How do we know it's clear if we can't see a damn thing? We're going to be ambushed."

"We can't let these bastards run rampant through our city," Donovan said. "Come on, follow me."

The next two alleyways were clear as well. Some of the ten sounded annoyed, others relieved.

"Alright, we're heading to the City Gate, let's go," Donovan said. Before his voice even finished echoing down the alley, an arrow clipped his side. "Take cover!" his shout rang through the night as he ducked behind a rain barrel. The air hissed as more arrows whizzed past, making *thunk!* sounds when they hit wood, followed by the mechanical rattle of crossbows being wound back up.

Cries of pain came from somewhere. Donovan looked around—he'd been separated from all but one of his squad.

"You alright?" Arabella whispered. She crouched behind a wooden cart next to the barrel.

"Just grazed," Donovan replied. "Tech! Tech and teching damn!"

"Any ideas besides swearing?"

"I'm trying to figure out what's going on first. We cleared the alleyways, where did those shots come from?"

"Looks like the rest of the squad is a bit further back," Arabella noted. "Behind Tom's Smithy. We're pinned down here until we get some relief."

"I have an idea; get your crossbow ready."

"What are you going to do?"

Donovan peeked over the barrel, a few more shots rang out, and he ducked behind. He took in a breath, then stood and hucked his torch toward the direction of the shots. The faint orange glow revealed men with crossbows further down the road.

Arabella was right in step, firing her crossbow. The bolt whizzed through the air right into the heart of the one of the raiders.

They both ducked back behind the barrel and took a few breaths. "I didn't think that would actually work."

"Not half bad," Arabella admitted.

Donovan listened closely and heard footsteps moving away from them. He peeked over the barrel one more time—the Kaldarans were gone. He looked around and saw someone from the squad signaling them over to the smithy.

"They ran. Let's go."

Donovan and Arabella made a break for the back of the smithy. When they reached the rest of the squad, Emeline was on the ground, an arrow in her breast.

"Bag of bones," Donovan breathed out the curse.

"She's dead," Chadwick confirmed. "So are Henry and Celene. We're sitting ducks out here, soulburned."

"He got one of 'em," Arabella said.

"And they got three of us," Chadwick rounded.

"No more torches," Donovan said. "We know this city better than they do. Chadwick, I need you to take Steven and go down Butcher's Row to try to get their attention."

"Why there?" he asked.

"Because if they don't know the city and are trying to stay out of sight, it's the most obvious way for them to go to try and flank us. That street is never lit very well. Helena, you take Arabella and make a pass through the canal. It's going to smell like gol but try to stay out of the water and keep quiet. If they reach the end of Butcher's Row before Chadwick and Steven, you can come up from behind and crush them."

"What about us?" Andrew asked, gesturing toward himself and Rue.

"You two can use Technique, so you're coming with me. The rest of you, go, now!" Donovan ordered, and his squad scattered.

"Do you even know how Technique is used?" Rue asked.

Donovan bit back an insult. It was a fair question. "I know enough to have an idea. Stay with me."

Donovan took the two of them past Broken Street and down Caravan Way. The wide street made them easy targets, but it also allowed for the most visibility of any enemies moving. More importantly, the street was known for being loud. Sound from nearby alleys and streets always echoed into Caravan Way.

Donovan held up a hand to signal a stop and paused to listen. He checked the door to Linda's Soap and Laundry. Unlocked. "This way," he said in barely a whisper. The three of them went inside.

Donovan paused again to listen. He heard crossbows winding. "With apologies to Linda," he said, "Rue, cut through this wall as quietly as you can."

Rue nodded and whispered, "*Sunder*," and her sword began to glow an orange color. She then stuck the blade into the wall and started to carve out an opening large enough for a man. Donovan saw sweat forming on her forehead when she was about halfway through. The concentration and sacrifice to use the spell was taking its toll on her. But she stayed strong and finished.

"Now what?" Andrew asked. "The wall is cut, but still standing."

"Use your shield. Use *impenetrable* and break through it. Then charge forward. We'll only get a couple of seconds before they gather their heads."

Andrew paused to think about that, but nodded his head. "Surprise attack. I like it." He whispered, "*Impenetrable;*" his pained grin visible in the glow of his shield as he exchanged a piece of himself for power. He then charged forward and broke through the wall, sending rocks and mortar flying away as they separated from the large chunk.

Donovan and Rue were right behind, and they ran forward, encountering the marksmen that previously had the jump on them. They cut them down. It was odd for Donovan. The Kaldaran he had killed with his bow, but this time he was...opening up flesh with his sword. It felt wrong. But he remembered that three of his own were dead in the street. Did the Kaldarans feel any remorse over that? He doubted it. They chose to come to Nightingale. Nightingale would not take that lying down.

Now, there was only one more Kaldaran, on the ground, his weapon shattered in his hand. "Please, don't kill me!" he begged.

"Donovan, finish him," Andrew said.

Donovan hesitated. "He's surrendered. I can't kill a man in cold blood."

"Kaldarans don't take prisoners. They show no mercy and expect none."

Donovan considered that. If the Kaldarans did not take prisoners, they certainly did not deserve the same courtesy. "It doesn't seem right."

Suddenly, a stabbing pain went through his gut. The Kaldaran had risen up on his knees, a knife hilt in his hand and the blade end in Donovan's gut.

"Donovan!" Rue screamed.

He fell to the ground and caught a glimpse of Andrew cutting the Kaldaran clean open, blood on the knife in the dying man's hand.

"Is that...my blood?" he asked.

Rue was the first to lean down and check Donovan's wound. "This needs mending immediately," she said. "There is a half-fey mender back at the barracks. We need to go right now."

"We have to go to the City Gate," Donovan said in a weak voice. His mind clouded over as blood drained from his stomach.

"He's not fit for command," Arabella's voice rang clear. She and the others had reunited with Donovan's group. "Rue and Andrew, take him back to a mender. The rest of you, come to the City Gate with me."

"I'm fine," Donovan said. "I'm...I have to be fine...I can't...This isn't how I die...is it?"

Donovan stirred in his subconscious. He was in the throne room that he had seen in his dreams before. This time, neither the name plates nor the gods that belonged to them were there. But the king from before was, and he was studying Donovan carefully.

"Quite a scrape you got yourself into," he said. "You were a fool to give a Kaldaran an opening."

"Wow, thanks for stating the obvious," Donovan replied. "In case you didn't notice, I was trying to do what was right."

"No, you weren't," the king fired back. "You don't know what is right, as evidenced by the knife-shaped hole in your gut."

Donovan tightened his fist. "Who are you? Why are you in my dreams? To insult me?"

"I hardly consider that an insult. An insult would be if I told you that your beard makes you look like a goat so your mother must have been one."

"That's certainly one opinion. A false one."

The king smiled at him. "You can do better than that."

"I would rather have a goat mother than be king of nothing."

The king shrugged. "It's a start. Glad to see you have fight in you!"

Donovan scoffed. "Is that the point of these conversations? To make sure I still have fight in me?"

"Only in part," the king replied as he stroked his chin. "You will need a lot of it."

"Does that mean I'm not dead?"

"Not this time."

Donovan awoke from the strange dream. It left him with odd feelings he couldn't put a name to. It had felt like a long dream, but he only remembered a bit of the conversation he had, and that quickly faded away once he was awake.

Blinking so his eyes could adjust, he looked around. He was in a small room he did not recognize, but that looked like part of the barracks. A man in dark clothing and a black cloth covering all but his eyes stood at the entrance, the door behind him open. Donovan blinked once more. The man was gone, the door behind him closed.

"What in all Abaddon," he muttered.

A minute later, the door opened, and a half-fey man walked in. He wore a glove on his hand to protect himself from the iron of the door handle. Fey were allergic to metal, and half-fey sometimes took on that trait.

"Are you alright?" he asked. "My name is Eodius. Mender, at your service. You look a bit pale, but that is normal after a rough mending."

Donovan nodded and said, "I think I'm alright."

"Let me see you. Sit up." He put two fingers under Donovan's chin and lifted. "Your ley lines look well adjusted, especially for a soulburned."

"Ley lines?"

"I know, I know, I get comments about that one all the time. But humans have them too; you just have to know what to look for."

Donovan was too confused to press further on that. "Was someone else in the hallway when you came in? Dressed in all black?"

"No, I would have noticed that. Open your mouth for me."

Donovan did, and Eodius made a few thoughtful grunts before nodding. "You are in much better health than you should be. You almost died yesterday."

"Yesterday…the Kaldaran attack. Is Alexis alright?"

Eodius raised an eyebrow. "I assume you mean the Second in command? She is just fine. She came by asking about you a few times. Told me to go get her once you were awake."

Donovan sighed in relief. "I would like to see her."

"Just as well, I think she would like to see you. Allow me to fetch her."

Donovan nodded and Eodius went back out. He was glad Alexis was alright, but then remembered the soldiers who had died under his command. *Can I even remember their names? Emeline, Henry…Celene?*

A knock on the door, then Alexis came in. "Donovan!" She walked up to him, and for a second it seemed she was about to hug him, but she stopped short. "I'm glad you're well. Rue said you took a pretty good wound to the gut."

"Yes…Kaldaran bastard said he surrendered, then tried to kill me at the first opportunity."

"You should have known better—Kaldarans never surrender."

Donovan clenched his fist. "Well, we haven't exactly gone over that in training. And I didn't want to kill someone in cold blood, is that so bad?"

Alexis paused, then her eyes dropped to the floor. "I...I'm sorry. I was really worried about you. I should have told you sooner that Kaldarans never surrender. I should have prepared you for this. It's my fault. I should have pushed you harder."

Donovan furrowed his brow, then eased. "Wait, is that why you have been so tough on me? You were afraid I was going to die?"

"Of course." She brought her eyes up to meet his. "You're my best friend."

"But you've always wanted me to join the Guard."

"Not anymore. Not now that Kaldaran has chosen to attack us. I...I had a suspicion they were here for us. So I pushed you hard so you would be ready. Also, I knew the captain was going to take your training into his own hands if I didn't push your hard enough."

"I'm not sure Captain Gerald could have done me much worse."

"I'm sorry," she said. "I've put you through gol. I shouldn't have made your protection my responsibility. All that, and I still almost got you killed."

"I was wondering about that. You put me in charge above more senior recruits. Why?"

"Honestly, Donovan, because you're better than all of them."

Donovan brightened at that.

"It looks bad for me politically to put you in charge, but last night I didn't care. You're the best for the job. A lot of the guard has gotten lazy around here. But you came in full of fire and ready to learn."

"But I got four people killed. I failed."

Alexis shook her head. "Three, and you did not fail. You were just unlucky. The chances were good that one of the teams would get ambushed. We lost only two others last night. The crossbowmen you killed were close to outflanking us. You saved a lot of soldiers."

Donovan had a hard time with that. He couldn't see three dead soldiers as a good thing, five counting the other two. But Alexis knew combat. And she was blunt, which was admittedly annoying at times. But when Donovan needed to hear the truth, he could always count on her.

"Thanks," he whispered. "Do I...I mean, has someone—"

"Told their families? Yes."

Donovan nodded. "Thanks again." There was a pause.

"I think I owe you a drink," Alexis said. "How does tonight sound? Ramon and his new guy, Tybalt, are welcome to come too."

Donovan's smiled. "Sounds great."

"Good! See you at Safe Haven tonight."

Alexis turned to leave, but she paused on the doorway. She turned around and smiled at him for a moment. "Some good news—the captain has approved your promotion. You are now a sergeant and will be given a team to lead now and then, when needed. The promotion also comes with days off, your first being tomorrow. So no holding back tonight when I drink you under the table."

Donovan chuckled. "You're on."

Chapter Six

Donovan stopped mid-stride to avoid walking into a post. He was on his way home and still not fully awake. The mending had taken a lot out of him, and Alexis's smile was on his mind.

There was also the strange dream, and the man in black he saw in the doorway after. That had also been part of the dream, hadn't it?

His daydreaming was brought to abrupt end when he saw Emeline's husband, the blacksmith, now also a widower. The hot metal on his anvil looked like it was being turned into a sword. He looked up, catching Donovan's eyes. His face twisted. He set his hammer down and took a step toward Donovan.

"Rethink that move," a voice called out. The husband's eyes moved from Donovan to someone on the left. Toby took a couple steps forward.

"If it wasn't for this man, ya might be dead too, dontcha know?"

The blacksmith's eyes fell. He turned away without a word but went into his home instead of back to work.

"Thanks," Donovan said. "But how do you know what happened yesterday?"

"I fought alongside Alexis yesterday. Ya did good, I heard. Ya certainly don't deserve to get beat for it, dontcha know?"

Toby's kind words could not erase the guilt after seeing the hatred in the blacksmith's eyes. Three soldiers under his command, dead. *How many others in Nightingale are weeping today?*

"I'm not sure about all that."

Toby gave him a firm hand on the shoulder. "All this will be over soon, Donovan. Keep yer chin up."

Toby was gone before Donovan thought of something to say in response.

He made it home and saw a "back soon" sign hung on the shop window. Ramon and Tybalt were probably out to lunch. He walked in and upstairs. Martha was sitting at the table enjoying lunch on her own.

"Donovan!" she said as she rose.

"Don't get up!" Donovan said, but Martha had her arms around him almost before he finished speaking.

"Alexis sent me home this morning, or I would have been there when you woke. I made her promise to send you home the moment you were awake. How do you feel?"

"Tired, but well. Fey mending magic is a wonder I will never understand."

"Thank the gods you are alright!"

Donovan nodded, his eyes wandering.

"Something on your mind, *Sonna*? What happened in the battle? Are you still injured?"

Donovan chuckled. "One question at a time, please."

"Fair enough. Take a seat and let me get you some warm soup!"

Donovan smiled and sat across from Martha's place at the table. She set a steaming bowl of pork stew in front of him, then sat back down.

"What happened in the battle? I was so worried about you when I heard the alarm bells ringing."

"I was told my team did well but…three of my Guard were killed. I feel like I failed them."

"Your team? Is this the promotion Alexis told me about?"

Donovan's lips tightened. "Did you hear me? Three people died under my command."

"And many more were saved because of your command. Alexis told me that."

"Martha, I thought you of all people would be able to empathize with me on this one."

She paused her eating. "I won't help you in feeling sorry for yourself."

"I feel sorry for those who died and their families. Myself is the last person I'm thinking about."

Martha scoffed. "I don't believe that for a second. You did your job, and that's that."

Donovan didn't know what to say. There was reason in what Martha was saying; he was feeling sorry for himself. *But that look from Emeline's husband…*

"Did you speak with her today? What did she say to you?"

Donovan blinked back into focus and shook his thoughts away. "I'm sorry, who?"

"Alexis, of course!"

"She said I did alright. She invited me, Ramon, and Tybalt to Safe Haven tonight."

Martha smiled wide. "That sounds like a great idea. You've earned it. You've been carrying the weight of the world on your shoulders, and I don't like seeing that one bit. I hope Alexis stops pushing you so hard now."

"She told me she was worried I would get killed if she didn't train me well enough."

"I thought that might be the case. She cares a great deal about you. Try not to let her lessons get to you."

"Thanks," Donovan said, returning to the stew and his thoughts about the people who died.

"It never gets easy," Martha said a moment later. "Leading such promising young men and women into battle, only to lose some. You know, Lionel was a military commander in his younger years."

"Really? He never mentioned it."

"He didn't like to talk about it. All these weapons on the walls—they aren't collector pieces. They were all his. There's at least one life taken by each one; many, many more for some."

"Wow, I wonder why he never shared any of that. If I were him, I would be proud and sharing war stories with everyone I knew."

Martha smiled, her eyes starting to water with tears. "Honestly, Donovan, he was more proud of you and Ramon than anything else. He was never able to have any children. I know that hurt him deeply. But when someone brought you up in a conversation, the light touched his eyes."

Donovan felt the strain of tears in his eyes now. *Lionel was proud of me?*

"Thanks," he whispered.

"You're always welcome. Now then, how about I get some hot water going so you can bathe before your big outing with Alexis tonight?"

Before Donovan could protest, Martha was out of her seat, the water bucket in her hand. *That woman sure can move fast when she wants to.*

"Donovan!" she called from downstairs. "I bought some soap from Linda the other day you can use. It's in my desk in my room. Could you fetch it?"

"Why don't I do the heavy lifting and you fetch the soap," Donovan called back. Before he could take one step down the stairs, Martha was near the top of them with the first bucket of water to be heated.

"I need the exercise. Come on now, one side, Donovan."

Donovan chuckled but did as she asked. *I'll get the soap, then convince her to let me carry the water.* He walked to her room and opened the door. The bed was immaculate, of course. Big enough for two, but now used by only one. He sighed and looked over at the desk. Another one of the many gifts Lionel had received from his wood carving friend during his lifetime. Donovan walked over and opened the drawer, but between the pieces of paper, the inkwell and quill, and some scattered coins, there was no soap to be found.

"Where in the desk is it?" he called out, but Martha must not have heard. He knelt down and reached in the very back of the drawer. He felt something solid and tugged at it. There was a click, and below the desk, a hidden compartment dropped opened.

"What in the—" Donovan breathed out. A large steel…something was sitting there. He pulled it out and felt the heavy weight of it in his hands. It was a book, bound in steel, with thick pages pressed together by the weight of the binding. It was cast metal, with a design of a dragon and phoenix locked in battle on the cover. The eye of the dragon was a small, orange crystal, and the eye of the phoenix a white one.

"Elementium. Gol, this is illegal to have here."

"It's just in the top of the dresser, Donovan. Are you having—" Martha stopped when she saw him holding the book. "What are you doing with that?"

"You said the soap was in your desk."

"I said the dresser!"

"You definitely said desk. Martha, what is this thing? You know this is illegal, right?

Martha took in a heavy breath. "You weren't supposed to see that. Not yet, anyway. It's my responsibility until I die. Lionel made me promise."

"But what is it? What is your responsibility?"

Martha turned and shut the door, then crossed over to the bed. "Bring it here." Donovan brought it over, taking a seat next to her. She opened it, revealing thick leatherleaf pages with a foreign script. "This is the myth of one of the Crowned, the agents of the gods themselves."

"The Crowned?"

"Over five hundred years ago, the Kingdoms of Drannus and many other places were ruled by the gods more directly. The Crowned were called that, not only because they were the Queens and Kings, but also the agents of the gods. They had close communion with the gods and studied these ancient books to become more and more like the god they represented. That is why the Kingdoms took the namesakes of the gods."

"And how do we know any of that is true?"

"Donovan, please let me finish first."

Donovan nodded.

"The Crowned were wise and powerful fighters. Like the gods themselves, they preferred to have those under them do their business, but every now and then, a Crowned would fight. Those battles made up many of the legends you still hear today. Dragons in the west were brought to their doom. Great chasms in the ground opened from a mighty spell. Mountains came crashing down and the oceans rose far beyond their natural borders." Martha looked at Donovan, her expression now inviting questions.

"If they were so powerful, what happened to them?"

She smiled. "You already know." Donovan raised an eyebrow, so Martha added, "Many do not like being ruled by a god. They overthrew their god-kings and forgot their gods."

"So every kingdom rebelled? At the same time? And didn't they come against 'mountains crashing' and 'great chasms opening'? Like you said? If these Crowned were so powerful, how did ordinary men stand against them?"

"That would have happened, yes. But the secret of the Crowned was the ways and laws of their gods. And those ways were kept in books just like this one. Those books were found, stolen, and destroyed. The Crowned ceased to be because once the books were gone, the ways of the gods fell into obscurity. The rituals performed by the priestess of K'var in the chapel here in town are likely just a shadow of what the goddess herself taught her people to do."

Donovan considered everything Martha was saying. This was crazy talk, but Martha was not crazy. That didn't make any sense. She was one of the more skeptical people he knew when it came to gods and goddesses. *Could that be because she knows what the real thing is?*

"Martha, if this is all true, how did you get a hold of such a book?"

"Lionel gave it to me for safekeeping shortly before he died. I never knew how he got it. I never knew he had it until those last days with him. He spent the last of his strength telling me about it, about the history of the gods and their Crowned. He told me to guard it with my life, and when my time came, to pass it on to you or Ramon. He always thought Ramon was a better fit because of how much you dislike the gods, but he said you were someone special and that you might prove yourself more worthy of it."

Someone special? Donovan thought. That was a good feeling. But there were still so many questions.

"Martha, I was arrested during a search for elementium weapons. Something tells me the Guard isn't going to like that you have this book."

"The Guard doesn't need to know, and you're not going to tell them. If you do, then you lose all pork stew privileges."

He chuckled at that. "Martha, this is serious."

"I know, *Sonna*. If what Lionel said is accurate, then very bad men would do just about anything to get their hands on this book. Even destroy Nightingale for it."

A horrible thought clicked in Donovan's mind. "Bad men such as…those from the Kingdom of Kaldaran?"

Martha nodded slightly.

"That's absurd! How would they know you have it?"

"Donovan, I don't know. But what I do know is Lionel said he had seen a lot of magic in his time he could never understand, and that these books did not stay hidden forever."

"I still don't believe that this book is worth more than the elementium crystals in it."

"Perhaps a demonstration would help you," she said as she closed the book and placed a palm on the front cover. "You know that I never have been able to use Technique."

"Of course; not unusual for those who haven't studied it."

Martha closed her eyes and let out a breath. She breathed deeply in and out for several seconds, then the binding of the book began to shine with a faint, orange glow.

Donovan jumped to his feet. "Bag of bones! Martha…it's Technique!" She exhaled and the glow faded.

"Not exactly, but close. I think you can see the power these books have, though. They are a conduit to the gods."

"Martha, you must let me try this. I could use Technique again!"

"I don't think it will work for you, *Sonna*."

Donovan looked at her with a grave expression. "This is a major piece of what I've been looking for. I need it. What will it hurt to let me try?"

"Only your pride." She smiled weakly and handed the book over.

He placed his hand on the cover and took a deep breath. *This could be it.* He focused and reached deep inside himself for the power of human magic. He called out to his soul and demanded the sacrifice to be made. "Impenetrable," he breathed out. He felt his inner-man reaching for the power at the command.

And was struck once again by the feeling of deep emptiness.

Donovan gasped and dropped the book, thankfully missing both his and Martha's toes.

"I'm sorry, *Sonna.*"

He shook his head. "No, it's alright. I had to try. You know I had to try." He bent down and picked up the book, handing it to Martha. "What do we do with it now? Keep hiding it?"

"Lionel said he had been entrusted as the keeper of this book, to keep it safe until the god Orimin determined it was time for his chosen one to take it up."

"Orimin? No kingdom bears the name of that god."

"According to Lionel, Orimin belongs to no kingdom. He is the god of all, so the entire world bears his name in the ancient tongue."

"And how will we know who Orimin's chosen one is? What if we give the book to the wrong person? Can someone use it for evil, or only if Orimin was evil?"

"All very good questions, Donovan. But you are reaching the limit of my knowledge. All I know is that the book can be taken by evil men, and kept secret, so that good men can never use it."

He sighed. "So if everything Lionel told you is right, we need to keep the book safe, and that's all we can do?"

Martha nodded.

"Life is much less complicated without the gods."

"One day, you might understand their importance. But for now, we will put the book back where you found it. When I die, you will be its new keeper. You must keep it hidden. Secrecy is our best defense. We do not know for sure that Kaldaran is here for it."

Donovan did not think anything could warrant such fear from Martha, but Lionel had been a very mysterious man. If there was anyone in Nightingale who had kept a secret like this, it would have been him.

"Alright, Martha. I will do as you ask. But I want you to tell me everything you know about this book."

Martha nodded. "Yes, another time. For now, I want you to be thinking about your time with Alexis tonight." She closed the book and took it over to her desk, where she hid it in the secret compartment once again. Then she went over to the dresser, opened the top drawer, and fetched out a bar of soap.

"You definitely said desk, I know you did."

She laughed. "Maybe I did. But you smell awful, and you need this. Come help me finish carrying the water."

Donovan stood outside the Safe Haven Inn, still chewing over everything Martha had told him that day. He didn't believe in the gods—was well known for being one of the few people who didn't—but Martha was a smart woman. Lionel an even smarter man. When it came to myths, lies, and half-truths, there had been no one better at sniffing them out than Lionel.

If that was true, then why had he bought into this strange god?

Donovan resolved to stop thinking about the book and everything Martha had told him. *Just enjoy yourself. Ramon and Tybalt will be there too, so there's no pressure.* With that thought, he stepped inside.

Alexis was already there waiting, along with Ramon and the new guy, Tybalt. Ramon stood up to embrace Donovan in a hug before both of them sat down.

Alexis bought the first round, including drinks for Ramon and Tybalt. The more the ale washed through him, the more relaxed he felt, and soon he was laughing with the others as Ramon shared memories.

"So then, Jasper's brother, Jahan, squares up to Lionel and says, 'If you want to keep all your teeth, take your fur hunting business elsewhere.'" Ramon paused to take a long swig of blonde ale before continuing. "It went dead silent for probably the first time during working hours since opening. Everyone knew not to mess with Lionel, but Jahan was clearly drunk, and there were rumors going back and forth that they had been sabotaging each other's businesses. Well, Lionel didn't like being threatened one bit."

"Did he knock Jahan out?" Alexis asked.

"I kid you not, Lionel takes one finger, puts it on Jahan's chest, and pushes him clear back into a table. And you've all seen the guy—he's young and beefy. Well, Jahan's friends didn't like *that* one bit, so they rushed Lionel, and quickly discovered that the old man had way more strength than they anticipated. He swatted them off like flies, and before long, the barkeep was running—"

"More like limping," Donovan muttered.

Alexis and Tybalt laughed.

Ramon continued, "—out from the back and *roars*, 'That's it! I'm throwing all your asses out of here! I don't want to hear one more word!'"

Alexis rolled her eyes. "I get that he runs the place, but you must expect some fighting to break out anywhere ale is served."

"Well, to be fair, the table Jahan landed on snapped in half. Lionel made him a new one, though."

"Really?" Donovan asked. "Which one?"

Ramon indicated the very one they sat at by glancing down before taking another drink.

"I knew I always liked this table," Donovan said with a wide grin.

"Lionel was a woodworker?" Tybalt asked, in a quiet, gruff, but friendly tone. He was a Driggonite by the look of him, and that usually meant disaster. Driggonites usually stuck to their own and had strange cultural customs. But from what Ramon had said of him, Tybalt was a solid companion and a good hunter.

"Lionel was a master of many trades," Ramon answered. "He learned more in his eighty years than most men could if they had five hundred. Damn shame we lost him."

"I'll drink to that," Alexis said as she held up her tankard. "To Lionel, and to the gifts he left behind."

"Hear, hear!" Donovan said.

The four clicked their tankards together and started in on the night. There was a pause in the conversation as they drank their ale, felt the warmth of alcohol rush into them, and together remembered some good times. Donovan leaned back in his seat and took it in—the murmuring of the tavern, the smell of ale in the air, the warm glow of the lantern lights, and the occasional barking laughter from the barkeep, the same one who ran Lionel and Jahan out that night.

By the time Donovan turned back into his friends, Ramon and Tybalt had moved on to talking about what they needed to do when they got back to the shop. Alexis put a hand on his arm. He turned to her, and she smiled.

"What are you thinking about?" she asked.

"How nice everything is right now. Well, almost everything. Martha was telling me about…some of Lionel's past earlier today. It kind of rattled me."

"Does that happen a lot?"

"First time. The things she said were so strange it made me see her and Lionel in a different light, and I'm not sure I like it."

"I'm sure both of you will come around. Us women are…complicated at times. I feel like I'm less complicated than most, but there are those who would beg to differ."

Me being one of them, Donovan thought. *Friend and cruel taskmaster all at once.* He just smiled instead.

"What was the conversation about?"

Donovan considered her question. It wasn't safe to tell her about the book, but he didn't have to bring that up.

"You knew Lionel a little, did he ever mention his religious devotion?"

"Briefly, once. He said he served 'the god with no kingdom.' I first thought he was setting up a joke, but that was all he said."

"That sounds like Lionel."

"Is that what you and Martha talked about? Why would that make you feel rattled?"

Donovan leaned in. "Lionel and Martha have earned more respect from me than just about anyone else."

"What about me?"

"You as well. But let me finish. I've always looked up to them, but they never told me about their beliefs, and I never saw any idols in their home. I just assumed they were like me and didn't believe in the gods."

"And why is that such a problem?"

"I thought about it on the way over here and…and I just realized how alone I am in my beliefs."

"But you still hold to them."

"I know. But I can't force myself into believing something I don't. The way people use the gods—as excuses for bad things happening, or justification for war and violence, or to make money—this all seems insane to me. I just can't believe that these gods are real, and if they are, I want nothing to do with them."

Alexis looked away; Donovan felt a little guilty. He knew she was devoted to K'var. But a moment later, she looked back at him and surprised him with her response. "And did Lionel use his god as an excuse for bad things happening? Have Martha or I used our gods as justification for war, or to make money?"

Donovan took in a breath. "No, and that's part of why I like you and her. You are good people, and I think your gods have nothing to do with that."

A sudden crashing noise quieted the room. A drunkard had fallen off his chair and knocked over a table. He cheered like it was part of the party, but the barkeep was not amused.

"Uh-oh, looks like someone is about to get the Lionel-Jahan treatment," Ramon said, a little loudly. Enough people at the Safe Haven must have known about that incident, because they laughed, and laughed harder as the barkeep—quite literally—threw the man out.

"I think Ramon is a bit drunk," Donovan said loudly enough for him to hear.

"Isn't that the point?" he answered. "Another round, on me!" Ramon nearly fell out of his chair getting up, and he slowly sauntered over to the bar.

"He's not going to make it back with four drinks," Tybalt commented. "I'll go help."

Alexis watched Tybalt go, then turned to Donovan. "Just us for a moment." He felt nerves stirring in his stomach.

"It's nice," he said. She was looking at him, but somehow not staring. It was like her eyes were communicating with his. "How have you been with all this? Nobody expected Kaldaran to attack us."

She looked down. "Honestly?"

"I won't tell a soul."

She looked back up. "I'm a bit scared. I don't mind a fight—I've been spoiling for one—but the Kingdom of Kaldaran is over ten times our size, and K'var hasn't responded or sent help. It worries me."

"I didn't know K'var hasn't answered."

"Something I'm not supposed to tell anyone, so please keep that under wraps."

"Of course. Are you going to be alright?"

She suddenly grabbed his hand.

"Alexis," he breathed out.

"I'm glad you joined the Guard. I like knowing you're there. But please, do me a favor and stay alive? Please?"

Donovan smiled. A stray lock of brown hair had fallen over her nose. She was beautiful. "I promise."

Chapter Seven

A month had passed since Donovan's "promotion," which turned out to be more than a one-off. Nothing major since, just a couple small excursions to deal with straggler Kaldarans. But both missions were successful with no casualties. All the while, he could tell Captain Gerald kept a close eye on him, waiting for him to mess up. He didn't like being in the middle of the captain's feud with Alexis, but being in the Guard was going better than he expected. He still got nasty comments about "soulburned" this and "god hater" that, but he had earned the respect of enough soldiers that the pranks stopped.

The bitter cold of winter was sinking in. The war with Kaldaran had stayed very much the same. The Kingdom kept mostly on the outskirts and raided farms, merchant caravans, and the like. It was like being under siege, but not quite as strict. The effects were painful, though.

"How much for that chicken?" Donovan asked.

"Ten silver coins," Jenna replied. "I'm sorry, Donovan, things are so bad around here and my stock has run low. You know I always try to give fair prices, especially to you and your family. But this is the best I can do."

"My pay in the Guard isn't anything great, but it's all going to food. What's going on here, Jenna?"

"Too many farms have been raided, and most merchants are too scared to come through here. I'm...I'm scared too."

Donovan eased up at that and handed over the ten silver.

Jenna smiled and slipped a squash in with the chicken. "That's a little bonus for keeping Nightingale safe. Thank you."

Donovan wrapped up the food and put it in his basket before heading home. He suddenly felt a tug on his Nightingale tabard.

"Please, good sir. I haven't eaten in a week. Please!"

Donovan turned to the man. He was all skin and bone. A lot more beggars had appeared since the Kingdom of Kaldaran attacked. The cost of living was quickly outpacing available work.

"Here, it was given to me for free anyway," Donovan said as he passed the man the squash. His eyes lit up like a child receiving a new toy.

"Thank you, sir! Thank you!"

Donovan pulled his cloak tighter as a late autumn wind whipped through. He was nearly home when the bell rang out from the Nightingale barracks. That usually meant they were under attack, but the pattern this time meant a less urgent call to arms. He would be expected there within the hour. He rushed home to drop off the chicken to Martha, then quickly reported for duty.

Inside the barracks, the Guard had assembled. Donovan took a place along the wall and watched others come in. Captain Gerald had yet to make an appearance, but Alexis was there, her eyes quietly taking roll call.

"Where's Bryant?" she called out.

"Sick as a dog," another soldier called out. "He can hardly move, much less fight."

"That better be true," Alexis called back. "The rest of you, when I call your name, stand by me. We're forming up teams."

"What for?" another soldier asked.

"It's time to take the fight to Kaldaran," she announced. Cheers rose up to that. Until now, they had only been reacting to what was happening. Many had complained that there was no chance for action.

"I guess the captain finally changed his mind," Donovan said aloud.

"Finally," came Arabella's voice from next to him. She had been under Donovan's command for the last two teams he led and was one of his most reliable soldiers.

"Donovan, you're leading your usual team plus a couple others," Alexis called out. "Arabella, Rue, Andrew, Chadwick, Steven, Helena, you're with Donovan."

The seven of them gathered near the front. Chadwick crossed his arms and glared at Donovan.

"Something to say?" Donovan asked.

"Yes. I'm wondering why a soulburned is still in charge of anything around here."

"Your last two missions were successful," Alexis explained.

"Successful in arriving too late to do any real good. Both of those raids we responded to, we arrived after all the butchering, and only killed a couple Kaldaran stragglers in response. If we are going into Shiverpine to hunt them down, I'm not doing so under the command of a soulburned."

That was an exaggeration, but it was true that some farmers were wounded, and parts of their farms destroyed.

Donovan opened his mouth to explain this, but paused when he saw Alexis take a step towards Chadwick, "Are you defying a direct order, recruit?"

"You two are sleeping together, aren't you? Is that why this soulburned was promoted so quickly?"

"You swine!" Donovan barked out, but Alexis held up her palm to him.

"Fine. Jillian's team has room for you, Chadwick. You can go with her. But if I hear one more accusation that I have been anything less than professional with my soldiers, then I will take you to the baths and hold you down in the water until you learn to breathe it. Understand me?"

Chadwick slumped ever so slightly. "Yes, Second." He turned to take his position amongst Jillian's team.

"I can't believe him!" Donovan said.

"We're better off without him," Arabella put in.

"Attention!" Captain Gerald's voice cut clean through the chaos. He walked out of the hallway and took a good, long look over the assembled squads. "By now, you all know what's going on. This is retaliation. We are taking the fight to the Kingdom of Kaldaran and the nest they have built in Shiverpine."

The group sent up scattered cheers. Donovan remained quiet, focusing on the captain.

"Chances are good they will see us coming, so we need to move fast and not give them a lot of time to prepare. Your team commanders are Jillian, Fod, Donovan, Marshall, and Kane, and Alexis above all of those. Our scouts report that we have a good chance of putting an end to all of this. Second in Command Alexis will lead you all to Shiverpine and give you further instructions from there. Are we clear?"

"Hear, hear!" Chadwick shouted, and many others joined in agreement. Donovan simply waved for his team to follow him to get suited up.

"Something wrong, Donovan?" Rue asked.

"Why isn't the captain coming? Shouldn't he be leading the charge instead of passing this off to Alexis?"

"I thought that was strange too," Andrew said. "Captain Gerald has held his rank for nearly a decade. Do you think he's hiding an injury and can no longer fight?"

Donovan strapped a sword belt around his waist. "I think he's turned from captain into politician. I'm worried his number one interest is to find another job."

"Does it really matter?" Arabella asked. "Everyone has been asking for this. I personally don't care if the captain sits in his office and sips whiskey all day. As long as we get to defend Nightingale, I'm happy."

"Maybe we should ask Chadwick his opinion," Steven said. They all laughed.

"Chadwick's an ass," Arabella said. "He was sleeping with Emeline, and he blames Donovan for her death. That's why he hates your guts."

Donovan's stomach churned. "Did Emeline's husband—the blacksmith—ever find out?"

Andrew barked out a laugh. "Chadwick would be dead by now if he did, and no one would prosecute a blacksmith in a time of war."

Donovan crossed his arms. "Still, it seems like someone should tell him."

Andrew shook his head. "As awful as I think Chadwick is, I would rather have him out there fighting than his body rotting in a grave doing no good for anything but the flowers."

None of that sat well with Donovan, but Andrew did have a point. At the very least, he wouldn't have to deal with Chadwick anymore.

Another bell rang clear through the barracks. Donovan finished the last strap to secure a bow at his back. "Time to go."

Excitement and unease marked the troop of Nightingalens heading north to strike at the Kaldaran soldiers in Shiverpine Forest. Alexis hadn't given any orders on what the plan was when they got there, but Donovan knew they were going to split up into teams and attack that way. It was risky, especially for whichever team got targeted the most by Kaldaran defenses, but the rest of the teams would then have a big opening.

The cold gusts sweeping through the hills north of Nightingale felt surprisingly good. They had been on the march half the day with no break.

"My legs feel like porridge," Rue complained. "Why do these hills have to be so tall? How long have we been marching?"

"Not long enough," Donovan answered. "Shiverpine is close but we still have a little way to go."

Rue groaned. "I wish you hadn't told me that. How are we supposed to fight like this? The Kaldarans have probably been eating and drinking all day."

"All the better for us if they have been," Arabella put in.

"Alexis said we plan to camp close by and strike in the early morning light. You'll get a break, just a bit longer."

Rue gave Donovan a sideways glare. "Well, when you need Technique, don't come calling to me. At least not without giving me a break."

That comment stung more than she had probably meant it to. That's what Donovan told himself as he tried to let it slide.

"How many Kaldarans do you think are there?" Andrew asked.

"Best intelligence indicates anywhere from fifty to a hundred."

Arabella scoffed. "And by 'best intelligence' do you mean the ramblings of a random farmer?"

Donovan did not want to admit that Arabella had hit the nail on the head. Most of what they knew about Kaldaran came in from farmers who witnessed a raid and were lucky enough to get to Nightingale alive.

"Maybe someone should organize those farmers into a spy ring for us," Andrew said.

Arabella, Rue, and some of the other soldiers laughed. Donovan thought it wasn't a half bad idea.

"Yes, or perhaps we could—" Rue cut herself off when she nearly bumped into the person in front of her. The column had come to a sudden halt.

"What's going on?" Andrew asked. "Is it time for a break?"

"Finally!" Rue exhaled a sigh of relief and sat down. Donovan, a bit taller than the others, looked over their heads to see what was happening.

"Rue, get up, now!"

"Huh?"

"We're under attack!" Alexis called out. "Form up, now! On the teching double!"

"The Kaldarans are advancing on us?" Andrew frantically unstrapped his bow. "What the gol? Why would they do that?"

"Maybe to catch us off guard!" Donovan worked on readying his own bow. "Seems to have worked pretty damn well, wouldn't you say?"

"What should we do?" Rue asked.

"Follow Alexis's orders," Donovan answered.

The Kaldarans were coming in on horseback. They had used the hill as cover and charged up and over it when the Guard got close. There were fewer of them than the Guard, but they were mounted. Andrew, Donovan, and a few others good with the bow started firing. They picked off a couple, but the Kaldarans were on them. Swords at horse speed swung down.

Donovan tried not to lose focus seeing the brutal killings happening in front of him. He pulled another arrow and loosed it at a Kaldaran, then dove out of the way when the horse ran wild, dragging its dead rider by the stirrup.

Andrew had switched to his sword and breathed out, "Featherweight!" The sword glowed a faint orange, and the metal became lighter. It could still hit with deadly force—Donovan didn't understand that, but he had seen it before.

Rue had collapsed to the ground and Donovan couldn't tell if she was alive. Alexis was barking out orders, but the whole battle was chaos, and he couldn't hear her clearly. He was better with his bow, but the mounted Kaldaran soldiers moved too fast and were too close now. He drew his sword and readied his shield, but as they rushed past him, he spent more time evading than swinging. He felt useless. His couple kills with the bow were all he had still.

Arabella was handling herself the best and had killed a few Kaldarans while also helping Rue back to her feet. Donovan was relieved—Rue was still alive.

"Donovan, watch out!" Andrew shouted.

Donovan turned to see a Kaldaran racing toward him. He held up his shield and deflected the blow, but the force sent him to the ground. He pushed himself back up but felt an intense pain in his shoulder. The blow had dislocated it. He wrenched it away from his shield and turned to fight with the good arm he had left.

Arabella's scream tore through the air. Donovan turned and expected her to be cut open, but she had been disarmed and was carried away by two Kaldaran soldiers. They were retreating, but Arabella was in tow.

"We fought them back?" Andrew called out.

"For now," Alexis answered. "Status report: how many dead and wounded?"

Donovan rushed over to her. "They took Arabella! Why aren't we chasing after them?"

"We're not in any condition to give chase!" Alexis barked back. "And we're on foot and they on horseback, in case that escaped you."

"Teching damn, Alexis, she was taken alive! Kaldarans don't take prisoners, what do you think they are going to do with her?"

"I don't know! Now will you let me teching think?"

Donovan turned to Andrew. He knelt next to Rue, who was holding her bleeding gut.

He turned back to Alexis. "I'm not giving up that easily!"

"Your shield arm says otherwise."

Donovan ignored her and walked over to Rue. "We need a mender!" he called out.

Eodius was not there, but another half-fey soldier came out of the crowd.

"She is too far gone," he said. "She will never survive the mending."

"Just try it!" Andrew pleaded. The mender knelt and took hold of Rue's hand. A blue glow emitted from his palm. She screamed in agony, then her voice faded and her eyes closed.

"Teching gol!" Andrew grunted.

Donovan just stared, mouth agape, horrified. "The mending killed her?"

"The body can only handle so much," the mender explained. "She would have died either way. I am sorry."

Donovan's fist tightened. He wanted to cry out in bitter rage, but there was work to be done. Arabella had been taken away. He turned to the mender and indicated his arm. "Here, fix me." The mender looked annoyed; he was supposed to be taking orders from Alexis. "Do it," Donovan commanded.

He grabbed Donovan's palm and let the healing magic go free. Donovan grunted in pain. It was said that mending took all the pain you were supposed to feel during recovery and shortened it to a few, intense seconds. He moved his shield arm enough to know it had worked, then took off for one of the loose horses a dead Kaldaran had left behind.

"Donovan, get back in line!" Alexis ordered.

"I'm not losing anyone else. I'm saving Arabella."

"You are about to charge in like an idiot and die for nothing!" Alexis pleaded.

Before she had finished speaking, Donovan had dug his heels into the horse and pressed the beast onward. He looked back only to make sure no one was following him, and to his surprise Andrew had grabbed a loose horse and was close behind. He gave Donovan a quick nod and that was enough. The two of them were going into enemy territory ahead of the rest of the Guard.

Not long after, they made it to Shiverpine. The forest was named for the cold wind that would frequently sweep in from Mount K'var nearby, but now, the once familiar forest sent shivers up Donovan's spine, giving new meaning to the already foreboding name. He knew enough about tracking to pick up the trail of the Kaldaran soldiers, so if the ones that took Arabella went to the same place, he could find her.

He and Andrew rode together at a trot, slow enough that Donovan could keep track of where the Kaldaran soldiers went.

"What's the plan?" Andrew asked in a low voice.

"We get Arabella and ride like gol," Donovan said. He caught Andrew's frown and added, "I know that's not enough, but it's all I have for now. Once we get there and assess the situation, we can think of exactly how to get her and get out alive."

One of the famous cold winds suddenly swept through. Donovan and Andrew both grimaced and tugged at their cloaks.

"Damn, Donovan," Andrew said. "Truth be told, I don't think I've been this scared since I was a child. You?"

Donovan glared at him. "I don't remember being a child…"

"Right. Sorry. Just so you know, I never looked down on you for being soulburned. Gol, I'm not sure why people are so weird about it. Seeing you become a good soldier gives me hope that, should the worst happen, my life might not be over."

Donovan felt his spirit lifting at that. "You really think so?"

"I wouldn't have followed you this far if I didn't. Anyone who uses Technique should think so. I think most people are too stupid to really give it another thought, though. I had a cousin who soulburned, and he spent the rest of his life fishing down in Sokor. He was a tournament archer before that, but no one seemed to respect him after it happened. He found that the fishermen didn't seem to care about his condition. I can't say he was exactly happy, but…he had a decent life, all things considered."

"Had?"

Andrew frowned. "He got thrown off his boat in a storm. But he died trying to save someone else. He had more respect for that among his peers than he ever did from the tournaments. I'm damn proud myself."

Donovan nodded in respect. But he couldn't shake the thought that maybe Andrew's cousin was more willing to give up his life because he didn't value it as much as he should. *Way to stay positive, Donovan.*

The signs of Kaldaran activity increased, so Donovan signaled for Andrew to keep quiet. He nodded and they continued with extra caution.

After about half an hour, they heard voices in the distance. Donovan signaled Andrew to follow, and they rode over closer to the mountain.

"What's this?" Andrew whispered.

"An old hunting ground," Donovan answered. He brought the horse to a halt and dismounted. There was a hedge of thick brush, and he pulled some of it back and pointed. "There's a cave here. New plan: we hide our horses and possibly camp until the rest show up to attack."

"But what about Arabella?"

"We are going to get her and bring her back here, but there's no way we are sneaking in or out on horseback."

"Right." Andrew dismounted and the two led their horses inside the cave. The sun was starting to fade, and once they were a little way in, the dark concealed their horses. The horses were a bit spooked by that, so they took a few minutes to calm them down.

Donovan felt along the wall until he found a metal ring attached to the stone.

"Lionel made this so he would have something to tie his horse to. We can do the same."

"Pretty impressive," Andrew said as he tied the reins to the ring.

"He liked to have places to get safe out on hunts. Saved his life and mine at least once."

With that, the two of them went back outside and toward the Kaldaran camp. The sounds of Kaldaran men shouting and laughing grew louder and louder as they drew close.

"They are celebrating," Andrew noted.

"They definitely did more damage to us than we did to them."

The beating of drums started up, echoing into the night. Donovan was relieved at that; the sound would cover their approach.

A moment later, they could see the Kaldarans gathered around campfires. In the center of the camp there sat a large flat rock covered in blood and illuminated by torches. On the ground near the rock lay several bodies. Donovan swallowed hard at that. Some of the faces were familiar to him. No one he knew well, but people he had seen drinking at the Thirsty Horse and Safe Haven.

"K'var's blood!" Andrew breathed out. "They are performing ritualistic sacrifices!"

"Now we know why they took Arabella."

"Do you see her?"

Donovan risked taking another step forward and getting a better view of the camp. Off to the side, he saw Arabella. Her feet were chained to a wooden post, and she lay next to it. Donovan took a step back to Andrew.

"She's over on the right, her feet chained to a post."

"Is she alive?"

"I can't be sure, but no wound looks fatal from here. And if they are doing sacrifices, they will want to keep her alive for her turn."

"I can cut her chains with a *sunder*. Do you think we can get to her without being seen?"

"We need to try. I know a way we can get close—follow me."

Donovan led Andrew around another path by way of the mountain's rocks. They stayed in cover until Arabella was just twenty paces away, but that's where the rocks ended. Andrew let out a heavy breath.

"What now?"

"I think I can get a little bit further up and around, then I can create a distraction so you can get her free. I know these woods. Hopefully better than they do. I can get away and meet you back at the cave."

"That sounds terribly risky, Donovan." He looked over at Andrew.

"More than anything else we've done so far?"

"Good point, but yes, far riskier. Are you sure about this?"

Before Donovan could answer, two Kaldarans came over near Arabella. One of them had a tattoo of a serpent dragon down his right arm, and the eye of the serpent matched the eye on the Kaldaran tabard.

"Yes, this one will do fine." The dragon man grinned wide. "Ya did good."

"Thank you, my king." At that, Andrew jumped a little.

"King Santos is here?!" he whispered. Donovan glared at him to keep quiet.

"Thought ya might like another live one," the man standing next to the king said. "But, if you don't mind me askin', my king, when the gol do we get the tech out of here?"

King Santos turned toward him and furrowed his brow. "Are ya questionin' my authority?"

"O' course not!" the man fell to his knees. "I am only lettin' ya know, a lot of the men are wonderin' if K'var is gonna come soon. I ain't one to question ya or run from a fight, but it would do our hearts good like a fine drink to know if we're gonna move on before they show up."

"They aren't showin' up, ya damn idiot. I wouldn't be so stupid as to fight with them so far from our home. They're too busy fightin' those techin' burnin' beasty things with no hearts."

"The Barkodi?" Andrew whispered. Those were fire elemental creatures, and they did war with K'var often.

"Must be." Donovan nodded.

"My king, are you sure?" the groveling one asked.

"K'var ain't worried about Nightingale anymore. They are worried about survivin'. The Barkodi aren't dealing with those cliff dwellers these days. They are going after the Kingdom of K'var with full force."

Donovan hoped King Santos was lying. *But...gods...the king of Kaldaran is here. He wouldn't come out all this way if K'var was going to stop him. Would he?* King Santos suddenly turned back toward the camp.

"My fellow warriors!" his voice roared through the night. "Once again you have done well and have brought sacrifice for our god. To Kaldaran be the glory!"

"To Kaldaran the glory!" shouted all the rest in response.

"May his cloak of darkness cover us!" The tattooed one continued. "May his eye watch over us! May he fill our enemies with dread and bring his confusion and chaos upon them!" The drumbeat sped up in rhythm to his words. Donovan felt a hint of the dread the king boasted about. He looked to Andrew who was sweating in the cold, his face drawn back in panic.

"Are you alright? I need to you stick with me on this one. Arabella needs you."

Andrew nodded slightly.

"I know this is a longshot, but I'm taking most of the risk. Wait until—" a roar interrupted Donovan. He turned and saw the tattooed Kaldaran fighting with another. All the other Kaldarans gathered around and watched, no one jumping in to help their supposed King.

The fight only lasted a minute before King Santos scored a long cut across the chest, sending the other Kaldaran to his knees, his life bleeding out rapidly.

"Put him on the altar! He will die the same as anyone else who dares try and take my crown from me!"

"All hail King Santos!" resounded the Kaldaran soldiers as a few of them moved to do as their king ordered.

"These people are insane!" Andrew's breathing was ragged.

"One less of them to deal with, right?" Donovan forced a smile.

Andrew's panicked look remained unchanged.

"Remember the plan," Donovan said.

Donovan moved slowly until there was a good amount of cover, then picked up his pace. *Gods above, I know I'm not your favorite. But if you aren't the horrible, made-up things I think you are, please keep Arabella off that altar for another five minutes. Is it so wrong to ask for five minutes? That seems reasonable. And it's for her, not me.*

Thirty paces away there was a rock formation jutting out of the hill, and a large tree was stuck hanging on the edge of it. It was far too heavy to move, but it didn't look like it needed much of a push. Donovan was always a good climber, and he made to the top with ease. Upon closer inspection, the tree seemed to be swaying in the wind, waiting for just the right touch to come tumbling down.

Here goes, he said. He took one more breath and gave the side of the tree a swift kick, which pushed him back down to the ground with a thud. He looked up—the tree hadn't moved. *Alright, you little tree bastard.* Donovan approached one end, bent at the knees, and with all his might he pushed. The tree moved ever so slightly. He did it again and got a little more movement. Then he gathered his strength together and went for one final push. He put all of his strength into it, and the tree went crashing to the ground.

Distant cries of Kaldaran soldiers resounded in the forest. Donovan's hands were shaking, but he knew he had to move. He climbed back down, nearly losing his grip and falling the last few paces. But he made it, and he was on the run. If his distraction worked, Andrew would have Arabella soon and they would both be back in the cave.

The drums had stopped. That was good. Donovan tried to slow his breathing and focus on not making a sound. The camp was probably just ahead. He moved a hand to take sweat out of his eyes. His heart pounded so hard—he had to keep going. He came in sight of the camp and dropped prone. *They all left! It worked!* He wondered if just maybe some god had granted his prayer. But then his heart stopped.

I see Arabella, and no Andrew.

Donovan waited a moment for his fellow guardsman to appear, but there was no one. The distraction wouldn't last for long; it was a miracle it worked so well to begin with. *Where the gol is Andrew?* He had come too far to give up. He had to try. He needed to try. For Rue…for Emeline…and for Henry and Celene. All those who died under his command.

Donovan rose slowly and crept forward. He took a quick look around the camp, then bolted forward for Arabella. He slid the last couple of paces down to the ground next to her.

"Arabella! Are you alright?" he asked. He picked up her hand. Her face was bruised, her lips swollen. Still-wet blood stained her tunic, and her arm looked unnaturally bent.

No response. Donovan's heart sank. Then he saw the steady rising of her chest. *She's only unconscious!* He took in a breath. *Unconscious and still chained to this teching post! Where the gol is Andrew?!*

Donovan drew his sword and started slashing at the post. It was thick, hard lumber, and swords were not meant to cut wood. He struck again, and again, and again, but he had only made a notch. It was too tall for him to slip the chain to the top, and the post was just a tree that had been trimmed out. The stubs of cut branches along the way would make it take forever to work the chain around.

"Damn it, damn it, damn it to teching gol!" he breathed out. "Bag of bloody bones!"

"What's that?" someone shouted from far behind. They were coming. Donovan's hands quaked in panic and anger. Only one thing could save her now. A *Sunder* Technique. He focused his mind, concentrating on drawing power from his heart. That's how it was always done, that's what everyone told him. It's what he had tried with the book Martha had shown him. He imagined his blood pumping power through his veins, into his hand, his skin, into the metal itself, charging his blade with the magic of humankind. He felt something inside him well up, a tingling sensation in his gut rising up through his chest to his heart.

And once again, the painful emptiness struck him.

"Arabella, wake up!" he pleaded. But there was no response. She could use Technique. She could save herself with his blade. But she did not stir.

"It's coming from the camp!" said a Kaldaran. Donovan whipped around in that direction. Time was up. He stood up and raced for the rocks he had hid behind before. Andrew was nowhere to be seen. He peeked out from the rock and gasped as he saw Arabella's eyes opening. For a second, it looked like she locked eyes with him.

Then, out of the forest, the Kaldarans emerged. The tattooed one took several, swift steps forward towards her. She turned toward him and screamed. Grabbing Donovan's sword, she took a wild swing. But she had no chance. The Kaldaran kicked the sword out of her hand, and she wailed in agony.

"Found a sword, did ya?"

"Gods…no!" Donovan breathed out.

"No worries, little lass. You'll be in Kaldaran's arms tonight!" the man turned to his followers. "Put her on the altar!" The Kaldarans roared in agreement.

"All hail King Santos!" they said. Donovan turned away and sat with his back to the rock, catching his breath. It was too risky to move now. And maybe…just maybe they would all go to sleep and leave Arabella alive.

But as the hours passed by, Arabella's screams split through the night. They didn't just kill her like they had done the Kaldaran before. They tortured her. They tortured her and danced to the beat of the drums, celebrating their depraved ritual.

With every scream, Donovan's heart filled with more and more pain. Tears ran down his cheeks. The sensation was unbearable. He had failed. *I am a soldier without magic. What good am I? I have no past, and what future is there for soldier who can't use magic?*

The hours passed by; Donovan neither slept nor moved. Arabella's screams had given out at some point. He prayed her torment was over. He waited a little longer before risking a glance. He regretted it when he saw what had been done to her. The Kaldarans were gone, likely in the tents that were scattered about, bundled up and sleeping around campfires. There were a few watchmen with torches, but they weren't looking his way. He took his chance and moved back into the cover of the rocky path he had taken up with Andrew earlier. He made it and ran for the safety of the cave.

When he got there, Andrew was there, huddled against the wall.

"Donovan? You're alive?"

"*I* am. Where the gol were you?"

"I went there but…she…she was dead! She looked dead! I…I ran back for the cave thinking you would meet me here if you were still alive!"

"She *wasn't* dead!" spit flew from between Donovan's clenched teeth. "But she is now! You were supposed to be there to save her!"

"Oh gods!" Andrew breathed out. "Donovan, I swear I thought she was dead! After you left I watched her the whole time and she never moved! I…" He buried his face in his knees and started to weep.

Donovan took a few, slow breaths. When his rage had subsided, he sat down next to Andrew. "You…we gave it a good shot. It's more than anyone else did."

"What do we do, Donovan?" Donovan considered the question for a long moment before answering.

"Wait for the others to start their attack, then join them. Perhaps we can still do some good."

"I—I'm so sorry."

"No more than me."

Chapter Eight

The counterattack against the Kingdom of Kaldaran ended in a defeat, though the Kaldarans certainly paid the price. Alexis and her teams had showed up in the morning, as was planned. Donovan and Andrew joined in. What should have been a sound victory resulted in nothing but a chaotic mess.

First, none of the Guard worked together the way they should. No one could hear the orders Alexis was shouting. The Guard was never meant to be an organized army; it wasn't allowed to be, based on the peace deals K'var signed with the Southern Kingdoms years ago.

Second, scouting reports were way off. There were around eighty Kaldarans in the camp Donovan had seen, but there were more camps. Kaldarans flooded in through the woods, and things got bad quickly after that and Alexis called the retreat.

To top it all off, Donovan heard many soldiers quietly admitting they felt the same thing Andrew must have experienced. A sense of dread that shook them to their core. Donovan had felt a little of it, but nothing as severe as they described. Alexis said she watched soldiers deserting before the fight turned against them.

Still, some were calling it a success. Donovan wasn't sure. They killed at least a few dozen Kaldarans, and had similar casualties. But during the battle, no one could lay a hand on King Santos. The man was a damn good fighter, better than anyone Donovan had ever seen. The King of Kaldaran cut down everyone who challenged him in combat.

Donovan hadn't even tried.

Upon returning, he was promptly demoted. His disobedience ruined his brief stint as a team leader. But at the end of day, Nightingale couldn't do with losing more soldiers, so they didn't kick him out completely. He was assigned to work with the local farmers and help keep food supplies coming to Nightingale.

I have been reduced to the level of Chadwick. Kept on the Guard only to be a warm body...at least no one else will die under my command.

It had been a month since that ill-fated mission into Shiverpine. The war—as some had come to call it—had taken a turn for the worse. Captain Gerald kept promising they just had to hold on until K'var came to rescue them, but Donovan knew better. He and Andrew told the captain what King Santos had said, but the captain dismissed it outright. He also refused to believe that King Santos himself was there, even though Andrew corroborated the story, as did Alexis.

Regardless, the plan was to hold out for a rescue that Donovan knew would never come. He hoped that the might of Nightingale alone would be enough to save them.

It was now the dead of winter, but the day had been warmer than the past week. A warm, southern wind had blown in from Ladesh and given everyone a break from the cold. That would have been a relief if it weren't raining.

Donovan stood out in the rain and watched as more dead soldiers were carted back into the city. They were lucky. They weren't put on an altar and tortured well into the night,

Every other second, a raindrop hit Donovan's face, but he left his hood down behind his head. He was frozen in time, watching Officer Fod's troops returning. He had been assigned to a different team, and this time they weren't the ones attacked.

"You alright?" Alexis's voice sounded behind him.

Donovan turned to her. "No, but it's good to see you, regardless."

Alexis smiled and took a place standing next to him. She was wearing her white cloak, the one with the purple bird of Nightingale on the back. It was what all the ranking officials wore for what was essentially a funeral procession. "You're thinking about how you could have just as easily been with Officer Fod instead of Jillian today, aren't you?"

Donovan nodded.

"I think the same thing, sometimes," she admitted with a sigh. "That's the burden of the living—to watch and wonder."

"Wonder if there was any way to not get all my people killed."

"Five is hardly all of them."

Donovan returned to watching the Guard coming in.

"You look cold," she said as she reached past his face for his hood and pulled it over his head. He let her. Her touch was surprisingly gentle. "Donovan…I want to speak to you as a friend." He turned toward her again. "I'm worried about you."

His eyes fell. "I know."

"We've barely talked since what happened at Shiverpine, and I didn't get the chance to tell you that what you did—as out of line as it was—was the bravest thing I have ever seen."

"What do you mean? I failed, Alexis. I failed Arabella, and before that, I failed Emeline, and Henry, and Celine. I failed Nightingale. I am a failure. Chadwick was right to join another team. It saved his life."

"A lot of people have died that weren't under your command, Donovan. Chadwick has it easy. All he has to do is follow orders. He doesn't know what it's like to be in command. He never will."

Donovan considered that for a moment. Then he shook his head. "What difference does it make? You believe me about King Santos, don't you? You told the captain you did."

"I do, and while I doubt King Santos was speaking the truth entirely, K'var most likely isn't coming. They haven't returned our carrier pigeon messages, and our only messenger who came back said he wasn't allowed audience there. I think we are on our own, and the captain doesn't want anyone to know so they won't panic."

Donovan huffed out a breath. "When every Nightingalen is dead, they won't be panicking, either."

Alexis paused at that for a moment. "Would you like to do something about it? More than you are doing now?"

"I was ordered not to tell anyone what King Santos said."

"I don't mean tell people about King Santos. I mean get back into the fighting. I spoke with the captain, and we are short team commanders—"

"No. Alexis, just...no. I'm not getting any more Guard killed."

"You wouldn't have to worry about that." Donovan furrowed his brow.

"What do you mean?"

"I may not agree with many of the captain's decisions, but he saved up quite the war chest before all this went down. Nightingale has the funds to hire mercenaries, and we picked out some of the best to form a new squad. A couple of them were marksmen in Toby's crew. They said they wanted a change of leadership, so we snatched them up. The only thing they are missing is one Nightingale loyalist to lead them."

"You can't be serious.'"

"It's either hire mercenaries or..." Alexis turned her eyes to him, "everyone will start panicking."

He sniffed. "Captain Gerald is serious about this? He isn't worried I'm going to go rogue again?"

"We expect you to go rogue, that's why we gave you a team of rogues to work with."

"You know how I feel about mercs, Alexis. Yes, I liked Toby's crew. But they weren't at the whorehouse every night like most of them are."

"Donovan I..." Alexis stopped to take in a breath. "I don't trust anyone else to do this. You're an honest man and that's what we need to lead a group of mercs. Plus, you may not think anything of it, but you do have experience leading now. Yes, I get it, you think you failed, and it was made worse by your demotion. But so what? Are you going to try again or are you going to give up?"

Donovan turned to Alexis and pointed a finger at her. "You know I don't quit that easily!"

She shrugged and said, "Could've fooled me."

He opened his mouth but paused. She was getting him riled up so he would get back into the fight. He took in a breath gave her a slight smile; she smiled back. His heart always melted at that smile.

"Alright, you win. When do I meet them?"

"Tomorrow morning, just before sunrise. Thirsty Horse Tavern. I'll stop by after you've had a chance to make initial greetings."

Donovan muttered a curse and grabbed at his furs. The air had turned frigid overnight and was likely to stay that way. He stomped out his snowy boots under the sign of the Thirsty Horse Tavern. He was about to meet his so-called team, flaws and all. He paused for a moment to look up at the old, squeaky, wood plaque that swung lightly in the damp, morning breeze. It displayed an image of a horse, winking and eating from a nosebag that had *ALE* written in letters large enough so even a blind old bastard could read it.

A then-young Patrick Doll had built the alehouse over five decades ago. It was the oldest building in Nightingale, barely. Madame Silva's whorehouse was constructed just a few months after. Before that, it was horses, carts, and whatever makeshift shelter traveling merchants set up while taking a break from their journeys.

"Surprised we aren't meeting there," Donovan muttered sarcastically toward the whorehouse as he opened the door to the Thirsty Horse.

Upon entry, the familiar smells of stale beer and hints of vomit hit Donovan's nose. It was all mixed together with the scent of sweat on old wood, and a few candles Patrick the owner had lit earlier in the morning that had not yet burned all the way down. A thin line of cold blue light came in through the center lines and slats of the shutters, but everything was closed up for now.

The old floorboards creaked under Donovan's boots as he strode in, leaving a fresh trail of muddy prints over slightly older ones. He had been here many times before with Ramon, whenever Safe Haven was too crowded for them, or when Patrick had an especially good cask of dark beer.

Sitting on the far end of the tavern, around two tables that had been pushed together, were the six men and one woman that made up Donovan's team. They all looked him over once, and apparently, that was enough to size him up.

"So," one of them spoke up. He had long, reddish hair and green eyes. He wore dark clothing that hid his frame a little, but it was still obvious he was strong. He looked to be mid-twenties, with a mix of nationalities. His skin was a couple of shades darker than the others, which might have meant Corrick blood, but the eyes and hair pointed to a more foreign ancestry combined with Kaldaran blood. Donovan had seen only one other man that looked anything like that, and he was from Velmar. "The first meeting of the Thirteenth Division has begun."

The Thirteenth Division. Nightingale had twenty-three divisions of soldiers to divvy out protection of the trade routes and occasionally go fight off a small group of raiders on a farm. Soldiers not in divisions yet served in teams or squads, and recently squads were mainly used, as the divisions had to be broken up to serve other needs.

In reality, though, Nightingale had only ever had twenty-two divisions. The Thirteenth Division was a title never used due to superstition about numbers being bad luck.

"Abaddon wielded thirteen swords, had thirteen wives, thirteen military commanders, and thirteen assassins," was an old saying that had survived from the days when gods ruled over the kingdoms directly. To avoid the number supposedly cursed by the dark god, Nightingale never had a thirteenth division. Donovan thought the name fit him quite nicely.

"What's your name?" Donovan asked.

"Rohawk."

"You have Kaldaran blood in you?"

"Of course, but only half," he said, producing a pipe from his clothes and starting to pack it with some cut tobacco sitting on the table. "My father was from Deldamore, my mother from Kaldaran. Is there a problem with that? If you knew Kaldaran, you would know I have no love for the people I share blood ties with."

Donovan crossed his arms. "What about this Deldamore?"

"In Velmar. I know, I know, you Drannussians don't know anything about Velmar. I suppose I shouldn't expect a very high level of education out of this group."

One of the other men smiled. "You'd be surprised, Rohawk," he said in a slightly high-pitched voice with an aged rumble beneath it. He had big, gray, caterpillar eyebrows and a full mustache to match. Not only that, but he seemed lucky enough to have most of his hair, though it was hidden underneath his cavalier hat.

"I don't much mind that you are Kaldaran, but I don't want people lying about who they are here. I don't care if you walk out this door and tell everyone you're the reincarnation of Borek himself—in here, we have honesty. Understood?"

There was a collective nod.

Donovan nodded at the oldest of the bunch, the one who had commented to Rohawk, and said, "Introduce yourself, if you don't mind."

"Lysander," he answered. "Yes, the same one who designed the wall down in Corrick, though that was many, many years ago. Now I'm a sword for hire, a spellsword is probably the most accurate description. I know nearly every Technique there is to know, and more importantly, I know how to use them with minimal effort." Donovan took a seat at the table but left a little distance between himself and the others.

"What do you mean?"

"Only use what you need," Lysander said as he tapped his sword. "A Technique blade, designed to make it easier to channel into the edge of the weapon only. Perfect for *Sunders*. And of course, timing is key; not channeling longer than you need to." The old man narrowed his giant eyebrows. "How do you not know any of this, Donovan?"

Donovan swallowed hard, not knowing what to say.

"Maybe he just doesn't want a lesson from an old man right now," said another one of the men, his tone somewhere between jest and insult. His age was hard to pin down, and he had peculiar gray eyes that seemed to look past Donovan even when he was looking right at him. His light shirt revealed bare arms that had a slightly blue tint, and his left arm was callused between the wrist and the elbow, like a bracer had been tightened over it again and again. He was a marksman.

Lysander smiled despite the slight, and said, "Sometimes I forget I'm the old fogey in the group."

The gentle, self-deprecating response seemed to garner a little respect from the marksman. He smiled a little, then said, "I am Wyndell. I used to run with Toby's gang, before he started becoming a pain in the ass."

Donovan furrowed his brow. "What happened?"

"He started ranting and raving about something related to Kaldar and restoring the old glory days. It creeped me out, so I bailed."

That doesn't sound like Toby at all. Is this Wyndell lying?

"Also, I'm a quarter fey, so please don't ask me if I'm getting enough air, that's just the way my skin looks all the time. I'm a marksman, if that wasn't obvious. I can shoot accurately up to three hundred paces if I'm well-rested and have a longbow. But I'm guessing that situation would be rare, so it should suffice to say, I can make most of the shots you need, or just provide some cover."

An odd bunch so far. Not like any of the mercs I'm used to seeing around town. Except for this Rohawk fellow—he seems as mercenary as they come.

"I think Kristine has similar abilities to me," Wyndell added, nodding toward the one woman in the group. She was young, probably early twenties, with long blonde hair wrapped in a single braid down her back. She was thin and fit, and her blue eyes were like the beauty of a winter snowstorm. Donovan was surprised—women who were that pretty didn't become soldiers. Alexis was beautiful, but tough. This woman could be a lady in a court. Yet...there was something. A dark past. Possibly trauma. Maybe she watched family members die in front of her. It wasn't the only explanation, but something about those frosty eyes spoke of great turmoil that had been put in the past by sheer strength of will.

"My name is Kris. Between Wyndell and me, you should have all the ranged cover you need, whatever you plan to have us do. Though I admit, I probably can't shoot as far with a longbow, unless I use Technique to compensate, which isn't hard."

Donovan nodded. The comment was a slight. *Wyndell can't use Technique.* But Wyndell didn't seem to mind the slight, which meant that he was attracted to her. *No...wait...it wasn't a slight,* Donovan corrected himself. *It was a friendly jab...are they together?*

Donovan took a sudden inhale of breath as he forced himself out of his head. He was trying to cold-read all these mercs, but in the end, the best he could do was just let them introduce themselves and try not to over-read everything now. He turned to consider the next person, a strong fellow with short brown hair and a pair of axes strapped to his back. He looked like he was a woodsman for years before turning to mercenary work—a similar path to that which Donovan had chosen.

"And you are?"

"Godell. A pleasure to meet you, Donovan," he said in a gruff baritone. "I will be joining you on the front lines. I can track, hunt, and hide, all skills I've heard you can do as well. Most importantly, I can fight. I can fight multiple opponents at once."

"Your axes don't look very defensive," Donovan noted. "How do you plan to do that?"

Godell grinned and said, "You ever heard of Magnetic Technique?"

"It's unreliable at best," Lysander huffed.

"Not if you've mastered it," Godell replied, grinning knowingly.

"What's it do?" Donovan asked.

"Draws your blades to your enemy's. They can't hit you if your axes are moving faster than a hummingbird's wings."

Lysander crossed his arms. "I will believe it when I see it, but if what you say is true, I am impressed."

"I hope the Kaldarans will be equally impressed right before they die," Donovan noted. "Any more frontline men here?"

"That would be me," said a black-haired man. His clean-shaven face had more than one small scar on it. "Faith is the name. I am the son of a priest, and I suppose he thought it funny to give me a woman's name. Things didn't turn out as he planned when I turned to mercenary work. I can use a shield and just about any one-handed weapon suits me well."

"A priest turned mercenary," Donovan said. "Never heard of that before."

"Will that be a problem? I know they call you the god-hater."

"That name gets around, huh?" There were a lot of problems with this group, and Donovan thought Godell and Wyndell were a bit overconfident. Also, none of them used spears, which meant they all had to be skilled with Technique to compensate against mounted opponents, and Kaldarans loved their horses. He paused for a moment to regain control of his thoughts and not get too judgmental. It wasn't easy.

Some team, Alexis, Donovan complained to himself. *I bet Toby's crew could run circles around us.*

"And what about you?" he asked the seventh and last member. The person looked up, and Donovan realized that there were actually two women in the group. She had her brown hair cut short and her small breasts were hidden by her tunic. But now that her head was raised, her feminine features were clear.

"My name is Banner," she said. "I grew up on the streets here. I've stolen from most of the merchants around here just to survive, even from Lionel a couple of times. Never from you, but that's mostly because I heard you had a bad temper. Found more opportunity at some of the thriving merchant stands, anyway."

Donovan sighed. "Well, it looks like we have a random bunch of skills and are hoping to fare better than the guards who have trained together for months if not years."

There was an awkward pause in the room.

"Well, it sounds bad if you put it *that* way," Faith commented. Rohawk and Lysander laughed; the others grinned.

Donovan tried to shake off the nasty mood he knew he was in. "As long as you are all aware of the trouble we are in, then I'm fine going forward. Nightingale needs the help. I just don't want anyone running into this blind."

"We all know what we signed up for," Godell said, but his eyes were drifting to the window. "Lot of people milling about outside."

"It's the whorehouse next door," Rohawk said, then added, "so I've heard."

Lysander and Kris looked annoyed at the whorehouse comment. Godell looked more curious than interested—Donovan wondered if he had spent the night there and was trying to hide it. Wyndell looked like he was trying to look annoyed but really didn't care.

"The women there are actually really nice," Banner said in a kind tone. "It's a bit of shame what they've gotten themselves into. I've hid from the guards a few times in there and they always played along."

Lysander's jaw dropped.

Rohawk just grinned. "I can sure vouch for them!"

Lysander turned to him. "I don't think that's what we are here for, if you don't mind."

Rohawk shrugged. "Well, it's certainly not why we are in this tavern, yes. But that could change."

"Alright, here's how this is going to work because I think it's the only way it can work," Donovan said in a tight voice. "You will always obey my orders to the letter. If we work together, we can help keep Nightingale safe, and you can get paid, which I'm guessing is far more important to all of you." Another bit of awkward silence. *Teching gol, am I really this bad at this?*

"Some of us do care about Nightingale," Lysander said. "This is a place of trade, and with trade comes the exchange of knowledge. I would hate to see this town go to ruin. I took the mercenary track simply because I'm too old to be part of the Nightingale Guard, and I can't commit to it long term, anyway."

Donovan paused and took a breath. Lysander's friendly, even-toned comment reminded him that there were possibly good people in the group. Toby's group was solid. He reminded himself he had wanted to join that group not long ago. And making enemies was going to help nothing. If Chadwick could be a warm body fighting to save Nightingale, these mercs couldn't be worse.

"I'm...sorry," Donovan breathed out. He couldn't believe he was saying the words.

Rohawk finished packing his pipe and lit it. After a long draw, he exhaled smoke, put his muddy boots up on the table, and said, "We're not the smoothest bunch, but we're the best Nightingale's got."

Donovan smiled just slightly. "If that's true, we're all doomed." Everyone seemed to pick up that he wasn't entirely serious, and a few chuckled. "Let me start over a little. I don't know what your motivations are, but our orders are to help defend Nightingale based on the intelligence we receive from Second in Command Alexis. I am going to do everything in my power to make sure this division accomplishes that goal. I know you are all probably used to working alone, but we have to try our best to come together on this. If that's a problem, say so now."

There was some uncomfortable shifting around in chairs, but no one got up to leave. "Good. Second in Command Alexis will be here soon with our orders. In the meantime, here are a few things to keep in mind. Discretion is an absolute must. Please don't talk about what we are doing with anyone else."

Rohawk let out a puff of smoke. "I don't know what your experience has been with soldiers for hire, but around here, in Nightingale, we're pretty good on our word."

"The word of a mercenary," Donovan mumbled, but it was clear that everyone heard it.

Rohawk looked at Donovan with a level gaze. That gaze might have been respect, understanding, anger, contempt—any number of things either good or bad.

"Is that better or worse than the word of a soulburned?" he asked.

Donovan glared at him, but was spared from the tension in the air when Alexis arrived. She handed him a sealed envelope and left. It was for him to decide how much to tell the rest of the group. He was already regretting what he said, but he thought it best not to turn back, and just focus on what was in the envelope.

"Bag of bones," he breathed out halfway down the letter. He finished reading, then looked up and told his team, "Crandall's farm has been taken. No one knows if Crandall or any members of his family are still alive."

"Sounds like you need us, then," Banner said with a hint of triumph. She added to it by standing up, producing a dagger, raising it to the sky, and with a grand gesture she proclaimed, "The Thirteenth Division has its orders!"

"This is serious," Donovan said, but he wasn't scolding her. She may have been trying to insult him, but a little enthusiasm didn't hurt. "I knew things around here were getting bad... Crandall is a good man with a family. His farm didn't do great this year, but he has a lot of food stored up still, food that Nightingale needs, that we have to keep out of Kaldaran's hands."

"And how do you know his farm didn't do well?" Godell asked. "You keep up with the local farmers regularly?"

The sarcasm in Godell's tone was evident, but Donovan responded with a matter-of-fact "Yes" while his eyes stayed on the letter. When he had finished reading, he added, "Alright. It's about half a day's ride to the farm. If there are any survivors, there won't be for long. We leave immediately."

"It's mostly flatland between us and that farm," Rohawk said as he suddenly leaned forward. "We'll be spotted well before we make it there."

Donovan took a mental note that Rohawk knew the landscape. "Not if we take another quarter of the day to go wide and come around from the north. There's a hill on that side of Crandall's farm. It can give us some cover and possibly provide a spot for our marksmen to shoot from."

Lysander smiled. "Impressive bit of knowledge, but we still don't know how many are at the farm, yes?"

"At least six," Donovan explained as he looked back at the letter to make sure he had read it correctly.

"At least?" Faith asked. "Not exactly holy scripture you have there, huh?"

"Look, chances are this isn't a Nightingale Guard scout reporting," Donovan said in a dry tone. "This is probably some neighboring farmer who ran for his life and was lucky enough to get away. But your comment does make a good point. We need to treat this situation like there are triple that number there."

"If there's triple that number, we shouldn't be going," Wyndell complained.

Donovan sighed and said, "You're not wrong, but that's the state of play right now. We need some big victories, or Nightingale is finished."

Donovan looked over at Banner, who grinned at him expectantly. He shook his head, but in spite of his better judgment, said, "The Thirteenth Division has its orders."

Chapter Nine

The air of tension was tangible as The Thirteenth Division rode out of Nightingale. They were an odd-looking bunch, and people took notice of that, but mostly they just moved to the side of the road to let the eight horses through.

"You know, eight is a lucky number," Faith said.

Donovan looked over at him. "How so?"

"Eight is the number of Fortina, a minor goddess of luck. She was said to have eight husbands and eight children and...eight of something else I can't remember."

"Eight husbands sounds excessive," Kris said.

Faith nodded. "Old gods are described in this way often, it's not necessarily literal. When one of Fortina's sons was killed, it brought about a tragic series of events. Fortina killed all of her children by accident due to massive misunderstanding, and when she found out what her actions had done, she killed herself. There were eight different times in the story where, if Fortina did not have a massive stroke of misfortune, one or more of her children would have lived."

"Wow, that sounds like amazingly good fortune," Donovan said.

Faith chuckled. "Agreed, but the luck she was denied, she now grants to us from the afterlife."

"I thought you said you *used* to be a priest," Godell put in. "What's with the mythos lesson?"

"I said I was the son of a priest."

The conversation continued, but mostly between Faith and Godell. Donovan was thinking about what they would find at the farm.

"Must be a good day to be a fur trader," Lysander stated. Donovan thought he meant that a fur trader could choose to stay home, but then Lysander pulled his cloak over his chest and added, "Don't quite remember it ever being so cold at this time of year."

"That's why I've been talking to so many farmers," Donovan explained. "I was assisting with fixing the food distribution. Too bad there wasn't much I could do about it."

Someone in the crowd yelled, "Get 'em, boys! Kill those Kaldaran bastards!"

Cheers and cries of "hear, hear!" followed.

Donovan's expression froze, and not because of the cold.

"What's wrong?" Rohawk asked.

"How did he know what we were going to do?" Donovan asked.

"It's pretty damn obvious," Godell said after a scoff.

"I still don't like it." Donovan's voice was quiet, cold steel. "Maybe I'm paranoid."

"Being paranoid isn't entirely bad right now," Rohawk said quietly, to Donovan alone. "Just make sure to keep your wits, lad. We'll get through this, and we'll laugh it up at Madame Silva's before you know it."

Rohawk's words were encouraging to Donovan, despite the lascivious reference which he did not care for. He turned and looked down Broken Street, where a man in black clothing stood, watching him go by. He briefly locked eyes with Donovan before turning into the crowd.

"That's the second time," he mumbled aloud.

"I'll keep an eye on ya," Banner said, very close to Donovan's ear. He jumped a little. She had risen in her stirrups so she could speak close. "I know you don't like us mercs, but we're tryin'. I saw that guy lookin' at you. I know all kinds of things about the underworld here. And they know I cause enough trouble to not be bothered with."

"Uh, thanks," Donovan got the words out with a bit of a struggle. He didn't like the idea of Banner looking out for him, and he doubted she truly had a fierce reputation in the so-called underworld. But all of a sudden, his mercs were reassuring him and supporting him. *Have I earned their respect? Are they just buttering me up?*

As they came close to the City Gate, Donovan looked over at the statue of Borek. Faith produced a silver coin from his pocket and flicked it with his thumb, sending the token whizzing through the air and hitting the base of the statue with a loud *ting!*

"The god of trade and rogues," Lysander nodded as he spoke. "A bit of a duality considering one steals from the other."

"Just figured it might give us some good luck," Faith explained.

"If you wanted good luck for battle," Godell said, "you should go to the Chapel of K'var and pay tribute to one of the gods of war."

Donovan chuckled a bit sardonically and said, "K'var has forgotten us, and maybe that's a good thing. I'm tired of fighting with the gods. Life would be a lot better without them."

Faith frowned at him, but Rohawk said, "Agreed. Let men be men, and the gods can go deal with their own affairs."

"I think you'll find the god's affairs frequently involve men," Wyndell, who had been quiet up until now, put in. "Fey too, for that matter. No one escapes from their games."

Donovan chuckled. "Well, let's give it a try."

It was barely night by the time the Thirteenth Division made it around the hill and into position around Crandall's farm. Their horses were stabled one farm over for now. The group had discussed it and they decided stealth was a better option rather than a frontal assault. That, and the horses were tired out and not ready for battle yet.

A peek over the top of the rise that overlooked the north side of Crandall's farm revealed men in Kaldaran tabards riding a patrol route, torches in hands, looking out into the night for anything that moved.

"Well, I see ten men out on patrol, keeping a pretty tight radius around the farm," Rohawk noted, his body pressed down flat on the snow and peeking over. "They aren't all that well organized, but we won't get past the sheer number of them without being spotted. Your instinct to come around from the north was good, Donovan."

"Yes, but now what?" He whispered the question. He, too, was pressed flat on the ground, the cold of the snow seeping into a few spots his furs didn't cover. "How many are in the house? And the barn?"

Rohawk brought a hand up to scratch his nose. "A couple at least in the barn, and there's a lot of movement in the house and near the stables. I couldn't get a good head count, but I would say around two dozen or more, counting the patrols."

"Bag of bones! Why are they running such a tight patrol route? And this many men? Are they *this* low on food? Crandall's harvest was not good this year, but it was a full farm's worth, which is plenty for a small army."

"Any food they take from Nightingale is worth way more than the food they have to work for themselves," Faith pointed out.

Donovan narrowed his eyes. "Yes, thank you. I had no idea," he said in a dry tone.

Faith looked a little embarrassed.

Donovan looked over toward the barn and the attached grain bin and pointed. "Actually, you might be on to something, Faith. Everyone knows how important the food is. Why are all the patrols around the house and none around the food?"

"Maybe all the food is in the house," Wyndell said.

Everyone turned to Wyndell.

"You can't store a season's worth of grain in your house," Godell said with a soft chuckle.

Wyndell's lips went tight. Before he could answer, Kris said, "But something as valuable as that could be in there."

"What could be more valuable than a season's worth of food in a time of war?" Lysander asked. "We can't just wait out here all night—are we moving or what?"

"Getting stiff, old man?" Godell asked.

"Quiet!" Donovan warned. "Something is happening."

The door to the farmhouse swung open, and two sconces hung nearby revealed a man Donovan did not recognize. There was something unusual about him. Even at a distance, he had an air of authority about him, and for some reason, the very sight of him sent a twinge of dread through Donovan.

Behind this man was another man, who was carrying a bundle of something with the help of another.

"Bag of bones," Wyndell breathed out. "He has a serpent tattoo. The King of Kaldaran really is here."

"I don't see any tattoo," Lysander said.

"I've got better eyes than you, than all of you. Perks of being part fey. I'm sure it's there."

"K'var's bloody sword," Donovan cursed in barely a breath as he tried to push himself further into the dirt and snow. "No wonder there's so many Kaldarans here." All went silent as they watched a Kaldaran bring King Santos a horse.

The King nodded and mounted. He bellowed out a call, and the ten horsemen on patrol all gathered toward where the King was headed—the well. The two soldiers carrying the bundle followed on foot. All of them crowded around the well, and it seemed like they were exchanging some gear and drawing water. The sounds of laughter, of the wooden bucket hitting the sides of the stone well and splashing into the water, of horses whinnying and hooves clopping onto dirt—all these noises echoed across the snow.

Donovan was still frozen, trying not to breathe too loudly.

"Wait, those two men were carrying something, where did it go?"

"What are you talking about?" Banner asked. It took Donovan a second to answer; he had forgotten she was there. *Bag of bones, she really is a sneaky one.*

"Wyndell, you saw it, didn't you?"

"Yes, but not what happened to it. Is it in the snow?"

Suddenly, the horsemen and King Santos rallied and charged off toward Shiverpine, not far from the hill Donovan and his companions had taken.

"He took eleven soldiers with him?" Lysander hissed in disbelief.

Donovan couldn't believe it either—why would Santos need eleven bodyguards, and why would he risk leaving the farm unprotected?

"Now might be our only chance," he said. "Kris, Wyndell, stay here and provide ranged support from the top of this hill." His order was clipped and disciplined. "If the fighting looks like it's going to happen inside, then move in as fast as you can. The rest of you, follow me."

"Where are we going?" Faith asked, but he was already following.

"To the barn, and the attached granary. We are going to secure the food first, then clear out anyone left. Rohawk, Banner, when we get close, you two go in and kill any Kaldarans inside, then send me the all clear. We need to be done in the barn fast in case any more from the house and stables come this way."

"Understood," Banner said with a nod, at the same time Rohawk spoke a curt, "Right, on it."

The group of six reached the barn without being noticed by anyone from the house. They came up on the north side, where there were no torches or lanterns to show what they were doing. Without a word, Banner jumped up and into one of the windows.

"Kaldar's balls!" Rohawk muttered as he hurried to follow her.

Despite his insistence that he had not followed his father's way of the priesthood, Faith looked uncomfortable at Rohawk's strong oath.

"I'm no good with all this cloak and dagger stuff," he complained.

"You'll get your chance to fight soon," Donovan assured him. He crept along the edge of the barn to peek toward the front, which faced west. The farmhouse and stables were farther southwest, and from that direction came four men on foot with torches in hands. Their faces were grim.

Have we been spotted?

Wyndell or Kris must have thought so, because an arrow bolted through the air and struck one of the guards in the shoulder.

The man screamed, and his three companions jerked to attention, searching the landscape for the source of the arrow.

"Bag of—" Donovan bit off the end of the oath.

"They didn't even kill that one!" Godell growled. "Aren't they supposed to be crack shots?"

As if in answer, another arrow whipped through the air and struck the neck of another Kaldaran, killing him instantly.

"We're under attack!" one of the others shouted. The three still alive made a mad sprint for the house. "Kill the teching family!"

Another arrow sailed by. The one who had shouted was struck in the back and killed, but the other two made it to the farmhouse.

Donovan's heart pounded and his hand went to his scabbard. "We have to do something, or—" he was cut off when he felt a hand on his.

"It's a bluff," Rohawk whispered.

Donovan jumped and bit off a curse. "Rohawk! What the gol? What happened in the barn?"

"Banner and I killed three. The shouting was a good distraction."

"What about Crandell and his family?"

"Kaldarans don't keep prisoners except for ritual sacrifice. The king would have taken one with him for sure if he had any alive. It's common for the king to be the one to perform the ritual sacrifice."

Donovan knew that to be true. He had seen it for himself.

The thought of Farmer Crandall and his whole family being dead in that house made him feel sick. He pushed down the sensation and said, "How many more Kaldarans are in the house? We are going to have to kill them to secure the farm."

"You say that like it's a bad thing." Godell cracked his knuckles.

Godell's confidence was refreshing, but Donovan did not share an ounce of it. Something felt wrong. He didn't know what command to give next, so he waited. But there was nothing else happening. Silence had descended on the farm. The only sound was the lowing of cattle inside the barn floating out on the frozen air. The night was now completely upon them, and the long sickle of the quarter moon hung like an icy dagger. It was ominous, haunting—Donovan didn't like it one bit.

Another quiet moment passed, and it was only more maddening. The Kaldarans were waiting—five of them had been killed now—two foot soldiers and three guarding the barn—but Crandall's farmhouse was large. *How many are in there? If only we hadn't blown our cover. We needed the element of surprise. Maybe they aren't watching one of the doors? Maybe...* A smile came across Donovan's face.

"What's the plan?" Lysander asked. Then he looked around and added, "Where's Banner?"

Everyone but Donovan looked at Rohawk, who seemed to realize at that moment that he last had track of her.

Donovan turned to the group, still wearing that grin. "Is she in the tunnel?"

Rohawk looked even more confused.

"There's a tunnel connecting the barn to the farmhouse. It was built by the original owner," Donovan explained. "That could be our way in, and maybe where Banner went. Let's go!" The five of them went around through the door of the barn.

Donovan was the first in, and he nearly tripped over the body of one of the three Kaldarans Rohawk and Banner killed. Two sconces in the center of the barn gave off just enough light for him to see and step over the corpse. He walked farther inside but saw nothing except cows and hay. A pitchfork and shovel hung on wall pegs. Donovan grabbed the pitchfork and started moving some of the hay around.

"Smells foul," Faith said.

"You and Wyndell need to get out more," Godell said.

"Should someone go tell them what's happening?" Lysander asked.

"Do you really want to climb that hill on foot?" Rohawk asked.

Lysander glowered at him. "I didn't mean me. I want to help find Banner."

"How do we know this tunnel even exists?" Godell asked. Everyone turned to Donovan.

"Crandell said it saved his life from the stone lion he killed a while ago."

Faith crossed his arms.

"What if that's made up?"

Donovan shrugged. "Farmers tell tall tales, but they rarely outright lie." That seemed to be enough to convince everyone to help look. A moment later, Donovan saw a stall that was gated off but had no livestock and barely any hay. He looked over the gate and saw a wooden trap door with a metal ring on the top. "Over here!" he called out. The other three came running and went inside. Donovan pulled on the ring, then grabbed the wooden door and propped it open the rest of the way. "Come on," Donovan said as he grabbed a torch off the wall. "Let's get moving."

"What if this isn't where Banner is and its full of Kaldarans?" Faith asked.

Godell readied his axes. "Sounds good to me."

The five of them descended into the hatch, down the old, cracked, stone steps.

Donovan waved his torch in front of him and reeled backward. Nine terrified faces, alongside Banner's calm demeanor, stared back at him.

"Donovan?" Farmer Crandall asked. His voice quivered with fright but hope gleamed in his eyes. "Oh, thank all the gods above, it's you!"

"You need to get your family out of here, Crandall." Donovan's warning conveyed both his surprise and his relief that the farmer and his family were alive.

"How?" The farmer sounded desperate. "Even if you killed the guards in the barn, won't they see us?"

"Maybe not if you leave now. What about going to your neighbor, Keith? His farm is where our horses are."

"I was worried maybe they got to him too."

"It's about to be a warzone in your house," Godell cut in. "Do you really want to be here, farmer?"

Crandall looked back at his family.

"I know it's dangerous, but we have people who will cover your retreat until you're well on your way to Keith's farm," Donovan said.

Crandall's wife nodded to her husband.

"Head out the eastern exit of the barn," Donovan instructed, "and give us a minute or two to start the fighting so they're distracted and won't see you. There are archers on the rise behind the barn, so give them the Nightingale salute so they know you're with us." He put his fist to his chest and tapped three times.

"Do we even have to clear out the house?" Faith asked. "We can get out right now with the farmer and his family, perhaps provide them some protection, and our mission will be done."

"Our mission would not be done—we still have our orders to retake the farm and the food," Donovan answered. "Crandall, how many men are in the house?"

"I...I don't know. When they first came to the farm, there were around twenty-five of 'em. But we heard noises a while ago—sounded like there were more here."

Twenty-five? Donovan thought. The house was large. *Is there any chance that many men could still be inside? And why had King Santos been here? Why did he leave and...is he coming back?*

"Even with those we've killed, that leaves quite a few for us in the house," Faith noted.

Donovan exhaled. "We watched a bunch of them leave, and now is our best chance. Faith, you and I will go in first with our shields. Focus on creating space for Godell and Rohawk to strike killing blows. Lysander, I want you in that space as well, using Technique to cover any weakness you can identify. Banner, I want you to go out and around to the house and climb up on the outside to the second story and flank from there, but wait for us to start making noise so they don't suspect you."

She nodded and ran off toward the barn hatch.

"This could be suicide," Rohawk advised.

Donovan's eyes drifted in thought for just a moment, and when they refocused, they were on Rohawk. "Are you ready?"

"*Den bekkin ha bekkin,*" he said.

Donovan had heard the phrase before. It was an ancient tongue and a common prayer amongst Kaldarans. It meant, "Born in blood, die in blood."

"Go, Crandall," Donovan ordered. "Get your family to Keith's farm."

Crandall nodded. "Best of luck, Donovan." He turned to herd his wife and kids out of the barn. Donovan considered that the luck of Borek might have been upon them, because Crandall's newborn lay quiet, asleep in his mother's arms, even amidst the chaos.

If the gods were going to meddle, the least they could do is some good. *I'll take whatever I can get.*

Donovan and Faith led the way through the tunnel and up the stairs on the other side of the door that went into the house, Lysander right behind them. Donovan gave a sideways glance to his shield-mate.

"Ready?" he asked. He checked to make sure Godell, Rohawk, and Lysander were close behind.

Faith nodded and whispered, "Ready."

Donovan pushed gently on the hatch at first. There was something on it.

"What's the hold-up?" Godell whispered.

Donovan pushed a little harder and heard a wobbling noise. Something wooden was on the hatch. He pushed again with more force, but still slowly. Around halfway up, there was a thud as something fell off the trapdoor and onto the ground. The room was dark, but flickering orange light seeped in through door-shaped lines on the far wall.

Donovan heard Faith come up the stairs next to him. "Through the door," he whispered. "Let's go!" They readied their weapons and Donovan opened the door. Two Kaldarans came down the hall in response. He and Faith each struck with their swords, killing the two men.

Lysander, Godell, and Rohawk were close behind, but it quickly proved unnecessary as they made their way through the kitchen. The rest of the house appeared empty, except for the Kaldaran who'd been wounded outside, and he lay bleeding on the living room floor. One of his trembling hands held a sword pointed toward Donovan.

"What in Abaddon's Den," Donovan muttered. "Where are the rest of your people?"

"Stay back!" the Kaldaran shouted as the sword shook in his unsteady grip.

"There were only three of you in here?" Donovan asked, indignant. "Bag of bones! Why would you leave so few to defend a source of food?"

The Kaldaran wore a look of insane satisfaction. He was hiding something.

"Stay back! Ha! King Santos will kill all of you!" The man sprang to his feet and lunged with his sword toward Donovan.

Godell swooped past Donovan and parried the oncoming sword with an axe, then buried his other axe deep into the Kaldaran's chest. He fell to the ground, dead, his remaining blood spilling out.

Banner appeared coming down the stairs. "All-clear up there."

"Search the rest of the house, just in case," Donovan ordered. "Faith, go give the all-clear to Kris and Wyndell."

Banner, Rohawk, and Lysander all obeyed without a word and Faith went out the front door. Godell stayed behind for a moment.

"You did well," Donovan responded to the unasked question.

"Right," Godell said curtly before heading back to help search the house.

Donovan listened for shouts of alarm from any of the others, but there was nothing. After a minute, Rohawk's voice sounded the final all-clear Donovan suspected. He looked up and down the room before settling back on the dead Kaldaran Godell had cleaved open.

"So few men...what am I missing?"

Chapter Ten

The Thirteenth Division was in high spirits. They had successfully ended the Kaldaran presence on Crandall's farm, saved the farmer and his whole family, and secured all the food except for what had been taken from the pantry. All without losing a single soldier. It was a resounding success.

After spending the night at Crandall's farm, and deeming it safe for now, they rode back to Nightingale. Donovan asked for two to stay behind in case Kaldaran came back. Kris and Wyndell volunteered. Donovan reluctantly agreed. He didn't trust those two together, but he could tell no one else wanted to do it.

The rest of them were in a celebratory mood as they rode back into town, save for Donovan. Despite many comments that he should lighten up, he felt like a piece of the puzzle was missing.

Perhaps they had done well, regardless of what was yet in the future. He simply couldn't get over how lucky they had been to strike right at that moment, when King Santos was pulling troops away. He looked over at the statue of Borek as they passed by on their return trip into Nightingale. He remembered the tribute Faith had paid on the way out. *Could it be that simple? Was luck on our side? Why would a god need human coins, anyway? I suppose that would fit how fickle they seem to be.*

The triumphant return of The Thirteenth Division was massively overshadowed. Not that anyone knew what had happened on the farm yet, but now it wouldn't matter. A crowd gathered in the town center, all eyes on the mercenary Toby as he held the head of a man who looked unmistakably Kaldaran. The mouth was frozen unnaturally wide open in a scream.

"Hear, oh citizens of Nightingale!" Toby shouted. "Me men and I have killed the King of Kaldaran. Santos is dead!"

The cheers from the crowd unnerved Donovan. He should be celebrating as well, but this didn't make sense.

"Toby got the king?" Godell asked. He seemed to share Donovan's level of uneasiness. "How could that have happened? Did he just get lucky and ambush the king right after he left the farm?"

"Are we sure that's really King Santos?" Faith asked. "None of us got a good look at him, except maybe Wyndell. Do we know for sure we even saw him last night?"

"It should have been," Rohawk said. "I saw the tattoo as well. Kaldarans don't just tattoo that on anyone. It's part of their religion."

Faith scratched his chin. "So is the ritualistic worship of chaos. Wouldn't it cause more chaos to have a king and a double appearing as king?"

"That sounds like it would cause more chaos for the Kaldarans than anyone else," Lysander put in.

"Come all!" Toby shouted. "See the severed head of the man who has terrorized Nightingale and join me in celebration! I call for music! Let there be dancing and good drink for all! King Santos is dead!"

The Nightingalens didn't need much more encouragement than that. Someone had already started playing the lute and wood was being piled for a large fire to keep everyone warm outside.

"Everyone seems to think we've won," Donovan said.

"We haven't?" Banner asked. "Toby's pretty damn good at what he does—everyone around here knows that."

"And maybe that's why we had such success at the farm," Lysander added. "Kaldaran is weakened and dying. Good days are here for Nightingale again." Donovan frowned. Something was off—he knew it. Godell was already drinking mead and joining in the festivities. Rohawk, on the other hand, looked thoughtful.

Donovan prodded his horse closer to him. "What do you think?"

Rohawk eyed the crowd for a moment. "I would like nothing more than to join in, but we could have a big problem on our hands still."

"What do you mean?" Lysander asked.

"Keep in mind, this is all religious ramblings, but the people of the Kingdom of Kaldaran believe in it," Rohawk explained. "Their mythology says that whoever is King of Kaldaran receives the spirit of Kaldar. In the old days, people called it 'being Crowned by a god.'"

Donovan recognized the terminology. It was the same Martha had used.

"The spirit of Kaldar makes the mortal king incredibly powerful. In the moments when Kaldar and his Crowned are closest, the Crowned can unleash magic without sacrifice, and cannot be killed. You could stab him in the heart, and he would smile back at you."

"So what does all that mean?" Donovan asked.

"It is believed that, so long as the King of Kaldaran continues to satisfy the wishes of his god, obeying his commands and satisfying his desires, then he will remain king. But if someone kills the king, then the Kaldarans will believe that king was weak and not satisfying Kaldaran's desires."

"So with every death their new king is better than the last?" Banner asked.

Rohawk shrugged. "It is what they believe."

"And what do you believe?" Faith asked. "Do you think that Kaldaran still watches over his kings and gives them power if they satisfy him?"

Donovan thought Rohawk was going to laugh and say it was all hogwash, but to his surprise, Rohawk answered, "I've seen too many weird things in my life to discount it entirely."

There were shouts of joy and Donovan looked over to see Toby receiving gifts of gold and jewelry. *Toby has always been a straight shooter, but is this a scam? Could he have taken the head of any Kaldaran and presented it just to strike it rich?*

"Let's go somewhere not so wild," Donovan said. He prodded Chomper to a trot, and the Thirteenth Division moved down Broken Street where the festivities were not so loud. All except for Godell, who was partying.

Once they were far enough away from the noise, Donovan said, "Let's say all of this is real, that there is going to be a new king of Kaldaran better than the last one, and let's say that this god Kaldar blesses his new servant with power. Is there a way to kill a Crowned?"

Rohawk looked terrified, but only briefly. He quickly smiled, then laughed—seemingly genuinely. "I would be careful about putting those words in the air."

Donovan sighed, then rephrased, "What would happen if someone killed the new king while he was Crowned? In the full strength of his power?"

"I don't know if it has been done," Rohawk answered. "According to the old ways, the only thing that could kill a Crowned is another Crowned."

"Well let's hope that's not the case then." Donovan halted when the group came around to the barracks. "I have to give a report to Alexis. The rest of you can take the day off."

"What if we are still needed?" Faith asked.

"Kris and Wyndell are still at the farm and Godell is probably already drunk. It will have to wait."

"Donovan!" Alexis stood near the entrance of the barracks. "Glad to see you well!"

"I was coming to see you," he said. "Got somewhere quiet we can go?"

"Back at the barracks. Just you, though."

"Wouldn't want to get between you and your mistress," Rohawk jabbed. "You'll see me tomorrow," he added. Others in the group echoed similar sentiments—minus the lewd comment—before taking off.

Donovan dismounted at the same time a stable boy came to take his horse. Then he and Alexis walked together toward her office inside. A lute was playing there too, and judging from the hollering, the rule against booze in the barracks was being broken.

"Mistress, huh?" Alexis said with a playful smirk.

"Rohawk likes to imagine things," Donovan said, trying to make his tone as mild as possible. He was a little uncomfortable with the comment. "What do you think of Toby killing King Santos?"

Alexis said nothing more until they had walked the rest of the way to her office. The fire was lit, and the warmth was heavenly. An iron pot sat on the hearth near the fire.

"I made some soup, would you like any?"

"You made soup?"

"I like to make my own food now and then. Better than what the kitchen around here serves." She ladled out a helping into a wooden bowl, then passed it Donovan's way, along with a spoon. Donovan took a seat and tried it.

"It's good. Really good. Thank you."

Alexis nodded. "Jillian said she saw your band come in, so I went out to look for you. Are Kris and Wyndell alright?"

Donovan gave a detailed report, explaining that Kris and Wyndell were left behind as scouts. He made a point not only to mention King Santos, but that the captain should have believed him before when Donovan said he had seen the man. Alexis mostly nodded along, taking notes and asking questions when Donovan wasn't clear about something. When he finished, she sighed.

"I can't be sure, but my gut has been telling me Toby didn't kill King Santos, and after your report, I doubt it even more. Even if he did intercept the King and kill him last night, I don't think this is nearly over. But I guess I can't stop people from celebrating at this point. It's nice to have some happiness in Nightingale again, I just hope it won't double the pain when people find out that the Kaldarans have selected a new king and nothing has changed."

"Rohawk was telling me about it."

"I figured. He was the one who told Captain Gerald and me. He's the best informant on Kaldaran culture and religion we have, which is part of the reason I picked him for your...Thirteenth Division."

"The name got around?" Donovan asked, a little worried. That was said in what was supposed to be a private meeting, and Alexis hadn't been there for that part.

"Patrick, the Thirsty Horse owner, told me," Alexis said, unamused. "It's hard to keep secrets around here, but he promised he didn't tell anyone else. I believe him. That old bastard probably knows everyone's secrets around here."

"Why is Rohawk your informant on Kaldaran, though? Toby probably knows more."

"Apparently not," she said, continuing with the unamused tone. "He clammed up when we tried asking him. He thinks that if he tells us, we'll then tell everyone, and that will give other mercs an edge over his group. Then Jillian tells me he's laughing it up in the town square acting like some big hero. He's only out for himself, if you ask me."

"I didn't know he was giving you so much trouble. He was always good to me at the store."

Alexis shrugged. "He's a merc. It's what they do. I'm surprised you're so friendly with him after the backtalk you gave me about your team."

Donovan looked down at his feet. "Maybe I was wrong about him, but after Lionel died, Toby brought us some animals to work on so we wouldn't go out of business while we figured things out. I didn't think someone who was only out for himself would bother to do that."

Alexis nodded. "Regardless, you did very well, Donovan. Re-securing that farm eases my concerns about food for a while. I will order Jillian to go today, and I would like you and your division to join her tomorrow. When she gets there, I will have her send Kris and Wyndell back so they can get some sleep and join you tomorrow."

"Thank you," he said. For once, Donovan felt a bit proud of his leadership. He had a good team, but he didn't get any of them killed for a change.

It worried him, though. What Rohawk said about the Crowned. He unintentionally corroborated what Martha had said, and those two were as different as any two people could be.

Alexis must have picked up on his thoughtful expression, because she asked, "Is there something else you're not telling me?"

"Rohawk was telling me about the Crowned of old. He said that if the King of Kaldaran pleases Kaldar, he is given power. Do you think there is any truth to that?"

"I kind of doubt it. Someone was claiming the god Driggon had chosen a Crowned a few years ago, but if he did, then nothing came of it.

"What do you mean?"

"The so-called Crowned of Driggon gained a large following in his kingdom. Riled up enough followers to lead a small army against Sokor. It was just raids at first, no real opposition. But when the King of Sokor got his act together and sent his army, the Crowned and all his soldiers were killed in the first battle."

"So that disproved his claim, I'm guessing."

"Not only that, but if the Crowned really existed, why don't we see them? I would think the gods would want champions."

"But you believe in K'var," Donovan pointed out.

"K'var, yes. The Crowned? I doubt it. I think the gods' influence is much more subtle than that."

Donovan nodded. "People have been using the title to gain followers and establish themselves as political leaders. Just another way these so-called gods make everyone's lives worse."

"Of course you would think that...but I guess in this case it's more or less true."

"What do you mean by that?"

"I know how you feel about the gods, Donovan."

"So does everyone else in Nightingale, but it's never bothered you."

"I suppose," Alexis said as she handed Donovan the folded parchment. "Please give this to Jillian on your way out."

Donovan paused a moment. He realized he had offended her, but didn't know what to say. He stood up and took the letter.

"Alexis, I...I'm..."

"That letter is important. You are dismissed."

Donovan nodded and walked out, letter in hand. *Great. Way to go, Donovan.*

After a short conversation with Officer Jillian, Donovan headed home. He felt the odd sensation of being directionless. The last few months had been training, working, and fighting almost non-stop. This was his first day of real downtime for a while.

The celebrations happening in the town did not lift his spirits any. The scent of fresh beer wafted through the air and there was a cacophony of different instruments being played in all parts of town. He caught a little bit of several different parties echoing through the streets. The last time a celebration like this was held, Donovan had been there drinking alongside Ramon and Lionel and having the time of his life. Now it just felt...empty.

He passed behind a few people sitting on a bench and recognized one of the voices. He kept walking, but ducked behind a building and listened.

"Look at the lot," Toby said. "Completely unaware what's comin' next."

"Are you sure about this, Boss? It's not too late to change yer mind, dontcha know? I know we're Kaldarans, but we turned away from that life a long time ago."

Toby stood up and waved his hand forward. "It is much too late for changin' of minds. Kaldaran is calling us home. Our people need us." With that, they were off into the crowd.

This sounds like what Toby was talking about that day at the shop. What's wrong with him? He sounds...sad. And what did he mean Kaldaran is calling him home? Is he switching sides, or... Donovan swallowed hard. *Is he planning to die?* Both of those thoughts were bizarre. No one in Nightingale served their old gods this seriously. In Nightingale gods were there to serve you. *Is Toby serious about his religion?*

Donovan set aside those thoughts for now. Martha might know more about the Kaldaran religion, or Rohawk might. Maybe they could make sense of what he just heard.

As he was nearing the front door of the shop, Donovan produced a key from his pocket. Ramon and Tybalt were probably out hunting, and Martha kept the shop locked when it was closed. He stopped suddenly, hand halfway to the door. The lock had been broken. His stomach sank. His sword was back at the barracks. He opened the door slowly, as quietly as he could manage. So far, nothing. He grabbed a hand axe from the supply room so he was armed, then made sure the bottom floor was clear before looking to the stairs. He knew where to step to avoid creaking noises. Martha was a light sleeper and he had come home late many times. He crept up them, watching each step and taking them lightly. He opened the door to the main room.

No one was there. The window clapped loudly in the wind.

One of the chairs was knocked over, and there appeared to be droplets of blood leading into Martha's bedroom.

Donovan vaulted the chair and darted toward the bedroom. He flung open the door and saw Martha lying on the ground in a pool of her own blood. She was dead.

He only had an instant to process the image when he felt a knife enter his back. He elbowed whoever had stabbed him and tumbled forward but was stabbed again—a shallower cut, as he pulled free almost in time. He rose on his feet and turned around to see a man dressed in all black from head to toe.

"Where is the book?!" the man demanded. "Surely it is not worth your life?"

"Why don't you come get it?" Donovan said as he readied the axe.

"I will spare you if you tell me where the book is," the assassin reiterated. "It's a very generous offer—one I only make because the Master said he has plans for you."

"The Master?" Donovan breathed out.

"Are you not the vampire? I know he is in the city, but he would not take the job. Is that because he is you?"

Donovan had no clue, but he thought maybe he would seem stronger if he stayed silent.

The assassin grew impatient with Donovan's lack of response. "Gol, I was hoping to settle both matters at once. I will have to settle for just one— where is the book?"

"Go die," Donovan growled as he raised the axe.

The assassin lunged and grabbed Donovan's wrist before he could bring the axe down. Donovan moved to dodge the sharp end of the knife coming at him, but realized too late that the assassin was not trying to stab. Instead, he feinted the stab and brought the blunt end of the knife handle up, smacking Donovan in the mouth, hard. Donovan reeled from the blow, unable to retaliate, and crumpled to the ground.

The assassin kicked the hand axe away, then knelt, picked Donovan up by his collar, and hissed, "Why do you resist? Where is the teching book?"

Rage filled Donovan to the brim. He was entirely consumed by adrenaline and emotion. Anger, grief, pain, and misery all mixed and spewed forth as he fought. He wrenched himself free from the assassin's grip and punched him in the groin. The assassin toppled and dropped his knife. Donovan kept his footing and lunged forward, grabbing the assassin by the neck and bringing his head smacking down on Martha's wooden desk. A hidden compartment below the desk swung open, revealing the book Martha had shown him. Donovan grabbed it.

"You want the book?" he roared. "Take it, then!" He slammed the steel binding across the assassin's face. The man stumbled backward, crashing through the window and falling to the ground.

Donovan ran to the window to look down. It wasn't a far drop, but the assassin had landed poorly, and his head looked like it wasn't in the right position. He wasn't moving. Donovan dropped the book as tears streamed down his face. He turned to Martha, knelt beside her, and took her hand.

"Martha," he said to her lifeless face. "Mother," he breathed out. He felt the sting of the stab wounds and warm blood running down his back, but agony overwhelmed him, and he felt dizzy.

He had killed her attacker, but somebody had sent him, somebody had given him the job. But he would have to find out who, while also continuing his service to the Guard, to Nightingale, to Alexis—to Emeline's husband and everyone else who had loved ones no longer alive because of the war. He was among them now. He couldn't believe it. Martha was gone.

I will be gone too, if I don't do something, he thought. He felt his head swimming. Blood was going out of him too fast. He ripped his tunic and wrapped it around his cuts, then pulled it tight. He could barely breathe. He heard commotion outside—someone had discovered the assassin's body. He would have help soon. He dropped to the floor next to Martha and took her hand in his.

"I swear, Martha, I will kill whoever sent this assassin." Donovan's voice was quiet, raspy. He barely had the breath. "I...I swear it!"

Ramon grinned at the revelers in the streets as he and Tybalt walked toward the shop. The hunt had been unsuccessful, but that didn't dampen his spirits.

"Let's go get a drink," Tybalt suggested.

"Sounds good, but we need to stop by the shop, put the cart away, get some coins first." Ramon said. They turned the corner toward the house just as a body flew from the upstairs window—Martha's room.

"What the—" Ramon took off at a run, pausing briefly by the body to confirm the man was dead, then dashing inside and up the stairs, Tybalt close on his heels.

Donovan lay passed out on the floor in a pool of blood—his mixed with Martha's.

"Are they dead?" Tybalt gasped.

Ramon checked Martha and shook his head, then turned to Donvan.

"He's alive! We need to get him to the mender, quickly! Help me!"

He and Tybalt carried Donovan's limp form down the stairs and put him on the cart, then wheeled him as quickly as they could to the mender at the Nightingale Barracks.

Eodius met them at the door. "Donovan!" he exclaimed as he ushered them in. "What did he do to himself this time?"

"What do you mean, this time?" Ramon asked.

"He's a frequent visitor in this place," Eodius said. He led them down a short hallway to a room with a bed. "Put him here."

"Will he be alright?" Ramon asked.

"I won't know until I try. I need to focus. Please, give me space. Wait out front and I will come get you as soon as I can."

Ramon was about to protest, but Tybalt put a hand on his shoulder. "We've done all we can, Ramon. We need to stand aside."

Ramon nodded and the two walked out into the entryway. A middle-age clerk glared at them, but Ramon didn't care. Martha was dead. Donovan might not make it. *What in all of gol happened? Martha...she's gone.*

"Are you alright?" Tybalt asked.

"I always knew Martha's time would come. But…never would I have thought it would be like this." Ramon sat down and put his head in his hands. "Bag of bloody bones…"

"Can I help you two?" The clerk was standing next to Tybalt, his arms crossed and his foot tapping on the floor.

Tybalt turned his deep green eyes toward him. "Yes, leave us the tech alone. I won't ask twice."

The clerk blinked and swallowed hard, then returned to his desk.

"Being from Driggon has advantages at times."

"We should have been there," Ramon lamented, ignoring the whole scene. "I knew Donovan had been getting into some risky business. I was worried that it might end up in trouble coming our way. I just didn't think it would be this bad. I can't believe Martha is dead."

Silence hung in the air. Ramon's eyes rested on the floor of the barracks, out of focus, his mind lost in thought. Someone had kicked a small rock inside, and he absently moved it around with his foot, thinking about everything he had seen in Martha's room when he and Tybalt had entered.

"An assassin going after Martha does not seem logical," Tybalt noted. "I wonder what happened."

"We won't know what happened unless Donovan survives…Gods, I hope he pulls through."

"Eodius seems like a skilled mender."

"You and I both know that's not always enough," Ramon said in a soft voice.

"Look," Tybalt said. Ramon raised his head to see Eodius coming out to see them.

"His wounds are closed—that part took only seconds," he explained. "I have spent a few minutes watching him, examining his breathing. He is weak, but I think he will survive."

"Thank K'var," Ramon exhaled.

"He is your friend, yes? You should keep a close eye on him. He has had several close calls. I fear the gods might be angry with him."

"He is not on the best terms with them."

"You need to try to convince him otherwise."

"What good will that do? Martha is dead! What god is going to bring her back now? Will one of your fey gods answer our prayer, mender?"

Eodius did not respond.

"What good could I do anyway? Donovan doesn't give a damn about the gods, no matter what it costs him."

"I'm not dead, you know," Donovan's voice came down the hallway. Eodius whipped around to see his patient standing in the doorway, leaning on it for support.

"You have the strength to walk?" Eodius asked, a single eyebrow raised. "You should be resting, Donovan."

"Probably should be, but I need to speak with Ramon, alone."

"I insist you rest for the sake of your life," Eodius replied in a stern tone.

Donovan put a little emphasis on each word. "I need to talk to Ramon."

"I hope Ramon remembers those words when you collapse and I am questioned about doing my job," Eodius said, but he walked away as he did.

Donovan watched Eodius leave, then turned his gaze directly to Ramon.

"No matter what it costs me, eh?" he asked in a low tone.

Ramon turned his face away. "I'm sorry. I'm...overwhelmed right now. I'm glad that you are alive, Donovan."

Donovan took in a deep breath. "But you also meant the other part. You think my beliefs are bringing misfortune to our household."

"I saw you ride out yesterday; you had a bunch of mercs with you. Is this because Toby turned you down? You weren't good enough for his team, so you made your own?"

Donovan bit back words he wanted to spit at Ramon. "I'm under orders from the Guard. The mercenaries are my new team."

"And which one of them did this to Martha?"

Donovan's eyes seethed rage as he took one step forward; Tybalt put himself in between the two. "Out of line, Ramon."

"This is a family matter, greenhorn."

"No, he's right," Donovan pressed. "That assassin did not belong to anyone from my team, and it's insane that you would accuse them of something like that without any evidence."

Ramon couldn't believe what was happening. *I'm firing Tybalt's ass for this.* He opened his mouth to say something, but remembered the last time he and Donovan had an argument like this. It was when Lionel was alive, the old man had separated them and ended up scolding Ramon.

He wasn't ready to let either person off the hook, but he decided walking away was best for now. He turned and walked outside into the cold, his direction aimless. *Anywhere will do for now.*

Donovan watched Ramon go. He knew that his friend must be seething, but he respected the fact that he walked away instead of getting angrier.

"Donovan, can we speak privately?" Tybalt asked.

Donovan nodded and waved for him to follow. The Nightingale baths were connected to the barracks, and not open today. "What is it?"

"Where did Martha get that book?"

Donovan froze. He had no chance to hide it again.

"I put it out of sight when Ramon wasn't looking. I don't think he saw it. But I know what's it worth, and that it's illegal here."

"Tybalt, you aren't supposed to know about that book. I'm not supposed to know about it."

"I agree on both accounts. I just wanted to let you know I saw it, I know what it is, and I can keep a secret."

"How do you know what it is?"

"I only meant that I know its value, and that it's not legal to have it here. That's all."

Donovan thought Tybalt was lying, but he didn't think there was anything evil behind his words. He hoped not, anyway. "Alright. Thanks for taking care of it."

He turned, but Tybalt said, "What do you plan to do with it?"

"I will try and figure something out. For now, I need to hide it better, and we need to keep an eye out for each other, and…" Donovan hung his head. "And bury our dead."

Footsteps drew their attention to the doorway. There was Eodius.

"You're not going anywhere the rest of the day, or the Second will ream me. I saved your life, it's the least you can do."

"I will find Ramon and work on funeral arrangements," Tybalt said.

Donovan nodded. "Thanks."

Chapter Eleven

A few hours of restless sleep later, Donovan was awake in the infirmary. Eodius was tending to some of the other wounded. When the mender left, Donovan decided he had enough rest. It was evening—hopefully of the same day—and he wasn't going to waste it.

He got up and grabbed his cloak that had been lying on one of the beds. The cold outside stung, but he wouldn't be in the cold long. By the sound of it, the celebrations had continued through the day, but had moved to another part of town.

Somewhere in his mind, he knew Martha's funeral needed planning. But Tybalt said he would take care of it, and the man meant what he said. Still, Donovan knew it was wrong to not go check on preparations. He didn't care.

He arrived at the Thirsty Horse and found it quiet. He sat the bar and rested his elbows on it. He still felt weak, but he could rest here as well as anywhere.

Patrick saw him and brought over a bottle of Corrick fifty-year whiskey, setting it down on the bar. The thick glass bottle hit with a dull thud.

"I can't afford this," Donovan mumbled.

"Nobody can," Patrick said. "That's why it's always given as a gift. I heard what happened. I'm sorry, Donovan. Martha was a good woman."

Patrick said nothing more and left Donovan to it. He poured two fingers into a glass and examined it. He rarely got drunk. He didn't like it. The idea of blacking out and forgetting anything—he didn't know why anyone would ever want that. Memories were precious to him. But now he thought about what it would be like to soul-burn Martha away. It wasn't possible to control the power like that, but if it had been, he would have considered it.

But that would also erase all the good memories he had with her.

"I will settle for painkiller instead," he said as he sipped at the whiskey. Rich caramel notes and hints of apples flooded across his senses, and the liquid itself was smooth, coating his tongue on the way down.

"I didn't think you were one to drink your sorrows away," Alexis's voice sounded from behind him.

Donovan did not turn around. "I've never experienced sorrow quite like this before. It was hard with Lionel. But this…"

She looked around and took a seat next to him. "Donovan, I...I didn't think anything like this would happen. I'm sorry."

"Not your fault."

"I hate what I'm about to say next but—"

"I need to go out tomorrow," Donovan said. "You'll have more trouble convincing Eodius than me."

"I outrank him...but I'm not sending you out tomorrow, either. I want you to take at least a day to rest, and to have a proper funeral for Martha."

"Didn't know Nightingale had any proper funerals left in her after all this."

She put her hand on his. He looked over at her.

"We will make an exception," she said.

Donovan gave her a hint of a smile. "Thanks."

She squeezed his hand and let go.

He took another sip. "How are you holding up?"

"Don't worry about me."

"Impossible."

Alexis blushed. "I um...I'm worried these days. Things are getting bad around here. You brought back the first good news we've had in a while."

"Except for Toby."

Alexis shrugged. "We've gone over that one already." She absently turned the bottle of whiskey around then gasped. "You bought this?"

"A gift from Patrick. I'm guessing every drop out of it has gone to some poor soul in a situation like me."

"Do you think he will mind if a less-poor soul finishes what's in your glass?"

Donovan smiled and pushed the drink toward her. "I believe we agreed to share a drink sometime when we had the chance."

Alexis sipped at it, gave Donovan a very obvious expression of approval, then said, "Let me know if there's anything I can do for you."

"Right now, your company is about all I need."

She smiled warmly, but sadness was in her eyes. She took his hand in hers again. "When this is all over, do you plan to stay with the Guard?"

The question caught Donovan by surprise. What was the answer she was looking for? The warmth of her hand seemed to indicate that she...wanted him. But he had also just lost someone dear to him, and he did not want to read too much into her sympathy.

"I think so. But I don't know. This is all a bit too much for me. I thought I would fight some battles, win some fame, and return to being a fur trader with more stories to tell and a reputation as a hero. I didn't think it would involve losing Martha."

"But you want to stay in Nightingale?"

"I don't know how I feel about Nightingale, to be honest."

Alexis nodded. "Well, this may sound presumptuous, but I think *I* know how you feel about Nightingale. You chose to stand up and fight for it. And you're still doing that. That's incredibly brave. When this is over, I think those left in Nightingale are the ones who really cared all along, and that will lead to a bright new future."

Alexis took another sip. She was thinking deeply about something. She always was when her brow furrowed in the way it was doing now. Donovan thought it was cute.

She took one more sip, then continued. "Even though K'var allowed women in their army, I never liked it there. I shared the same dreams many women there had—to be a soldier, fight against the Kingdom of Fire, protect K'var, and earn a name for myself. But I realized I was more interested in helping people than fighting. I came to Nightingale and decided I could do more good here. I was no longer just another soldier girl. I've been able to leave my mark here."

Donovan nodded. "Do you regret leaving K'var at all?"

"Not at all. Especially not now that the Kingdom has abandoned its duty to Nightingale."

"They didn't totally abandon us—they sent you, and that's pretty good."

Alexis looked to her drink and blushed. "I wouldn't say they sent me. But that's really sweet of you."

Donovan kept his eyes on her. The way she spoke and squeezed his hand sent lightning bolts through his skin. *Is she just being nice because...of Martha? That's not like her, though...she says what she means.*

"Alexis, I—" Donovan was cut off when Alexis's eyes darted past him and she suddenly let go of his hand.

Captain Gerald strode into the Thirsty Horse like he owned the place, and when he spotted Donovan and Alexis, he made his way over and pulled a chair with him so he could sit down.

"Damn fine work at Crandall's farm, Donovan," he said. Then his eyes moved to the whiskey bottle and his brows rose. "Teching damn, you really pulled out the big stuff tonight. I heard about Martha. Very sorry to hear that." The captain swiped Alexis's now empty glass and started helping himself to Patrick's thoughtful gift, and quite a lot of it too.

"Captain Gerald, it is a pleasure," Donovan said, trying to mask the fact that it was most certainly not. "Thank you for your condolences."

"More work like that and we'll have this whole thing wrapped up in no time. Can finally get trade going around here again." The captain downed his drink in one gulp.

Donovan glanced over at Patrick. The bar owner's expression was like a mother who just saw her baby get dropped.

"Your pal Ramon managed to snatch up one of the best warriors before all this started. Damn shame. Tybalt is very skilled. I tried to get him to join the Guard. Most Driggonites are insane religious zealots, but if you can find one with a good head on his shoulders, they make for damn fine warriors. Like you."

"Yes sir," Donovan said. Patrick was suddenly there, with another bottle of whiskey.

"Captain Gerald, times are tough right now. Might I offer you my only bottle of Corrick Seventy-Five?"

"You're alright, Patrick," the Captain said as he leaned back and watched the barkeep swap out the bottles. "Two more glasses for my friends."

Patrick gave Donovan a sideways glance but went to go get the glasses and returned to the table with them. The Captain wasted no time pouring all three, passing two to Donovan and Alexis.

"To Nightingale, and to the Guard," he said as he raised his glass. Donovan shrugged and raised his, Alexis did the same, and the gentle clinking of glass rang out into the tavern. The Captain slammed his drink again. Donovan took a sip, then looked over at Alexis to see her reaction. She had a good palate, and he could tell that she, like he, had noticed that the supposedly Corrick Seventy-Five was more likely a Sokorian un-aged batch.

"Best damn whiskey I've ever had!" the Captain roared.

Donovan looked back at Patrick, who looked relieved. He sighed. *Clever bartender.* He glanced over at Alexis who was now occupied talking to the captain. It was the usual conversation—professional and polite, but with undertones of political combat. The captain at least seemed a bit more relaxed than usual.

Donovan sighed quietly to himself. The words he was about to say to Alexis were now trapped in his chest and slowly died out as the night went on.

A sunny day was the best Donovan could have asked for with a winter funeral. It was a small crowd. Too many had died recently, and everyone was tired of burying the dead.

The grave keepers lowered Martha down in the ground. Ramon wiped the tears from his eyes. "It's just too much, Donovan."

"Yes, I know," he whispered.

The priestess of K'var was there to perform burial rites.

"May the warrior goddess watch over you in the afterlife, dear sister," the priestess spoke.

"You let this loon in here?" Donovan whispered.

"Martha was always more religious than us. I thought she deserved something from the gods."

"She deserved better than dying like this, I know that for sure." Donovan's gaze wandered and came to a stop when he saw Rohawk standing on the outskirts of the graveyard. Banner and Lysander were with him, and they all gave Donovan a Nightingale salute when they saw he noticed them.

After the ceremony, Donovan went over to talk with them. "You didn't have to stand on the outside if you didn't want to."

Rohawk shrugged. "It didn't seem quite right, you know what I mean?"

"But we had to do something," Banner put in. "Gotta let you know we have your back."

Lysander nodded. "My condolences, Donovan. Martha seemed like one of the best of us all."

Donovan smiled just a little. "Well, that's very kind of all of you. I hope you're ready to go back out tomorrow."

"Ouch, all business?" Banner asked. "We thought we would buy you a drink or something!"

Donovan grimaced. The captain had forced more way drink on him last night than he had wanted, and his head still ached. "How about next time."

"I don't think I ever heard what got her," Rohawk said.

Donovan felt a little incensed over such a causal comment, but he saw the sincerity in Rohawk's eyes. "Some man broke in looking to steal things. He killed Martha and tried to kill me when I walked in on him."

Banner shook her head. "Bastard," she muttered.

Donovan raised an eyebrow at her.

"Don't look at me like that! I never hurt anyone. I just take what I need to get by, and from crooks if I can. Now that I'm a merc, I don't need to do any of that anymore."

"I'm sorry to hear all that, Donovan," Lysander said. "It was many years ago, but I lost my father when a horse broke loose and ran wild through the town. Knocked him to the ground as it sped by, and he died that night. It doesn't mean his life or Martha's was any less than ours. Sometimes life is just…cruel and random."

Donovan shrugged. "I suppose. Only weird thing is the man said he was looking for someone called the vampire. Never even heard of that."

Rohawk looked a little pale.

"It's an old Kaldaran myth," Lysander said. "Vampires were creatures that looked mostly human but could drain the life out of others and spend that power on Technique. But that's an old tale used to scare children. The man was probably high on dream shrooms or something."

Rohawk patted his vest. "I have some of those if you ever want to try them."

Lysander narrowed his eyes at him.

"Well, that explains it a little," Donovan said. "I should go back and talk with the others. Thank you for coming by." The three said their goodbyes to Donovan. He turned to walk back toward the grave, but felt the hairs on his neck crawl. He looked back at the same time Rohawk was looking back at him, but the merc quickly averted his gaze. *There's more to this. Rohawk knows it. I intend to find out.*

The rest of the funeral was mostly just Donovan and Ramon talking to Martha's friends. The priestess of K'var had stuck around. She seemed sincere in her beliefs, but the whole thing irked Donovan. Martha did not believe in K'var. She believed in Orimin. Where was a priest of Orimin to fulfill her wishes?

Donovan walked over to her grave. She had been wrapped for burial, and the time to bury her was near. This was the last chance.

"Orimin," Donovan mumbled, then looked around to make sure no one could hear him. "Orimin, if you exist, then forgive me. I am not the one to say this prayer, but I am the only one who can. Please take Martha into your arms. Please treat her well in whatever afterlife you may have for her. And please give her the justice she deserves, to find whoever sent that wicked man to our door. If you are real, and you are the kind of god Martha said you were, then prove yourself to me. Bring justice for her, and for Nightingale."

Donovan woke when a sunbeam landed on his closed eyes. "What time is it?" he mumbled as he forced his body to respond. He had no intention of drinking that night, but later at home, Ramon and Tybalt had drinks and tobacco ready for him. They stayed up late drinking and smoking the night away. Ramon had apologized for the argument the night Martha was killed. Donovan was more than ready to forgive. It was hard enough losing Martha; he didn't want to lose his friendship with Ramon.

Tybalt, despite being the newbie, blended right in with the two of them. The man had a deepness to his soul that surprised Donovan. He was wise, respectful, and insightful. A welcome addition to the group.

After all that had happened, it was a very good night, but not befitting of a soldier on call.

He forced himself to sit up on the edge of the bed. The barracks was so quiet. He vaguely remembered that he decided to stay here. Tybalt had one extra bed at his place for Ramon, and no one had slept at Martha's since it happened.

Most everyone in the Guard was out on duty or off on a mission. Donovan had never heard silence in the barracks before. It felt a bit wrong, like the whole world had passed him by while he was sleeping. But that couldn't be true; it looked to be a couple hours before noon. He cracked a wide yawn and wiped the sleep from his eyes. The silence remained.

"Hello?" he mumbled. "Hello?" again, a little louder. "Is anyone here?"

"I'm coming, I'm coming." Eodius walked in and came over to Donovan's bed. "You look relatively well. Alexis has been asking me if you are fit to go out again. How much did you have to drink last night?"

"Probably too much."

Eodius frowned. "Well, at least you're being honest." He handed Donovan a wooden cup. "Drink this. It's made of herbs from the fey wilds."

"Herbs?"

"Believe it or not, fey try to avoid mending as much as we can. Plus, there are some things that herbs are far better at. You need some water in you anyway. So, drink up while I get you another."

Donovan nodded and followed orders. It tasted awful, but he felt like he was waking up more and more with every sip. When Eodius returned, he downed it in one gulp.

"Easy," Eodius said. "Let me check your eyes." He put a hand to Donovan's face and pulled on the skin near the eye socket, then did the other one. "You are in much better shape than I would have expected. You might have a little fey blood in you somewhere." He chuckled.

"Did Alexis say she wants to send me out today?" Eodius crossed his arms.

"She said she would defer to my judgment. It's much safer to keep you here at least a few more days, but I know things in the war aren't going well." Eodius paused and raised a hand to scratch his chin. "If it was up to you, what would you like to do?"

"Stay here, honestly. But I have people relying on me, and Nightingale needs us."

Eodius nodded. "I will tell Second Alexis you are well enough to fight. But if you die, I will share some of that guilt, so stay alive and don't come back to me for a while. Agreed?"

"Fair enough."

"I cannot speak for the Second, but my guess is she will want you out right away. Take a few more minutes while I get you another herb mixture, then you should suit up. I will return shortly."

Donovan sighed and laid back down, but didn't feel like going back to sleep. Instead, he stared at the ceiling and thought. Martha was gone, Ramon had a new hunting partner, and Nightingale was in grave danger. *So much change in such a short time.* He wanted nothing more than for things to go back to normal.

"Soldier," Alexis said from the doorway. Donovan shot up. "Easy there, no need. I was just teasing you." She walked over, shoving some of his gear on the floor out of the way with her foot, then sitting down next to him on the bed.

"I apologize; it was a late night. I did not keep my quarter well."

Alexis shrugged. "You're practically a merc now, in a way."

Donovan grimaced, and Alexis chuckled. "Wow, I guess I should have known I would get that reaction. I like to think you're setting a new standard for what the mercenaries around here could be."

"Speaking of…"

Alexis nodded and said, "Eodius told me he cleared you, which was a surprise. I'm not happy about it, to be honest. But we need you and your team out there. If it were up to the Captain, you would have been out yesterday. You sure you're alright to go out today?" Donovan sighed.

"I think it's time."

"That's what I thought you would say. I already alerted your team, and they are getting ready to meet you here. Get geared up and I will have a stable boy fetch your horse."

"Thanks, Alexis." She rose and walked out, all the while Donovan debating if he should say what he did not get to say the other night. But she was gone, and so was the moment. It wasn't the best time, but he wondered if any given day would be the last he saw her.

By the time Donovan had all of his gear on, his team was waiting outside with his horse. Rohawk was the first to see him, and gave him a loud hello.

"About damn time we get back in action!" he said. "Godell and I have a bet going on who can kill the most Kaldarans."

"How do you know we're going to kill more Kaldarans?" Donovan asked as he put his foot in the stirrup. "What if we are assigned to sweep the streets of Nightingale and keep the peace?"

"Please!" Rohawk bellowed. "Why would they waste such good talent on peasant keeping? I already know we're going back to that Crandall farm. I'm good for a second helping of what we had last time."

Donovan settled in his saddle and groaned. *Rohawk is such an ass. I hope he doesn't get me or anyone else killed.*

"The Kaldarans sent a scout back to the farm the other day," Kris said. "Wyndell and I killed him."

"You mean I killed him," Wyndell said.

Kris rolled her eyes. "I spotted him. You can't kill what you don't know is there."

"Is everyone ready?" Donovan called out. A general collection of nods and agreement. "Alright, to the Crandall farm. Officer Jillian will let us know what to do from there."

The ride back to the farm was uneventful, to say the least, but it went by quicker now that they were approaching it directly from the south. It was still only mid-afternoon when they arrived.

The first thing Donovan noticed was a group of soldiers standing around the well. Officer Jillian was with them, and she had a sour look on her face. He thought at first it was because of the sorry-looking "army" she had at her command—which looked like farmers and beggars with pikes—but when he got closer, he realized she was only giving occasional glances to her soldiers and was directing her ire toward the well itself.

"Thirteenth Division reporting," Donovan said when he got close enough. "Officer Jillian, what seems to be the problem?"

"I'm glad you're here, Donovan. We could use the help of your most nimble soldier." She glanced at Banner. "Take a look at this over here." She motioned toward a tree stump draped with a white cloth.

Donovan dismounted and followed her over to the stump. She motioned to another soldier who handed her a cup, and she poured out water over the cloth.

"The water is…a bit pink?" Donovan asked, confused.

"Our best guess is some wounded animal fell into the well and is bleeding into it. Something broke the bucket off the rope and we had to tie on a new one to get a load of this swill. We've been getting water from the neighbor's farm in the meantime, but you can imagine it's a bit of a walk."

"Bones," Donovan mumbled. "And you want me to go get the animal out?"

"Doesn't have to be you. I thought maybe you had someone in your group who could do it. Alexis gave me the rundown of your...Thirteenth Division." The way Officer Jillian said the name wasn't so much disdain as reservation. "All the men here are either not agile enough for this kind of thing—which makes me question their abilities in battle—" Officer Jillian took in a long breath—"or they are too spooked to go down the well."

"You're worried that this is a sign from the gods," Donovan surmised.

Officer Jillian crossed her arms and gave a curt, "Yes. Can you help or not?"

"Banner?" Donovan looked back as he said her name.

"On it, Boss," she said without missing a beat. "Been a while since I've done this." She untied the rope from the bucket and tied it around her waist instead, then started to climb her way down the well. She pressed her body and legs against the walls to lower herself slowly.

"Godell, grab the other end of this rope—you too, Faith," Donovan ordered.

"You don't need to worry about me," Banner said. "I just tied it around my waist so it's handy when we need to lift the animal carcass out of here. This is how I used to get away from the Nightingale Guard when they caught me stealing." Her voice resounded in echoes from down the well farther and farther away as she descended. Faith and Godell shrugged but held the end of the rope loosely.

Seconds passed in silence.

"Teching damn!" Banner suddenly screamed. The mess of slack rope on the ground quickly whipped into the well. Godell and Faith tightened their grip and held fast. The rope went tight; Godell and Faith gave a light grunt.

"We've got her," Faith said.

"Banner, are you alright?" Donovan called out into the darkness of the well.

"Are you sure you have her?" Lysander asked. He sped over to the well and investigated it with Donovan. "Banner?"

Silence.

Officer Jillian's face was pale, and she said, "I knew this was a sign from the gods!"

"Could something be down there?" Donovan called out to anyone who might have an answer.

"Donovan?" Banner's voice came up from the well. Barely. She must have been far down.

"Banner? What happened?" Lysander called out.

"I messed up. I slipped and can't get my footing."

Donovan signaled to Faith and Godell. "We'll get you back up."

"Wait, not yet. Get me a light down here."

Donovan held up a hand for Faith and Godell to wait and relayed the order to the others. A few soldiers worked to fasten a lantern on a second rope, carefully lowering it down the well. A vague shape appeared near the bottom, and the rope stopped swaying as the light was taken from it.

Banner said something, but Donovan couldn't quite hear it.

"What is it?" he asked as he leaned in.

"I'm going to tie this other rope around something. Wait for my signal."

Donovan relayed the order. Rohawk and Wyndell grabbed the second rope and waited to pull. Lysander went to help Godell, but he said, "We got it, old man."

Lysander seemed a little put off and backed away.

"Whose bright idea was this anyway?" Kris asked.

"I think people who like drinking water," Faith answered.

Kris glared at him.

"Alright, pull me up first to give it some space," Banner called out. Donovan made a twirling motion with his finger, and Faith and Godell pulled Banner up and out of the well. When she reached the top, she plopped out rather ungracefully and moved away with a few careful steps before handing the lantern back to a soldier and sitting down on the ground. Donovan gave a slight nod and Rohawk and Wyndell went to work pulling the other rope.

Banner brought herself up, shivering. She was wet from the waist down.

"Bring her some blankets," Donovan ordered to no one in particular, but a couple people started to work on it. "Your face is a bit pale," Donovan noted as he knelt next to her. "Are you alright?"

She nodded in between breaths, which were a bit strained. "I haven't slipped like that in a while."

"You did well. Just be more careful next time."

Anger flashed on Banner's face, but when she locked eyes with Donovan, she softened. Her cheeks went a shade redder. "I...well, just be prepared for what you're about to see. It doesn't bother me that much, but it will probably bother you."

"I would be a lot more prepared if you would just tell me what—" Donovan stopped when he heard gasps and shouts coming from the camp. He turned around to see a headless corpse being raised out of the well and set onto the ground.

"Bag of teching bones," Rohawk said, "this must be King Santos."

Donovan heard someone retching and looked over to see Officer Jillian bent down, hands on her knees. She wasn't the only one. They were probably the ones who drank some of the water before noticing its color.

"How do you know that without the damn head?" Kris asked. "Wait, the dragon tattoo."

"That's like the one I saw the other night when we first came here," Wyndell said.

"Bones," Donovan muttered the curse and scratched his chin. *We saw King Santos leaving the well. How can this be his body?* Donovan's eyes grew wide. "Rohawk, you said the King of Kaldaran is a test of strength, that whoever kills the king becomes the new King Santos, right?"

"That's how it works."

Donovan processed all of this. Toby had always been a decent man, but Donovan did not know him all *that* well. And there was the conversation he overheard the night before, when Toby said weird things about the people of Nightingale not knowing what was coming.

"I know who the new King Santos is," he said.

"Who?" Wyndell asked.

Officer Jillian had recovered enough to rejoin the conversation, and she also looked curious.

Donovan shook his head in disbelief. "Toby. It's teching Toby. It must have been him that we saw here the other night. He was dumping the body into the well, that's what we saw those Kaldaran men carrying out of the farmhouse. He was telling the truth in Nightingale; he did kill King Santos."

Kris looked incredulous. "Wait, why would he make such a show of it in Nightingale, then?"

"He sure profited a lot from it," Donovan pointed out, "but there might be more to it. Maybe he wanted Nightingale to lower its guard, or…"

"This is all nothing but wild guesses," Officer Jillian noted.

"Perhaps not," Rohawk countered. "Chaos and confusion are methods of warfare for those who serve Kaldar."

Officer Jillian crossed her arms. "And would killing King Santos cause confusion?"

"That alone wouldn't," Rohawk admitted. "But if Toby is the new King Santos, then that certainly would cause a lot of confusion."

"That makes sense," Officer Jillian admitted. "Is there any way to confirm this?"

Donovan's eyes drifted to a Nightingalen horseman who had crested the hill to the north. He was coming dangerously fast, and when he got closer, the arrow in his shoulder and red blood on his tabard were clear. "Already confirmed," he mumbled.

"They're coming!" the rider shouted. "On horseback!"

Chapter Twelve

"Formation!" Officer Jillian yelled. "Hedgehog! Get those pikes in line or you're all dead!"

Shouting filled the camp, a mixture of oaths from all different kinds of cultures. One soldier was daft enough to mumble "Abaddon's cock" near Commander Jillian, and she took four valuable seconds to ream him for it before continuing preparations. That would have been his last day on the Nightingale Guard if it wasn't for the fact that he wasn't in the Guard—he was a peasant.

Donovan circled his team around and fired off orders. "Kris, Wyndell, take your positions on the roof of the house and rain gol on them."

"I should go to the roof of the barn instead," Wyndell said.

"Fine, go," Donovan ordered. Not worth the time to argue.

Kris and Wyndell turned to run to their respective vantage points.

"As for the rest of you," he went on, "I want Banner at the bottom of the barn with Lysander and Rohawk. Hide there until they commit, then flank the skot out of them. Faith and Godell, stay with me and the Officer's soldiers. Chances are, they will break our line at some point, and we need to be here to fight them back."

Officer Jillian's hedgehog was a basic pike formation—the front line lying down, then the second line kneeling, and the third standing, all holding pikes outstretched to protect the people in front of them. If the line could be kept together, it was highly effective.

About thirty horsemen crested the top of the hill and paused. They were dressed as usual—no real armor. Just furs for warmth, and some had even gone shirtless altogether.

A man with a crown rode in the center of the group, and even at a distance Donovan could make out a black tattoo on his forearm.

"Could it be…Toby?" Donovan muttered to himself.

"Looks like your little detective work was pointless," Godell commented. "But nice job putting it together."

"Just keep formation with me," Donovan grumbled.

Godell just grinned at him.

Something odd happened next. There was laughter coming from the riders, and the crowned rider took the crown off and passed it around. They took turns wearing it.

"What the gol?" Donovan asked.

"They are trying to confuse us," Faith said. "The one with the tattoo on his arm is the real king!"

There was no way they heard Faith, but right after he said that, seven or so of the Kaldarans pulled up their sleeves to reveal tattoos. At a distance, there was no way to tell which one was the real one.

"Now that's just not fair," Faith groaned.

"Just kill all of them, then!" Godell roared.

Godell they probably did hear. They roared back and charged, horses thundering down the hillside.

Donovan looked for Toby, but it was a chaotic mess. He didn't know for sure Toby was in the group, but it made a lot of sense.

A few arrows flew at the coming charge, but nothing seemed to make a mark. "Come on, Wyndell, Kris," Donovan said to himself. "Get your act together and kill them."

The horsemen came closer, and two of the men in the hedgehog formation chickened and broke away to run for the barn.

"Back in line, now!" Officer Jillian yelled, but before the words were even out of her mouth, the Kaldarans turned and rode those two down, killing them effortlessly with horseman's picks. As long as they held the line, they were protected against the charge.

"Hold the damn line!" Donovan roared. He turned to the sound of metal striking metal. An arrow stuck out of the back of Faith's cuirass. He gasped for breath and tumbled to the ground, groaning in pain. "Abaddon's teeth!" Donovan shouted. "Where did that—" He looked back at the farmhouse to see Kris loading another shot. She was the only one back there. *Wait, what? Why would...*

Donovan remembered they had been part of Toby's crew. *And they still are.*

He looked over at Wyndell in time to see an arrow pointing down at the Nightingale troops, toward him. He raised his shield, but he was not the target. Godell turned around just in time to take Wyndell's arrow to the face. He was dead.

"Traitorous bastards!" Donovan grunted.

"Keep formation!" Officer Jillian cried out again. And for once, it held. The Kaldarans picked an angle and charged, but the attack stopped against the pikes. Half a dozen riders were killed and a few unhorsed. But a voice with a Kaldaran accent called out orders to regroup. Donovan tried to see who that was, but to no avail. The riders moved back to where they had come from, then dismounted for an attack on foot.

What are they doing? It didn't make sense that the Kaldarans would so easily give up their mounted advantage, but on second thought, Donovan realized a possible explanation. The Nightingalen forces were mostly untrained, and they didn't know much more about combat than defending against a cavalry charge. *And Toby would be aware of that.*

Still, it did help a little now that they were off horses, and Donovan didn't bother to curse good fortune. When they came in, he could charge them with Chomper, but there was still the threat from behind he had to deal with. He turned to look at Kris, who almost had another arrow ready.

"Damn it," he mumbled. He turned and broke formation, charging toward the farmhouse and narrowly avoiding Kris's next arrow. He made it to the front of the home and skidded Chomper to a halt before he jumped off and tried the door. *Locked.* He put his kite shield forward and slammed into it, splintering the jamb. Now inside, he ran up the stairs and over to the ladder that led to the attic. He climbed up it, and saw Kris' footprints in the dust leading to the roof access, and there was just one more ladder with a hatch to the roof. He pushed on it, but a weight was holding it down.

"Don't try it, Donovan," Kris's voice came through muffled from above.
"

"Kris!" he shouted. "Why would you do this? Was Nightingale gold not enough for you?"

"Nightingale gold pales into comparison to the power of a god! Toby has figured out a way to get it!"

Well, that was the confirmation about Toby he didn't really need.

"You know that's complete bullskot!" Donovan roared back. "If Toby betrayed Nightingale, how do you know he won't betray you?"

"He knows who his own are, Donovan. That's why he turned down your offer to join us. You will never be one of us!"

Donovan realized that with every second that passed, the Kingdom of Kaldaran was killing more Nightingale soldiers, and he wasn't there to help fight them. But letting Kris shoot freely from the roof would lead to even more deaths. He had to find another way up. He had to get her talking for a while. He had to distract her and he had to act fast.

"So that's it then? A sad girl with a sad past clinging to the first man who showed her anything like fatherly love?"

"You don't know anything about me, Donovan! If you knew what I've seen, what I've—"

Donovan moved slowly down the ladder and toward a small casement window. He would need to move like Banner to make this work, but he was always a damn good climber. He opened the casement and slipped outside. He was close enough to grab a corbel propping up the edge of the roof, but only if he jumped for it. He made his way out of the window, grabbing on to the inside for as long as he could. He could hear Kris still shouting back at him through the hatch.

Donovan let go and sprang upward, grabbing the corbel with both hands and moving his grip one hand at a time to the top of the roof. He swung over it, and saw Kris turn around at the noise. She quickly loaded an arrow and fired—Donovan brought his shield to bear just in time. She let out a grunt and dropped her bow for a sword. Donovan readied his and engaged her.

"Kris! Surrender now or I will be forced to kill you!"

"Toby has promised us the power of the gods, Donovan! What hope do you have against that? I will become like the gods, and no one will ever take advantage of me again!"

Kris lashed out with a wild blow and Donovan side-stepped it, bringing his sword around. She screamed, falling to her knees holding her stomach.

"Bag of bones," Donovan breathed out. She was bleeding through her stomach fast. The blood seeped through her arms as she tried to hold her wound tight. She was going to die.

"No...this can't be right...can't be like this..." Kris whimpered. "This is...how I die?"

Donovan huffed out a breath. "It didn't have to go this way."

Kris rolled around, clutching a dagger and screaming out the *Sunder* Technique as her eyes burned orange. She lunged at Donovan. Her knife went into his shield and cut clean through it, taking off a corner, narrowly missing his arm. He brought the cross guard of his sword around and smacked her across the chin. She dropped the knife and fell to the roof, screaming in agony.

"What's happening to me? Where am I?" she cried out.

Donovan froze. *She...she soulburned herself? Does this mean she doesn't remember being a traitor?*

"Please, someone, help me!" she screamed.

Donovan knelt beside her and tore off a piece of her tunic, trying to make something to bandage her wound. "My name is Donovan, I'm here to help. Just take it easy."

"Who are you? What have you done to me?" She struggled against his grip, but within seconds, she weakened. Her body went limp. She was dead.

Donovan dropped her. He took a few steps back, horrified at what he had seen. *She shot Faith and tried to kill me. But...was she still that person when she died?* He shook himself out of his thoughts. There was a fight going on. He looked over—Nightingale was struggling against the much more veteran Kaldaran soldiers.

Donovan looked over to the top of the barn and saw Rohawk dropping Wyndell's body to the ground. The rogue looked over at Donovan and gave him the Nightingale salute.

"There's some good news at least," he said as he moved for the hatch. He raced through the house and was back on Chomper, turning toward the fight.

As Donovan neared the edge of the battle, he saw Kaldaran's plan to approach on foot had been successful. They were overpowering Officer Jillian's larger—but mostly untrained—army.

Donovan moved in and brought his sword clean through a Kaldaran's head. He was still mounted and had the advantage. He pressed that advantage and killed another, but that drew the attention of some of the others. A few Kaldarans turned on him, and Donovan tried to whip Chomper around to avoid running into the three. But Chomper was not trained as well as a war horse, and he stumbled. Donovan tumbled to the ground, and a panicked Chomper fled from him.

Donovan got up to meet one of the Kaldarans on foot. The enemy soldier brought a horseman's pick down. Donovan still had a good chunk of shield, and he caught the pick with it. The pick pierced through, the menacing sharp end coming close but missing Donovan's arm flesh. Now he had control of it. He cranked his shield and yanked the pick out of the Kaldaran's hand, then brought his sword around in a circular sweep—a moulinet—and cut the man's chest open.

Donovan looked where to go next. Officer Jillian was flanked and about to be killed. He charged toward her, just in time to slice through the hand of her would-be killer. The Kaldaran had the gall to grab a dagger with his other hand, but Donovan brought his sword around for the killing blow.

The Kaldarans had a bit more reach with their horseman's picks, but Donovan was not going to be trifled with. Another Kaldaran came within measure and made the mistake of going for a heavy swing. Donovan did not risk blocking this time. He stepped into the Kaldaran, trapped the man's weapon arm with his shield hand, and brought his cross guard around into the man's face. His skull collapsed against the blow of the pommel.

Donovan might have been able to best the Kaldarans one on one, but he was being surrounded and was without a tight line to watch his flank. *Where are the others?* He looked up to the top of the barn, but Rohawk wasn't there anymore. Banner and Lysander were also nowhere to be seen.

Donovan looked over at Faith, who lay on the ground, gritting his teeth as life flowed out of him. Godell's body lay next to him. With mending Faith might survive, but the Kingdom of Kaldaran had to be dealt with first.

Officer Jillian cried out for a reformation of anyone left to fight, and the Nightingale soldiers rallied in a surprisingly good line. Then, the Officer called for the line to move forward.

The Kaldarans either had to cut and run or turn and fight. Donovan knew which one they would probably choose, and he was right. The Kaldarans moved back into the battle. It was a bloodbath, but the line was holding. About a dozen Kaldarans turned and ran back for their horses; Donovan was shocked by that.

"We need to charge them," Donovan called out.

"Hold!" Officer Jillian called back. She glared at him. He knew he was right but…she was working with inexperienced soldiers and did not want to risk breaking their line. It was a miracle they had reformed in the first place.

"Where is Toby?" Donovan breathed out. He did not see the dragon tattoo on any of them, but there was so much blood on all of them, it could have easily been covered. His shield hand itched. He looked down to see someone had gotten a cut on him he had not noticed. Blood soaked his padded jack. But he felt strong and alive, and paid no mind.

"Is this how the god of chaos fights?" he called. One of them turned his head, and Donovan realized he locked eyes with Toby. The mercenary…smiled at him. It wasn't what Donovan expected at all. The smile was confident, but somehow sad. If Donovan was reading it right, the Kaldaran man thought he was going to win, but did not like having to kill Donovan.

"Well, at least a little sympathy before he tries to run me through," he said to himself.

The Kaldaran cavalry regrouped and turned around for another charge. The Nightingalens outnumbered them at least four to one at this point, but they persisted. Officer Jillian called for the pikes to be steady.

The new King Santos, King Toby, rose in his stirrups, then put his feet all the way up on the saddle. He was postured to jump from his horse.

"What is he doing?" Donovan asked those around him.

"Suicide," one of the soldiers answered. "He's been driven mad by the teachings of Kaldar!"

Donovan's gut told him that was not quite right. Something was wrong. Nothing about Toby's actions now made sense to Donovan, but he knew the once-mercenary was smart. Very smart. He knew something none of them knew.

A sudden sense of dread permeated the air. Something had changed. There was a new presence on the battlefield.

"Kaldar!" Toby roared. "Heed my call!"

The Kaldarans reached the line and either lost their horses or were themselves impaled by the remaining pikes. But King Santos jumped from his mount and brought a horseman's pick down on Officer Jillian, killing her instantly. He'd gotten impaled by two pikes on the way down. When his feet were on the ground, he just…kept going. Pikes and all. They turned into improvised weapons, and he flailed wildly about, smacking people with the blunt ends.

"Why won't he die?" Donovan grunted. He tried to get there to fight the king, but there were still too many Kaldarans in the way.

Annoyed with the pikes, King Santos finally stopped and pulled them out. He should have been gushing blood, but the only sign of it was smeared on the pikes. It looked like nothing flowed from the holes in his body.

King Santos took the pikes and threw them at Nightingale soldiers. One of them went clean through, wood splintering to pieces and the sharp sticking into a man behind.

Donovan froze, his breathing ragged. "Gods above...he's Crowned." The dread was creeping in, but something inside of him pushed back against it. *Who better to kill an agent of the gods than the god-hater himself!*

Donovan decided no matter what stood in his way, he was killing Toby. He fought his way through, his sword arm aching from the stress of battle, his shield hand cut but still grasping firm what Kris had left him with.

When he neared, Toby turned toward him. "Old friend. Sad you do not share blood with me."

"You have betrayed Nightingale!" Donovan shouted. "Mercenary!"

"I ceased to be a mercenary when I came home to Kaldar!" Toby spat back. "I respect your strength, Donovan. It will bring Kaldar great pleasure when I kill you."

Toby lunged; Donovan decided the best way to block that horseman's pick was not to be there. He quickly moved out of the way, feeling the force from the hammer side of the pick coming awfully close. Instead of letting the momentum go to waste, Toby brought it back around in a moulinet and brought it toward Donovan's head.

It was all Donovan could do to get his shield in the way. The angle saved his life; the hammer slid off the shield, but even then, the blow was massive. Donovan groaned in pain and felt his arm go numb, but he did not break concentration. He brought his sword to bear before Toby had time to rein the pick back in. Donovan twisted his hips as his sword cut clean across Toby's chest, a deep cut that skittered off of bones.

"Mortal weapons!" Toby roared at Donovan. His voice had an echo to it—it sounded like two voices speaking at once. "You cannot defeat Kaldar's chosen! Become his next sacrifice!"

Toby brought the hammer around. Donovan backed up out of the way and tripped over a body. He felt pain somewhere when he fell. His head ached. He had just enough time to see that the body was Faith. Toby sprang forward, but his advance was halted when an arrow appeared in his neck.

"Donovan, run!" Rohawk's voice cut through the air.

Donovan grimaced at the pain in his arm. Running would not be easy, and maybe not fast enough. He looked around; a loose charger trotted by and he sprang into action, struggling to mount it with one good arm, but succeeding. He turned to look at what was happening with Rohawk and King Santos. The two were several paces away from each other, squaring off.

"You betrayed me, Son of Kaldar!" Toby roared with his two voices. "Half-breed weakling! I should have known your Deldamore blood would call you away!" Rohawk flourished his katars. It was the first time Donovan had seen them. Each one looked like a large, long, white tooth that came to a point, with handles attached for grips at the bottom.

"Or maybe I just don't like insane cult leaders besmirching my father's bloodline." Despite his taunting, Rohawk sounded ever so slightly panicked.

King Santos was the first to move. He brought his pick around on his right, but it was a feint. Donovan had no time to call out the move, and for a split second, he thought he was about to witness Rohawk's end. But before the horseman's pick came around, Rohawk vanished.

King Santos let out a primal roar that shook the ground. Donovan had no clue what just happened, but he'd stayed way too long already. He urged the horse to full speed.

"Damn the fates! I've got to get out of here," Donovan said to himself.

"Donovan, you look half dead!" Rohawk said as he neared him, also on horseback.

"What in Abaddon? Where did you come from?"

"From gol, that's where! Let's get the Abaddon out of here." Rohawk dug his heels in the horse's side, and they bolted off. The sense of dread that Donovan had felt earlier began to fade. He noticed Rohawk looking more and more relieved the further away from the farm they got.

Donovan said nothing for the first hour of the ride. He had smacked his head a bit when he fell, and he had seen things that made no sense. He killed Toby. Others had killed Toby. But none of the killing blows did anything.

Finding the right words to describe what happened seemed impossible, but finally, Donovan decided he needed to try. He was about to say something when Rohawk said, "Bit of rotten luck about your horse, eh? At least Mongoose is still good." Rohawk patted his horse's mane.

Donovan noticed a quiver in his voice. Rohawk had been panicked.

"Poor thing is a bit tired, though," Rohawk added.

Donovan absorbed that for a few seconds then shook his head. "He cannot be killed, Rohawk. He...he was Crowned, wasn't he?"

"Who, King Santos?"

"Who else would I be talking about? Are you purposefully being daft? We are the only ones left alive."

"Not true. A few probably escaped. Banner is alive. I watched Lysander helping her escape on our way out. You were too busy to notice. Looks like you took a knock to the head, too, and that arm will need mending. You should recover—Banner isn't so lucky, though. If she survives, I'm guessing she will have a limp for the rest of her life, even if she gets her leg mended soon. I worry about her. It's like taking the wings off a bird."

"Godell is dead," Donovan said, "I saw him get shot in the face. And I don't think Faith could have survived how much blood he was losing...both were killed by Kris and Wyndell."

"Godell is alive, at least he was."

Donovan blinked. "What? He had an arrow in his face."

"He got up and made a break for it. I've seen people survive getting shot in the head. Granted, I've seen a lot more die from it."

"Well, I hope he made it. That's something. I wish I could have done something for Faith."

"You did pretty damn good, I think. You stood up to King Santos."

"For all the good it did," Donovan muttered.

"I didn't see anyone else get as far as you did," Rohawk said. "Holding a pike and hoping to get lucky isn't the same as going toe to toe with…" His voiced drifted off.

Donovan looked over, but Rohawk just cleared his throat and added, "Good job with Kristine. I was a little worried about her and Wyndell, but I had heard they were on the outs with Toby. And I didn't know Toby was a traitor to begin with. I should have said something before the fighting started but…I wasn't sure, either."

"I sure didn't see it," Donovan said.

"It wasn't your job to catch that stuff, it was mine. Alexis was worried about rogue agents. She wanted me to look out for you. I told her I'm not anyone's babysitter, but I ended up doing what she wanted anyway."

"Why?"

"Because you came along and you seemed to care a whole lot about what happened around here. Do you think Captain Gerald gives a damn? Corrick's looking to poach him to be the Captain of the Guard for the Royal Palace there. They will, too, the moment this gets too hot for him. Which is probably now. After today, most of the Nightingale Guard is going to be ready to call it quits."

"We have to hold on, though."

"That's what I find fascinating about you, Donovan. You care. Nobody I know besides Alexis is like that. It's respectable. That's why I vouched for you with the other mercenaries; that's why they were looking out for you. We needed a good man to lead our little band of villains."

Donovan let out a faint chuckle that sounded like weak *has*. "For all the good it did you. Three dead, two wounded."

"We came out of something alive that we shouldn't have. Your strategy worked, by the way. Lysander and I probably killed more than all those farmers combined. Banner helped too. She watched our backs, but that didn't stop one of them getting close enough to clip her leg."

Donovan nodded slightly, then clenched his teeth as the horse jostled his arm.

"You look a bit pale," Rohawk noted. "A bruise is taking shape near your face too. That can't be good. Hang on and we will get you help first thing once we get to Nightingale."

"Very kind of you," Donovan groaned.

Rohawk laughed. "Teching damn, Donovan! That was stupid of you to fight King Santos. You're lucky to be alive. Very lucky. There are dead men back at that farm that were a thousand times more careful than you."

Chapter Thirteen

Donovan faded in and out in terms of attention, but he was awake the whole ride home. His head did ache. Rohawk must have been right about whatever bruise he saw.

It felt like forever before they made it to the safety of Nightingale. The sun had set, and the city was quiet. When the townsfolk saw Rohawk and Donovan, many gasped, some turned away, and a few pointed and whispered to one another.

"Something's not right here, Donovan," Rohawk said. He turned around and bit off a curse.

"What?" Donovan asked.

"Gods, you don't look so good. How do you feel?"

"Pretty woozy."

"Little further," Rohawk said as they turned toward the barracks.

He dismounted, then helped Donovan down, and then inside.

"I need a mender right now!" Rohawk shouted. "And somebody find Alexis immediately!"

The clerk behind his desk flashed a "not again" expression and got up, going down the hallway. Within a moment, Eodius came out.

"What is going on? Who needs my—" he froze when he took a closer look at Donovan. Then he looked at Rohawk. "Bag of bones, I know this man. Looks like he is doing his best to break his promise. What has happened to him?"

"Hit his head and has taken a few cuts," Rohawk answered. "Not sure what's worse. Can you mend him?"

"I will have to examine him first. He looks like he has lost a lot of blood; human medicine might give him a better chance. Bring him back to the infirmary." Rohawk followed Eodius through the barracks and to a room with a few dozen cots. He put Donovan on an empty one.

"What's happening?" Donovan asked.

"Getting you better," Rohawk answered.

Eodius came over with a knife to cut away at the padded jack and leather jerkin. "Hm," he mumbled.

"Arm hurts," Donovan said as he indicated his left arm with his chin.

"Broken, I think." Eodius looked over the arm, then back at Donovan's chest, neck, and head.

"Do you want to stand around and study him or make him better?"

"Donovan, I can try to mend you, but without knowing what's going on with your head, it could be risky."

"Work your magic, boss," Rohawk said.

"It is Donovan's decision," Eodius said pointedly.

Rohawk threw up his hands and stepped away. Donovan thought a moment. His head swam. He wasn't well enough to make this decision, so he thought to go with Rohawk's answer.

"Do it. Mend me."

Eodius looked very uncomfortable, but he nodded. "You were not awake last time, but this will hurt like gol. Brace yourself."

Donovan opened his mouth to say "just do it," but before getting a word out he gasped as a sharp cold flooded his veins. The pain he felt spread to his entire body, but was sharp in his head and immense in his broken arm. Donovan remembered what happened to Rue. Was he also about to die? Was the mending too much? It was so intense. He felt that he was on the brink of slipping out of this life. He screamed and called out for Eodius to stop.

"Easy there, I am already done," Eodius said. "Mending is harder when you have so many in such a short period of time. Your body is strained."

Donovan regained his senses and the pain faded away. "Gods..." Donovan moaned out.

"Is he alright?" Rohawk asked.

"He's alive and talking, so yes. Mending either kills or heals."

Rohawk nodded. "Good. Thanks."

"I do not appreciate being ordered around by a merc like you. Who do you report to?"

Rohawk pointed to Donovan.

"Fine, I will tell Officer Jillian. She will listen to me."

"Joke's on you—she's dead, and so are all of her men."

Eodius looked like the half-fey version of pale.

"We lost Crandall's farm, his neighbors are probably going to get taken as well. That means no more food from the north. That's why I asked for Alexis when I came in. Did that clerk go get her?"

"He did," Alexis said. She walked up and stood over Donovan. "I can take it from here. Will the two of you excuse us?"

"That includes me?" Rohawk asked, either being offended or feigning it. Alexis nodded.

"Alright, but you better make sure he's alright so my hard work doesn't go to waste." Rohawk walked off, but Eodius remained.

"He will be alright for a few minutes, yes?" Alexis asked him.

Eodius took in a deep breath and said, "If nothing else happens to him, then yes. But I don't think even the gods can keep up with this one. I will be back with some herbs." Eodius gave the Nightingale salute and turned to leave.

"Glad saving me was worth it to Rohawk," Donovan said coldly.

"His pride won't let him say that he didn't want to see you die."

"I suppose you want to know what happened."

"I already know most of it. Lysander and Banner were here a couple hours ago." Alexis took hold of Donovan's hand. "Are you alright? What happened to you?"

"A lot of things. The battle was the worst I've seen so far. So many dead and wounded. We lost Faith; I'm not sure if Godell made it. Kris and Wyndell betrayed us. They were still loyal to Toby. And Kaldar."

"Toby? Lysander said Kris and Wyndell turned traitor, but what does this have to do with Toby?"

"Lysander didn't tell you that part? Toby is the new King Santos of Kaldaran. The first night we were at the farm, he was there with his crew, killing King Santos and taking control."

"I always knew something was off about him, especially after he paraded the old king's head around. But he did a lot of good during his time as a merc, and I didn't think he was a traitor. What happened to Kris and Wyndell?"

"They fired on us. I went after Kris and...killed her. Rohawk killed Wyndell."

"Lysander said the battle was going in our favor until the final charge from Kaldaran. What happened?"

Donovan carefully considered his answer. "King Santos was Crowned, Alexis. I saw it. I teching saw it. He was skewered twice and acted like it was nothing. I cut him deep and there was no blood coming out of him."

"Are you sure of what you saw?"

Donovan considered that. "As sure as I can be. Either I'm completely insane or King Santos is Crowned. Take your pick. Either way, I ran for it. But if I'm insane, Rohawk's probably insane too, then. Just ask him."

"I will, but I don't believe you're insane. I just…if the Crowned still exist—if they have always existed—it affects everything I thought I knew."

"How do we fight against that? How do we fight against someone with the power of the gods?" Donovan felt his hand get squeezed tighter. He looked back at Alexis, and she was crying. "Alexis?"

"You're leaving," she said in between tears. "I'm sorry. I can't do anything about it."

"What?" Donovan asked. Her words filled his stomach with butterflies. "What do you mean? What does this have to do with Kaldaran?"

"Nothing with Kaldaran, I just…couldn't keep the thought inside anymore. I know that the captain sees this as another failure from you. He was there with me when Lysander gave his report. Kris and Wyndell's betrayal and the loss of the farm…he is a politician and is looking for someone to blame. So he is discharging you from the Guard and making you a mercenary."

Donovan clenched his fist and said, "I had nothing to do with our loss at the farm. Nightingale is my home. I've fought for this place, bled for it! The bodies of my fallen friends are not even cold and the captain is worried about who to blame?"

"Donovan, I know," Alexis whispered, but he went on.

"I looked into the eyes of a Crowned and cut him—for Nightingale! I've buried my loved ones here! And now I am being sent out into the night like a dying dog? I know that I wasn't born here, that much is clear, but I have made a life here. What am I supposed to do?"

"The captain has another mission for you. You take it or he throws you in prison."

Donovan's mouth moved but no words came out. Nothing was right in his world. Nothing he could say would change that.

"I've nowhere else to go," he whispered. "The captain knows that." He paused and inhaled a few deep breaths. "What is he sending me to do?"

"You are going to the Eastern Fey Wilds, to Fallavon, the capitol of the Lion Clan."

"He's sending me to the teching fey?"

Alexis chuckled. "I had a similar reaction. But King Beldon has been to Nightingale once before, and we have had good communication with him. We helped broker the peace deal in his last war. It is a longshot, but we are going to offer him suzerainty of Nightingale in exchange for his help. The same deal we have with K'var, since they've broken their end of the bargain."

"I suppose it's as good as anything else we can try at this point." Donovan sighed. A thought came to his mind. He was no longer part of the Guard. He was considered a mercenary. "Alexis."

"Yes?" Her breathing seemed to quicken. Donovan did not know if he was about to add insult to literal injury or not, but he took a deep breath. *Gods be damned, I'm doing this.* He slowly sat up and gestured for Alexis to sit next to him. She did.

"I…I'm no longer part of the Guard. You are no longer my superior officer."

Alexis suddenly stood up. "Donovan, not now. Not with you leaving."

"What?"

"I know what you're about to say. Please promise me you will say it again when you return."

"Why not now?"

"Because if you promise me you will say it when you return, that means you will return. I know it's silly, and childish. But please, just indulge me in this."

"Why wouldn't I return, Alexis?"

She took in a deep breath. "I think Captain Gerald is sending you to Fallavon because he thinks whoever he sends will die. We have had a good relationship with King Beldon, yes. But the king there does not have absolute power. He shares his rule with a council, and the Grand Magistrate is known for his hatred of humans."

"If the captain wants to get rid of me, why doesn't he just hang me, then?"

"A lot of people around here still respect you. I think he sees this as a more diplomatic way of solving his problem. And in the off chance you are successful, then he will take credit for getting the fey to help us."

Donovan sighed. "Politics. I don't even speak the teching fey language."

"King Beldon and many of his fey soldiers speak the common tongue. You should be able to get by. We would send you with a translator, but Eodius is the only one we have, and we need him here."

Donovan nodded slowly. "Gods above, I don't want to leave."

"I want to give you something." Alexis reached at her neck and pulled a glass locket that was hung on a small silver chain. She held it out in her open palm. "There is a little portrait of me in here. I know that sounds odd—that I would be wearing it. My father made it. My mother stopped speaking to me when I told her I was leaving K'var, but my father always supported me. He said, 'I want you to remember the look on your face when you told your mother. I want you to remember that courage and strength.' Well, now I want you to think of the same."

Donovan carefully took it out of her palm. "I will treasure it. Thank you."

She smiled. Donovan slowly stood and pulled her into an embrace. They held each other for a minute, but Alexis started to let go.

"I need to let you rest. You are going to be busy tomorrow with preparations. So will anyone from your team who is willing and well enough to go."

Donovan took her hand and she locked eyes with him. "I don't care if this is a suicide mission. I will convince the King of Fallavon to help, and I will return to you. I swear it."

Donovan rustled through the back room of the shop, looking for anything else he might be forgetting for the journey. He saw a leather strap under a pile of old tools and dug it out, sneezing a couple times from the disturbed dust.

A spare bridle for Chomper...

Chomper's fate was unknown. Ramon nearly went out looking for the horse, but the Guard stopped him. It wasn't worth his life. They were right, and Donovan hoped that the horse would find his way home.

The Guard had assigned him a new horse for his trip to Fallavon. It was lean, fast, and trained to flee from pursuers even on rough terrain.

It just wouldn't be his.

He sighed out a hot breath in the cold air of the first floor. He would miss the winter festival while he was gone. It would likely be small and sad with everything going on, but the thought of asking Alexis to dance…

"Making preparations?"

Donovan turned around. He had left the door to the shop unlocked, and Lysander and Banner let themselves in. Banner's leg was wrapped up and she had a cane at her side.

"Look, I'm old!" she said as she demonstrated her limp by walking slowly back and forth. Donovan tried not to laugh, but it was pretty damn funny.

"Glad to see your sense of humor isn't wounded," he said.

"It will be a different life for me, but the mender said I have a chance at full recovery. He recommended I…" she paused. "Get away from the war."

"Then I imagine the two of you will not be coming with me to Fallavon?"

"We hate to abandon you, Donovan, but I'm getting too old for this kind of all-out war," Lysander explained. "I was quite the warrior in my younger days, and that has stuck with me much longer than I expected. But my granddaughter and I—" Lysander froze. "I mean—" Banner rolled her eyes.

"He probably already knows, grandpa."

Donovan chuckled and said, "No, but you two did seem a lot closer than two strangers would be. Now that you mention it, I can see a resemblance." Donovan's eyes wandered as somebody else came by the shop. "Godell, you almost look like you haven't been shot in the head."

Godell crossed his arms. He had a patch on his left eye and some bandages around his head. He was fighting off a smile at Donovan's comment. "You're an ass," he said, but a chuckle broke through.

"I know it's worthless to say, but I'm sorry," Donovan said. "I should have known Kris and Wyndell were traitors."

Godell turned toward Lysander and Banner. "I knew it! It was those two lovebird marksmen! I told you! They turned traitor and shot me in the eye."

"Sounds like you three have been making plans," Donovan noted.

Godell looked back at him. "As short as our time together has been, you're a damn fine soldier, Donovan, and I appreciate that. But I'm not interested in going into the Fey Wilds. Those fey creep me out. Figured I would go with these two and make sure they make it back to Corrick alright."

"You got a home there, Lysander?"

The older man nodded. "Of course. I'm a war hero back home, and the architect of the greatest wall known to history."

Donovan threw a rope and a thick canvas into a bag. Sleeping outside would be brutal, but he knew how to make a workable shelter. "Where's the last one?" he asked.

"Rohawk?" Godell said. "Haven't seen him since the battle."

Banner poked him. "Are you keeping an eye out for him? Oh wait…"

Godell narrowed his one eye. "Watch it, kiddo."

"Looking for me?" Rohawk said as he walked in. "Sorry I'm late. I didn't think all of you were going to Fallavon!"

Lysander, Godell, and Banner all hesitated, but Donovan said, "they're not."

"But what about the Thirteenth Division?"

"It's done, disbanded. I'm going to Fallavon alone."

"You can't be serious, Donovan!" Rohawk took a step closer. "Those fey are not like us. They'll hang you high just for stepping on a single leaf."

Donovan knew there was a possibility of exactly that happening. "Someone must try to get help for Nightingale. Latest word from K'var is that they are 'still coming.' Everyone knows that's a joke."

"But the fey helping out humans?" Lysander said incredulously. "Donovan, if that kind of thing has ever happened, the last time must have been hundreds of years ago. I fought some of the fey clans for Corrick, and they are barbarians in battle."

Donovan dropped his sack of supplies and turned. "Look, I don't have a choice. The captain took me off the Guard, labeled me a merc, and said if I don't do this, he will have me arrested and put on trial as a traitor."

"Then why not just come with us?" Banner asked. "We'll take ya!"

"I can't," Donovan said, his eyes downcast. He shook his head and ran his fingers through his hair. "There's too much here that I love. I have to try."

Lysander took a heavy breath. "You are a damn fine man, Donovan of Nightingale. Should you ever find yourself in Corrick, come find me. We will give you shelter."

"Not sure if we will ever cross paths again, but if we do, I have your back," Godell added.

"Thank you," Donovan said. He turned to Banner. She looked like she wanted to say something. Instead, she slowly moved over to Donovan and hugged him tightly. He smiled and returned the hug. "Best of luck to you, young lady. Don't give up."

"Same to you." She released him, and what remained of the Thirteenth Division left Donovan's little shop.

Except for Rohawk.

"Where are you off to next?" Donovan asked as he picked up his sack of supplies.

"What do you mean? I'm going to Fallavon with you."

Donovan chuckled. "You can't be serious. You're a mercenary, Rohawk. You're the most mercenary of all of us. Going to Fallavon is a suicide mission. Dead men don't get paid. Whatever they offered you, they only did so because they know you won't come back to collect."

"There's a Seer in Boroshard's Folly, and we will be passing right through that town. I have some questions that need answering."

"You seem to be the kind of man who has more answers than questions."

Rohawk pulled away, feigning offense. "What do you mean by that, Donovan?"

"You're just...secretive. It's annoying. Besides, I would save your silvers. Those Seers are all trash. Nothing but charlatans."

"She's not like the other Seers. Not even close. Haven't you heard of Lady Renna?"

Donovan paused at that. "Now that you mention it, I have. But what makes her so special?"

"She's accurate, that's what. Some call her the king maker, though that's only happened twice."

"She predicted a couple kings rising to power? How many of her predictions has she whiffed?"

"None."

Donovan's irritation subsided a little. He was done with fortune tellers and their scams—but the ones he had seen had all been from or going through Nightingale. What if this lady was the real thing?

"How do we get an audience with her?" he asked.

"Now you're talking! But that's part of the problem. She sees whom she chooses. I've already been to the Folly several times and never been picked."

"Encouraging."

"But we need to go through there anyway to get to Fallavon, so it's worth another shot."

"That's the only reason you're coming? Are you going to turn back after we get there?" Rohawk crossed his arms.

"Believe it or not, I don't want to see Kaldaran win any more than you do. Plus, I heard the women in Fallavon—feylas they call them—are absolutely stunning!"

"Are you sure it's worth risking life and limb for some ogling?"

Rohawk's brow furrowed. "Donovan, this isn't just any ogling. The fey women are the most beautiful in the world. You need to learn to live a little."

Donovan shrugged. "Well, I can't argue. I would love some company."

"Certainly better than going it alone," Rohawk said, his voice taking on a hint of seriousness that spoke to something in his past.

"Good to have you on board. I have to take care of one more thing before we leave. Can I meet you at the City Gate in an hour?"

"North or South?"

"North, the South is the Highway Gate."

Rohawk nodded. "One hour. See you then."

Donovan waited to make sure Rohawk was gone, then went back to preparations in case the half-Kaldaran had picked up on his nervousness. The man was sneaky enough to spy on him, and what he had to do next, Donovan wanted as few people as possible to know. After a few minutes, he went upstairs.

The house was so quiet without Martha. He imagined her welcoming him as he reached the top, but she wasn't there. Ramon had cleaned up most of her blood, but a shadow of red still stained the floorboards. He carefully stepped around it as he entered her room. It was still a mess from the attack. No one had been through her things yet. He didn't want to do it; Ramon certainly didn't, either. At this rate, maybe no one would. Ramon and Tybalt were going to be fleeing the city soon. His friend had told him that when Donovan had told him he would be leaving. Merchants weren't soldiers, so it wasn't deserting for Ramon and Tybalt to run, but Donovan wondered how long before no one would be allowed to leave.

But there was one possession of hers Donovan had to take care of. He went over to the desk and unlatched the contraption that held the book. It dropped open with a thud, and there it was. The steel binding shone, and the gems glittered in the light coming through the window. Donovan took the book and hid it inside a satchel.

He had been advised to not take any unnecessary iron into Fallavon. It was offensive to the fey. Elementium was the exception; fey could touch it without harm. But there were still cultural taboos around iron, even enchanted iron.

Donovan sighed. He dreaded what he was about to do, but the book was not safe at the home. He wasn't going to risk Ramon's life over it, and he wasn't positive Tybalt could be trusted. So he decided to take a chance with the most religious person in Nightingale.

Snow flurried around him as he stepped outside and made his way to the Chapel of K'var. Despite the shame the captain had brought upon him by kicking him out of the Guard, the people of Nightingale seem to look on him with gratitude. Some even gave him the Nightingale salute as he walked by. He smiled a little. It reminded him why he had joined the Guard. For all her faults, Nightingale had some good people.

The cobblestone building that was the Chapel of K'var loomed over the other structures around it. There were no services today, but the priestess was there at all hours, ready to serve the people of Nightingale. Donovan pressed at one of the large, double wooden doors and went inside.

The high ceiling made the chapel seem vast. No other building in Nightingale was that tall, and they were always split into multiple levels. An arched window on the far end let in multi-colored light through its stained glass, an image of the warrior goddess K'var gently touching down on the world. In one hand she held a sword of fire, and in the other, a sword that commanded the wind and lightning. As the legend was told, those swords became sentient and turned on her, leading to the creation of the wind and fire spirits that the Kingdom of K'var was constantly at war with.

The priestess knelt at the altar, her long, brown hair down over the back of her green robe. She had a sword at her hip which was the custom of a K'var priestess during a service.

"My goddess," she said. There was no one else in the chapel, but she still spoke loud enough to be heard. "I will always be ready to fight. Ready to stand against the spirits of wind and fire. Ready to stand against wicked men. Ready to stand against even my own sisters, should they betray you. Grant me your blessing to stand strong in the day of war."

Donovan took a few steps forward and sat on a bench near the back.

"What is it you seek?" the priestess called out. Donovan did not know if she was asking her god or him. He waited until she stood up and turned around. "Yes, I am speaking to you." She paused, recognition lighting her face. "You are Martha's son, yes?"

"In a way," he answered.

"I am sorry for what happened. Martha died in battle, and so deserves the blessing of K'var. If it had to happen, that is how I wish to die someday."

"I like living," Donovan answered.

"It is nothing to K'var for a man to die in battle, unless you die in service to her kingdom. Then there is a small reward for you."

"A reward? After dying?"

The priestess raised her chin. "Do you doubt the existence of an afterlife?"

"I'm not sure how I'm supposed to know something I cannot see."

The priestess walked over and sat on the bench in front of Donovan. "Do you believe in justice? The concept of justice, I mean."

He thought about the question. "Everyone does. Whether or not their perception of justice is correct is another thing."

"But assuming your perception is correct, there are still those who do wrong or do not pay for it in their lifetime. Do you agree?"

Donovan thought about Toby. There was still time for him to pay. But what if that didn't happen? What if Toby lived to a nice old age, enjoying all the comforts of life in the meantime?

"Yes, it is possible," he said.

"Then there must be an afterlife to correct those injustices. The goddess influences our world but does not control it. When we die, then K'var will deal with us."

"How do you know it is K'var who will deal with us and not another god or goddess?"

The priestess smiled. "I will be honest, I do not know. That is a good question I am still seeking the answer for." Donovan raised his chin a little.

"I did not expect such honesty from a religious zealot."

"Zealot is a bit strong. I prefer priestess."

"Says the woman who gives sermons holding a sword."

She smiled. "You still haven't answered my question. What is it you seek?"

Donovan took in a deep breath. This was a big risk, and now was his last chance to back out. But he couldn't think of another way to keep Ramon and the book safe.

"I need you to safeguard something for me. I'm not sure if K'var would be happy with this or not, but you're the most religious person I know."

The priestess looked curious as Donovan pulled out the book from the satchel. Her eyes widened.

"A holy book!" she breathed out. "Not belonging to K'var. The gemstones are wrong, as is the engraving."

"It belongs to an old god, one who does not have a namesake amongst the kingdoms of Drannus. I want you to keep this book safe while I go to Fallavon. There are men out there who would kill for it."

"You know this because they killed Martha, is that right?"

Donovan's brows raised. "You put that together?"

"These books are worth killing for. What makes you think I would honor your request? I do not serve this god, and it would put my life at risk."

"I know. I know it is asking you a lot. But you just said you do not know if K'var will take you when you die. Wouldn't it be better to…diversify a little?"

The priestess tilted her head. "You have a funny way of viewing the gods, Donovan."

"Priestess, I am going on a mission to Fallavon that could very well cost me my life. And I have already put my life on the line multiple times for this place. I'm not saying you owe me, but…a lot of people around here have taken a turn either risking their lives or losing them."

"So you're saying I owe it to Nightingale."

Donovan thought about that for a moment. "Yes, I suppose I am."

The priestess examined the heavy metal binding for a moment. Her eyes were searching. They moved from the book to Donovan. "My name is Anna, and I accept your request." She reached out with her hands, and he placed the book in her grasp. She rose and took it to the front of the chapel, where sat a large wooden chest. She produced a key from her pocket and turned it in the gold-plated lock. With a click, the top popped open, and she placed the book inside.

"It is against the law for anyone to open this besides me. Punishable by death, if I ask for it. Your book is safe."

"Thank you…Anna."

Anna rose and nodded at Donovan. "Blessing of K'var upon you, Donovan of Nightingale. I hope that you return to us ready to fight another day."

Chapter Fourteen

"We made good time!" Rohawk said as he and Donovan rode into the town of Boroshard's Folly around sundown. It was their second day of travel, and the first night camping in the wild had been rough. Rohawk was a decent frontiersman, though—he had clearly spent some nights under the open sky.

"Good time?"

"I used to make this ride at least once a month, and I expected you to slow me down more than you did."

Donovan narrowed his eyes at Rohawk. "Whatever you say. Anything I should know about this place?"

"Watch out," Rohawk said. Donovan looked behind them and was slapped in the face by a low branch.

"Bag of bones, that hurt!"

Rohawk laughed. "You wouldn't know it in winter, but there's a reason they call this place Leatherleaf Forest. The leaves here are good material for clothes and many other things. It's one of the reasons the town has flourished. That and Lady Renna."

Donovan looked around at the town they were coming into. Many of the people walking around had cloaks made of thick leaves sewn together.

"I guess fur hunting isn't as popular around here."

"To answer your previous question, though," Rohawk added, "here's what you should know: the Folly has very few laws, but they are important. Don't kill anybody on someone else's property, Arcane Imperium Currency only, and whatever you do, don't mess with Lady Renna."

Donovan blinked. "The Folly?"

"It's what everyone around here calls it, so start calling it that and you won't look like a total outsider. Didn't Lionel ever bring you here?" Donovan shook his head.

"This is as far east as I've ever been."

"Huh," Rohawk said, but didn't add anything else.

"So...how do we get to see Lady Renna? What does she charge?"

"I don't think coins are a factor for her, but I could be wrong. She owns a lot of the land around here and makes income as a duchess."

"And you know this because you've become some kind of Lady Renna expert?"

"I much prefer expert to sycophant, so I will take that as a compliment. Look!" Rohawk pointed to a wooden sign that read, *The Trade Inn*. "That's my favorite hideaway. Let's stop for some food and drink while I try to figure out an audience with Lady Renna. They have a stable we can trust with our horses too."

Donovan sighed, but agreed. After sending their horses off with the stable boy and a coin for his trouble, they went inside.

The Trade Inn looked like it had either seen better days or never had them to begin with. The wooden floors were old and rotten in some places. Fresh vomit lay in a corner, and no one seemed to be bothered with it. There was a constant rattle of dice games being played, and shouting after a roll was counted.

"How is anyone supposed to sleep in a place like this?" Donovan asked, but Rohawk was already at the bar, talking to the barkeep.

Donovan sighed and took a seat. The chair felt like it was about to fall apart. He leaned on the table, but that was also unsteady. *I guess if it's survived all the drunks in here, it will survive me.*

Donovan's eyes turned to watch a grizzly looking man descending the stairs with a curvy, plump-breasted woman whose outfit revealed a generous amount of what the gods had given her.

"Where the gol has Rohawk taken me?" he asked himself.

"What'll ya have?"

Donovan turned; a barmaid was at his table waiting to take his order.

"I, uh…my friend is already at the bar making our arrangements."

The barmaid glared at him. "Look, I don't mean any disrespect, but if you're gonna take up a table and not pay for anything, my boss is going to come and kick you out. How about some mead?"

"I don't—"

"Great! I'll be right back with it." She was gone before Donovan could protest further. He looked back at the bar—Rohawk was gone. *Well, if I'm stuck here waiting for him, then I'm drinking something.*

The barmaid returned with a tankard and Donovan tossed her a few copper coins. She took them, then glared at him. "Right, Arcane Imperium only." Donovan fished through his satchel for the right marks and handed them to her. She still took the other coins her gave her. He sighed and took a drink of the most watered-down mead he had ever tasted.

"Traveling alone?" a kind, feminine voice sounded to his right. Donovan looked over his shoulder and saw a thin woman standing near him. She was dressed like the other girls there, but Donovan took more notice of how gaunt she looked.

"Might as well be," he said, a little bit annoyed.

"Well, I could give you some company, for a little while."

Donovan looked back at her. She was smiling, but it didn't touch her eyes.

"I'm not very expensive," she added.

He sighed. "Here," he said as he handed her a few silver coins. "Just take it. Do yourself a favor and sleep alone tonight."

She looked stunned. "Th-thank you," she stammered.

Donovan nodded and shooed her away with a gentle hand flick. One mead turned into three, and still no sign of Rohawk. He was tired of waiting. The whole place smelled rotten, and he had a small satchel of the best tobacco Nightingale had to offer. A parting gift from Lysander. He went outside, choosing the cold over the smell, and walked a dozen or so paces from the tavern.

It took him a minute to stuff the pipe properly, but when he had it filled, he lit a stick on a nearby torch and put the flame on the tobacco. A few quick puffs, and the flavor rolled over his tongue.

"A bit too loud for you in the tavern?" A woman's voice cut through the cold.

Donovan turned, prepared for another prostitute. This woman was maybe in her early twenties, hair as black as midnight, skin light brown and nearly flawless. She wore a thick cloak, but peeking out from underneath was a dress that clung to her curves and revealed a lot in the chest. She did not look quite like the others, though. Her eyes told the story of someone who was not owned by another like most of the prostitutes were.

"Something like that," Donovan answered.

"I understand," she said, and gave a subtle indication to Donovan's pipe.

He caught the gesture and offered it to her. She smiled and took it, enjoying a few draws before passing it back for Donovan's turn.

"Not a lot of women who smoke. Have you lived here your whole life?"

"Well, well, aren't you sharp," she said, her tone bored, sarcastic.

Donovan chuckled at himself. "Alright, you just want to smoke," he said as he held out the pipe to her. "I already offered once, so I suppose I'll continue being polite."

She shrugged. "Not many around here wearing as many furs as you. You seemed interesting—I guess I was wrong."

Donovan narrowed his eyes. "Too bad. I thought the same thing about you."

To his surprise, she smiled a little. "You think the way to a woman's heart is through insults?" she asked, feigning offense.

"Not interested in your heart," Donovan said after a draw. When she raised a brow, he added, "Nor any other part of you, to be honest." That wasn't completely true, but he meant it. The locket from Alexis was hanging beneath his undershirt. "I am wondering why you're talking to me, though. You have a reason you haven't made clear."

"Oh?" she asked. "And what would that be? If you can tell me, I will reward you handsomely."

Donovan thought for a moment. "This is some kind of game. What are you trying to pull?"

She didn't respond. Donovan thought a bit longer. He doubted she had any kind of handsome reward to offer, but it was fun. At least it gave him something to do while he waited for Rohawk.

"Well?" she asked, that one eyebrow raised again.

"Donovan!" Rohawk's voice sounded from the door of the inn. "I've made accommodations. Bring your whore and come get some sleep. We've gotta get up early tomorrow."

"Can you wait a minute?" Donovan called back to Rohawk.

"I can wait if you give me a few silvers," he said after he took a few steps closer. "I need it to cover everything. I spent half of my silvers trying to figure out how to get a meeting with Lady Renna. I thought most of the people were con men, but...it was a chance I was willing to take."

"We've been here a couple hours and you've spent half of your silvers?"

"We'll have all the accommodations we need when we get to Fallavon, so we can spend what we need to now." Rohawk turned to the woman and grinned. She looked away, uninterested.

Lady Renna, Donovan thought. He looked back at the woman and caught a glitter around her neck. *A diamond...if there was any person who could afford it—and wear it without anyone messing with her...*

"I know who you are," he said.

"Time's up, you lose!" she fired back, gently tossing the pipe back to Donovan. "But good effort, you were closer than most," she added as her goodbye.

"Wait!" Donovan called out, but she was faster on her feet than he expected and was gone in seconds. "Teching damn!" he muttered.

Rohawk's brows shot up. "I didn't think you were one for that kind of language. I should have given you a few drinks when we first met."

"That was her, that was Lady Renna!" Donovan said.

"That wasn't Lady Renna," Rohawk said as he rolled his eyes. "She's a bit older than that."

"Well, whatever. It just would have been fun to beat that woman at her little game."

Rohawk laughed. "You can't beat anyone at their own game around here. Everyone cheats. Come on now, the keeper is probably getting antsy to sell the rooms I told him to hold. Let's get him paid and get some sleep."

The mead seemed to have been enough for Donovan to fall asleep without too much trouble. Waking up, however, was a different story. He opened his eyes sometime in the wee hours of the morning and saw three shapes silhouetted in the dim light in his room. He reached for his arming sword, but the shape in the middle held it up.

"Looking for this? You won't need it." Donovan recognized the voice as the woman outside the inn.

"This is why you were talking to me?" he asked. "I was your mark?"

"Yes, but not in the way you think," she said as she walked over and held out her hand. "Lady Renna will see you now."

"You *are* Lady Renna," Donovan said, a bit smug. Rohawk was in the next room, and Donovan was already thinking of bragging about it when morning came.

The woman chuckled. "She is not here. I am her daughter. These two are my bodyguards, and will be yours as well for the next hour. Lady Renna wishes to see you, and I intend to take you there."

Donovan considered it. This could still be a ruse; she could be luring him outside to rob him. But that didn't make sense because she had him pretty good now, and all his belongings were in the room already.

He was about to say yes, but remembered Rohawk. The man had chosen to go with him when everyone else scattered, and this was one of the major reasons he came. It wasn't right to leave him behind.

"I'm sorry, but Rohawk, my traveling companion, needs to see Lady Renna."

"The invitation is for you only," the woman said coldly.

Donovan opened his mouth but paused. The way Rohawk talked about Lady Renna made it sound like when she wanted to see someone, she saw them. Had anyone ever turned down her summons? Would she allow being rejected? Something in Donovan's gut told him that the lady was very controlling and wouldn't take no for an answer."

"Then I suppose you will have to tell her that you failed to get me to come."

The woman crossed her arms. "These two men next to me could just drag you there."

One of them smiled and cracked his knuckles.

Donovan nodded, buying himself a few seconds. She called his bluff. He stifled his nervousness and continued. "Sure, but…isn't that just so much more inconvenient? I'm heavy and tend to catch easily on small rocks."

The woman's lips tightened at first, then loosened into a smile. "You're more fun than I thought. Fine. Go get your friend, but be quick about it. And I can't promise him that Lady Renna will give him a reading."

"Miss Nyla, are you sure?" one of the bodyguards asked.

"I will explain it to Mother."

Donovan smiled, then nodded and jumped out of bed.

One room over, he knocked softly at the door. When there was no answer, he entered the room.

"Rohawk, come with—" Donovan stopped himself when he saw Rohawk in bed with the woman he had given the silver coins to earlier. He sighed and shook his head, then walked over and kicked Rohawk in the leg.

In the blink of an eye, a naked Rohawk was out of bed and had Donovan pinned against the wall.

"Donovan!" he said in a voice just above a whisper. "What in Abaddon's Den are you doing? You shouldn't wake me like that. One more tenth of a breath and your blood would have been on the floor. What do you want?"

"The Lady wishes to see us," Donovan grunted. "And speaking of breath…you seriously need to cut back on the stinky mead."

Rohawk released his hold on Donovan's neck and nodded without missing a beat. He started to pick up his clothes and put them on. "Yours is no better, just so you know. But more importantly, how did you manage this?"

"That woman I was talking to earlier is her daughter. She's outside with a couple of thugs, ready to take us to Lady Renna."

"Bones! You're more clever than I thought." Rohawk put on his undershirt. The girl stirred but did not wake.

"Can you hurry up? This whole situation makes me dreadfully uncomfortable. Why are you putting your pants on last?"

"Not true—the cloak is last," Rohawk said as he finished with the pants and tossed his cloak over his shoulder. The steel of his anelaces caught the moonlight for a split second before disappearing underneath somewhere. "Alright, let's go."

Lady Renna's estate was on the northern edge of town, and it was heavily guarded. Donovan counted five sentries on horseback and a dozen more foot soldiers keeping a tight perimeter around the house. The manor itself was more like a fortress. It was made of carved stone stacked and mortared, well maintained, and even had a short, cobblestone wall around the perimeter. Moss covered the short wall but it looked sturdy. Donovan now understood Rohawk's comment about Lady Renna being a duchess of sorts.

He thought about what he was going to ask the Lady. He could ask her the same thing he had asked every other fortune teller. He wanted to know who he was in his past. But the fate of Nightingale was resting on his shoulders now.

He was undecided. *Will she answer more than one question if we pay her?* Donovan had been wondering if he was going to have to pay at some point—Nyla didn't say, but the money to build something that could withstand an attack from a band of soldiers was not commoner money.

Donovan blew out a low whistle, and said, "Rule three: don't mess with Lady Renna. Is all this necessary?"

"It is after King Ferdinand tried to force his way in to see the Lady," Nyla answered. "She was kind enough to spare him his life, but we have fortified ourselves more after that."

"King of Dadock—he's a total idiot," Rohawk mumbled to Donovan.

"I know!" Donovan quietly snapped back. "I'm not ignorant of kingdom politics."

Rohawk just grinned.

When they had gone past the gate and across the courtyard, the front door of the manor opened for them.

A voice sounded from inside, "Come in!"

Rohawk took a step and was immediately stopped by the guards. "I'm getting mixed messages here," he said with a tight grin.

"Search 'em," one guard bellowed out in a gruff voice.

The guards patted Donovan down, but found nothing. They had already taken his arming sword.

They looked up at Nyla, who gave them a slight nod of approval. Then they turned to Rohawk next and removed his cloak.

For the next few minutes, the guards searched Rohawk up and down, finding more knives and pulling them out. One of the guards was shaking the cloak vigorously, and every few seconds another knife would fall out. When five knives were on the ground, they all turned and eyed him suspiciously. They patted him down one more time.

Donovan knew Rohawk's anelaces must still be on his person somewhere. A guard started patting near his inner thighs.

"Are we done?" Rohawk asked, annoyed. He reached out for his cloak and the guard pulled it back.

"Relax," Nyla said as she put a gentle hand on Rohawk's shoulder. "You will get it all back when the reading is finished."

Rohawk did not look satisfied, but shrugged and said, "Your house, your rules. When you come to my house, you will follow my rules."

"Does one of those rules involve removing all clothing?"

Rohawk looked a little shocked. "Bones, you got your mother's gift, woman!"

Nyla did not reply to that. She led them farther inside, down a long hallway lined with large paintings on both sides. More than one depicted a king or queen, and a few others showed generals leading armies into battle. One had a humble looking middle-aged man who was overseeing construction of a wall.

"Lysander?" Donovan said to himself.

"These are the greatest people my mother has given readings to," Nyla explained.

"Should I plan to stay late to model?" Rohawk asked.

"I wouldn't," Nyla fired back.

Rohawk chuckled.

At the end of the hall, Nyla opened the door and waved Rohawk and Donovan in. The room was a bit small, with dark red curtains hung to cover the walls. In the center was a round wooden table, three chairs, and a middle-aged woman's face lit up by the small candelabra in the center of the table. Dark curls spilled down from underneath a red headscarf.

The woman sat in one of the chairs, the empty two were opposite her.

"Two chairs, mother? How did you know?" Nyla asked.

Lady Renna smiled. "You know why. I have been expecting both of you." She looked at her daughter. "Thank you, Nyla, you may go."

Nyla bowed and closed the door behind her. It was now just Rohawk, Donovan, and the Lady.

"Please, sit," she said as she motioned to the empty seats. Like Nyla, she had light brown skin, and must have borne her daughter while still in her youth. She did not look older than forty. "You insisted your friend come or you wouldn't, Donovan. Why?"

Did someone go tell her everything while we were being searched? Donovan wondered. *It would explain her knowledge just as well as mystical powers.*

"I mean no disrespect," he started, "but I thought *we* were supposed to ask *you* questions."

Rohawk shot a burning glare at Donovan, but Lady Renna chuckled and said, "In due time. For now, please, indulge me."

"I owed him one," Donovan answered. "Maybe more than one. And I'm not sure you can help me."

"But you do not know what I am going to say, so how could you know that?"

Donovan leaned back. "I've met a good number of fakes. But Rohawk told me your words are true. It seems you have given me a chance; I will give you a chance."

Lady Renna nodded slowly. "It is good to be open to knowledge; it comes from unexpected places at times." She looked over to Rohawk. "Well, well, well, Shadow Walker. What is so important that you had to see me?"

The turn in Rohawk's face nearly made Donovan gasp. He hadn't seen such seriousness since...since Rohawk killed Wyndell.

"Lady Renna," Rohawk addressed her as if she was a queen, "Will I retake my kingdom?"

"It was never yours in the first place, Shadow Walker. Do you think a shadow can reign as king? Will the shadows of *Harm Ta* agree with you when you next meet with them?"

"Um, what?" Donovan asked.

Rohawk leaned forward, ignoring him, and said, "I only work in shadows when evil men are allowed to do wickedness in broad daylight." The air in the room turned cold. "That kingdom is mine, regardless of who has possession of it right now. Again, I ask, will I retake my kingdom?"

"You failed to retake your kingdom because you are a shadow, and a shadow cannot exist without something to block the light. That something is your cousin. No, you will not retake your kingdom. Not with the shadow in your soul."

Rohawk looked as if somebody had punched him in the gut. Hard.

"What the gol is she talking about?" Donovan blurted out. Rohawk just stared into nothing.

"Now you," Lady Renna said, looking Donovan straight in the eyes. "What do you wish to ask me? Keep this in mind: you are the envy of many kings right now. I recommend you make your question a good one."

"Nightingale seeks an alliance with Fallavon. How can I make that happen?"

Lady Renna smiled. "I'm afraid my gift doesn't work that way. I cannot tell you what to do, only what your future holds. What you do with this knowledge is up to you."

Donovan nodded slowly. It's not the question he really wanted to ask, but he had been disappointed time and time again. He was losing his nerve, and he had a duty to Nightingale. That was more important.

"Will I succeed in making an alliance with Fallavon and Nightingale?"

Lady Renna closed her eyes for a few seconds, took in a deep breath, then exhaled as she slowly opened them. "You will see success in Fallavon, but that is not what you should concern yourself with. A great, dark shadow follows you." Her brow suddenly furrowed. "A powerful entity."

"A dark shadow? Does this have anything to do with Rohawk?" Donovan asked.

"No, not him. Another. Someone much more powerful. A single eye that burns with intense hatred. A serpent's eye."

Kaldar? Donovan thought. He swallowed hard.

"The eye is what you should be concerned with. That is all I am seeing."

Donovan nodded. "Alright. This was fun."

Lady Renna smiled and reached out her hand to take Donovan's. He suddenly noticed how beautiful she was. A bit older than he was, but time had served her well. There was something dangerous in her eyes.

"Surely that is not the only thing you want to ask me?"

Donovan glanced over at Rohawk, but he was still staring off into nothing. He looked back at Lady Renna, who was grinning wide at him. There were a few women back in Nightingale who had flirted with him, but nothing so forward as this. He had to say something.

"I'm not interested."

"But I can tell you everything you need to know. Do you have any idea who you are saying no to?"

"You can't tell me what I want to know. No one can."

She raised her chin slightly. "What do you mean?"

"I am soulburned." Donovan thought she would pull away from him at that comment, but she seemed even more intrigued. "I want to know who I was in the past."

"I've never had a soulburned here before. Let me see..." Lady Renna closed her eyes and started swaying back and forth, gently. The smile returned to her face. "I see now. You are surrounded by fire, but it does not burn you. Great winds are stirring up the fire, causing it to grow, to jump, to burn brightly. The flames are in your mind, but they are healing. You...you will remember who you are."

Donovan felt a thrill in his chest. "When?" he asked, leaning forward.

Lady Renna kept swaying. "The gods are being particularly playful with that part of the question. But I know how to speak to them." She swayed back and forth with more intensity now, like she was moving to unheard music.

Suddenly, she stopped cold, her eyes opening wide. "When you remember," she started, "You will strike them with the fury of the heavens...everyone...will die...Everyone will die." She repeated the words over and over with increasing speed. Her gentle grasp on Donovan's hand suddenly turned to a bear grip. "Everyone will die, everyone will die, everyone will die!" Then she shrieked and said, "*You* must die! Guards, kill him! Kill both of them!"

Chapter Fifteen

"What?" Donovan ripped his hand out and jerked back from Lady Renna's enraged gaze.

"Guards!" she called out again.

Rohawk suddenly came to. He pulled Donovan up with him, running for the door. The room must have had thick walls, because the guards outside looked confused—they had not heard the Lady's orders. Rohawk and Donovan shoved past, the Lady's orders following them out.

In that moment of confusion, Donovan and Rohawk made it to the front door. A burly guard stood in the way, but before he could draw his sword, Rohawk smacked him across the face with the butt of an anelace. He grabbed his cloak hanging on a nearby wall, then flung the door open and ran through.

A horse with a cart still in tow was stationed outside, the cart being unloaded of its various late-harvest vegetables shipped from a warmer region in the south. It was just before sunrise, and this was the morning delivery.

Rohawk ran for the saddle, while pointing for Donovan to get in the cart. Donovan obeyed, not realizing until after he landed that it might have been easier to just hop on the back for the horse. Rohawk dug his heels into the horse's flanks and pushed for a full charge down the hill, toward the inn on the other side of the Folly.

Lady Renna's voice rang out into the air calling for the closing of the gate. In response, an arrow struck the cart Donovan was in, barely missing him. They made it out the gate before it could be closed, though the arrows continued from behind the half-walls. Donovan took a pumpkin and tried to shield himself. An arrow appeared in it with a *thunk!*

The two of them had gotten outside the range of the archers when Rohawk yelled back, "I hope you're ready to leave, because we're grabbing our horses and getting the gol out of here!"

"I don't have my weapons or my gear!" Donovan shouted back. "I just got that new arming sword."

"I still have a few weapons and we'll get you something in Fallavon. We broke rules number one and three, and as soon as anyone in town hears about it, we're dead!"

"Speaking of dead," Donovan shouted and pointed at one of the horseman patrols charging toward them. The guard had a couched lance and was aiming for Rohawk.

"Bones, bones, bones!" Rohawk mumbled as he reached around for his hidden daggers. They were all in his cloak, which had been emptied. "Damn it, I need something I can throw, I don't have any of my balanced knives!"

Donovan grabbed a squash, and, steadying himself with one hand, he chucked it as hard as he could with the other toward the oncoming rider. It landed way too short, but a knife appeared, stabbed into the man's lance arm. The lance fell toward the ground, and the rider grabbed tightly to the reins to stay on the horse. The motion caused the horse to stop abruptly, sending the rider flying off.

"Never mind, they missed one," Rohawk shouted back. "Probably my last, though." He drove the horse and cart onward at the same pace, much to the dismay of Donovan, who bounced around like the vegetables he had taken residence with.

Donovan forgot how much time it had taken them to walk to Lady Renna's. The ride back to the inn felt agonizingly long. No doubt more mounted guards were headed their way, and Rohawk knew it. The two arrived at the stables right as a sleepy-eyed stable boy was beginning his shift.

"Here, lad!" Rohawk shouted out in a jovial greeting. "Groom the fine boy here and park that cart somewhere. The vegetables are yours!"

"This horse is a mare," he said, still wiping the sleep from his eyes.

"Groom the fine *girl*, then!" he said in the same tone as he flipped a silver coin to the boy. "For your trouble!" he added as he dismounted. He and Donovan then ran into the stables, grabbed their respective saddles, and geared up their horses. It took only a few minutes, but Donovan was sweating—hard. Each minute was one less in the precious little time they had before Lady Renna's men would arrive.

They rode out of the stables at full speed, clipping past two of Lady Renna's guards who were not prepared for them to come flying out quite like that. The guards turned their horses and chased them out of the city, but after a short pursuit, they gave up. Their horses were not quite as rested, and they had no hope of catching Donovan and Rohawk without fresh steeds.

"Phew!" Rohawk said to Donovan as he slowed Mongoose down to a more reasonable speed. Donovan slowed down his steed, Hansel, as well.

"Teching bones, Donovan, Lady Renna saw something about you she did *not* like."

"I can't say what that would be, honestly can't," he replied. "It didn't sound good, though. It was like she was seeing the beginning of the end of the world."

"Her premonitions are very accurate," Rohawk said, "but they don't always manifest in the way that she and her audience think."

"'Everyone will die'?" Donovan repeated her words. "I have a hard time interpreting that any other way than the obvious meaning."

"Sometimes cataclysmic events in visions just mean that the world is changing in significant ways," Rohawk explained. "I once read a book written in an old Velmarian language, and it spoke of a prophet who had predicted the world coming to its end in a massive cold snap. The result was supposed to be four hundred years of winter. It never happened, but around the time it was supposed to come to pass, the Crowned were pushed out of their places as rulers, and most human kingdoms were ruled by men and women who had no connection to the gods."

"How do you know all this?"

"I told you, I've been trying to get an audience with Lady Renna for years. I've been studying not only her visions, but also the nature of visions in general for quite some time."

There was a pause as Donovan considered Rohawk's knowledge.

"There's just one problem with your interpretation, Rohawk."

"What's that?"

"Wouldn't Lady Renna have known all of this? That her visions are not always what they seem?"

"Of course," Rohawk said with a nod.

"Then why did she go insane on me?"

Rohawk considered this for a moment. "I see what you mean, but I need a little time to think about what Lady Renna said. I wouldn't worry too much about it. Perhaps her visions have made her insane. For now, check our backs every few minutes to make certain we aren't being followed."

"You're telling me not to worry, but you seemed pretty worried about what she had to say. What was all that about, anyway? All that talk of light and shadow and retaking your kingdom?"

"I...I'm still not sure," he answered.

"But what did you mean when you asked if you would retake your kingdom? What kingdom?"

"Donovan!" Rohawk snapped. "Teching gol! Not another word about her vision for me! I need some time to think on it."

Donovan watched Rohawk carefully for a moment. It looked like he might be starting to cry, and when he saw Donovan staring, he looked away.

"I told you to watch our backs," he growled.

"Right. My mistake."

Donovan held a steady gaze upward as they topped what was probably the last large hill before reaching the Fey Wilds. A wind strong enough to lift a twirl of the heavy, dense leaves blew across the road. The closer they came to the Fey Wilds, the more the snow and cold faded away.

Donovan hadn't said much to Rohawk since Boroshard's Folly. They talked a little sitting around the campfire the night before, but not about anything important.

Donovan inhaled the aroma of damp leaves. "I wonder how Banner's doing. Did you see that painting at Lady Renna's?"

Rohawk shot him a glare.

"I'm not bringing up her vision again; just wondering if you saw the painting outside."

"Of course I did. Not many things surprise me anymore, but that one. That old man was and is full of surprises."

The awkward silence resumed. Donovan thought for a moment, then said, "It's not like I don't have a lot to think about, either."

Rohawk looked over at him, his expression softening a bit.

"I've wanted nothing more than to remember my past. And the very moment I receive this promise that I will remember, it also comes with this looming curse. Are Lady Renna's visions set in stone?"

Rohawk took in a long breath, then answered. "I don't know for sure. I know that people who have tried to avoid her predictions end up falling into them in some unfortunate way. Years ago, King Banard of Corrick received a prediction that he was to soon die at the hands of an assassin. He immediately fled to his fortress in the Corrick Mountains. And you know what happened? Near the top of the mountain, on one of the narrow roads, his horse got spooked and bucked him, sending him tumbling down to his death far below."

"So, he didn't die by an assassin?"

Rohawk laughed. "The horse!"

Donovan narrowed his eyes. "That seems like a stretch. It sounds to me like her vision didn't come true entirely."

"That's how her visions work. They aren't always what you expect, but they do seem to work themselves out." Rohawk sighed. "I suppose we both have things to dread from her words. I had a sinking suspicion that no good could come out of hearing her predictions."

"Then why did you want to go?"

Rohawk looked away.

"Well, if the gods are anything like I think they are, they aren't above playing petty games. Maybe they give Lady Renna some insight, but it probably has strings attached. I say forget her and the whole lot of them. We will choose our fate."

Rohawk chuckled. "I like your attitude, Donovan."

At the top of the hill, the first goldenleaf tree stood out like a woman in a red corset at the Thirsty Horse. It was smaller than the maples surrounding it, but its spade-shaped, golden-colored leaves glittered in the sunlight. Its trunk was a healthy-looking light brown with thin, papery bark.

"Remarkable," Donovan commented. "I had heard they were quite the thing to look at, but did not expect this."

As they prodded their horses down the dirt road, the goldenleaf trees became more numerous. Donovan felt the temperature gradually shift, until both he and Rohawk were removing their cloaks and furs one by one.

"Where is this warmth coming from?" Donovan asked.

"The trees."

Donovan noticed more wonders—flowers of violet, blue, pink, and red grew all over as wild as weeds grow in unattended fields. Various types of vines—normally an invasive nuisance—grew in like colors and looked like flawless paintings on the canvases of goldenleaf bark. Then there was the smell, the sweet scent that was simply wonderful. It was like strawberries and peaches and apples all blending perfectly. It seemed as if the plants and the wind had agreed to work together and sew up a quilt of good scents and blanket the Fey Wilds with it.

Donovan closed his eyes and inhaled a deep breath. "This is winter?"

"Donovan, pay attention," Rohawk chided. "We have company."

He opened his eyes and saw, by quick count, about eight to ten fey partially hidden in the trees, now coming out into the open of the road. They looked much like the others he had seen in Nightingale now and then. This was the most he had seen at once, and in a group, their deep, mysterious, gray eyes were intimidating. Their skin varied in the colors of the rainbow—and in different shades.

Their hair color also ranged in the same way. The shade humans called red didn't even come close to the actual red hair that one of the fey bowmen had. Their ears were pointed, but did not stick out very far, not as far as Donovan remembered. Perhaps that varied too. Each fey in this group was at least a head taller than Rohawk, and probably a little bit taller than Donovan.

All of them wore black tabards fringed with gold and bearing a gold, roaring lion on its hind legs in the middle. Their armor was black leather that matched their tunics.

About half of them had two swords drawn, some with short swords while others held long blades steadily in each hand. The blades looked odd, and when they came closer, Donovan saw that they were carved out of wood. He remembered that pure-blooded fey were allergic to iron, and even some half-breeds couldn't touch it. It wasn't instant death, but it would leave a burn. The fey who did not have swords drawn had bows with arrows notched at the ready.

One of the bowmen, a red-skinned fey with light blue hair, was the first to speak; it sounded like the native fey tongue.

"Do you know any of their language?" Donovan asked. "Feyspeak it's called, right?"

"A little." Rohawk cringed, then said something in the fey language. The fey soldiers looked confused.

"What did you say?" Donovan asked.

"Either, 'we mean no harm,' or 'we need to poop.'"

"Judging from the looks on their faces, I'm betting on the latter," Donovan said as he reached in his pouch for the letter of introduction Alexis had given him. The fey looked on guard until they saw the scroll come out of the pouch.

The first fey who had spoken took the letter, then crumpled it up and carelessly stuffed it in one of his side pouches. Then he seemed to speak what was an order in his language. After he did, the four male fey of the group—*feynars,* if Donovan remembered correctly, while the females were called *feylas*—sheathed their swords and ran up quickly to seize Donovan and Rohawk. They searched Donovan for weapons but found nothing sharp. He had left everything in the Folly.

"Why are we always being searched?" Rohawk asked.

One of the *feynars* looked surprised when they found the anelaces up his sleeves. They started to rip at Rohawk's clothes and he jerked away.

"Don't be hasty!" he protested. "I can remove these myself." The fey took a step back as Rohawk fiddled with the cuffs of his tunic, removed the two anelaces hidden underneath, and threw them to the ground. The fey soldiers picked up the blades quickly and put them with the rest of the weapons. Donovan glared at Rohawk.

"This is why we are always being searched."

Rohawk shrugged.

The red-skinned bowfey, who was clearly the leader, put his bow away and pulled out one of his two swords. He waved with his hand for Rohawk and Donovan to move, and the fey formed a barrier around the two humans and marched them deeper into the Fey Wilds on foot, their horses being led with them.

Another one of the fey, a green-skinned one, walked at pace with the red-skinned commander in the back. Donovan and Rohawk could hear them talking to each other; Rohawk leaned over to Donovan and whispered, "They're talking about us, if that much wasn't obvious."

"No kidding," Donovan said dryly. "Any idea where they are taking us?"

"Where are you taking us?" Rohawk asked loudly.

Donovan shook his head and said, "The gods really don't like me, do they?"

"If this is how you treat all guests in your kingdom," Rohawk went on, "I guess I should be thankful I'm not an intruder." He chuckled at his own sarcasm. The fey shot him a few glares, but nothing more. It was hard to tell if they understood the common language or not. "You know, this is a violation of Nightingale law—K'var will be knocking on your doorstep for an answer."

"You should keep your mouth shut, human," the red-skinned fey barked from behind. His accent was there, but not thick—he knew the common tongue well. "We are of a higher honor than your blood, and you will get your chance to speak. But for now, remain silent!"

Rohawk looked over at Donovan and whispered, "My fault, I had no idea they were 'of a higher honor.'" He rolled his eyes.

Donovan looked over at the one who had yelled at them, and he looked furious. "I think they can hear you."

"Good."

The group walked for quite a while without much talking, except a little amongst the fey. Occasionally, one of them would talk in an excited or a dry tone, and the rest of them would laugh uproariously. Their smiles usually faded when they seemed to remember Rohawk and Donovan.

Donovan kept noticing something strange in the distance in between the trees from time to time, but he could not make out what it was until the group reached a small clearing. It was thick hedge that looked made up of hundreds of small trees that grew with twisted branches.

"It's...a wall?" Donovan said aloud before he realized he had. He had never heard of fey cities with walls.

The leader of the fey walked to the front and motioned for them to keep moving. All of them walked up to the wall and the leader muttered something in feyspeak. When he did, the branches shrunk until there were large openings between small plants. The group walked through and into the fey city, which was now completely visible. Donovan gaped at the sight.

The beauty of the inside of the city made the outside seem simply pleasant. The buildings were made of much larger golden trees that twisted through the air and were hollowed out to form what looked like houses. All kinds of flowers and large mushrooms like those outside grew in even greater abundance inside. Purple, blue, yellow, red, green, orange—every inch of the city was filled with every kind of color. It was quite the contrast from Nightingale, where most things were functional, and aesthetics had to come after quality and price—which usually meant not at all.

The fey people also seemed to be lovers of sculptures—there were many shaped out of the trees. One large sculpture depicted a male lion mid-strike, about to kill a prone human man. That did not make Donovan feel at all more comfortable about his current situation.

It was the afternoon hour, and the fey people were going about their daily routines. Donovan and Rohawk received all kinds of different looks from those passing by. Some glared at them as if they were worms, others looked frightened, others confused, while some seemed to be excited by the visitors.

The common outfits for the men were loose-fitting tunics of various colors, all with deep V-necks at the top. Their breeches were baggy and varied in color, though some wore more plain clothes that seemed better suited for manual labor. The women wore colorful silk dresses of many colors and various patterns. Donovan once read a book that had described them as "hauntingly beautiful" and that wasn't too far off. He had always taken a liking to feyla, but they rarely came through Nightingale and never without a feynar on their arms.

"Beautiful!" Donovan said, a bit breathless by all of it.

"You might not be seeing much of it, human," said the presumed leader of the pack.

Further into the city, the aesthetics transformed into more basic housing and the number of onlookers increased. Some shouted questions in their native tongue and received harsh responses from the guards.

"I think we're causing quite the stir," Rohawk whispered to Donovan.

"They don't seem to like us," Donovan whispered back.

"Don't be so glum. This could get very interesting. I'm already entertained." The fey guards kept on marching until they all came to a grouping of buildings that seemed to be carved out of a single large tree. On the first step inside, Donovan noted that, though hollow, there were no tool marks on the walls. He also noticed that it looked like a prison.

There was no clerk there, just a few prison guards dressed the same as those who had escorted them. They studied Donovan and Rohawk with those placid gray eyes.

"Well, this prison already seems much better than most human dungeons," Rohawk said.

"How?" Donovan asked.

"It doesn't smell like rot or blood. It smells like trees. And look: windows!" The windows Rohawk talked about were only small round holes, far too small for anyone to squeeze through, but they did allow him to see the light of day.

One of the prison guards saluted and greeted the others. One of the fey escorts said something in response, his tone implying that he'd said it thousands of times. They exchanged words for a moment before the prison guards stepped aside and allowed the soldiers access to the prison cells.

The cells had wooden bars, but they looked thick and sturdy. The guards shoved Donovan and Rohawk into the first cell. Suddenly, one of them began to yell at the other and point to a fey prisoner who was already in the cell. They argued for a moment, then finally dragged Rohawk back out and down the hallway.

"Why did they do that?" Donovan wondered aloud.

"It is against the rules," said the fey prisoner.

Donovan turned his head quickly, surprised that the feynar knew common. His light blue skin shone pale in the reflection of the sun, and his long, ruffled, orange hair looked as if it hadn't been washed for a week or so. He had a yellow *sarta* across his bare chest, a birth mark that all fey had in different colors. Donovan had always heard it called a "a tattoo of a ribbon" and that was a close description. This one ran from one shoulder down toward they feynar's heart, then curved around his back. It looked like a large crack in a rock, but smoother on the edges.

The feynar's face was sturdy, though a little thin from hunger. He had the same gray eyes all the other fey had. They were a little unnerving, staring at Donovan the way they did. He appeared to be tall, but that was hard to determine with him sitting down.

"What is?" Donovan asked.

"To have three prisoners in a cell—it's against the rules around here—at least the ones King Beldon established a year ago. Whether or not those rules are enforced seems to change from day to day. Today they are, I suppose." When the feynar said the name King Beldon, he said it in such a way that gave Donovan the impression that the King was not a good one. "What is your name, human? Why are you here?"

Donovan hesitated to answer. The bitterness in the feynar's voice was deterring, but he knew very little of where he was and what his fate would be. Perhaps the feynar would be willing to trade questions and answers, and at the very least, they were fellow prisoners, which meant there was some kind of bond.

"Donovan," he answered. "I am on a mission from Nightingale to try and secure allies. Kaldaran is attacking in force, and we need help."

"Ah, so you are no friend of the Kaldarans. That is good. Very good. But I am not sure how much help you will find here, human—I mean, Donovan. My name is Glyn. It is some kind of honor to meet you, I am sure."

Donovan held out his hand for a handshake, but Glyn only stared at it. "What?"

"Human gesture," was all Donovan said as he lowered his hand. "So, where am I exactly?"

"You do not know?" Glyn asked as if Donovan was an idiot. "Well, I suppose you *are* a human. You are in Fallavon, the city of the Great Lion— that means it is the capital of the Lion Clan and the city where the King resides."

"I knew that," Donovan explained, trying not to sound annoyed. "What I meant to ask is, why am I here in prison? Is this how your kind treats all diplomats?" Glyn sighed.

"Diplomats, you say? You have come at a bad time. Are things in Nightingale also bad?" He laughed.

Donovan shifted his eyes a little. "Do you think this is funny?"

"I should not, I suppose," Glyn said with a thoughtful, crooked frown. "Kaldaran soldiers are everywhere now, and I am in here when I could be doing something about it. Excellent use of a soldier, putting him in prison. Two of us, I suppose. You look like you've seen some battle."

"What do you mean Kaldaran soldiers are everywhere?"

"You said they were attacking Nightingale. They've been raiding the edges of the Fey Wilds too. Why Fallavon has not declared war on them is beyond me. King Beldon is too afraid of the Gledalai, I suppose, after what happened last time."

"What happened last time?"

"Stick around and you will find out," Glyn said as he crossed his arms.

Donovan shrugged, and asked, "Do you know where they are going to take my traveling companion?"

Glyn narrowed his eyes and looked at the small round window for a moment. When he spoke, it seemed like he had not heard Donovan's question. "Under rare circumstances, you might be welcome here. Under normal circumstances, they would send you away and warn you not to return. But under these direst circumstances which you have fallen into..." Glyn's eyes turned to the hallway.

A few guards passed by. They each shot Donovan a glance as they walked, but did not say a word.

When they had gone, Glyn continued, "The Grand Magistrate is in rule while King Beldon is away. He is the one responsible for putting me in here—unjustly, I might add. He thinks humans are weak, but worse for you, he thinks all humans are enemies of the fey. Many in Fallavon agree.

"You're not one of them, I imagine," Donovan said with relief, but Glyn gave him a hard stare. His eyes were half glazed over. He was remembering something. Donovan did not want to know what it was. "Am I a dead man?" he asked.

"It is politically advantageous for him to kill you," Glyn replied with cold speculation. "Allow me to make this clear for you, Donovan: Fallavon is on the brink of civil war. The Grand Magistrate wants King Beldon's crown. It is not what you would call public knowledge, but many in the Great Tree—that is, the King's palace—have caught on by now. Surprisingly, the King has not found some way to have the Grand Magistrate executed, though he would have to be crafty to make it happen by law. And King Beldon certainly seems to enjoy doing things by the law, as stupid as it may be."

Glyn stood up to get a better look out of the window. "Unless one of them, King Beldon or Grand Magistrate Vinson, dies soon, the city will likely be thrust into civil war. If the Grand Magistrate lets you live, it will show weakness on his part."

"How?"

"Many fey think the king is being weak by avoiding war with Kaldaran. If the Grand Magistrate lets you leave alive, it might look like he is also avoiding the same thing. Granted, I am smart enough to know the difference between a Kaldaran and another human, but many in Fallavon might not see it that way."

"I have nothing to do with all this!" Donovan snapped, as if Glyn was the one who was going to do the harm. "By Driggon's Teeth!" he mumbled the oath. "I am an emissary of Nightingale, and the fact that your kind locked me up like some kind of common criminal is an egregious offense as is, and now your so-called pathetic Grand Magistrate is going to kill me for some political gain?"

Glyn's expression was caught somewhere between surprise, fear, and anger.

"If I die," Donovan continued in a low, strained tone that was like murder itself, "then good luck fighting Kaldaran."

Glyn's face flashed with emotion, but he reined it in quickly. "There is a Fah Rellion thunderstorm in Fallavon right now, Donovan, and you and I both are ships far from the harbor."

Donovan backed off a little, realizing that Glyn had no power to change what was happening.

"Fah Rellion. Fey god," Donovan said. "Does he treat you well?"

Glyn scoffed. "Not as of late."

A sound from the hallway drew Glyn's eyes to the outside of the cell. Donovan stood next to the bars and looked as well, toward the prison's exit. The red-skinned fey leader had returned with his band of soldiers. He sent half further on—probably to fetch Rohawk—and the other half stayed with him. He grabbed a rope and indicated Donovan with a hand gesture.

"You are to be given an audience with the Grand Magistrate immediately," the leader said in a commanding voice. "You must submit to having your hands bound."

Donovan put his arms out. "As if I have a choice."

Chapter Sixteen

It didn't take long for Donovan and Rohawk's arrival to cause a stir in Fallavon. Mothers, children, soldiers, merchants—all work or play of any kind seemed to pause for a moment when the two humans were brought down the road. Some stopped what they were doing to follow and watch.

Rohawk kept eyeing the guards as if he still had weapons up his sleeves and could somehow stop all of it or get away. He knew how to use Technique, but doing so without metal took a lot of sacrifice. Maybe he was still armed.

Donovan was thankful that the half-Kaldaran kept his mouth shut. He did not want violence. They were protected under Lion Clan law, and he still hoped this Grand Magistrate would not openly violate it. But the looks some of the fey gave Donovan made him realize that there were people there who wanted him dead. He hoped the Grand Magistrate was not one of them, despite what Glyn said.

Donovan slowed his step when a feyla emerged from the crowds. It was not her looks that made him pause, though she was very beautiful. Her eyes were covered by a black blindfold that he almost didn't notice because it blended in with her dark blue skin. Long, silky purple hair that flowed over her shoulders made her skin look like a backdrop while her hair was the painting. A three-stringed compound bow was strapped to her back, along with a quiver. *A blind feyla with a bow?*

Donovan's thoughts were interrupted by a sudden kick in the back, which sent him forward to the ground. All the guards around laughed, all except the leader. Donovan looked over at the blind girl. It seemed like she was noticing him.

"That is what you get when you stop moving, human!" the guard with the thick fey accent mocked.

"Help him up!" the red-skinned leader commanded in the human tongue.

The guard replied something in the fey tongue, but suddenly the leader pulled his sword and held it at the soldier's throat. The blade was wooden, but it did have an edge, and getting smacked hard with a blunt end would not feel good either.

The guard didn't look happy about the blade at his neck, but he nodded slightly. The leader pulled his blade back, and the guard turned and helped Donovan up.

Rohawk raised an eyebrow at the fey leader and said, "About time you fellows showed a little decency."

The leader turned his attention to Rohawk and said, "Decency is becoming rarer and rarer as of late. My name is Deltra, and you might say that I am a friend. The only friend you have right now."

Rohawk sniffed. "Sure."

"We don't have many options," Donovan pointed out. "Thanks," he said to Deltra. "My name's Donovan."

"What about you?" Deltra said to Rohawk. "You have a name?"

"Rohawk. You've heard of me, perhaps?"

Deltra blinked in non-recognition.

"Hm, probably a good thing."

"You have not been convicted of anything," Deltra said. "Therefore, you deserve humane treatment. Some of us need to remember our manners..."

"You didn't seem too fond of us earlier," Donovan said.

Deltra's eyes shifted around before answering. "There is a lot going on here you know nothing about. I am trying to keep up appearances. What I did just now might cost me, but I have my limits."

They hadn't gone much farther when a feynar, dressed in leather and strapped with swords and a bow, charged toward them with swords drawn in both hands. He shouted something, eyes glaring daggers at Donovan. All the fey guards had their twin swords drawn before the man even came close. Deltra shouted at the man in feyspeak, but he still stalked toward the group, shouting.

Deltra replied calmly, but kept his swords raised with a firm grip, and even pointed with them once or twice. The feynar stopped for a second, then shouted again and lunged toward Donovan. Deltra was there in an instant. His first strike broke one of the feynar's swords with a crack, then he followed up immediately and batted the other sword out of the feynar's hand.

Deltra sheathed one sword so he could grab the feynar by the neck. He leaned in and spoke with a tight voice before shoving the feynar to the ground.

The mad feynar breathed hard, with Deltra's hand pressing him into the dirt, but he calmed down and muttered something.

Deltra let him go. The attacker got up and walked away slowly, but not before the twisted glare on his face moved between Deltra, Donovan, and Rohawk.

"Did he...want to kill me?" Donovan asked.

"Undoubtedly," said Deltra. "But the Grand Magistrate will decide what happens to you, not the common folk. I hope he deals more kindly with you."

"This is just a prelude to our execution, isn't it?" Rohawk said sharply. "Some friend you are."

"If I was not a friend, would I have bothered to learn your language?" Deltra asked with a weak smile. He barked orders in feyspeak to get the group moving again. Donovan noticed the subtle tightening of their formation. They were more on guard now.

"Does this mean you'll help us?" Donovan asked. "Maybe put in a good word?"

"Your fate is not up to me," Deltra answered. The tone of his voice let on that there was more to be said, but not in mixed company.

They turned another corner, and Donovan's jaw dropped at the largest tree he had ever seen. It could be none other than the Fallavon Great Tree. The trunk itself looked like it could fit over a hundred men pressed up against it, connected by outstretched hands. Then Donovan noticed that the tree was not just one, but that there were some other trees grafted into it that looked like later additions. Some of the golden leaves on the large branches were the size of a man's shield.

"Impressed?" Deltra asked. "Believe it or not, I have seen fey with the same expression when they saw a human castle, but none of them would admit to being impressed with anything made by men."

Deltra led Donovan and Rohawk to the entrance of the Great Tree, two large wooden doors, with a giant root that formed a ramp leading up to them. Banners bearing the golden lion were set up along the sides of the stairs, which were lined with soldiers bearing the same lion on their tabards. The tailoring looked immaculate, yet they still were no comparison to the lion on the doors themselves. It was like a carving, but it must have been shaped by fey magic.

The group walked up the ramp, and the guards at the entrance opened the large doors after receiving a nod from Deltra. The great lion on the door parted to give a view of the entryway. A fine smell wafted from inside and fell on Donovan like a light sheet. It was neither too sweet nor too musky—like the smell of cinnamon and evergreens.

"Curious scent," Rohawk said.

Donovan wondered if that was a compliment.

"Only one of the rarest and most elaborate perfumes known to Drannus," Deltra said, looking a little bit surprised at Rohawk's seemingly underwhelmed response. "The Queen makes batches of it using her own secret recipe. All the servants here spray a little of it on themselves in the morning, and the smell permeates the place."

"Well, it makes my nose itch," Rohawk complained.

"I will be sure to bring that up with the Queen when she returns," Deltra said in a tone dryer than the ash mounds in the Valley of Dragon Bones.

A servant came up to Deltra and asked a few questions. Deltra responded, pointing at Donovan and Rohawk once or twice, then the servant nodded and left. "I have told him to announce us in a few minutes."

"Why the wait?" Rohawk asked.

"Because you two are going to need a little bit of preparation—that is, if you are to come out of this conversation without a death sentence." Deltra barked out some orders to the guards. About half the soldiers bowed quickly and left. "Just making sure those who speak common are gone. Rohawk, you like to speak your mind—that will not get you far. Donovan, you seem too nervous or awestruck to say anything right."

Rohawk grinned and looked away, trying to suppress a chuckle, then turned back to Deltra and said, "I know how to handle myself before royalty."

"Still, you should listen," Deltra said. "The Grand Magistrate is a prideful man. If you stroke his ego enough, it will get him on your side—more accurately, it will seem like you are on his side. He will see you both as evil humans, something to be eradicated. If you can show him that you are lowly and recognize your low-born place in this world, he may decide you are not worth potential trouble with K'var by killing you. Above all else, never forget that he has complete power over you."

"Right," Donovan said at the same time Rohawk said, "We're doomed."

Donovan glared at Rohawk. The half-Kaldaran frowned, then said, "I will do my best, but I don't intend to go down like a dog. I have an angle that will work if you follow along."

"Last time I lied to an official, it didn't go well for me."

Rohawk opened his mouth to respond, but turned his attention to the footsteps of an approaching servant.

"The Grand Magistrate will see you now," he said.

"I thought we had more time," Deltra said as he exhaled a breath. "Follow me," he added as he waved a hand forward.

The wide double doors to the throne room were shoved open, and at first sight, Donovan felt like he was entering a temple. The throne room was large, circular all the way around. The ceiling appeared to be twenty-five paces from the ground, supported by four tall, circular, wooden pillars that looked like separate trees. Carefully carved designs of lions crowned the pillars at the top and circled them around the bottom.

Along the walls were windows similar to the ones outside, except every other one was stained glass with a picture depicting some kind of fey king with strange, ribbon-like wings. In between the windows, large tapestries of various colors with different emblems were hung. One larger tapestry hung above the goldenwood throne, bearing the golden lion of Fallavon for the Fey King Beldon.

But right now, none of the things surrounding the throne, nor the throne itself, was nearly as important as the one who sat upon it. The Grand Magistrate wore beautiful white and gold clothes wrapped around his true yellow skin. When he looked at Donovan, he gathered his long, dark blue hair away from his face with a commanding hand then brushed two fingers along his white *sarta*, which ran across from his left ear down to the bottom right of his jaw.

Suddenly, Donovan was overwhelmed by a waking dream, a vision. He almost lost control of himself as he saw the bronze king from his dream back in Nightingale. The image was superimposed over the Grand Magistrate, and it took all the self-control he had not to cry out. Instead, he stood perfectly still and prayed the vision would end. He saw crowns on the ground, smatterings of dried blood on them, just like the dream.

What is happening to me? He felt a cold bead of sweat running down his back.

"He's not going to believe you," he heard the bronze king speak. "He's already made up his mind."

Then it ended. The voice of the Grand Magistrate calling Donovan and Rohawk to approach broke through the vision and restored Donovan to reality.

When they reached the throne, Deltra quietly told them to bow, but Rohawk was already doing so and Donovan was following Rohawk's lead.

"Arise." The Grand Magistrate's tone was cold steel.

Donovan and Rohawk stood back up. Donovan squared his shoulders when he saw Deltra and Rohawk doing so.

"Your names and where you are from," the Grand Magistrate ordered.

"Donovan, of Nightingale. And this is—"

"Rohawk, of the Kingdom of Sokor, your lordship." To Donovan's surprise, Rohawk imitated the Sokorian accent perfectly.

The Grand Magistrate eyed them carefully, studying their appearances. "Tell me, what would a Nightingale mercenary and a Sokorian be doing together in the Fey Wilds?"

Donovan had not stated his profession, but the Grand Magistrate seemed to assume that anyone from Nightingale was a mercenary, or perhaps Donovan had the look of one. Technically, he was right.

Rohawk opened his mouth to answer, but Donovan spoke quickly, saying, "We are on official business in service to Nightingale. We came requesting help from King Beldon. Nightingale is being routinely attacked by Kaldaran soldiers, and we need aid. Rohawk was hired as a guard for me."

Rohawk glared at Donovan, but the Grand Magistrate continued on without notice.

"What made you think that the Fey Wilds would so much as welcome you, never mind honor your ridiculous request?"

This time, Rohawk spoke up quickly to stop Donovan. "High One, we are ignorant of the ways of your people, and we were told to come to you seeking aid or forsake our orders under penalty of death." Rohawk's accent wasn't the only difference in his speech. He spoke with strong elegance as if he had spent a lot of time in royal chambers. "If, by your grace, great ruler, you would consider our plight and look over our offense—"

"No," the Grand Magistrate said calmly. "You expect me to believe that Kaldaran is attacking Nightingale when I know full well their attention is on the Fey Wilds? If you were going to make up a story, why not say that Corrick had moved on you?"

"I *was* going to say that," Rohawk breathed out quietly through gritted teeth.

The Grand Magistrate did not hear Rohawk and continued, "I will most certainly not look over your offense. It is clear that you intend to spread misinformation in my kingdom to cause confusion."

"We have done no harm; we are here as diplomats!" Donovan pleaded. "And everything we have said *is* true." He realized that Rohawk's Sokorian angle was a lie, but hopefully that would go unnoticed.

The Grand Magistrate waved his hand. "No more. I have heard enough. I hereby sentence you to death, come tomorrow morning, on the account of," he paused only briefly, "being spies for the kingdom of Kaldaran." The Grand Magistrate looked past the two and nodded at Deltra.

"What?" Donovan shouted. "This is your version of justice? I'd find more honor in a den of thieves and more chastity in a whorehouse!"

"Get him out of here!" the Grand Magistrate shouted back. "Get these wicked people away from my presence, until I request it once more to remove their heads from their necks!"

"Bastard!" Donovan spat out.

Deltra slapped him across the face. "The Grand Magistrate has spoken!"

The force of it sent Donovan to the ground. He cupped his hand to catch the blood drizzling from his nose. Not broken, or at least it didn't feel broken, but there would be a bruise, for sure. He took his bloody hand and pressed it against the white rug, not only to help himself up, but also as one final act of defiance.

Deltra immediately ushered the two of them out of the Great Tree and back toward the prison. He seemed angry, but did not say a word.

Along the way, Rohawk gave Donovan a curious look, a look that could have been interpreted as respect. "Guess it was you who didn't want to go down like a dog," he said. There was no hint of his usual sarcasm, and Donovan was unsure how to feel about the compliment.

Upon reaching the prison, the two were returned to the same cells as before. Glyn was still there, and his eyebrows raised in curiosity as he observed Donovan's bloodied face.

"Is that the extent of your punishment?" he asked.

"That bastard wanted us dead before he even saw us," Donovan said with a growl. "He trumped up some charges to accuse us with and sentenced us to death."

"I thought he might, but, if it makes you feel any better, I had hoped that he would show mercy."

"I thought the fey people were honorable, Glyn. Gods, I thought Nightingale was filthy, but I suppose I was ignorant of true filth. Shame on me."

Glyn said nothing for a moment, then finally spoke. "Say what you will, but it will not make a difference. Even if the Grand Magistrate has done wrong, and is deserving of death himself, he has power. Power is greater than sin." After a hollow laugh, he added, "I learned that the hard way. I wanted to discover the source of the Grand Magistrate's power, so I made my way deeper and deeper into the secrets of Fallavon. I was not careful enough. His men caught me and threw me in here. So you see, for the time being, we are actually on the same side."

"I'm not on anyone's side!" Donovan shouted. "Not the Grand Magistrate's, not yours!"

Glyn spat on the ground. "It will not matter much, will it? When we are both dead? Show some decency, Donovan, and share this one bond of death. Speak no more ill of me."

"*Both* dead?" Donovan asked slowly.

"Do you think the Grand Magistrate has forgotten about me? No, I am certain he has not." With that, Glyn sprawled out on the floor and closed his eyes without saying another word.

Donovan did the same, though he didn't expect to sleep much, especially since it was only late afternoon. Instead, he stayed awake for quite some time, thinking over his life, and the little bit that was left of it. *Why did I try to become a soldier? Why did I go to Shiverpine and find things I wasn't meant to? My heart is only heavier—the burden I sought to lift from my shoulders has been doubled and placed back upon me.*

"I do not know if there is comfort in this life," he said aloud. "But I can say for certain that I have not found it. The glory I sought has destroyed my soul."

Glyn opened his eyes just a little. "That is the pain of this life, Donovan. To know the prison of the soul. At the very least, your burden will be lifted soon. So will mine."

Donovan opened his eyes into another vision. He had a sense that he was awake, but the images were superimposed over his sight, as they were when he had spoken with the Grand Magistrate. He saw an armory before him, but everything was fey craftsmanship, which meant wood and leather.

He watched as strong feynars and feylas came in and out of the room, examining swords, plucking bowstrings, and grabbing quivers with arrows. They all had grave looks on their faces, as if they had been told to dress for death. *Is the city under attack?* he wondered. "Am I still in the prison?"

"I would hardly call this place a prison," a voice sounded from behind him.

Donovan turned, thinking he would see Glyn, but it was a different person standing there. It was the bronze king, only he looked more like a normal human. A little, anyway. His skin was leathery instead of bronze, and his hair was a brown-red instead of gold.

"You called it with the Grand Magistrate."

"You think so? I thought your fiery speech was pretty good. Would have convinced me."

"Who are you, and what am I seeing?"

"I'm a friend. This is what's going on behind the scenes in Fallavon. Something is brewing, and it could destroy the Lion Clan."

"Well, if it's Kaldaran related—"

"It's not, though. Those raids are hardly anything."

Donovan watched more of what was happening. The fey he was so angry with looked like they needed help.

"I don't wish any ill to the people of Fallavon, but they aren't my favorite right now, and they certainly aren't my duty."

The bronze king stroked his beard. "But they need your help."

Donovan chuckled. "They are going to kill me."

"You do not know for a fact that you will die soon."

Donovan sniffed. "I know it as much as any man can."

"Yes, but that was true before you came here. No one knows when they will die. Perhaps some have a better idea than others."

"I'm one of those now."

The bronze king smiled. "We'll see. What did you do with the book?"

Donovan blinked. "You know about that?"

"Of course."

"Left it with the Priestess of K'var back in Nightingale."

The king was taken aback. "You are full of surprises! Good! I like it!" Donovan felt strangely encouraged. Even if what was happening was only a figment of his imagination, it was a figment from the part of him he soulburned. He knew that. The bronze king was unlike anything he had ever thought of before.

"Our time's up. Stay strong, Donovan. Don't lose your fighting spirit. There's plenty of fighting to come."

With that, the vision was gone. Donovan once again saw the prison he was in. He thought he had spoken aloud in the vision, but even if he had, Glyn was still asleep. A quick look through the window showed the hints of sunrise. Donovan had slept away most of his final hours. *The bronze king doesn't seem to think I'm about to die, and he...knows things. Maybe there's hope.*

Loud footsteps sounded in the hallway, which awoke Glyn. He looked over at Donovan, and said, "You say odd things in your sleep. I'm surprised I got any."

"What kind of things?"

Before Glyn could answer his question, the fey soldiers were at the cell, unlocking it. Deltra was not present, and that sent chills up Donovan's spine. One of the soldiers said something in feyspeak that sounded grim. Donovan looked over to Glyn, who sighed and nodded slowly. The soldiers entered the prison and bound Donovan's and Glyn's hands. From down the hallway, other guards returned with a hand-bound Rohawk walking in front of them. His feet were also bound loosely, so he could only take short steps. They must have figured out he was a slippery one.

The group merged, and as one, exited the prison. Donovan thought they would be executed inside, but they were being taken somewhere else.

"Where are we going?" Donovan asked Glyn.

"Probably to the center of the city, to execute us publicly," he replied.

Donovan took in quick breaths. "I know it as much as any man can," he mumbled to himself. The man in the vision seemed to agree with that—did that mean Donovan was wrong? And what about Lady Renna's vision?

Would he remember who he was, then die? *Could that be what she meant by the world will end? My world will end?*

"It is illegal to execute prisoners publicly," Glyn noted.

"And the Grand Magistrate is doing it anyway?" Donovan asked.

He was surprised when it was Rohawk who answered. "To show that he is the new lawmaker in this city. He's becoming more open with his defiance to the king."

Glyn gave Rohawk a look somewhere between respect and caution.

"Where is the king?" Donovan asked.

"Gone, been gone for a month," Glyn answered.

"Great timing," Rohawk said. Then the walk continued in silence for a little while. Onlookers gathered again, this time with much more expectation. Some of them were grim, while others cheered openly.

"Bag of bones, is this how I die?" Rohawk said, half to himself. "I thought I should live longer, to see Lady Renna's vision through, one way or another."

Donovan shook his head and said, "I guess she is a liar then."

Just ahead, Donovan saw a chopping block on the ground and the Grand Magistrate standing nearby with a large axe in his hands. The arrogant fey leader looked upon Donovan and Rohawk as if they had each slept with his daughter. The place of execution was the market, which was now turned into a viewing arena. As the three prisoners neared the chopping block, the Fallavon guards surrounded them and formed a barrier between them and the now roaring crowds. Donovan saw the strange blindfolded feyla there. Her lips were tight, her hand even tighter on her bow, as if she intended to use it in a few moments.

"Quite a mixed crowd, eh?" Rohawk commented.

"Makes it easy to spot who is still loyal to the king and who is loyal to Vinson," Glyn said.

"What do you mean by that?" Donovan asked.

"Those who are cheering are probably the Grand Magistrate's people. The ones who look on with disapproval are more King Beldon's sort."

"Bring them over here!" the Grand Magistrate bellowed in the human tongue. The guards forced Donovan, Rohawk, and Glyn over to the chopping block, where they stood like sheep to the slaughter. The Grand Magistrate looked Donovan straight in the eyes.

Donovan glared back, summoning all his courage. He was beginning to understand what Rohawk had meant earlier about not going down like a dog. If this was to be his last moment, he would leave this world with a gesture of defiance.

The Grand Magistrate raised a hand, and the crowd fell dead silent. A mere cough from somewhere in the back turned the eyes of half of the soldiers. The Grand Magistrate said something in feyspeak, then repeated himself in the common tongue. "These three men are guilty of insurrectionist crimes against the government of Fallavon," he announced, "Their penalty is death by public execution, to make an example of what happens to anyone who tries to usurp the authority of the Fallavon Great Council."

"I am innocent," Donovan shouted, his voice reverberating with strength and conviction.

"Put *his* head on the block first," the Grand Magistrate snarled. "It seems that even in his last few minutes of life, he remains a liar," he added as he locked eyes with Donovan. That comment was not meant for anyone else. The Grand Magistrate was enjoying this.

One of the fey guards grabbed Donovan and forced him forward. Many in the crowd cheered. Donovan looked over at Rohawk and saw that the binds on his legs and wrists were still there, but loose. He was about to act. Donovan braced for what was to come next, but there was a sudden blare of something that sounded like trumpets. The crowd fell silent, except for Vinson, who started speaking frantically in the fey tongue.

The guards acknowledged Vinson's order and pushed Donovan forward, but they stopped when the crowd began to grow uneasy.

Vinson's eyes widened a bit. He gave another order in his native tongue.

The guard grabbed at Donovan yet again, but Donovan sensed the tide turning, and resisted by mule-kicking the guard in the shin.

Rohawk laughed and shook away from his binds, the ropes falling off him like they were made of hot butter. "That's the way to do it, Donovan!"

The guards drew their swords and converged on Donovan and Rohawk, but they all stopped short, frozen by the sight of something, or someone. They dropped their swords immediately and bowed low.

Donovan turned around and saw a group of about a dozen fey riding on giant wolves. Each rider looked like a soldier, armed with leather jerkins, tabards, wooden swords, and bows. The two riders in the middle stood out the most. They had captured everyone's eyes, as well as everyone's respect. All the fey in the crowd bowed low and kissed the ground in the presence of those two.

One of them was a feyla dressed in a white skirt divided for riding. To say she was beautiful would be an understatement equal to saying the frozen, bitter winds at the peak of the Kaldaran Mountains were cold. Her yellow skin shone like polished gold, and her long pink hair radiated in waves as it blew in the wind, framing her symmetrical face in brilliant color. Her eyes commanded the flowers to grow, and her smile would raise the sun before the night had ended.

Donovan got to see that smile for only a second, but it seemed directed toward him.

She asked a question of the crowd as she looked up and down, over the people, finally resting on the tree stump and Vinson standing next to it with his large axe.

When no one answered her, the feynar next to her dismounted. When his feet hit the ground, it was as if a great beast had set foot upon the world, or perhaps a god had fallen from the heavens to the ground. Lightning—the yellow *sarta* on one of his red thighs looked like a bolt coming down to strike the dirt.

If his steps had not been thundering enough, his voice was, as it boomed through the city. He was demanding answers. It was clear now that this feynar was the king, and he took a few steps closer, toward the Grand Magistrate and locked eyes with him.

By now, everyone, including Donovan, had knelt in respect. Except for one. Vinson remained standing. He seemed so preoccupied with King Beldon's untimely entrance that he had forgotten to show respect.

"Have you become so high and lofty that you do not bow to your king, Vinson?" King Beldon said, now in the human tongue, as he brushed his long, white hair out of his face. Donovan remembered that there was a fey ceremony that turned a king's hair white.

Vinson blinked in surprise at the king's comment, then bowed reluctantly. "Are you so low and fallen that you address me in the vulgar human tongue?" he asked.

"This matter concerns humans, does it not?"

"King Beldon, your majesty!" Vinson said, suddenly shifting to groveling. "You should be pleased to know I have discovered three insurrectionists here in Fallavon. I was about to execute them myself when—"

"A public execution?" King Beldon shouted. "Are we barbarians now? Are we without law? Have we grown the fangs of animals and turned on each other like cornered wolves?" The king turned away and guffawed. He addressed the onlookers in the fey tongue, perhaps repeating what he just said. Some seemed roused by his comments, voicing their agreements. Others remained stone silent.

Donovan glanced over at the queen. She looked concerned, and she kept looking over at Rohawk and him. When she looked, Donovan turned his gaze away, but he knew she must have caught him staring once or twice.

King Beldon turned back to the Grand Magistrate and said, "Let me make this clear, Vinson. You know that it goes against all honor—and the law itself—to have a public execution here in Fallavon! Who made it right, *Grand* Magistrate? Who made it right?"

"I made it right!" Vinson shouted, his face twisting with rage. So much for groveling. "It is my decree, and you should abide by it!"

"*I* should abide?!" King Beldon shouted, louder than Vinson had. Something was strange about the King's voice—it had changed slightly. It sounded like some kind of faint, dark echo was with it. It was the fey magic coursing through his veins.

"You forget who is king and who is magistrate, Vinson!" The king stepped closer to Vinson until he was in the feynar's face. "I have abided by the Council's decisions plenty of times, but I will not stand in the presence of your despicable, unadulterated power trip and be lectured on who should abide by whom! One more word of defiance from you, and I will put your head on this stump right now!"

The Queen gasped and quickly approached her husband, putting her hand on his shoulder. The Grand Magistrate shook with fury but held his tongue.

King Beldon kept his eyes on him for a moment, then looked over at Donovan, Rohawk, and Glyn. "I was right to say these are the three to be executed?" he asked. He sounded as if he had just got done chasing a rabbit around and finally gave up. He looked back at one of his wolf riders and commanded, "Take them to the Great Tree immediately, I wish to judge them myself."

No sooner had King Beldon said the words, did the Grand Magistrate erupt, "But I have already judged them! Would you hold court again and defy my judgment?"

In the blink of an eye, King Beldon had Vinson by the throat and forced down onto the tree stump, making him drop the axe.

There was a collective holding of breath from the onlookers. "I will hold court when I please!" King Beldon breathed out. "Did you summon the Council when you held this false court of your own? I see none of them present, besides Lord Jaager and yourself, Vinson! The Grand Magistrate cannot pass condemnation by his own word, but *I* can! Do I make myself clear?"

The Grand Magistrate held his mouth shut tightly now.

"Love, please," the queen said in a low voice.

King Beldon released his hold on Vinson and pushed him up to his feet, away from him. Then he looked at the guards standing near Donovan and said something in feyspeak. The guards nodded and promptly removed the ropes from him and Glyn. They seemed bothered that Rohawk was already out of his, but said nothing.

From the look on the Grand Magistrate's face, Donovan thought there was a chance the feynar was going to pick up that axe again and try for a swing at the king. Instead, he let out a fraction of his frustration in an exhaled breath and walked away. His band of bodyguards formed a circle to escort him back to wherever he came from. There was no need for them to push through the crowd. The citizens of Fallavon had given Vinson's group a rather wide berth, enough for a company to pass through with ease. Few wanted to be near him.

King Beldon sighed and nodded back at his riders. Three of them prodded their wolves over and held out hands to help Donovan, Rohawk, and Glyn onto the backs of the animals.

The queen gave an additional command, and the riders all put a fist to their chests and gave a slight bow.

The wolf riders said something that sounded like a command, and the wolves began to run and pick up speed. Donovan nearly fell off at first, but grabbed tightly onto the rider in front of him. He thought the feynar would curse him off, but he didn't say a word.

Riding on the wolf was exhilarating. Donovan smiled with relief as the beast took him and the rider around corner after corner, away from the execution ground. The beast was agile, tearing up the dirt with its fierce claws and going faster through the city than any horse ever could.

When they had arrived at the Great Tree, the guard dismounted first and reached out a hand. Donovan grunted as he moved his legs around, already a little sore from the bumps and turns. The feynar laughed, but not the mocking laugh Donovan expected. Instead, the man was genuinely smiling. He even gave Donovan a firm pat on the shoulder.

"You seem to be a much nicer sort," Donovan complimented. The man laughed again and motioned for him to follow.

"Anyone who makes the Grand Magistrate *that* upset is a friend of mine," he said. "You looked like you had him pretty worked up. Promise me, if the king lets you go, you'll share a drink with me and tell me about it. The name is Kellen, by the way."

Donovan smiled but was feeling a little uneasy. *If the king lets us go?*

Chapter Seventeen

Donovan expected to be rushed to the throne room a second time, but instead, he was ordered to take a hot bath. His only hesitation was surprise, then more surprise when he found out that he had his own private bath connected to the guest room he was put in. The bathroom alone was as big as the upper floor of his home in Nightingale. Several small windows illuminated it with the warm, late-morning light, reflecting in many colors off glass bottles set near the bath.

Donovan lay in the marble tub, which was sunk into the ground, with steps on one end for easy entry. A nearby shaft poured in the fresh, hot water when opened. Several kinds of herbal soaps had been placed in their trays for him to use at his desire. One was all he needed. A sweet smell surrounded him as he scrubbed away days of traveling dirt and mud.

"And here I thought Linda's stuff was good," he said as he inhaled a scent better than all the flowers in the city.

Donovan was unsure if he was still a prisoner. His room was guarded, but the feynar had given him plenty of space. The past week or so had been a nightmare. This was like waking up.

Then he felt again at the glass locket around his neck, and the nightmare crept in again. He worried about Alexis and all of Nightingale. Escaping the crazed Grand Magistrate was only a temporary reprieve if Nightingale fell. He had to convince King Beldon to help.

A knock at the door from the bedroom drew Donovan's attention. The guard there answered and exchanged a few words with someone, then poked his head in the room.

"Sorry to disturb your bath. A feyla named Selena requests to see you. Should I let her in?" Donovan was confused.

"Someone wants to see me? Do you think she means me any harm?"

"No, sir."

Donovan shrugged. "Give me a minute to get decent."

"I am happy to do that, but I do not think it will be an issue." Donovan raised an eyebrow.

Is this some weird cultural difference?

"She is blind," the guard added.

Just like that feyla with the bow and the blindfold.

"I would still feel better being dressed. Give me a moment." The guard nodded and returned to the main room.

Donovan got out of the bath and grabbed a towel. He pressed it to his skin and froze.

"Bag of bones, it's the softest thing I've ever felt." He dried off, then reached for the new clothes on the counter. They were a gift from the queen—silky, purple, loose-fitting tunic, with a green shirt and breeches that supposedly went with the purple. The colors were odd, but perhaps acceptable amongst the fey.

The socks felt smooth and fine, which was a rare comfort. Donovan released a sigh of pleasure as he put them on. *I hope this means they don't plan to kill me.*

Everything in the bedroom looked like it had been grown in place. That must have made renovation a nightmare, but it was beautiful. The bed had curved spirals on the tops of the posts resembling ferns Donovan had seen once. The sheets were purple silk. There was a desk in one corner grown with a large counter and thin underneath to allow for one to slide in the chair. A stack of papers and a quill with an inkwell sat ready for use. On the far side, near the door, two chairs were grown around a table that resembled a lily pad. It had green hues that were different from the goldenwood everywhere else.

"Sir?" the guard asked. "Are you ready?"

"Yes."

The guard opened the door and in walked the feyla he had seen earlier, the one with the bow and blindfold. She indicated to the guard for assistance, and he guided her to one of the two chairs. She took a seat, and her dark blue hand pulled back her purple hair, revealing the hint of a pink colored *sarta* that ran up from under the blindfold and across her left ear, back to where Donovan couldn't see it.

Donovan took the chair opposite her and sat down.

"Hello," she said. "My name is Selena. And you are?" Her accent was light. That sometimes meant well travelled or well educated amongst the fey.

"Donovan."

"It is nice to meet you, Donovan. I am here because I want to ask you to leave."

He blinked. "It must not be *that* nice to meet me, then. But it doesn't matter. Even if I wanted to leave, I'm under orders by the king to stay."

"Right, sorry. I am nervous about all that has been happening. I mean to say that I worry for your safety and the safety of Fallavon. Your arrival is bad timing. There are many in Fallavon who want to kill you. My brother, whom you met, might be one of them."

Whom I met? Donovan wondered. "Do you mean Glyn?"

"Yes."

"I'm not saying you're wrong, but Glyn did not strike me as someone who wanted to kill me."

"That may be, but he is angling for political gain. I am betraying his trust by coming here and telling you all this, but I cannot agree to what he is doing. Promise me you will leave when you get the chance."

"I can't promise you anything right now, but I don't plan to stay long. If my meeting with King Beldon goes well, I will be leaving later today or tomorrow."

Selena's shoulders relaxed. "Oh, that is great news. Thank you, Donovan. Please write me sometime from Nightingale. My assistant Twyla reads letters to me."

Donovan chuckled. "Should I address them to the sister of the feynar who wants to kill me?"

"That…would not help."

Donovan realized that Selena was upset about the whole situation, and his sarcasm was not helpful. "Sorry. Thanks for the warning."

"You are welcome." With that, Selena stood and made her way back towards the door.

Donovan realized he might be missing an opportunity. "Wait!" He called out as he rose. "What can you tell me about King Beldon? How can I get on his good side?"

Selena paused a step from the door. "I do not know. But I do know that he is a good feynar. If you are a good human, then you are already on his good side."

"Oh. Good," Donovan said as he watched her go. He was puzzled by what just happened. He knew coming to Fallavon was a risk, but now Deltra, Selena, and King Beldon himself all seemed to be protecting him.

That is, of course, if King Beldon was planning to let him go.

A servant appeared at the door and spoke quickly to the guard. He nodded and turned to Donovan. "The king will see you now."

Rohawk exhaled slowly as he stepped into his hot bath, finally. It had taken him a while to convince the guard to let him have some privacy. The guard was rather displeased when Rohawk asked him if a serving girl could be called to help him with his bath. He was only joking, or at least mostly.

"These fey just don't understand good humor," he mumbled as he rolled his eyes. He glanced over at the bathroom table and saw a silky purple tunic paired with a bright blue shirt and breeches.

"Hasn't anyone around here heard of black?" he mumbled as he reached for the soap. "Even a dark brown would suffice." He began to rub the soap on his shoulders when he caught its scent. *Perfect, if I wanted to smell like an uppity feyla.* He grabbed at the other bars and smelled similar things, but finally settled for one of them. He didn't like the scents any more than the bright clothes but reasoned that diplomacy might be better than stealth in this situation.

He briefly considered trying to run and get out of the city now, but the hot bath melted any planning from his thoughts. It had been a long time since he had experienced anything so luxurious.

Closing his eyes and inhaling a deep breath, he changed his mind about the soap. It was heaven. He tried all of them, lathering up and putting them back after.

The hot water calmed Rohawk's muscles and his mind, and he began to think that maybe everything was perfectly alright. But it could never stay that way for long. Not for him. Not for the one with a shadow in his soul.

"Damn you, Lady Renna. Couldn't you just have given me a hint of good news? Or at least have the decency to lie?"

There was a knock at the door to the main room. The guard answered and spoke with whoever it was, then walked into the bathroom and fixed a glare at Rohawk.

"The king has ordered you to his throne room, immediately." The guard barked that last word rudely.

Rohawk sighed. "Alright, fine."

The guard turned away slowly, keeping his eyes fixed on him as long as possible.

Rohawk jumped out of the side of the bath, planting his feet firmly on the ground without slipping one bit. He eyed the fresh fey clothes on the table, then looked at his old, soiled clothes sitting in a lump on the ground. He picked up his breeches and smelled them, abruptly tossing them back on the ground.

He looked back again at the table of the fey clothes and shrugged.

"At least they're royal clothes. Clean, not-smelly, royal clothes."

Donovan was brought to the throne room and left there waiting, which didn't help his nerves any. A few servants were dusting and cleaning the windows, and another two looking at the blood stain in the white rug and probably discussing solutions. One of them looked his way and he immediately turned his head.

The guards that stood at all entrances and exits seemed to glance his direction now and then, but nothing more. Donovan swallowed hard. He had not been this nervous a moment ago, but reality was setting in. Nightingale's fate rested on this conversation. He had to say everything perfectly.

He resisted the urge to pace. He assumed the king would be coming right away. Perhaps he was hiding somewhere already, watching. That seemed silly, but Donovan shifted his shoulders a little uncomfortably. He felt like *someone* was watching.

King Beldon walked into the throne room from a side entrance. He was adorned in a bright white shirt with like breeches and a black tunic that bore the golden lion of Fallavon on the back. There was something about the way he walked. It was as if at any moment he could bring down the Great Tree with one step. Yet, despite his powerful gait, he seemed calm, maybe even in a good mood. He sat down on the throne and smiled at Donovan, who was already bowing.

"Arise, please," King Beldon said. "I sent for you before the others to give me time to speak with you first. I apologize for the display I made with the Grand Magistrate. I am growing tired of that feynar, and my temper got the better of me." Donovan was incredulous.

"A king apologizes to me?"

"You are the official emissary from Nightingale, yes? In court manners, it would not be uncommon for a king to apologize for the sake of diplomacy. Besides that, no one is above mistakes, Donovan. Not even one's ruler." He eyed Donovan for a moment, then said, "Tell me about yourself."

Donovan paused to remember everything correctly, then said, "Nightingale is under attack and—"

"You may not know it," the king gently interrupted, "but I understand the urgency of your situation. We will get to that in a moment. For now, I am asking you to tell me about *yourself*, not why you are here."

"I…" Donovan was caught well off guard. *Why does King Beldon want to know about me? What's appropriate to say? What would Rohawk do?* His eyes drifted to the spot of blood, a reminder of what happened when he had said the wrong thing.

"Yours?" the king asked.

Donovan's eyes snapped back to the king, and he nodded.

The king tensed then took a deep breath. "I see. I am more sorry now than before. But please, answer my question."

"I am a soldier from Nightingale, and before that, I was a fur trader."

"Since childhood?" The king asked, with what seemed like genuine interest.

"No clue. Soulburned."

"Not something I can sympathize with, but I am sorry to hear it."

Donovan let out a muted sigh and looked over his shoulder at the servants and the guards.

"Privacy, please!" King Beldon called out. The servants moved quickly to the exits, and as soon as they were out, the guards exited and shut the doors behind them. "I understand that can be a sensitive topic. We will stick to recent history. What made you decide to join the Nightingale Guard? Why did you choose to come here?'

"I didn't say I was part of the Guard. I used to be, but now I'm just a mercenary. I joined the guard because I wanted to earn some respect."

"You didn't have respect before?"

"No respect for the god-hating soulburned," Donovan said with eyes low. "Not sure what the equivalent in your culture would be, but suffice it to say, I was pushed around a lot."

King Beldon nodded but did not respond immediately. He seemed to be studying Donovan thoroughly. His gray eyes were a bit unnerving. Thoughtful and wise, but in them was a hidden fire. Donovan hoped that fire would not come against him.

"You have killed in your memorable life, yes?" the king asked.

Donovan blinked but composed himself quickly. "I'm not proud of it, but yes."

"So you committed murder?"

"No, of course not. I've killed people in the war against Kaldaran."

"Then we have that in common. In fact, Donovan, I think you and I are very much alike." King Beldon stood up and walked over toward one of the windows, his white hair shimmering behind him. Donovan caught a glitter of blue fey magic in that hair as it moved.

"You're a good soldier, are you not?"

"I've made a lot of mistakes."

The king smiled. "Here, please look out this window. What do you see?"

Donovan stood next to the king and looked. Outside, he saw a bustling street in the city of Fallavon, with markets and homes lined up on the sides.

"I see a street in the city, fey people, homes, markets. Feynars, feylas, children..."

"Is that all?"

"It is rather beautiful. I could go on about the flowers, the houses, the trees...is there something in particular you want me to notice?"

King Beldon smiled, a little sadly, Donovan thought.

"When I look out this window, I see the darkest hearts and the brightest souls. I see the strongest hate and the most overwhelming love. I see people in want, and I see people with plenty. Do you want to know what I believe separates the two?"

"Probably gold, or family."

"Perhaps. But I believe it is the ability to forgive and receive forgiveness."

Some things can't be forgiven.

"You don't agree?" the king asked.

"You're the king, I'm supposed to agree, aren't I?"

King Beldon raised his chin, a slight smile across his lips. "Young and full of fire," he said softly. It sounded like he was quoting someone else.

The main doors to the throne room opened, and in walked Rohawk and Glyn. King Beldon motioned for Donovan to take a stand before the throne, while he sat down upon it. When all three of them had bowed, the doors to the throne room were closed again. King Beldon told them to rise.

"Welcome. Before we speak further, I owe each one of you an apology on behalf of the Lion Clan. Grand Magistrate Vinson should know better than to act as he did. His actions place his position on the council in jeopardy, and he will not escape his time in court." King Beldon paused, expecting one of the three to speak.

"We forgive your people," Rohawk said elegantly, in the same Sokorian accent he used on the Grand Magistrate.

"Please, Rohawk," King Beldon said with a chuckle, "There is no need for your fake accent. You may speak straight with me."

Rohawk seemed a little surprised, but he quickly contained it. "Forgive the habit, King Beldon. I am used to court politics."

"A mercenary used to court politics?"

"It was a different time," Rohawk said, each word weighted with hidden sorrow.

The king nodded slightly. "I have given the three of you an apology, and I think it fair that you give me the truth. First, Donovan and Rohawk. I want to hear in your own words what happened when you arrived in my land."

Rohawk summarized how they were ambushed by fey just outside the city and taken directly to the prison, then to a quick trial in the throne room where the Grand Magistrate sentenced them to death. He exaggerated a bit here and there, which irritated Donovan, but Rohawk was still more or less telling the truth.

"I see. And what brought you here to begin with?"

Rohawk opened his mouth but Donovan wasn't going to let him go off again. "Nightingale needs your help."

Rohawk shot him a frustrated glare, but then shrugged it off.

"Kaldaran soldiers have made their way across the Great River," Donovan continued, "K'var has ignored our cries for help with empty promises that they will come soon. I would like to emphasize that this is not merely a request for charity—if you help Nightingale, we are willing to offer you sovereignty over the town. K'var has failed us, we are seeking a new Suzerain."

"It's true, your majesty," Rohawk jumped in. "I single-handedly rescued this one from certain death in one of the battles against the current King of Kaldaran."

Donovan scowled a little bit at Rohawk, but behind his bragging, he was still speaking true. King Beldon paused for a moment, his expression a thoughtful one. He ran his eyes across the three of them and stopped at Glyn.

"What about you, Glyn, Son of Lord Jaager? Why did my Grand Magistrate want to execute you?"

Glyn tugged at a strand of his orange hair. "My tongue was...loosened a little after consuming a few glasses of wine. I spoke ill of the Grand Magistrate in a rather boisterous manner. It seems someone overheard me and relayed it to him. He did not find it at all to his liking."

Donovan wondered if Glyn was telling the truth. He said he had been put in prison unjustly, but speaking ill of the king or other officials was a serious crime in some places.

"Everything you said about him was true?" the king asked.

"Perhaps a bit exaggerated, but all warranted. Not a word of slander."

"You walk on thin branches, Glyn. You know it is our law that you cannot outright lie about a council member or the king."

"I would have been happy to prove my points if I was given a court of more than the Grand Magistrate's ego."

The king raised a hand to his chin, but Donovan caught a hint of a smile before he did.

"Normally, I would have your accusers brought before you, along with witnesses. But I have already taken time to gather a few testimonies of those involved, and, by my authority as King of Fallavon, I hereby declare you two," he indicated Donovan and Rohawk, "innocent of all charges the Grand Magistrate has levied against you."

Donovan exhaled a breath he hadn't realized he was holding, and Rohawk opened his mouth to, no doubt, give an elaborate thank you. But before he could, King Beldon continued.

"However, I do find you both guilty for trespassing in the Fey Wilds."

"What?" Donovan asked, confused.

King Beldon ignored Donovan and continued, "Glyn, in light of the Grand Magistrate's rush to judgment, I hereby find you innocent of any accusations held against you. You are free to go as you wish."

"Thank you, your majesty." Glyn sounded rather haughty, but he bowed anyway, before he turned around and left.

Donovan's mouth was still open, and he closed it with a click. King Beldon turned back to Donovan and Rohawk.

"As for you two, your punishment is that you must remain in Fallavon until I decide what to do about Nightingale. You will stay here in my guest rooms, dine with me for meals, and have conversation with me when I summon you."

"Wow that sounds…brutal?" Donovan said with obvious sarcasm and relief, but Rohawk seemed a little annoyed.

"Your majesty, I don't want to sound ungrateful, but we are to return to Nightingale as soon as we can."

"I understand, but I need time to consider your deal. All humor aside, you are free to go, but if you leave now, then I will deny your request for aid."

"And if we stay and you deny our request anyway?" Donovan asked.

"That is the risk you take. But keep in mind, if I say yes, I am taking a great risk. Gol, I am taking a risk just keeping you here."

Donovan crossed his arms. "How so?"

"A lot of my people do not like humans. Things used to be better between our races, but after the war with Kaldaran, anti-human sentiment spread like root blight. I want you to stay while I make my decision and see if you can get a few people to consider the idea of friendship with humans again. It helps that you struggle against the Kingdom of Kaldaran, as we did not long ago."

Donovan took a step forward. "Your majesty, I am thankful that you would consider our offer, but Rohawk speaks true. We have a duty to return and fight. Nightingale is on the brink of utter ruin."

"So is Fallavon," King Beldon said. It was only three words, but the weight behind them spoke to the soul. "I will not change the terms of my deal."

"King, forgive me, this is such an odd request," Rohawk said. "I know enough about fey culture, but Donovan is completely ignorant. He will be a poor lost soul here."

Donovan glared at him, but the king spoke instead.

"I know my request does not make sense to outsiders. But ever since the war, my people have turned inward, and the rot has been ongoing. I do not mind that they have love for the Clan, but we need trade and alliances with humans to survive. Perhaps a couple of honorable humans could be the beginning of something good."

"I never claimed to be honorable," Rohawk said flatly. "And I think your idea won't work."

"Rohawk!" Donovan chided.

"He is speaking his mind," King Beldon put in with a tone that said no harm was done. "You may be right. But that is the deal. Surely you must realize, becoming Suzerain of Nightingale will not do me much good for long. Sokor, Ladesh, or Corrick will likely challenge my claim, especially since they all want Nightingale on their respective sides for their own wars. Not to mention the fact that if I am lucky enough for them to leave Nightingale alone, K'var will doubtless challenge the deal you are making with me once they settle their current conflict. I will be powerless to stop them if they try to reclaim Nightingale by force."

Donovan had not thought through how bad of a deal King Beldon would be making, and he now wondered why the king would make it at all. Nightingale was a large source of wealth paid in tribute to its Suzerain, but the king made a good point. The chances he would maintain control were slim.

"If we do save Nightingale with your help, then what?" Rohawk asked. "Will you make us return here? I am a free agent for Nightingale and am doing this for pay. I cannot be bound here forever."

"I will likely request your return later, but it is not part of this agreement specifically."

"Alright, I can do that," Rohawk agreed.

"And you, Donovan?"

"I will stay, but I expect both of us to be well equipped for the journey back to Nightingale when the time comes. We had to leave Boroshard's Folly in a hurry and lost many of our belongings."

"Ah, so I am guessing that little seer gave you trouble."

Rohawk chuckled. "That would be putting it mildly."

"Alright," King Beldon said, confirming the agreement. "Before you go anywhere, there is something else I would like to discuss."

"You have our ears, your majesty," Rohawk said.

"I have been assembling a small army of soldiers I can trust. I train them separately from the rest of my warriors so I can keep their operations hidden from the eyes and ears of the Grand Magistrate. Because both King and Magistrate have access to the armies of the Lion Clan, I felt it necessary to build a group of soldiers whose abilities are known only to me, to leverage some strength over control of my kingdom."

"It won't be such a secret if you tell people you just met," Rohawk said, but he sounded a bit curious.

"True, but I am sure that Vinson knows about it already."

"Can't he use that against you?" Donovan asked. "Stir up the council and say you are hiding soldiers that the council has part ownership of?"

"He could, but no one would believe him. And I keep it secret enough that he doesn't know the specifics of what I have. Besides, the people I have tucked away have seen Vinson for what he truly is, just like you. Would someone in your shoes serve him after that?"

"Obviously yes, or you would have no opposition," Rohawk said flatly.

King Beldon looked surprised, then he smiled and laughed.

"It has been a long time since someone was brave enough to speak to me so bluntly. Though courage requires knowledge, and you do not yet know me. Take note of that. For now, do you agree to work with me and with my soldiers?"

Rohawk grinned. "Sure. You've got me curious."

"But how do we fit in with your secret army?" Donovan asked.

"You might not fit in. But for now, it is enough to know that I would like the two of you to go visit my soldiers soon, perhaps tomorrow. They need some encouragement, and I think they would enjoy your company."

"I am damn good company," Rohawk said.

"Excellent," King Beldon said coolly, though he seemed at least a little excited. "I will have the servants prepare a meal for all of us immediately. Please, feel free to roam the halls of the Great Tree or explore the city as you wish—I would recommend the library—but do not go far. The meal will be ready soon."

"What about the Grand Magistrate?" Donovan asked. "He's not going to send some assassin after us, is he?"

King Beldon looked confused, then nodded slowly with recognition. "Assassinations are unheard of in Fallavon, unheard of in all Fey Clans. The

Grand Magistrate hides behind his twisted interpretations of the law, but even he has some honor. Fey do not use assassins. It would be like selling your soul to *Gol Malden*."

Rohawk did not seem convinced, but all he said was, "Thank you, your majesty."

"If there is nothing else, I will see you two again in a little while." King Beldon arose from his throne and walked out of the room, immediately replaced by servants who came to show Donovan and Rohawk the way to their rooms.

"We get to be treated like royalty!" Rohawk said as they walked.

"I'm worried about what will happen to Nightingale, to Alexis."

"Donovan, it takes time to assemble an army and move them. Let's enjoy this place while we wait. We said our piece on wanting to leave."

"That's not the point. I don't want to be here when I could be there, helping."

"Donovan, our chances that the king would agree to send help were slim to none. Now he's at least considering it. You should be celebrating!"

"How can I celebrate when—" Donovan cut himself off, but Rohawk eased back his head in recognition.

"Ah. Your concern for Alexis isn't just concern for a friend, is it?"

Donovan turned away. "I suppose there is no law against it now that I am no longer part of the Guard. Still, Captain Gerald hates me and might try to say Alexis and I were romantic while I was still part of the guard."

Rohawk shrugged. "I wouldn't worry about what the Guard or anyone else thinks. Captain Gerald can go off himself for all I care."

Donovan cringed a little at that, but it was Rohawk's way of saying something nice. "Thanks."

"I might go draw another one of those baths," Rohawk considered aloud. "That was heavenly."

"I wonder how bad things are, for King Beldon, I mean," Donovan half-asked and half-wondered. "He looked so sad when we were looking out the window together."

"When was this?" Rohawk questioned.

"Just before you and Glyn arrived. He called me in early on purpose, though I am still unsure why."

"Ah yes, Glyn. The one who was in the cell with you…"

"He seems a bit like a mercenary; at least he reminds me of one. A bit like you."

Rohawk nodded slightly. "Yes, I got the impression he was a rather dangerous friend to have."

"You're seriously just going to bathe again until the meal?"

"I don't see why not. Just as good as anything else to pass the..." Rohawk's voice trailed as the two went by an incredibly beautiful feyla in the hallway. She smiled a little at Rohawk and kept walking. "Wow. By the moon and sun *that* was an incredible creature."

"Indeed," Donovan said, a bit stunned himself.

"Alright, this one is my room. Watch yourself, Donovan. I think the king underestimates how far the Grand Magistrate is willing to go."

"You may be right about that one."

Rohawk stepped inside his room, and Donovan was left alone. His room was only a little further down, but the king did recommend the library. Donovan asked a few servants passing by for directions until he found one that spoke common.

The inside of the library wasn't large. Endless rows of bookshelves had swallowed up the space. They were not quite like human libraries that formed neat rows on the left and right. Instead, they were curved around, as if they rippled out from the middle, with the wall of the library completely made up of one giant bookshelf. There were flaws and variations in the shelf sizes. Smaller books had been placed in areas where the shelves were shorter.

Donovan glanced at the books but passed up most of them. They were all written in feyspeak. It was a welcome surprise when he noticed a book that had some words written in common on the spine. He smiled as he removed it from its place on the shelf and opened it. *A Brief Description of Fey Culture.*

Donovan looked at the title, then put his fingers up against the thickness of the book, measuring three fingers thick. *Whoever wrote this has a tenuous grasp on the word 'brief.'* He shrugged and cracked the book open, scanning the pages. Clans, festivals, marital arts and...mating rituals. That was enticingly creepy. One of the largest sections was about great wolves and racing them.

"Interested?"

Donovan closed the book with a start, which sprayed dust into the air and caused him to sneeze a few times before finally turning to whomever spoke. There stood an older feynar, who wore a bright white robe over his dark purple skin. He looked almost like a priest of K'var, except that he was fey and male. He had a white teacup in his hand and lines of steam rose from it.

"It doesn't hold up to its promise on the cover."

The feynar nodded as he took a sip of his drink. "I feel the same way about many books. Tea?"

"No thanks, I'm having dinner soon; not sure I can stay for tea."

"Well, that is good, because I was only being polite. I hate it when people say yes. I offer them one cup of this," the feynar indicated with his teacup, "and they never ask again."

"Then why do you drink it?"

"Medicinal purposes," the feynar took a sip and winced. That reminded Donovan of the herbal mixtures Eodius had given him. "My name is Alden, and you are?"

"Donovan."

"You caused quite the stir with your entrance yesterday. I was impressed."

"Impressed? With what exactly?"

"That you would have the gall to come here at such a time as this."

"I wish I could claim that, but I had no idea what I was getting into. I was ordered to come here."

Alden raised a brow. "Why is that?"

Donovan smirked. "Medicinal purposes."

Alden's lips parted into a wide grin. "Well then, I look forward to dining with you this evening at the Great Tree. Until then, I have a few things to finish before the king summons us both."

"It was good to meet you."

Alden nodded and waved goodbye. Donovan figured that gesture must have crossed over to fey culture. Or maybe it was the other way around. Before he got far, though, Alden turned around.

"Donovan, one more thing."

"Yes?"

"If the king agrees to your request, he could lose Fallavon. You know that, yes?"

Donovan furrowed his brow. "He didn't mention that; he just said he was taking a risk."

"Yes, a very large one. If it had been up to me, I would have done exactly as the Grand Magistrate tried to do. You are lucky I am not king."

Alden turned once again to walk off. Donovan didn't say anything more. The tone in the feynar's voice held a strange lack of animosity for what was just said. Alden was speaking rationally, while the Grand Magistrate had acted out of self-interest. *Is King Beldon really considering risking it all...for Nightingale?*

Chapter Eighteen

The meal branch did not look like Donovan expected. It was very small, not at all like the great dining halls of kings Donovan had imagined. He asked one of the servants about this, who explained that major feasts and festivals were held in the courtyard outside. This was the more toned down, private dining quarters of the king and queen.

The oval shaped room had four windows, two on each of the long sides, which were currently covered by long white curtains. Even with the leaves breaking up the light and the curtains drawn, the light of the setting sun still made it through.

Donovan was shown to his seat, which was a patch of grass grown in a large circle. Sticking up out of the grass in front of him was a wooden stand shaped like a vine, growing out of the ground with a petrified goldenleaf the size of a small shield budding out near the top.

He was the first one there, and it felt awkward to just sit and wait. It wouldn't hurt to look outside. Donovan walked to the nearest window, moved the curtain with the back of his hand, and saw the courtyard the servant had mentioned.

A few dozen feylas were out there dancing, their long, colorful dresses streaming through the air, mirroring their movements. They were stunning, both talented and beautiful. He had always been told the fey were barbarians, but apart from his spat with the Grand Magistrate, he had seen nothing but beauty.

Perhaps the Grand Magistrate represents more fey around here than I realize.

Donovan watched for several minutes, then returned to his place. He stood next to the petrified leaf and leaned down to run his fingers along the details.

"Admiring my handiwork?"

Donovan turned and saw the queen had entered the room. He bowed. "Your majesty."

"My name is Philantha. Welcome to our home." This feyla, Philantha, spoke similarly to Selena—flowing, yet deliberate. "Your manners are appreciated, Donovan. But please, be seated. You are a guest here." Queen Philantha walked over to the walls and pulled on the strings connected to the white curtains, opening them wide and allowing the pleasant glow of the setting sun to illuminate the meal branch. Her yellow skin shone like gold in the light, and her pink hair took on a deeper hue in the orange light. "There, that is much better," she said as she brushed some dust off her white silk dress. "We usually do not open all of them. This is the first time in a while we have had real guests in Fallavon."

"I am thankful for your hospitality."

"It has been a long time since anything human has been in Fallavon," Queen Philantha said. "I think the last time was when Lady Samara brought in a group of masons to build her estate. You are a most welcome sight."

I am? Donovan wondered, trying to figure out what she meant. The queen turned her head and smiled when King Beldon entered the room.

"Where are our other guests?" he asked, a bit perplexed.

As if in answer, Rohawk entered, bowed quickly, and sat next to Donovan.

"It is good to see the both of you again," King Beldon said. "I hope you have had a little bit of time to relax and get comfortable."

"Not sure about comfortable, but intriguing," Donovan answered. The queen cocked her head in a questioning pose.

"Intriguing?"

"I met the librarian." Both king and queen nodded slowly in recognition.

"Your city is nicer than most," Rohawk put in. "I've seen fey clans that live in tents."

"I am glad we could offer better accommodations than nomads," the queen said with half closed eyes. Rohawk grinned, but she added, "I will take your comment as an approval of my work."

"Your work?" Rohawk asked.

"It is my job to make sure that the city looks and is beautiful," she answered. "Much of Fallavon was grown with only function in mind, as is fitting for a struggling clan. But we are not strugglers in these Fey Wilds. It has taken years of work, but the beauty of our Great Tree is a testament to the changes around here. The old one was purchased by the Grand Magistrate."

"Very ugly, that thing," the king added. "I think it went to the most fitting person around here."

"Beldon," the queen gently scolded. King Beldon walked close to the Queen and put his arms around her, with his head above hers and resting on her soft hair.

"All the more of a reminder for me how fortunate I am to be married to the most beautiful creation in the world."

Queen Philantha chuckled and received the compliment warmly while her eyes glazed over. Then, at the same time, the two seemed to remember there were others in the room.

"I hope tonight is the first of several meals we will get to share together," the King said to Rohawk and Donovan. "Please get comfortable. Our other guests will be here soon."

"Other guests?" Donovan asked and was answered when Glyn walked in the room. He was a bit surprised; the king had made it sound like this was to be a private dinner between him and the delegation from Nightingale.

The feynar bowed quickly, then stood up straight and said, "My father thanks you, King Beldon, for your intervention today."

Rohawk sniffed. "So is this a 'I'm sorry my Grand Magistrate tried to have you killed' dinner?"

King Beldon chuckled. "That title is more or less accurate, but a bit long to fit on an invitation. Glyn, please be seated. Deltra will be here soon. He is my right-hand feynar, and I would like all of you to get to know him."

Deltra showed up around a minute after King Beldon made the comment. After giving his apologies for his lateness, he took his seat. Food was immediately brought in, and Donovan's hunger was rekindled when he caught the smells of it. There was venison for sure, along with beef and turkey, accompanied by a lot of strange fruits he did not recognize. One looked like a large pear, except it was a golden yellow with blue dots. Another was something like a tomato, but it was also the same golden yellow as the pear, and it appeared that the vine was left attached to it and it been fried for eating.

Apples were the one fruit Donovan found familiar, and the hot green beans were also something he had enjoyed before. When one of the servants came to Donovan's tray with the last of the food, the plate was filled with more than he could eat.

He wondered if he was supposed to eat with his fingers, and looked around for utensils. A servant left a pair of pointed, wooden sticks on his tray. Each was about half the length of an arrow and as thick as the pupil of a man's eye. Donovan looked over at King Beldon and saw the feynar spearing the food with the sticks to bring them up to his mouth.

There were a few minutes of just eating then King Beldon started the conversation.

"So, Donovan, tell me—do you know where you were born? I have been to Driggon more than once; you look like you could be from there."

"That is everyone's guess."

"Well, where did you grow up?" Queen Philantha asked.

"To be honest, I don't remember."

King Beldon leaned over and whispered something to the queen, and she gave a nod of acknowledgment.

"That is very odd indeed," Deltra said suspiciously. "You don't know anything about your past?"

"Do not be rude, Deltra," Queen Philantha chided. "It is a byproduct of human magic."

Deltra nodded and said, "Forgive my rudeness, Donovan."

"It's alright," Donovan said dismissively.

"Where do *you* come from, Rohawk?" the queen asked.

"Velmar," Rohawk answered with food still in his mouth. He seemed far less concerned with court manners now than before.

"What part of Velmar?" King Beldon added.

"Deldamore."

"Ah yes," King Beldon said. "I have heard good things about that place. Is it true that the people there live by a code of honor?"

Rohawk's green eyes looked cold. "The people do. Their rulers do not."

"If the ruler does not please the people," Glyn started, "the people should take matters into their own hands and put a new leader on the throne."

"Good luck," Rohawk said in a dry tone.

Deltra seemed pleasantly intrigued by Rohawk. Glyn, on the other hand, studied the man with a look that sized him up as a possible threat.

"Speaking of wine, this is excellent," Rohawk said as he held up his silver cup and took another drink.

The queen chuckled at his obvious change of subject.

"I heard fey had the poorest taste for drinks," Rohawk continued, "but this is making me reconsider."

"I had it brought out for this special occasion," King Beldon said. "However, that does not mean there are no other drinks worth having. I encourage you to try some of our ale—you might be surprised."

"With your recommendation, my King, I would most definitely be willing to sample any drink. Send some to my room tonight, preferably strong."

Everyone in the room laughed at least a little. There was a quick, unspoken interchange between Rohawk and the queen, and Donovan felt certain she'd picked up on the fact that he was serious.

There was some more light conversation after that, and when the meal seemed almost over, King Beldon dismissed the servants and ordered them to shut the doors on the way out. Donovan felt a shift in the mood.

"As long as we keep our voices down, we shall have privacy," King Beldon said. "After some deliberation with Deltra, I have decided to let Glyn in on our plans. Tomorrow, Deltra will discreetly take you three to the hideout. But before that happens, I figured it would be best if he told you a bit more about how our army is formed." King Beldon nodded at Deltra, and he turned to address Donovan, Rohawk, and Glyn.

"I am the Grand Magistrate's chief executioner," Deltra started. "Since most fey executions are private, unlike today, I have been rescuing people the Grand Magistrate condemns, instead of killing them as he orders me to. We've been hiding these people so that, while the Grand Magistrate thinks they are dead, they are increasing the size of our army. It has also provided me a safe way to spare their lives without Vinson discovering my secret."

"When were you supposed to do this for me?" Glyn asked.

"Like I said," Deltra answered slowly, "I did not think your execution would be public. And I never let anyone know what is going on before the time comes."

"Wait, I don't understand," Donovan started, confused. "King Beldon, why don't you just override all the executions, like you did today?"

"That has great political ramifications I need to avoid as much as possible," the king explained. "The Grand Magistrate is trying to paint me as some kind of tyrant, and I need to work against that image."

"I've been here for less than two days and I can see that's complete nonsense," Donovan said. He crossed his arms and added, "Why would anyone think that?"

"Politics," Deltra said, as if the one word summed up the entire answer. Perhaps it did.

"Could you not just order the Grand Magistrate to be executed?" Donovan asked. "Wouldn't that solve the problem?"

The room got cold.

"Teching Booooooones," Rohawk said, drawing out the word. "Donovan the black-hearted."

Donovan's cheeks went red. "I did not mean to be so blunt. Forgive me. I only meant that he seems to have done plenty wrong to deserve it, and that's the kind of thing that would happen in most human kingdoms."

"Likely," King Beldon agreed. "And in most fey clans, it would be the same way. But we have established a rule of law here in Fallavon, and without some sort of legal ground, it would be murder. And besides, if the heart of the people is not truly with me, they may not approve of the execution, and revolt."

Donovan uncrossed his arms, trying not to look uncomfortable. "He tried to kill me today, unjustly. That seems at least worthy of prison."

"I do not question that you would have some justification for doing so, Donovan," King Beldon said in an even tone. "But you do not know what you would do in my position, because you do not know everything that is at play."

Glyn cleared his throat. "I am not sure my father would approve of me being part of your stowaway army, my King. Is that where I would be now if everything had gone according to plan?"

"Not necessarily, Glyn," Deltra answered. "While the king was away, I only wanted to keep you alive, not draft you into our ranks. I had planned a pardon for you all along, but things got out of hand. We would like you to see what we have going on and let your father know. Lord Jaager's support is most appreciated in these uncertain times."

Glyn crossed his arms but looked more thoughtful than bothered.

Rohawk leaned over to Donovan's ear. "They want to make sure Lord Jaager knows which side is smart to be on."

"Glyn, we will force nothing on you," the king put in, "but if you would humor Deltra and myself for one evening we would like you to meet some of the people the Grand Magistrate has tried to murder. I think it will show you and your father exactly what kind of feynar he is."

"We will see," Glyn said, not committing one way or another with his tone.

"Yes, we will. I think perhaps tomorrow night would—" An urgent knock on the door interrupted the conversation.

King Beldon shouted, "Enter."

When the door opened, an out-of-breath servant ran forward and bowed quickly.

"What is it? Speak!" King Beldon commanded. The feynar replied frantically in feyspeak. King Beldon's face hardened, while Queen Philantha looked concerned. The king stood up quickly and said, "Deltra, come with me. The rest of you, stay here."

"I am coming with you," the queen said. King Beldon nodded at her, then the three of them left with the servant.

Donovan looked at Rohawk. He had his hands on the back of his head and looked a little bit tipsy, but he shifted his eyes and motioned toward the exit with his head. He tumbled backward from his seated position and popped up on his feet. Though not quite as graceful, Donovan mimicked the motion and was on his feet as well. Rohawk gave him a brief smile, then the two of them began to follow a little way behind King Beldon and the rest. Glyn came as well, and soon everyone was outside and headed toward the center of the city.

A crowd had gathered around a feynar who was speaking loud, angry words in the fey tongue.

When Donovan and the rest had caught up, King Beldon reminded them that they were to stay put, but he didn't make any more complaints when Donovan started asking questions.

"What is this feynar talking about?" he asked.

"He is complaining about how I rebuked the Grand Magistrate and let traitors into the Great Tree," King Beldon answered.

"Standard revolutionary propaganda," Deltra joked. King Beldon frowned at Deltra, but said nothing in reply.

Everyone kept listening intently, and it bothered Donovan that he could not understand what the man was saying. He was hushed every time he asked, which only made his curiosity and irritation worse.

The revolutionary turned toward him and Rohawk, standing at the edge of the crowd. His shouting intensified, accompanied by violent hand gestures. Donovan looked at King Beldon for an interpretation.

"He is calling you out for a fist fight. He wants to test your strength."

"Seriously?" Donovan asked. "Like a drunken brawl? Am I supposed to accept?"

"You can't seriously be drunk after only one cup of wine," Rohawk muttered.

"I was making a comparison."

King Beldon put up a hand to interrupt them and said, "It is your decision, Donovan. These kinds of duels are common under old fey customs, customs I have tried to do away with. But my people still honor them, so I must do the same." Donovan sighed but slowly stepped through the crowd of people and came face to face with the shouting feynar.

The feynar hit Donovan with a quick jab to the chest, sending him stumbling back. He realized that the feynar would see that as weakness and strike again. Quickly regaining his footing, he sidestepped the second punch and grabbed the feynar's wrist, using his momentum to throw him. The feynar recovered quicker than Donovan expected, and the fight turned into a series of blows back and forth.

The first major hit was when Donovan landed a solid punch in the feynar's stomach, which caused him to double over in pain. Donovan was going to press his advantage, but he felt his sight blurring. The feynar looked like...*Toby?* Donovan thought. It was Toby, sort of. His eyes were replaced with the eyes of a serpent.

"Come on, let it go," Donovan said to the feynar. He did not like these strange visions and was worried he would lose control like he did with the Grand Magistrate. "Let's just resolve this and walk away."

The feynar did not accept. He recovered and swept a leg under a confused Donovan, who fell to the ground in a daze. He heard cheering and more shouting in the fey tongue.

A voice broke through it all, saying, "Donovan? Are you alright?" It was Queen Philantha's voice. Donovan snapped out of his thoughts and opened his eyes. Her beautiful yellow face filled his view. She looked worried.

Meanwhile, the ugly crowd had moved on as their cheers and jeers sounded from farther and farther away.

"Why did you stop fighting?" This voice was Glyn's. "You had him with that punch. You should have forced him to surrender, not ask him politely." Donovan didn't answer that. It would have been difficult to explain all his thoughts, and he had no interest in sharing them with Glyn anyway.

"What was he yelling about after he knocked me down?"

"About how humans are weak, and I am weak for trying to ally with them," King Beldon answered. "He is nothing but rabble, using the fight to make his point seem conclusive."

"I guess it worked," Donovan said with a moan.

"Perhaps," King Beldon said. "Perhaps for those stupid enough to follow along."

"Do not say such things, my husband," Queen Philantha calmly rebuked. "People will not follow a king who believes them to be stupid."

King Beldon only nodded in agreement, but Donovan could tell that the matter was not settled. The queen gave her husband a strange look, and it seemed there was some sort of unspoken conversation happening between her and the king.

"Not yet," King Beldon said to her.

"Yes, not yet," she said.

"In the meantime, we should all return to the Great Tree. Deltra and I will meet to properly assess what just happened."

While Donovan was being taken care of, or, more accurately, mothered, by the queen and a few servant girls, Rohawk had slipped away to follow King Beldon and Deltra. He wanted to know what the king meant by meeting to "properly assess" the situation. It sounded like the kind of thing powerful people say when they are about to kill someone.

King Beldon and Deltra had gone to a private room in the Great Tree. Rohawk had figured out that speaking the common tongue was a trick the king used to enhance secrecy, and he was hoping that was the case now. He pressed his ear up against the door. It was grown with a fey enchantment called knockwood, which made sound difficult to pass through. Many human kingdoms brought in fey craftsmen to make it. Deldamore had one, back when he had been allowed in the castle there.

There was a trick though. Rohawk put his ear up to the door and put a palm flat on another section. He felt a tingle as the fey magic gently sang through his body, and with it came sound from the room.

"I shall keep my concerns as brief as possible, your majesty, so as not to waste your time." Deltra's voice came through, muffled but definitely him. "Do you think it at all wise what you are doing with these humans?"

"What do you mean?"

"Beg pardon, your majesty, but you saw what happened today. Your people's hatred for humans has been stirred ever since you led your campaign against the Kaldarans ten years ago. And can you blame them? The Kaldarans attacked *us*! You were the hero-king who was known for killing humans. Now they see you as a pacifist, trying to ally with other human kingdoms."

"The war was just in many ways, but I was greedy in my conquest," King Beldon said with a sigh. "If Kaldaran goes to war with us again, we will have very little help. I wish the people of the Lion Clan could see that. I have burned a lot of bridges, and the fey clans willing to ally with us are few and small."

"And you think this Nightingale delegation is the answer?" Deltra asked. "Defeat the Kaldarans attacking Nightingale and people will see you as strong."

"That was part of my thinking. It seems a good option to fight Kaldaran without being officially at war. And those who interfered with our war last time will not fault us for protecting a city in need. But it is a risk, and it still does not solve all our other problems. I wish the people of Fallavon could see there is so much untapped potential in the human spirit. If you could see the castles they have built, the machines and the tools they use to harvest food and gold, the fine weapons they craft—they are unlike anything the fey have ever made. How can we as fey stand a chance against these human kingdoms, fractured as we are, and with little to no innovation in our warfare?"

"What we lack in tools we make up for in strength."

"If that were true, the humans would not outnumber us ten to one in Drannus. I may be foolish, but I believe that the answer to our problems here in Fallavon lies deep somewhere in human ingenuity. Nightingale has that ingenuity. Merchants pass through there all the time selling human fighting machines. You told me yourself when you were there years ago."

"But do you think it will be enough to build a pact between human and fey? The Grand Magistrate offers war and pillaging as his method to strengthen our clan. It may be barbaric, but it is what the people know. They do not understand human technology, nor the idea that their machines could make us any better. And every king who has tried to unite the clans has failed, you know this."

"Yes, I do," King Beldon said, his low tone hinting at the gravity in the statement. "But a lot of fey are already moving away to live in human kingdoms, and some are even interbreeding with them. A time is coming, Deltra, where tribalism will be extinct, and nations will be made up of people from all kinds of blood. I have heard Velmar is already more like this."

"Perhaps you should ask Rohawk how that has worked out for him, then. He did not seem too pleased with Deldamore."

Rohawk was annoyed by that comment, but it was accurate.

"If we keep identifying ourselves by our tribal bonds, we will be snuffed out," the king continued. "Not necessarily by war, but by the prosperity of the kingdoms wise enough to see that tribalism leads to no good end. Despite the wars popping up right now, the humans have been trading and learning from each other, and their lives are better for it."

"And you think these two humans will do that? Show us all how to better our lives?" Deltra sounded annoyed. "Forgive my skepticism, your majesty, but as your military advisor, you said you wanted me to challenge your thinking."

"I think these two newcomers have great potential," King Beldon said with excitement. "Both are very intelligent. Donovan is soulburned, but has more spirit in him than any non-burned human I have ever met. Rohawk is a bit worrisome, but he knows a thousand times more than he lets on. I think he is a Shadow Walker."

Rohawk nearly gasped. King Beldon was far wiser than he had originally attributed.

"I do not agree with your assessment of Donovan. His shrouded past is good reason for more skepticism, not less. Do you know he is telling the truth? The Seal of Nightingale he came with checked out, but that doesn't mean he is personally a good man."

"I understand your doubts well, my good friend, but did you not see what happened? He hesitated on that feynar when he had the chance to press the attack. That means he can control his strength. Should we not follow his example?"

"What do you plan to do, then?"

"I plan to be good on my word to Nightingale, but while we make preparations, I would like to see Donovan and Rohawk interact as much with our people as possible."

"Even Rohawk? All the man does is take baths."

Rohawk stifled a laugh.

"There is much more to him than that. He needs his curiosity piqued in order to act. And even if he does us no favors, I do not think he is going to turn to the Grand Magistrate. I saw defiance in his eyes at the execution, and he had already slipped his restraints."

"What if this does not all go as planned? What if the people of Fallavon hate Donovan and Rohawk and this whole thing backfires and starts the war?"

"Do not worry about those things for now. We will teach Donovan a few things, along with some skills for fighting in the fey style, and that will be a good start. I want him to know how to work alongside our soldiers for the upcoming battle. Once we liberate Nightingale, I plan to ask for his help here in Fallavon."

"But you did not make that part of the deal. How do you know he will accept?"

"I have a way, Deltra. That is all you need to know for now."

"As you wish, your majesty," Deltra said.

Rohawk was about to leave, fearing Deltra was coming out, but as he was pulling his hand away he heard the king say something and he pressed his ear and hand to the door again.

"One more thing, Deltra. I want to be clear on this."

"Your majesty?"

"If this leads to war, I am ready. And if anyone thinks I have grown soft since fighting Kaldaran, they will be the first casualties in the fight."

Chapter Nineteen

"Wear these," Deltra said as he handed Donovan, Rohawk, and Glyn a set of large cloaks, one a bright red, another a bright orange, and the last one a solid blue. "You will blend in better with those, trust me. Just keep the hoods up so no one can see your faces."

It was the day after Donovan's fist fight with the feynar on the street, and they were gearing up for their trip to visit the so-called secret army.

"Yes, best keep the feylas from swooning," Rohawk said as he flipped up his hood.

Donovan smiled and did the same. He had to adjust it a few times to get it to fit just right, while Glyn and Deltra put their cloaks on with mechanical familiarity. Deltra motioned them to follow, and the group left the Great Tree. Donovan was a bit nervous, but the other three were as calm as ever.

How does Rohawk manage to stay so cool in unfamiliar situations? he wondered.

It was now afternoon. The sun poured down in between the tree branches, which were pruned to allow more sunlight in during the day. Breakfast that morning had been excellent in terms of food, but lacking in conversation. The king and queen were too busy to attend, and the dialogue between Donovan, Rohawk, Deltra, and Glyn had been flat. Rohawk was the only one who had offered any bit of enjoyable remarks, but it was only because he told some wild story about catching a runaway horse. He was good at storytelling—even Glyn laughed once.

The center of Fallavon was no quiet place, being the hotspot for all the vendors. The heart of Fallavon's economy beat rapidly to the noise of the wooden coins sliding across desks, interspersed with the chatter of people haggling. A drink bought here, a shirt sold there—it all felt familiar to Donovan. No one took much notice of them. Deltra had been right about the cloaks blending them in.

After a while, the noise began to die out ever so slowly, and Donovan noticed how quiet the space around them had turned. They were entering a much sleepier part of Fallavon. By the time Deltra said they were nearing the hideout, there wasn't much to be heard. Fey quietly shuffled around in their ratted clothes, dirt across their faces and hands. Their backs were bent, some from age and others from what seemed to be the lack of will to stand upright. They passed by a feynar who was staggering his way back to wherever he slept.

There were a few who brightened at the sight of Deltra, and one man, a beggar by the looks of it, actually ran to Deltra to embrace him. It was obvious that he was excited amidst the flood of fey words that Donovan did not understand. Deltra spoke to the beggar and introduced Donovan, Rohawk, and Glyn. The beggar nodded with instant acceptance for each name and face.

The group started moving again, now with the beggar amongst their numbers, and Donovan decided it was time he was given a little explanation about this place.

"Where are we?"

"The poorest slum in all of Fallavon," Deltra said.

"I can't believe Queen Philantha allows this," Glyn said indignantly.

"You may want to change your tone," Deltra warned. "This section of the city is managed by the Grand Magistrate."

"How does that work?" Rohawk asked.

"The Lion Clan is ruled by both king and council, which I know is unheard of for a fey clan. The council consists of six members, including the Grand Magistrate, who is the council's head. The council members are the noblefey. Each one is in charge of governing his or her section of the city, while the king governs them all." Rohawk scoffed.

"Why, in the names of the gods, would you have the blasted hideout amid the Grand Magistrate's direct control?"

"A bird may as well build his nest on the ground," Donovan added.

"Maybe not," Deltra countered. "Out of all the people in Fallavon who support the Grand Magistrate, you will find almost none of them here. They know firsthand what it is like to be under his rule. They don't want to see more of it."

"This is unbelievable," Glyn said. "I never liked the Grand Magistrate but I did not know how bad it was. Someone needs to change this."

"Are you offering?" Deltra retorted.

"Put me in charge," Rohawk joked. "Or better yet, what about Donovan? He would make quite the Grand Magistrate!"

Everyone but Donovan laughed, even the beggar chuckled when he could tell the others had heard something funny.

"I'll pass on that," Donovan said with a sigh.

Deltra slowed down to a stop and whistled a tune to the surrounding trees.

"What is that tune?" Rohawk asked.

"You will see," Deltra whispered. "For now, silence."

Rohawk seemed genuinely curious for a moment, but then skeptical as the silence hung in the air for a good ten seconds.

Before he could speak up, the whistle was answered by another. Then Deltra whistled one more time, and a couple of feynars came out from behind a nearby tangled mess of tree roots and rocks.

"This is it," Deltra answered. "Come."

At first, it looked like Deltra was leading them into the impassable overgrowth, but the two new feynars concentrated with their hands outstretched to the roots. A strange blue aura emitted from them. The overgrowth bent away to reveal the remains of an old stone courtyard. Time had worn down what had clearly been a marvel in its day. Wild grass had taken its vengeance on the old stones and roots grew up and around, as if the stone wasn't there to begin with.

Donovan imagined what kind of festivals might have taken place upon the old stone. It seemed like a shame to see it aged and destroyed.

Glyn seemed to pick up on that, and said, "There was once great joy in this place. That time is gone."

"Deltra, why did you bring us here?" Donovan asked. While he was still speaking, there came a clicking sound and a rumbling from underneath. A piece of the stone shifted and revealed stairs descending into darkness.

"You will see," Deltra answered. "Come." The group shuffled down the dirty stone steps. The darkness swallowed them all as their eyes worked to adjust to the low light provided by fey torches—floating orbs held in place with glass cases attached to the walls, made up of pure, magical fey energy that emitted a soft blue glow. The glass was a type of crystal that contained the energy for a day or two until it needed to be recharged.

Deltra and Glyn both removed their hoods, so Rohawk and Donovan did the same.

A little bit farther in, the air turned musty. The air in Fallavon seemed so clean and sweet, and now there was the scent of dust, mold, and dirt. The steps ended and they entered what looked like a wooden tunnel.

The group took a turn around a corner, and immediately came upon a giant room, perhaps the size of the throne room, but with a much lower ceiling. The rings, marks, bumps, and colors on the floor looked like they were made from giant roots that been grown side by side, then hollowed out.

The room was half-filled with several dozen feynars and feylas scattered all over, each paired off with someone for skirmishes. Everyone had something to practice with, even if it was their own hands. It didn't take long for Donovan to notice that many in the room had stopped their sparring to examine the newcomers. Others didn't seem to care, and continued their practice as usual, lost completely in the focus of their close matches.

There wasn't much for furnishings in the room. One side had six tables set low for people to sit on the ground and eat. A dozen barrels with weapon racks on the walls above were opposite that, all grown in place. Dull wooden weapons stuck out of the barrels and a few bows were on the wall racks. The rest were in the hands of fey doing archery practice on the far end, opposite the entrance. A small barrel—this one not grown in—was filled with the feathered fletching of arrows sticking out of the top.

"Deltra, it is good to see you," said a feyla, who stopped her practicing to say hello. She smiled, but her kindness seemed a bit out of place with her strong, orange arms, tight with black veins from intense practice. Her purple ponytail rested upon very out of place plate-mail shoulder pads, connected to a shimmering chest piece that bore the symbol of a howling blue wolf. The eye of the wolf was an intense orange color and pulsed with enchantment. Elementium metal was safe to the touch for fey, but it was rare and hard to come by. Even rarer for a fey to have a full suit of armor.

When the feyla had taken a few steps closer, she rested the spear tip of her large halberd on the ground and leaned a little bit of her weight on it. A brown colored stone was embedded into the base of the axe head. "What brings you here today, friend?" the warrior feyla asked. "And with..." her expression soured when she looked at Donovan. "With such strange company."

"These are some of King Beldon's special guests," Deltra answered. "Perhaps you would like to introduce yourself?"

"If I must," the feyla said to Deltra, then turned her eyes past him to Donovan, Rohawk, and Glyn. "Hail to you, brothers. May your back never be to your enemy. My name is Altera, First Wolf to King Selor of the Wolf Clan in the West."

"It is good to meet you, Princess Altera," Rohawk said with a grin.

Princess? Donovan thought. *Is that what First Wolf meant?*

"My name is Rohawk, of Deldamore in Velmar," he added.

Altera's expression softened a bit. She seemed intrigued—or maybe impressed—by Rohawk. She said nothing more to him, though, and looked over at Glyn. He gave a curt greeting, and she responded in kind. She turned to Donovan last.

"My name is Donovan, I am a soldier and, I suppose, a diplomat from Nightingale." Altera turned her nose up.

"A Driggonite, by the look of you, yes?"

Deltra suddenly cut in. "We are here to speak with the good general. Where is he?"

"General Kadin is in the meal branch," Altera said, her eyes still on Donovan. "He is enjoying what he calls a break."

"Heh, when the general takes a break, everyone gets a break," Deltra said as he eyed a couple of feynars sitting against a wall. He shouted at them in feyspeak, and they jumped to their feet and resumed practice. Altera shook her head.

"Do not be so uptight, Deltra. General Kadin works us all hard enough as is. A little rest will not hurt anything."

"Fair enough." Deltra called out again in feyspeak, and this time everyone in the room took a break. "Everything will resume when we are done speaking with General Kadin."

"It most certainly will," Altera said, still glaring daggers at Donovan. She moved over to a group of feyla soldiers who started helping her out of her armor.

"Chilly in here," Rohawk mumbled to Donovan.

"My thoughts exactly."

Deltra led the group toward a doorway on the opposite end of the room, away from where some of the now-resting fey warriors were heading. General Kadin sat cross-legged on the ground eating a loaf of bread and drinking some cheap ale. Donovan could tell it was cheap because, after taking a gulp, he tossed the mug against the wall and muttered a curse. His skin was a light shade of green, and his hair hung down in red strands. Many scars cut back and forth on his large arms, and there was one on his cheek.

"General Kadin," Deltra addressed.

General Kadin's sour face untwisted into a smile when he saw his friend. He said something in feyspeak that sounded like a greeting, then looked at

Rohawk and said, "Humans? Why do you have humans with you? The last time I saw humans I was chopping them up limb from limb!"

Donovan felt very uncomfortable with that, but Rohawk didn't seem to mind. He stepped forward and introduced himself.

"I'm Rohawk, and don't worry about forgetting it. It will be on the lips of every maiden in Fallavon soon enough."

General Kadin laughed, a scratchy yet hearty belly laugh. "A sly one you bring me, Deltra!" He laughed more, then turned his eyes to Glyn.

"Glyn," was all he said. "We have met before." General Kadin eyed him carefully but nodded.

"What about this last one?" the general asked, noting Donovan.

"Donovan, I'm from Nightingale."

"That all? The other human gets the lips of maidens and all you have is Nightingale?" General Kadin smiled, but Donovan felt a sting in that comment. *I can't remember anything* but *Nightingale...*

"General Kadin," Deltra started, "please tell these three everything you know about Vinson's army here in Fallavon."

"That is a long list, Deltra," General Kadin said with a sigh. "Can I trust human blood? I still remember when his father and I," the general's head motion indicated Glyn, "shed it across the golden leaves. And from what I have heard in the West, there have been quite a few altercations between humans and fey. Corrick has been encroaching on fey forests there now. We thought they had it bad when it was Driggon."

"These two humans were sent by King Beldon himself," Deltra said.

General Kadin nodded. "Alright, then, I will question it no more. You all may as well sit down." The other four joined General Kadin on the ground. "It was not all that long ago when King Beldon decided it was time to restore the relationship between fey and humans. Have you heard of the war we had with Kaldaran?"

"Yes, I've heard of it," Donovan answered. "It started about fourteen years ago and lasted for four. Not exactly ancient history."

"Especially for the fey," General Kadin added. "Kaldaran attacked the Fey Wilds without provocation—but that was and is Kaldaran. They are a barbarian kingdom and have only grown so large because of their tenuous connection to the god for which the kingdom is named. If it were up to me, they would be called Bastardians, but my suggestion was kindly rejected the last time I offered it."

"Nice," Rohawk mumbled.

"King Beldon himself was much more of a charging bull back then, when it came to beginning wars, but Kaldaran had it coming. Our most eastern city, Feydun, was sacked, and survivors reported feylas being dragged away. It was that second part that sent King Beldon into a rage."

"A rage?" Donovan asked. He thought about the king he had seen back at the execution block.

"He has a mighty temper, he does," the general answered. "Beautiful thing to behold. It was under the power of that temper that King Beldon led us to victory again and again. When the Kaldarans returned, we repelled them. Their iron weapons and human magic gave us trouble, but our great wolves—we call them *Ferlons*—ran circles around their horses. We pressed our advantage, attacked the forward camp they had established, and reclaimed our prisoners. Most of them, anyway."

"Most of them?" Donovan asked.

"Wish I could say all. So does the king. I have never before seen a feynar as angry and as strong as King Beldon. He was unstoppable in battle. I once watched him kick a charging horse hard enough to stop it in its tracks. I never laughed so hard in my entire life. Nearly got killed doing so."

"You or the king?" Rohawk asked. The general put his finger on the ground like he was drawing out a map of the battles.

"Both, at the time. But I am getting sidetracked. Having pushed the Kaldarans back through a series of victories, King Beldon went to rally the fey clans together under one banner, to attack Kaldaran and destroy it, once and for all. But they refused, and that is when the king declared that he would unite the clans by bloodshed. It was all-out war with the Lion Clan against all others—almost. Our one ally was Queen Drusilla of the Goldenleaf Clan. She agreed that Kaldaran needed to be destroyed. Her alliance with King Beldon shocked the other clans—she was known for having a gentle and kind soul. But underneath her public image was a warrior. She was a fierce ally with a keen tactical mind."

"General, this is getting long," Deltra said.

"My apologies," the General said with a nod. "I have already left out great detail, but I will keep the rest brief. King Beldon's war to unite the clans was mostly successful, but Kaldaran rallied, and they pulled an act of trickery. They enlisted the help of the Gledalai, the water spirits, who then convinced Dadock that we were the aggressors. This new coalition of

Dadock, the Gledalai, and Kaldaran, reinforced the remaining fey clans. That was when we had a real war on our hands. With the arrival of troops from Dadock, our army had to fight its hardest just to keep the ground we had gained. We failed. We lost ground in the Fey Wilds day by day. We could have had one of our allies cut off the flow of Dadockian soldiers from the north, but there was one problem with that."

"Which was?" Donovan asked.

"We did not *have* any allies up north," Deltra answered dryly. "Only more enemies."

"Exactly," General Kadin agreed. "King Beldon refused to make peace or surrender. By that time, he had convinced a few small fey clans to his side, and he spat in the face of destiny. He rallied the Lion Clan, Goldenleaf Clan, Behemoth Clan, and Thunderbird Clan in one final push against the fortified Fox Clan city, Rahana. He nearly took the city, but he was not quick enough. Dadock pressed in with its cavalry and stopped King Beldon's advance. It was a horrible battle, and with King Beldon's coalition already weakened, and Dadock being propped up by the Gledalai, it became a bloodbath stalemate with both sides losing enough warriors to keep at equal strength. King Beldon was mortally wounded, bleeding out, and alone, too far behind enemy lines. Princess Philantha of the Fox Clan found him, and against his wishes, she mended his wounds."

Donovan leaned forward. "I think I am getting this confused—didn't you just say the Fox Clan was the one King Beldon was attacking? And how does the Lion Clan council fit into all of this? Did they approve of the king's actions?"

"You are not confused at all. Princess Philantha did a very noble thing that day. Some might say to aid an enemy is treason, but most saw it as a remarkable act of kindness. And no council existed in Fallavon at that time. It was only after that did King Beldon change his ways. He married Philantha, established the council of the Lion Clan, and decided to offer peace."

"And the other clans just accepted it?" Rohawk asked. "What about Dadock and Kaldaran?"

The next sentence came out of the General's mouth as if there was gravel in it. "To their credit, the Gledalai forced the other two human kingdoms to honor a peace treaty without taking the Lion Clan for all it was worth. The other clans agreed to peace after that. The clans will continue to honor it, but the peace between our clan and the humans is fragile."

"I don't mean to be rude," Rohawk said, "but why exactly are you telling us all of this?"

The General crossed his massive arms and looked over at Deltra. "The way Deltra explains it, you two are looking for help from the Lion Clan. I figure if you want our help, you should understand our history, and understand why you coming here has shaken up the city like a hornet's nest."

"No kidding," Glyn mumbled.

"The Grand Magistrate Vinson says the Lion Clan was 'too quick' to make peace," the general said over Glyn's mumbling. "And that the Gledalai cheated us out of our right to have our war with the humans. The worst part is, he is completely right about the Gledalai cheating us—even King Beldon himself still harbors anger toward them. But the king is insistent on prospering without more war, at least for the moment. The Grand Magistrate wants to reunite the clans who had joined us before, and possibly get the rest. Then he would lead a unified fey clan and go destroy Kaldaran before the Gledalai and Dadockians can even do anything about it."

"Why not do that, then?" Donovan asked. "I have no love for the Grand Magistrate, but Kaldaran is out of control. They are attacking Nightingale and provoking war with K'var—which I find incredibly foolish. But they will get away with it if everyone else stands idly by. The fact that the Gledalai are doing nothing about that is absurd."

"I agree, but the wounds from the last war have yet to heal," Deltra said slowly, calmly. "That is why King Beldon wants to help Nightingale. It is our chance to show the world Kaldaran is a blight and fight them in the process."

"If we want a fight with Kaldaran, this is the worst way to do it," Glyn said dryly. "I think King Beldon should attack the Kingdom of Kaldaran while they have so many troops away in Nightingale."

"Yes, that is what your father wants," Deltra said to Glyn, his eyes locked in a glare. "He would like nothing more than to see King Beldon killed while attacking Kaldaran."

"No, that is completely untrue," Glyn rounded but remained calm. "I want what is best for Fallavon, and if King Beldon does not do that, then yes, I would be happy to support my father."

"You would do well to remember your true allegiance!" Deltra snapped.

"Easy, Deltra," the general said.

Glyn glared at Deltra. "There is a difference between allegiance and being a lapdog."

Deltra reached for his sword, but the general shouted, "Stand down, soldier!" His voice boomed through the underground like thunder. The sound of chatter coming from the halls outside suddenly ceased. Deltra slowly obeyed.

"Yes, General."

"Glyn," the general started, "thank you for speaking your mind. I think you should reconsider your position. I am a warrior myself, and I stand with King Beldon. You may think he is weak, but the lion is getting prepared to roar."

Glyn did not respond.

There was a short pause, then Rohawk asked, "So Fallavon is on the brink of civil war, but what are the people waiting for?"

"Impossible to say for sure," General Kadin said, knuckling his chin as he thought. "Most likely some act of violence will trigger the chaos, but a direct order may come about from either the king or the Grand Magistrate."

"How much support does the Grand Magistrate really have?" Rohawk asked.

"Majority of the noblemen, which is where the power lies," General Kadin answered in a grim tone. "Lady Samara is on our side. Lord Jaager is neutral."

Donovan noticed a shift in Rohawk when the General mentioned Lady Samara. He looked lost in thought, his brow furrowed in concentration.

The General was focused on Glyn, who shrugged and said, "My father would be angry if you said his allegiance was to anyone but King Beldon. However, I agree with your assessment."

"Lord Gorm is a major supporter of the Grand Magistrate, but his influence has been slipping," Deltra added. "However, that still leaves Lady Anna and Lord Acton who have shown the Grand Magistrate steady support. As far as the citizens, it is a jumbled mess. Vinson tends to pander to the poor in public, proclaiming that poverty would not exist here if Fallavon would go back to war and take what is 'rightfully ours.' He then turns around and says to the nobles that in order to keep the lower classes in firm control, they need to follow him. We have had little success warning people of his double-speak." The general nodded.

"Those who fought in the war want to fight Kaldaran again, but they are also smart enough to know how foolish it would be to fight Dadock and the Gledalai as well. But there is another concern that has recently come to my attention. I have it on good word that the Grand Magistrate has secured some elementium weapons."

"What?" Glyn breathed out. "From who?"

"We have been trying to figure that out," Deltra replied. "Our source on this is good, but did not get a good look at the weapons. All the source saw was steel being smuggled into the Grand Magistrate's estate, and if they were not elementium, then it would make no sense to get them."

"Do you have a plan for dealing with this?" Glyn asked, suddenly concerned.

Deltra raised his chin and seemed to be considering whether or not to answer. "Once we know where he is keeping these weapons, we will steal them."

"General?" Altera's voice sounded from the doorway. "The soldiers are getting lazy."

"Break time is over!" the General's voice boomed. The sound of rustling in the main room was the answer to it. "Good timing, I was hoping to see these three fight."

Donovan froze, his only movement to lick his suddenly dry lips.

"Fight?" Rohawk stretched. "About time I'm offered something fun."

"I suppose it has been a while since I last practiced," Glyn said in agreement.

"Then what better way to put you all to the test, but by the Hundred Blades? Come, let us get started!" General Kadin let out a good-hearted laugh and patted Donovan firmly on the shoulder.

"What's the 'Hundred Blades'?" Donovan asked.

"Come! We will show you!" General Kadin motioned with his hand. "Hundred Blades!" he shouted. The fey lined the outer wall of the room in a circle. General Kadin walked over to the barrels in the corner and withdrew two dull, wooden swords from one of them. He tossed both to Donovan, who was caught off guard by the action and failed to catch either one. General Kadin cringed; some of the fey laughed. Donovan tossed his cloak aside before reaching down to pick up the swords.

"A little warning next time," he mumbled.

"Donovan, take your place in the center of the room," General Kadin ordered. "There are about a hundred fey here with one blade each. They will come after you, trying to land a blow, beginning with one at a time, then two at a time, then they will be coming and going so quickly you won't be able to count. But I will be counting, all the way to a hundred. Your goal is to parry or avoid every single attack. Do not let one blade touch you or you fail."

"This is insane," Donovan complained, but he took his place in the middle of the room anyway.

"Listen to him complain," Altera said from her position along the wall. The feynar standing next to her laughed.

That made Donovan's blood boil.

"Ready?" General Kadin called out. The fey on the edge of the room readied themselves.

"I think so, but—" Donovan was cut off when General Kadin yelled something in feyspeak and one of the fey came running to where Donovan stood. His instinct kicked in and he easily turned the first attack.

"Excellent, Donovan!" General Kadin shouted. "Keep going!"

Donovan looked around, keeping his head on a swivel so he wouldn't be caught off guard. Another feynar charged, and Donovan blocked the attack with the same ease as before. The next dozen were about the same. He wasn't good with two-weapon fighting, but so far, he didn't need his left hand to keep up.

Then the practice intensified. Two fey came at the same time, and Donovan could only block one of their blades before he fumbled his offhand weapon and was struck in the back of his knee. He fell to the ground with a thud and a groan. All the fey laughed uproariously. The blow had felt sharp—the blade had not been nearly as dull as the others, and he was bleeding.

Altera, the one who had struck Donovan said, "Not nearly as tough as I thought."

A vision clouded Donovan's eyes, and Altera morphed into a human man—but not Rohawk. The man was pale, with long black hair and the eyes of a dragon. With the speed of a lightning bolt, Donovan grabbed Altera's hand and pulled her to the ground, smacking her hard into the floor.

Donovan then held his hand at the feyla's throat, and breathed out, "Why did you follow me here?"

A collective gasp echoed through the room; Donovan felt the same sense of dread in the air as when he had faced King Santos.

The man—though part of him knew it was still Altera, all he could see was the man—got Donovan's hand off his neck enough to breathe out, "You cannot escape the wrath of Kaldar so easily! The shadowed one won't be there to save you the next time you catch my gaze!"

Donovan quickly regained his grasp, and shouted, "You're nothing more than a man! I will find a way to kill you!"

A blow to the head knocked Donovan out of the open vision and onto his back. He recovered and saw Rohawk standing next to Altera, who was struggling for air, but as the seconds went on, it seemed that she was regaining her breath.

"Are you teching insane?" Rohawk asked. It was one of the rare occasions he looked shocked.

Donovan was confused. Altera was giving him a death glare. He knew what he had done, but his mind was hazy.

"Twenty-one." General Kadin called out as he walked over to give Donovan a hand up. He took it, but the general spun his arm around and locked it against Donovan's back. "You need to learn to temper that anger before you hurt someone. Do you understand me, pup?"

"Yes," he agreed, but the general raised Donovan's arm and he grunted loudly at the pain.

"Do. You. Understand. Me?" he repeated.

Donovan took a second despite the agony. Was this his true nature coming forward? Had he been someone bad, like Kristine was, before the soulburn? Could he really promise the general that he could control himself?

"I swear it!" he said. "I swear it!" He was saying the words as much to himself as the general. Altera had been rude to him, but she certainly didn't deserve what he had done. It terrified him.

There was a brief silence before General Kadin released Donovan. "I think that is enough for the day, Deltra. Best not to overwork our guests."

Chapter Twenty

The group was quiet on the way out. Donovan was trying to work through what had happened. These visions had become debilitating since he came to Fallavon. *Is it something in the air? The water?*

He had come close to killing Altera. Rohawk was kind enough to explain that choking someone to death usually takes a few minutes, but it didn't help. Not much, anyway. The general didn't even offer a mender for his injury, and instead, Donovan had to settle for wrapping it in cloth and staying wounded. It was common for minor wounds to not be mended, but Donovan knew that it was part of his punishment, and he accepted it.

Donovan had never heard of anything like this happening with being soulburned, but that didn't mean much. No one knew a lot about the soulburned. Not too many of them lived long enough to tell their tales. Those who did had no tales to tell.

Am I insane? he considered. A shiver went up his spine. At the very least, one of the visions had been positive. The king from his dreams. Donovan wasn't sure if he could trust a fragment of his mind, but the king seemed like a likable person. *Maybe he is my father?* The thought brought a little comfort to him. Lionel had been like a father, and until he died, Donovan cherished his relationship with the old hunter more than anyone else.

Even after what happened, Glyn insisted on taking his turn at the Hundred Blades, so he stayed behind. Rohawk took Glyn's absence as an opportunity.

"Deltra, what do you know about this Glyn fellow?"

"Glyn? He is the son of Lord Jaager, one of the noblemen in Fallavon. He holds a good deal of sway amongst the nobles. As General Kadin said, Lord Jaager is somewhat neutral, though I worry he wants to use the Grand Magistrate as a cat's paw to get rid of King Beldon. Then, he would look very good by comparison."

"Really?" Rohawk laughed. "And you showed the feynar's son where your secret headquarters are? Why, in the name of the gods, would you do that?"

"Truth be told, if we do not have Lord Jaager, then we lose. But it was good timing that the General brought up the elementium weapons."

"How so?" Rohawk pressed.

"Glyn's reaction. He did not know about it. I have long had a hunch that the Grand Magistrate and Lord Jaager have been meeting and planning. But if the Grand Magistrate withheld that piece of information, it shows distrust. The more Glyn and his father distrust Vinson, the better."

"That still sounds like a long shot," Rohawk said dryly. "No, not sounds like—it *is*. Deltra, your king needs to play the game better."

Deltra shrugged. "For now, it is the play. Lord Jaager has a lot of *Sai'ents*."

"What is a *Sai'ent*?" Donovan asked.

"It is an ancient name given to skilled fey soldiers who swear fealty to a lord or king."

"Essentially, they are knights," Rohawk said quietly to Donovan.

Deltra picked up on the comment and said, "Yes, except we do not so easily give away the title of *Sai'ent* the way humans do with knighthood. Head over to the Corrick Capital, shout in the street for a minute, and you'll be sure to find a knight to rest his sword on your shoulder in exchange for a loaf of bread or a beer. Oh, but in K'var—well, *there* they protect glorious knighthood behind a fat coin purse! And if you're broke, you could go to Sokor and tell good ol' King Hendel a joke—of course, not *any* joke, it has to be especially funny!—and you will be rewarded with a crest on your breast and a suit of armor to cover any rotund, battle-virgin body. No swordplay required."

"Nice to know you respect foreign culture," Rohawk said, deadpan.

Deltra laughed. "It may be an exaggeration, but it's still close to true. My point is that the *Sai'ents* here are the best of the best fighters, and they hold a lot of sway in power dynamics."

Donovan was relieved the conversation was not about his actions, but he was barely paying attention. What happened worried him. He was lost in thought for a while, and when he came back to attention, Rohawk and Deltra were talking about something new.

"Routine, eh?" Rohawk asked, unimpressed about whatever it was.

"I will buy you some of Fallavon's finest ale if you come."

"Well, in *that* case...I mean, I suppose if it's as good as what King Beldon had..."

"Even better," Deltra said with a smile.

"What's this about?" Donovan chimed in.

"A job I would like Rohawk to tag along for. It would be best with just one of you." Deltra seemed hesitant to say too much, and added, "I also want to check in with King Beldon before I send you anywhere. He may want to speak with you."

When they returned to the Great Tree, Deltra told Rohawk that it would be another hour or two before they would head out, then left.

"This is dangerous," Rohawk said in grave tone.

Donovan's stomach dropped. "What is it?"

Rohawk looked around before leaning in and whispering, "They keep giving me time for more of those heavenly baths."

Donovan gave Rohawk a blank stare. "You're the last person I would have expected to say that."

Rohawk started to respond, but the two were approached by a servant feyla. "Donovan? The king requests your presence in his study."

"Alright," Donovan said, his stomach dropping for a second time. He knew what this was going to be about.

"Follow me," she said.

Donovan turned back to Rohawk, who gave him a mock Nightingale salute before he turned in the direction of his room.

The servant girl led Donovan to a large wooden door with the image of a lion grown into it.

"This is his majesty's study. Please excuse me, I must be on my way," she said before bowing and leaving.

"Strangely curt of her," Donovan mumbled as he knocked on the door. After waiting for a little while and hearing no answer, Donovan thought that maybe this door was made of knockwood. He opened the door and entered, immediately taking notice of King Beldon, who was sitting on the floor reading a book. He was wearing trousers that were loose and split along the sides. His yellow *sarta* looked bold on his leg.

"I've read that book," Donovan blurted out when he saw the title.

"Ah, Donovan!" King Beldon said as if he had taken notice of him only then. "Thank you for coming. Please, sit for a little while. If you would like, I could order the servants to bring us some tea."

"No, thank you," Donovan replied. King Beldon's eyes went past him, and it looked like he nodded at someone. But when Donovan turned around, no one was there.

"Please shut the door and sit down."

Donovan did so. The study was small, but it had a cozy feel to it. A few short shelves lined the walls, and a couple of maps hung above them. One side of the room was made up of a large window from the ground to the ceiling. Glass boxes were hung on the walls in open spaces, unlit for now. A large wooden desk that looked to be of human make took up most of one wall, and it was stacked with books. That was probably why the king sat on the ground to read. The most curious thing in the room was a brilliant, golden embossed chest that was anchored to the wall behind the desk, slightly hidden from view.

"How did your time with General Kadin go? I hope he was not too rough with you."

Donovan frowned a little. "He had me try...what did he call it? One hundred blades? Something like that. To be honest, I did poorly."

"That will change, in time," the king said confidently. "The fact that you tried it means a lot. Did anything of note happen while you were there?"

Donovan knew the King knew. "Yes, but I'm not sure I can explain it to you."

"Can you explain to me this book you have read?"

Donovan was relieved the conversation was moving on. "It's a book on Technique. I know enough to tell you that it is a bit lacking."

"But you cannot use it, am I correct?"

"No, not anymore."

"And that bothers you, yes?"

Donovan thought back to Arabella. "More than you know, your majesty."

"I know quite a bit, but this is something I admit I have no knowledge of. That is why I am reading about it. I cannot say with certainty, but it seems control is incredibly important for Technique."

"From what I know, yes. You can hurt yourself with it very easily if you do not know how to control it."

"Then why do you want to use it again?"

"You've fought humans. You know how strong human magic can be."

"I do. I have also seen bumbling fools waste it and collapse from exhaustion. Easy prey."

Donovan rankled a bit at that. For all his talk on wanting to form alliances with humans, the king sure had no problem bragging about killing them.

"Kaldaran prey," he clarified. "Kaldarans are savages. If you had come across someone like Rohawk in battle, it would not have been so easy."

The king kept a level gaze. "What would have happened with Altera if you could use Technique?"

Donovan felt like he had been punched in the stomach. He closed his eyes and did not answer. He hoped the king would say something, but the silence lingered.

"Donovan, please answer me."

"I don't know," Donovan mumbled.

"Say again?"

"I said I don't know," he answered quickly, irritated.

"It is alright, Donovan. You can be direct with me. It is clear to me that what happened bothered you a great deal. That tells me you have a good heart."

Donovan lowered his head, feeling unworthy of the praise.

"I know what it is to struggle with control. Do you know much about fey magic?"

"No."

"There are two parts to it: natura and adrenicka. Natura is the magic we use to grow, to mend, and to create light. It is the essence of fey magic given shape and form. The same way we grow and guide our trees is the same way we mend flesh and bone."

"I did not realize they were one and the same."

"Indeed. Not everyone is skilled or can even manifest Natura magic. Adrenicka, however, is different. It runs through the blood of every feynar and feyla. It is activated by strong emotion, usually through battle, but sometimes by love, sorrow, and rage. It increases our strength, quickens our reactions, and gives us power when we need it most."

"Similar to human adrenaline," Donovan commented.

"Yes, but even more powerful. When Adrenicka increases to a high level, a fey's body changes temporarily with it. It starts with a second voice, as if another voice is speaking a split second after, like a dark echo. Then, light begins to shine from behind our eyes, spilling out from just under the eyelid. And when the magic comes on strongest, a fey's back will sprout long ribbons of light shaped like wings and can fly with them." Donovan had never heard of that.

"That's incredible. How often does that happen?"

"Not often, and usually in the heat of battle. Any humans who have done battle against fey know that they have the early advantage. From what I have seen, Technique is always available, but it exhausts a human to use it. Humans lose strength in a fight, but fey gain it."

Donovan nodded. "I have heard that too, but never understood why fey increased in strength. It makes sense now."

The king smiled, then looked down for a moment before looking back up at Donovan. "Forgive the change of subject, but Deltra told me what happened—in case you were wondering how I knew—and I would like to hear your perspective."

"I...I don't know if you will believe me."

The king leaned forward slightly. "Try me."

Donovan nodded. "It started with a dream, a strange dream with a bronze king telling me I was his champion and I needed to remember. I had another vision of him when I was in prison here, but when I stood before the Grand Magistrate I saw...someone else."

"What do you mean you saw?"

"My eyes clouded over with a vision, and I could not control it."

"And that was what happened with Altera?"

"Yes. She looked like..." Donovan grasped at the memory, but it was already escaping him. "I am not sure. My mind was so hazy then. But I do remember she looked like a pale man, and whoever that man was, he wanted to kill me, and I him." Donovan shook his head. "I believe the man was King Santos. You probably think I'm insane."

King Beldon shook his head. "I have some experience with visions. I had one when I nearly died fighting the Fox Clan. I then attributed it to the fey magic that was coursing through my veins from the mending my now wife gave to me. But I think something else is at play here." The king rose and offered a hand to Donovan. "If you will join me, I would like to take you to the skirmish branch."

"I think I've taken enough of a beating today."

"Please humor me; there is a point to all of this." Donovan nodded and took the king's hand, then followed him out of the study to a very large room, probably about half the size of the throne room, which was massive. The floor, like the one in the meal grove, was nearly all grass, except for the outer edge.

The room was shaped like an oval, the door they entered through on one of the ends. On the right and left were giant windows that let in the late afternoon sun. The other long wall of the oval, opposite the window, was lined with wooden racks holding fey blades. The smallest were short swords, and the collection ranged up to swords barely smaller than a human claymore. Half a dozen quarterstaffs were hung horizontally on the wall, one above the other, and a few spears of similar size above those.

"What do you think of it all, Donovan?" King Beldon asked. "Not a bad collection, yes?"

"If I'm being honest, I've never been fond of fey weapons."

The king nodded slightly. "I will not lie and say it is better than human craft, but we can still kill with them. We will use the quarterstaffs. The worst you will get is a bruise, if that."

Donovan felt the sting of the wound on his leg and cringed. It wasn't awful—he could fight through it. It just wouldn't be pleasant.

King Beldon walked over to the wall and pulled off the weapons of choice.

"The quarterstaff is excellent for learning balance. Since you had so much trouble with the blades, I will not bother you with them any more today." King Beldon tossed one of the staves to Donovan, who made sure he caught it this time.

The king placed himself on one end of the grove and Donovan mimicked him on the other side. He put one end in the ground to quickly check the size. It was the correct length for him—the king knew his weapons well.

"Alright, I want you to give me everything you have got," the king said as his fists tightened around his staff.

"I don't think that's a good idea," Donovan explained. "This isn't a training tool; it's the real thing."

"I know that. If you strike me, it is my fault for being too slow." Donovan still did not feel comfortable. He thought they would just practice a few moves, not spar. What had happened with Altera was fresh in his mind. If that happened with King Beldon, it would erase any chance of getting help for Nightingale.

"King, I—"

The king closed the distance in two sudden passes, bringing his quarterstaff down from a high guard into a right hew. Donovan quickly shifted to block.

Crack! A perfect block. Donovan had acted fast enough to try a counter, but he did not know if he was supposed to.

"Good, good!" the king said as he stepped back. "Show me more!" He shifted to a mid-guard, then took a few steps into a short thrust.

Donovan blocked, saw he had the advantage, and brought his staff around in time to hit the king's thigh. It was a good hit, even though he pulled at the last possible split second.

"I'm sorry, King, it was just one fluid motion, I didn't—"

King Beldon hit Donovan in the ribs with the end of his staff. Then he slapped Donovan on the knee and brought him low.

"Why did you drop your weapon?" King Beldon asked, his staff pushed against Donovan's throat.

"I didn't mean to hit you, your majesty."

"Why, when I told you to come at me?"

"You are a king," Donovan said with a grunt. "It was dishonorable for me to strike you."

"I commanded you to fight me!" King Beldon shouted as he put his face close to Donovan's. "But you are a coward and dropped your weapon at the first sign of injury!"

Rage poured into Donovan like wine.

"I am no coward!" he grunted the words as he pushed King Beldon's staff away and grabbed his from the ground. The king rushed back at him and the two engaged in a flurry of guards and hews. Donovan's rage only increased as he grew more frustrated that he couldn't land another strike, angered that he couldn't prove he wasn't a coward.

Donovan roared and brought a high left hew. King Beldon blocked and put a quick thrust into Donovan's shoulder. That is when his vision went hazy. Donovan was no longer sure who he was fighting. It was just like with Altera. He noticed the delusion in time to take a few passes away, then slow down and breathe. It was not easy.

"What do you see, Donovan?" asked the man. He sounded vaguely like King Beldon but did not look like him.

"A pale man, dark hair, and eyes like a serpent," Donovan breathed out quickly, as if he had the characteristics memorized. "He has a serpent tattooed on his shoulder. The same one I saw with Altera."

"Who is that man?"

The sense of dread Donovan felt earlier returned. "The god of chaos," he answered without realizing the words coming out of his mouth. "Kaldar." With those words, Donovan's vision started to clear. He saw King Beldon again. His head swam. He slowly sat down on the grass and set his quarterstaff aside. "This is not one of my best days. Who am I?"

"A very strong warrior," King Beldon said with a calmness that would encourage a crying child. "These visions might not be as bad as you think. They can be overcome, and if you can control them, they may unlock secrets into your past."

"How would you know? You are not human—you cannot be soulburned."

"I cannot use Technique, but I know what it is to have deep, dark pain of the soul, and how that can affect the workings of fey magic—Adrenicka. I know you said you did not want tea, but I signaled Elania to go ahead and prepare it."

"That actually sounds nice. When will it be ready?" King Beldon raised his eyes, and Donovan turned to see Elania bringing in a wooden tray with the kettle and cups. Donovan welcomed the calming drink. His hands were still shaking, and he asked Elania to pour for him and not fill it to the brim. Donovan sipped at it. The taste was a bit rank, but he felt like it was calming him down.

"Are you alright?" the king asked.

"I'm not fond of what's happening to me. These visions are starting to ruin my life."

"Do not be so hasty to dismiss them, Donovan," King Beldon warned. "How long have you been a soldier?"

"Only about a few months. Depends on how much credit you give me for fur hunting."

"Could have fooled me. You fight better than most of my soldiers. Will you allow me a wild guess?"

"Sure."

"Deep down in your memory, is a warrior who has fought for a long time. I think you will need that warrior if you are to survive what is to come."

"And what exactly is that?"

"You must face the man in your visions. The Crowned of Kaldar." Donovan swallowed hard, and the king picked up on that reaction. "Surely you must have known this was inevitable."

"I suppose I was hoping someone else would figure out a solution for me and kill King Santos. Not to sound ungrateful for your consideration, King, but I am still hoping K'var comes to our rescue."

King Beldon sipped at his tea. "That would probably be best for everyone, but I doubt it will happen."

"Me too, but why do you say that?"

"Donovan, when you came to me with your request, I was already very well informed on what is happening with Nightingale. More than you, to be blunt. Infurion is attacking K'var in earnest. K'var is holding its own, but barely. I fear the kingdom will burn to the ground. Kaldaran is taking advantage of that. It is also on the brink of destruction."

Donovan scoffed at that. "For a kingdom on the brink of destruction, it sure seems to be doing well enough."

"You think so? Perhaps. But when Kaldaran accepted the terms of the peace treaty years ago, they suffered far more harm than we did. There has been non-stop civil war there. Religious zealots say there should have never been peace, while more reasonable Kaldarans say it was that or destruction. King Santos seeks to regain the lost favor of his god by striking at Nightingale, a place weak enough for him to capture. I did not think it would work, but if he is Crowned, then Kaldar is pleased with him. The kingdom has another chance at life."

"I hope you are wrong, for so many reasons."

King Beldon laughed. "Me too, friend."

Donovan felt warmed by that. He had a few good friends back in Nightingale, but other than that, he wasn't much liked. Maybe it was just something said in passing, but it was nice. That warm feeling grew and grew until Donovan realized his eyelids were heavy.

"What's in this tea?" he asked. His hand drooped and he spilled it out onto the grass of the Skirmish Grove.

"Something to help you rest. Do not worry. You are safe here."

Donovan's head dropped back and he crumpled to the ground in a deep sleep.

Queen Philantha walked in and saw Donovan slumped into slumber. "Was that necessary?"

"I was concerned about him," the king answered. "I had heard about what happened in the throne room with Vinson, and Alden suspected he was being plagued with visions brought on by anger when he heard about what happened earlier today."

The Queen crossed her arms.

"Do you not agree he needs rest?"

"I think he needs all the rest he can get, but he should choose it."

King Beldon shrugged.

The queen moved her hands to her hips. "Beldon of the Mountain, perhaps one day I will convince you not to play these silly tricks on people."

King Beldon stood, walked over to her, and took her in his arms. She protested a little at first, but eased into his embrace. "Philantha the Fox, perhaps one day you will stop being so ridiculously beautiful. But I do not see that happening anytime soon."

"Are you trying to calm me with your burly charms?" she asked, eyelids half closed.

"It has always worked before."

She laughed, then pulled herself out of his embrace. "I need to see that Donovan is taken care of. Elania! Come help me take our guest to his room!"

Chapter Twenty-one

Rohawk had used the last of the day's fading light to take a much longer, more relaxing bath. The hot water and fragrant soaps took him back to a better time when these luxuries were not so foreign to him.

Deltra had mentioned something about meeting, but Rohawk had forgotten all about it the moment he stepped into the warm, swirling waters. That was, until he turned to see Deltra standing at the entrance to the bathroom, and their eyes locked.

"There you are," Deltra said impatiently. "You have sure kept me waiting long enough!"

How did he get in here without me hearing him? Rohawk wondered. "It's uncomfortable to make eye contact during a bath," he said as he pointedly turned away.

"But if I was a feyla—"

"No changing the rules on me like that!" Rohawk rounded. "I suppose you are ready for me to come with you on your secret mission."

"You resent being placed out of the loop, I see. You have no reason to be upset; it will be fun. Come with me, and do not bother with the cloak this time. It would ruin the point."

"Why is that?"

"You are the bait," Deltra answered.

Rohawk jumped out of the tub and went for a towel and his clothes. "There we go; *now* we're getting to the good stuff."

When Rohawk was dressed, the two of them headed out onto the streets of Fallavon. The city was more alive than earlier in the day. The evening was fey leisure time, and much like humans, they loved to enjoy it with some ale at the tavern. Rohawk watched as a beautiful feyla walked past, a smile on her face and a spring in her step. He smiled back at first, then his smile quickly faded. "Women walk around alone at night here?" he asked Deltra. "Is it safe?"

"It is a lot safer here in Fallavon than most of your human cities. There are some bad parts of town I would avoid, and to be honest, even good streets are brimming with tension. But it is still safe. Some of those feylas are good fighters and can handle themselves." Deltra looked over at

Rohawk. "You were actually worried about her. You did not seem like that kind of man."

Rohawk shrugged and looked away.

Deltra led Rohawk to what was obviously a tavern. The ramblings of a drunk feynar staggering out of the door, the familiar smell of fine ale wafting through the air, and the sound of laughter and merriment coming from the inside—these things felt like home to Rohawk. Hanging on wooden chains above the door was a sign, which swung back and forth gently in the evening breeze. The name of the tavern was written in feyspeak, but the picture on the sign was clear: a golden leaf.

"What's this place called?" Rohawk asked.

"A New Leaf," Deltra answered.

"That's a human idiom," Rohawk noted. "How did this place get its name?"

"The owner was a feyla who had spent some time in Kaldaran owning a bar. She was also a merchant who sold her ale here in Fallavon from time to time, and eventually moved here altogether."

"From Kaldaran? That is pretty rare. Where is she now?"

"She sold the business when we had the first rumblings of war with Kaldaran years ago. Because she was from there, she feared for her life. I wish I could say her fears were unfounded, but things got messy during that time."

The two of them entered, and Rohawk's brows raised slightly. He had always heard that the fey were high and proper, and not so easily susceptible to human vices. But this place seemed as drunk and as bawdy as any other, and it was packed. Rohawk turned his head when a feyla waitress brushed past him, her large breasts doing most of the brushing.

The smell of ale from before was now mixed with freshly baked bread and pork being seared. "This is much better than that stuffy underground lair."

"We are not here to get drunk," Deltra warned, "just to eat and have a tankard or two."

"Who said anything about getting drunk?" Rohawk asked with his brow furrowed and hands held out in an innocent gesture.

Deltra chuckled.

The tavern had similarities to the meal branch. Grass covered the entire floor, and small leaf tables grew up out of the ground in circles around the room to provide places to eat with others. And across the room was the very human, very strong and sturdy, wooden bar. There were stools there to sit on, just like at the Thirsty Horse.

Several feynars crowded around a giant lily pad table in the corner, and the exchange of wooden fey coins after sudden laughter was language enough for Rohawk to recognize gambling.

"I'm glad to see the fey are not so conceited as to avoid some of the finest vices in life," Rohawk commented.

A couple of feynars got up to leave, and Deltra signaled Rohawk over. They took their seats on the ground behind a couple of lily pads.

Rohawk leaned in and grinned at Deltra. "So, this is the great mysterious mission? To eat, drink, and be merry?"

Deltra leaned forward as well and spoke in a much softer tone. "We are not here just for dinner and good ale. This is the most diverse tavern in all of Fallavon. It attracts people from all social classes. I come here often to see what kind of reactions I can get out of people, to determine what the attitude of the city is toward our king."

"Ah, so that's why I'm here, to cause trouble."

"You seemed good at it," Deltra said dryly.

Rohawk chuckled, turning his head to watch a barmaid walk toward them. She was an odd color, based on what he had seen so far— dark green skin with orange hair that was put in a single, long braid behind her. Rohawk felt his chest go a little tight as he watched her mostly bare green legs slide past the heads of feynars sitting on the floor. She greeted them in feyspeak and said something that made Deltra give Rohawk a sly smile. Deltra said something back, probably giving her his order.

Rohawk was already telling Deltra what he would like him to order when she turned and said to him, "And what would you like to drink?" She had a thick fey accent, but Rohawk thought it attractive.

"Give me your best drink, and make it strong."

Deltra glowered a bit at Rohawk.

"All our drinks are the best," the feyla said with a steady grin.

"Rum, then. And if I may ask, what is your name?"

"Freya," she answered.

"Freya," Rohawk said, eyes locking with hers. "That is certainly a lovely name. I admire things of beauty, and right now you have captured quite a bit of my admiration."

Freya smiled and laughed. "You know what else you are about to capture?"

Rohawk leaned in ever so slightly in anticipation.

Freya leaned in closer too, her blouse dropping a little and giving just a hint of a show. "My fist to your teeth if you do not watch your mouth, human!" She didn't sound entirely serious, but serious enough to sour Rohawk's expression.

Deltra, on the other hand, was laughing so hard he started pounding his fist on the table.

Freya turned and casually walked away, though she did look back once and flashed a grin while shaking her head.

"She did not rip your face off," Deltra joked after taking a breath. "That in itself is a good sign. She is one of ours, though. She is part of the queen's dancing troupe, so I expected her to be nice to you."

"I can tell she likes me," Rohawk said with a shrug. "But if that is liking, what is everything else?"

"Not the best. There was more tolerance for humans before the Kaldaran war, especially here. But right now, the people here do not seem happy. It probably doesn't help that you kind of look like one of the people they fought against."

"Do you really expect to get information just by looking at a few faces of the commoners? I know you said this tavern attracts all kinds, but I've seen raw power. It lies in the hands of soldiers, lords, and kings." Rohawk sighed for a moment before continuing. "The only soldiers, lords, and kings in this room are those on the playing cards."

"Oh, of course, the real kings gamble all their hard earnings away," Deltra said in a mocking tone. "But please. Show me what you got. You read the room."

"No no no," Rohawk said as he held up a finger. "One drink first, then I work."

"Will that not make the work harder?" Deltra asked.

"Oh, it makes the work good, Deltra. It makes work smooth, enjoyable, tasteful, and most importantly—bearable. Besides, it's just one."

"And your tolerance must be that of a Kaldaran barbarian."

Freya brought the rum over, and Rohawk downed it in a matter of seconds. He slammed the glass on the table, locked eyes with Deltra, and with a deadly smile, said, "Don't ever compare me to a Kaldaran ever again.

I was fine when you said I look like one, because that much is obvious, but no more. You get one warning, that's it." With that, he rose and made for the gambling table.

Rohawk couldn't resist a glance back at Deltra. He saw the feynar pat himself down, then pause and slowly raise his eyes to glare back at Rohawk. The half-Kaldaran held up Deltra's coin purse and shook it a little. Rohawk couldn't read lips perfectly, but he would bet the purse and then some that Deltra muttered, "Clever bastard."

"Gentlemen!" Rohawk stated loudly as he neared the gambling table. The feynars and their feyla companions all glared at Rohawk with looks to kill, but he pretended not to notice. "How about we up the stakes here a bit?" Rohawk did not know if any of them understood common, so he loosened the string on the pouch and poured the coins into his hand. He rubbed the wooden high marks around to make sure the fey equivalent of gold coins were clearly visible.

The feynars looked at each other, then smiled and laughed. The dealer dealt Rohawk in. One card. The back was bright orange with a yellow sunburst. Rohawk did not bother to look at the front right away but instead studied the reactions, or lack thereof, from the others when they looked at their cards. He wasn't getting much. This was a casual game, and the fey were betting moderately and enjoying the company of feylas and booze. He wasn't going to get anything from relaxed states of mind.

Rohawk looked at his card, hoping that it would match his desire to bid. A four—a rather low card. He gave the slightest hint of a smile but only for a split second. The turn came for his bid. He tossed a high mark into the middle like it was nothing. A few gasps came from the crowd. Only feylas gasping for now, but it was a start.

The feynar on Rohawk's left matched the bid, as did all but one of the others in turn. Another card was dealt to everyone. Rohawk looked at another four. He gave the slightest indication of a frown and tossed in only four marks—not high marks. These were equivalent more or less to silver.

The feynar across from him grinned and threw in four marks and one high mark. Everyone else put in a high mark to stay in, including Rohawk. Then the next card was dealt.

Rohawk had to work a little to not react to the third four. He kept his face neutral, in case anyone was reading him; he did not want to make it obvious he was faking his reactions every time. The betting stayed neutral that round, until the last card was flipped face-up on the table. The card that everyone had a claim to when they revealed their hands. It was another four.

Rohawk was worshipping Borek internally and smirked a little. Just a hint to show everyone he thought he had a good hand, but not so much as to announce victory. It was the bait.

The feynar sitting across looked a bit too confident and threw in another high mark. Rohawk thought maybe that one had a straight of four. It was a decent hand that still lost to his own.

The feynar sitting right next to Rohawk folded, leaving Rohawk and three others. He put his high mark to match and raised the bid by another, which drew out a few more gasps from those standing around.

The crowd that gathered to watch had been growing slowly and no longer consisted only of the gamblers and their feyla. The feynar on Rohawk's left put in only enough to stay in, but the one after him raised it by two high marks.

Two more of the fey folded, leaving Rohawk and one other still in the round. It was the one who looked confident. He laughed and revealed his hand: The Lion King of Fallavon, The Behemoth King of Rellivan, and the Fox King of Rahana, the three highest cards in the game to make three of a kind.

The confident feynar, the one with the incredibly lucky three cards, laughed and chuckled, clearly a little drunk on both booze and victory. As he reached a hand out for the marks in the middle, Rohawk snapped forward quick as a snake and gripped the feynar's wrist. The feynar locked his eyes with Rohawk and shook his wide-grinning head, but Rohawk dropped his cards on the table.

"Four fours beat three kings," he said plainly and coolly. Several fey standing around laughed as the feynar pulled his hand back from the stack, mortified at his loss.

Rohawk gathered the wooden marks slowly while reading the expressions of the others. Now the gamblers were getting nervous, and the real game would begin.

The next several rounds went rather smoothly for Rohawk. He had to fold on a few, but his stack of marks was increasing. Freya brought him more and more drinks throughout the night, and Rohawk threw them back like water to a man dying of thirst. He did not do any worse tipsy, and even approaching drunk; he was still outplaying his opponents. After a few more rounds, he had nearly taken all the coins from the fey at the lily pad table.

Suddenly, all the gamblers locked their eyes on Rohawk and stood up. At the same time, the one next to him punched him across the jaw. He almost fell back at the blow, but stumbled to his feet, instead. The feynar charged and grabbed him, but suddenly froze.

In less than two seconds, Deltra had made his way through the crowded tavern and drawn his fire elementium blade. He barked an order in feyspeak at the feynars who had looks to kill. When the man who had Rohawk in his grasp didn't move, Deltra pointed his sword at him and gave the command again. His face was still tight with anger, but he slowly let go.

Rohawk quickly holstered the anelace he had pointed toward the gut of the man next to him, hoping no one saw that he had been less than a second away from spilling black, fey blood.

There were grumblings, but the drunken fey left without causing more trouble. Rohawk had already gathered his winnings by the time they were gone.

"Come on, we should go," Deltra said as he sheathed his sword at his side. Rohawk agreed, and the two headed for the exit.

Rohawk looked back once more and saw Freya wink at him. He smiled as they left.

"I hope you know you owe me," Deltra said as the two walked through the Fallavon night back toward the Great Tree.

"I didn't need your help," Rohawk said.

"No, I mean you owe me the marks you took from me, plus interest. And I did not intervene to save you, I intervened to save *them*."

Rohawk chuckled and tossed Deltra the entire bag of marks. "It's fey currency anyway. Worthless anywhere else."

Deltra looked annoyed, but sighed and said, "I wish that was more of an exaggeration than it is."

"Where did you get that weapon? First Altera has a weapon *and* armor, then you brandish that sword in a crowded tavern. For someone so concerned about elementium weapons coming into Fallavon, you seem to have a few of them yourself."

"I am King Beldon's right-hand feynar. We have a few elementium weapons at our disposal, and Altera is royalty. She showed up with her weapon and gear."

Rohawk nodded. He had suspected that answer. Royalty in human kingdoms frequently had elementium weapons for the same reasons— power and gold.

"You really would have done it? Spilled fey blood?" Deltra asked.

Rohawk narrowed his eyes, then sniffed. "For the record, I didn't *want* to kill any of them. But, yes, I would have defended myself."

"Not surprising," Deltra said.

"What do you mean by that?"

"I know you think you have everyone here figured out, Rohawk. But I have dealt with your kind before. You are as human as they come."

"As human as they come, eh?"

"You cheat, fight, and steal your way through life and escape only until someone better than you at it comes along and puts a stop to it. Fey live a lot longer and are more concerned about our reputation than simply blowing through our lives doing whatever we wish until we pull a blade one second slower than the next person. You take more years when you take a fey life."

Rohawk spat to the ground. "Typical arrogant fey attitude, thinking a human life to be worth less than a fey. Not all humans fit in your little box. Donovan is a good man."

"But you are not?"

Rohawk considered that question for a second before realizing he was letting Deltra watch him think. He hated that. "That was good rum back there, wouldn't you say?"

Deltra shook his head. "I am waiting for someone to prove me wrong about your kind."

"Makes it a bit hard to be loyal to King Beldon, I bet, with all his talk of opening up greater diplomacy with human kingdoms."

Deltra stepped in front of Rohawk and stopped him cold. "Do not question my loyalty to King Beldon ever again. That is *your* one warning. Understood?"

Rohawk's brows raised. "Why are you worried about someone questioning your loyalty? Afraid you won't be able to defend it?"

Deltra looked angry for a split second, then shook his head and chuckled. "You have courage, I commend you for that. The king and I disagree on this matter a lot, but when I met you, I told you I bothered to learn your language because I wanted to be a friend. That has not changed." Deltra turned and motioned the way forward. "Can we agree to move on?"

Rohawk patted him on the back. "Of course. I can't be mad at a drinking buddy, can I?"

Donovan woke up in his room, in his bed. He had not slept so well in ages. A single light flickered on the opposite side of the room. It was dark outside—Donovan wondered if it was the middle of the night. He stepped out into the hallway, not realizing he was only in underclothes, and asked the guard, "What watch is it?"

The guard looked surprised only for half a second, and answered, "Late in the third watch, Donovan."

That meant just after sunset, Donovan knew. "Thank you."

"The queen requested your presence if you awoke before the fourth watch," the guard continued. "There is still time."

"Alright," Donovan replied, a bit slowly. He wasn't groggy from sleep, but he wondered if the guard meant the king had requested to see him. He didn't know what the queen would want.

"She is waiting for you in the courtyard. The appropriate attire was left in your bathroom, should you choose to attend. She recommended you wash up quickly and go there."

"Thank you," Donovan said again and closed the door. He went to the adjoining bathroom and saw clothes neatly stacked up for him. It was an elaborate outfit that looked kind of like the clothes he had seen on the dancers yesterday. The shirt was made completely of white silk, a white as bright as the king and queen's garments. The sleeves were loose, not like a robe, but halfway in between a robe and shirt. A deep V-shaped neckline ran down to the middle of Donovan's chest, with golden Lions embroidered on both sides of the V, as well as smaller ones on the ends of the sleeves. The trousers were the same flowing white silk, and they cut off just above the ankles. He thought the whole thing to be odd, but the queen was kind. He would comply with her request.

Donovan washed himself with a rag rather than taking a full bath and changed. The guard outside led him to the courtyard. This one was not overgrown like the one he had seen in the poor part of town. Large marble tiles made up the floor. The sun was slightly past set and lit everything with a faint, yet warm, orange glow. Dozens of fey lights were ready and lit along the edges of the courtyard to provide a blue glow beyond the natural light. A few dozen dancers practiced on the marble, but Donovan did not see a single feynar.

"What am I supposed to do?" he asked the guard. "And why am I the only man?"

The guard shrugged. "All I know is, you were invited personally by the queen. She will know more than I."

Donovan had charged into battle for Nightingale multiple times, but for some reason, this felt just as nerve-racking. He sighed and made his way toward the queen. Many feylas glared at him, but there were a couple that looked like they wanted him to take them in his arms for a romantic evening. He felt his cheeks turn red at that. These were probably noblemen's wives or daughters—they wore fine woven silk in many different colors. Most of the dresses made the women look like glass bells, beautiful and fragile.

"Donovan," the queen said in a musical tone. "I am glad you are coming to dance with us! Do not be so shy over there, come."

"This is...very unusual."

"Come now, Donovan, something tells me you know how to dance."

"A little, but why am I the only man?"

"Tonight is usually just the women. But I set the rules around here."

Donovan chuckled nervously. He wasn't great at social engagements where he was the clear outsider. His first winter festival in Fallavon had taught him to stick close to his friends, and here, the queen was the only person he knew in the slightest.

"How kind of you to make an exception."

"Exactly. I am in need of a partner to dance with, and my husband could not make it tonight. Will you dance with me?"

Donovan felt the blood rush to his head. "I don't know fey customs, but humans might consider that a little scandalous."

The queen laughed. "Good thing you are the only one here, then. What would you like? Something fast? Something slow?"

Donovan was about to ask what she meant, when he noticed her looking over to the musicians. "Slow, please. That will at least give me a chance."

Queen Philantha called out something, and the musicians started to play their curious instruments. Those with strings were strumming slowly or picking string by string. Others blew steadily into wooden flutes. The melodies had a sound to them he had heard in Nightingale described as "fey music." Something about the way they switched from high to low notes quickly.

The queen held out her hands and smiled. Donovan clasped them gently and stepped lightly about the courtyard.

"Show me a human dance. I am sure I can pick it up quickly."

"I don't know of many," Donovan said, blanking on the few he did know.

"Any will do."

Donovan felt very uncomfortable, but she was the queen and was to be obeyed. He started leading her in the one dance he strained to remember. Alexis had taught it to him one night during last year's winter festival. She had looked so beautiful that night…that was when Donovan realized he was falling for her.

He could only remember the next step as he finished the previous one, but he was maintaining his poise for the most part. The next part required him to pull her close to him.

"If the king asks, you asked for this," he said.

"Asks what?"

Donovan's answer was a hand on the small of her back, pulling her in closely. He heard gasps from the audience but ignored them. If he was going to be uncomfortable, ridiculed, and embarrassed, he was going to embrace it and go for broke.

The fey musicians wrapped up their song, and Donovan lucked into finishing by spinning the queen perfectly in time, avoiding an awkward finish. There was scattered applause.

"What kind of dance was that?" Queen Philantha asked coolly.

"Something from K'var, I think. But now that my reputation here is likely destroyed—" he was interrupted by a tap on the shoulder.

Donovan turned around, and a feyla held out her hand for a dance. She looked a little older than the queen, with kind eyes and a mischievous smile.

The queen said something in feyspeak and made a gesture like she was passing Donovan off.

He blinked in surprise. "Wait, don't do this, good queen. I don't know what I'm doing."

"Just go with it, Donovan! You can learn some of our dances!"

He opened his mouth to protest, but the feyla yanked him away, and the music began.

Chapter Twenty-two

Donovan all but limped his way back to his room. He had gone hunting hundreds of times, survived outdoors in the bitterness of the cold winter, killed a buck with a wooden club, outrun a wild boar—if only for a moment—killed a bear, and won dozens of arm wrestling contests at the Thirsty Horse Tavern. Yet none of these things had prepared him for what the feylas had him doing. They kept insisting it was normal for men to dance and stretch that way, but he felt anything but normal.

He groaned as he flopped down onto the soft bed. A straw cot would have been just as welcome at that point.

"They took advantage of me," he mumbled out to the air. The feylas seemed enticed with the scandal of dancing with a human man, and before long, he was being passed around like a meat platter. But it wasn't horrible. It felt a little good to be so well liked.

Exhaling a deep sigh, Donovan half-closed his eyes and nearly fell asleep. He shot up when the door to his room flew open without warning. His heart stopped when he saw a tall figure, probably a feynar, garbed in black from head to toe and standing in the doorway. He wore a wolf mask to cover his face, but it had horns and was twisted and red, like demons in some of the old myths. In his hands were two wooden short swords, pointed in a menacing way that could only be meant for killing.

Donovan rolled out of bed and stood, his soreness muted by adrenaline. His eyes darted to a vase across the room, the only possible weapon he could find. The feynar snarled, but instead of attacking, he tossed Donovan one of the swords.

"You could never kill an unarmed man, is that it?"

The feynar chuckled a deep rumble. "You are human, barely a person," his voice was like iced gravel, though something about it was familiar. "But the way of the warrior must be preserved if Fallavon is to survive. I take no pleasure in this, but I will do what I must." The feynar snapped forward with those words and Donovan swung his sword around to parry. General Kadin's words rang in his head again. *Turn every blade!* It was only one blade, but the feynar swung it so quickly, he might as well have had two.

Donovan was keeping up, but wearing out fast. The feynar was fresh—Donovan had spent everything and then some already. He made one final block, but did not have the strength, and the feynar's blade pushed through and slapped his knee. Only the blunt end hit him, but it sent him to the ground.

"Your strength is gone," the masked man breathed out. "Go ahead, soulburn yourself. I am not afraid of it."

Whoever this was did not know Donovan could not do that, both because he was already burned, and because Donovan had no metal to channel a spell with.

"Fine, then. Die!" The masked man lifted his arm to thrust the pointed blade. Survival instinct gripped Donovan. He reached out for Technique, but again, the same empty feeling came back to him.

"You will drop your weapon, or you will die." It was Rohawk's voice, sounding from directly behind the assassin.

The assassin's sword arm was as frozen as his mask, and the now-visible gray eyes behind it locked with Donovan's.

"Do I need to make that any clearer for you?" Rohawk asked icily.

"It would be a great honor to kill both of you," the fey breathed out. "But your cloak-and-dagger treachery has the best of me for now."

"You would attack a sleeping man and call it even because you tossed him one of those pieces of skot you call swords?" Rohawk growled. "To kill you would be nothing to me, but I won't risk our deal with the king. So, drop your weapon in the next two seconds, or I will disregard the consequences and paint this room black."

The feynar dropped his blade, then quick as a flash, he put an elbow into Rohawk's chest. Rohawk staggered back a step and the feynar darted out of the room and down the hall with blinding speed.

"Teching damn," Rohawk grunted. "Bones! He is fast."

"We should call a guard," Donovan breathed out.

"He's gone."

"But we have to find out who he is."

"Donovan, he's gone. No one will see him, they will only see us yelling and screaming about it. Now, are you alright?"

"I am. But…he almost had me."

Rohawk made his anelace disappear with a flourish and reached out a hand to help Donovan to his feet. "I know. I've seen that look many times. Just recently with you and the Grand Magistrate."

Donovan gripped Rohawk's hand tightly and still almost fell over when he stood up. "I'm still not sure I'm not dead. Wait a second, you said he tossed me a sword. How did you know that? Have you been here the whole time?"

"No, but someone gave it to you."

Donovan looked down and realized his grip on the sword was still tight. He let it drop. "Well, thank you. Any idea who that was?"

"Someone who doesn't like King Beldon, I imagine. Or you, for that matter."

"Do you think he will try again?"

"Probably. Oh, don't look so glum, Donovan. If they don't like you, they probably don't like me, either. And since I was the one who thwarted the assassin, they will likely come for me next time."

"Doesn't that worry you?"

"Nah."

"Oh, good," Donovan said sarcastically. *How can Rohawk be so sure of himself?*

"Don't sleep just yet—I was coming here for a reason before I saw that assassin."

"I'm not going to be able to sleep now, not after that. What if he comes back? We need to tell the king what just happened."

"He's not coming back tonight," Rohawk said as if it was obvious. "And I will go tell the king for you in a moment. I wanted to ask you what you thought about the people you've met so far."

"What do you mean?"

"Well, for example, King Beldon. I believe the fey king is trying to bait us into fighting on his side of this civil war. I have no problems with the thrill of combat, but should I fight a civil war for people I do not know?"

Donovan's brow furrowed. "No offense, but if they pay you, wouldn't you?"

"You know me as a mercenary, but gold is not my motivation."

"Then what is?" Rohawk just glared at Donovan.

"I'm keeping that a secret for now. Still, I want to know what you think about what's happening here."

"I'm keeping that a secret for now," Donovan said, mimicking Rohawk's voice.

"I should be annoyed, but your impression of me isn't half bad."

Donovan smiled. "Regardless of what the king decides, we are leaving soon, so I don't know what makes you think he is trying to get us involved in a war."

"I overheard a conversation between him and Deltra."

Donovan raised a brow.

"Alright, I was eavesdropping. The king plans on having us come back after we save Nightingale."

"Well, if part of that plan does, indeed, mean saving Nightingale, then I'm interested."

"Agreed. Nightingale first, then we will see."

"Sleep first, then we will see," Donovan groaned. "Not sure how I will get back to sleep tonight, though."

"I told you he's not coming back."

"And King Beldon told me no fey would dare send an assassin."

"Huh, good point. Alright, let's go tell one of the guards and ask for some extra protection for you. Will you be able to sleep if we do that?"

Donovan shrugged. "Worth a shot."

Dawn came, and Donovan was up far too early for all that his body had done yesterday. His bones ached, his mind ran through too many scenarios, and his dreams had been troubling.

He felt for the blade which had been near his hand all night and was comforted by the touch of the hilt. When he was awake enough to realize the hilt was metal, he looked to see that the blade was one of Rohawk's anelaces. He vaguely remembered Rohawk giving it to him the night before.

It took a few more moments, but Donovan made himself get up, out of bed, and dressed. He selected a purple tunic and brown breeches found in one of the dressers. He wondered what King Beldon would think about the assassination attempt. Last night they had given the report to Kellen, the king's guard who had brought Donovan to the Great Tree on his wolf after the king stopped the Grand Magistrate's execution. When Donovan opened the door to his room, Kellen was still there, standing watch.

"Good morning," he said in a gentle tone. "I sent a servant to let the king know what happened once he was awake. The king sent word to have you join him for breakfast."

Donovan thanked the guard and went to the meal branch. The king and queen were there, waiting for him to arrive so they could get started. Once the food had been served, the king and queen asked Donovan to tell them what happened. They listened intently as he told them of the masked feynar.

"This is worrisome," the king finally said. "I knew the Grand Magistrate was not above many...unsavory dealings. That is why I had a guard always posted to your room. I will need to check the watch schedule and find out what happened with that one."

"My King, I do not wish to be rude, but have you made a decision? It makes me uneasy that fey have tried to kill me twice since I arrived."

"You will abide by my deal!" the king said as he slammed a fist on the lily pad table.

Donovan shrank back, blinking. He did not expect that from King Beldon.

Thick tension permeated the room, but the queen placed her hand on the king's shoulder and said, "Donovan makes a fair point, my love. His life is in danger. We must do better if we are going to hold him to his agreement."

King Beldon sighed, then said, "You...are right. I am sorry. My anger was directed not at you, Donovan, but at those who would so blatantly violate my agreement with you. I did not think this would be such a problem. I do not fully understand human culture, but fey have rules about combat when we fight each other."

"I'm not exactly fey."

King Beldon nodded, then took in a deep breath and sighed. "An oversight on my part. I am sorry. If it helps any, you made a good impression on someone already."

Donovan furrowed his brow. "Who?"

"Altera."

"You must be joking."

"Not at all, Donovan," the queen put in. "We received word that she really liked your visit and wants you to visit again. She's not the one to lie or exaggerate. I think you earned her respect, which she does not give lightly."

"Then *she* must be joking. For some reason I don't understand, she hated me when she met me. Why would she respect me now after what happened?"

"Well, do you want to go back there today and find out?" the king asked.

Donovan picked at his food for a moment. "I suppose I should. If nothing else than to apologize to her."

"I will not make you," the king added.

Donovan could tell by the tone in his voice he was being honest, but he wanted him to go. "Alright. I will give it another try. But I'm not walking around unarmed. I want a sword and shield—iron ones."

"You think I have iron? It is an offense to fey." the king warned.

"I do not wish offense, I just want to be able to defend myself."

"Again, he has a point, my love," the queen pointed out. "Donovan, we could give you fey weapons. I know they are not what you are used to, but iron really is distasteful to our kind.'"

"I can agree to that," Donovan said.

King Beldon clapped his hands together. "Excellent. I will send someone to fetch those for you."

Beldon had gone out of the room quickly when Donovan left. Philantha knew that meant he was upset. She did not follow, not right away. But when nearly an hour had passed, she walked to the skirmish branch.

Beldon stood there on the grass, shirtless, with a quarterstaff in his hands. A cloth and leather training dummy lay in shambles nearby, displaying what had happened before she got there. He was taking deep, heavy breaths and clutching the quarterstaff so hard even his red skin was turning white.

"The Grand Magistrate needs to die," Beldon breathed out.

Philantha promptly closed the door behind her.

"I want to kill him with my bare hands!" he grunted and broke the quarterstaff in half upon his knee. He held the pieces in a death grip for a few seconds, then slowly opened his hands and dropped them. Her hand was on his shoulder. "Will it work, Philantha?" he said in a tight voice. "I have chosen to share my power with an elected council, and they use the power *I* gave them and turn it against me! This is *my* kingdom!"

"If this is *your* kingdom, it dies with you," Philantha said, her tone level and strong. "You cannot live forever. The Lion Clan must have a government that represents the people, not the whim of good and bad kings."

"I know," Beldon said, his breathing calming bit by bit. "But what good is it for the kingdom to outlive me if it falls apart while I am alive?" He chuckled sardonically. "What a masterstroke of irony that would be."

Philantha rested her head on his strong shoulder. "You are out of your element, my love. I grew up with political training, as did Vinson. But you are a warrior king. Your strength has saved this clan in the past, but now you fight a battle of the mind."

"My mind is not strong enough for this fight."

"You can learn," she said as she reached down to clasp his hand.

"In *time*, anyone can." Beldon's voice was low and weighted. "Is it foolish what I am doing with Nightingale? It is the only thing I can think of that will surprise Vinson and give us some allies in what is to come."

"I agree with both of those assessments."

"But will the people of Fallavon and the rest of our clan agree?"

Philantha shrugged and sat down. "Perhaps it is time to extend council representation to some of our clan outside Fallavon. The people in the border towns love you. You brought their feylas back from Kaldaran; they have not forgotten that. And they trade more with the humans. They are not quite so insulated as our people are here."

"That is not a bad idea at all, but I will need council approval. They will not like the idea of their votes being diluted like that."

"Neither will our people outside Fallavon like having their voices discounted. Have that messenger, Ivan, take detailed notes of that council meeting and send it to as many clan towns as possible. Let them know who it is who is blocking their representation. That will win them over to you twice as much."

King Beldon smiled and shook his head. "How did I get such a politically savvy feyla by my side?"

Philantha leaned over and kissed her husband, then rested her head on his chest.

"I am worried about Donovan. Even with the guards I have sent with him."

"And that is why you plan to send him away soon."

King Beldon nodded. "Yes. We will help Nightingale, but I am still waiting to tell him. General Kadin is making preparations, but I need to keep it as quiet as possible. If Vinson makes his move while the general is away, we probably lose. But I do not think he understands what we are up to and will not make a move in haste. Alden thinks so anyway."

Philantha chuckled, then asked, "What do you think Alden thinks of Donovan?"

Beldon smiled. "I heard the two talked and Alden was rude. I am not surprised."

"You know what he has been through. Give him some time."

"I know Alden wants nothing more than time, but I cannot give it to him. But I think he was just testing Donovan. To him, Donovan is a curiosity, and it takes a lot to make that feynar curious."

"I am amazed Donovan won over Altera."

"I think he did it by accident, but she respects strength. She respects fey and even respects humans, her enemies. Her past with Driggon is why she did not like him, but he proved himself. She will be a strong ally in the battle to come."

Philantha smiled. "I do not look forward to the day of war, but I must say, the thought of seeing you fight again..." She moved her hand down Beldon's chest, farther and farther.

Beldon pulled her in close and locked her in a passionate kiss.

A moment passed, then she pulled back and asked, "Perhaps we should go somewhere more private?"

"The secret passageways provide more than just a way of escape," Beldon said with a sly grin. "This way, my Queen."

Chapter Twenty-three

Nobody troubled Donovan on his way to the secret army base. Maybe his cloak blended him in well enough, or perhaps it was the fact that the king had sent soldiers to tail him along the way. He had noticed them halfway in, but one of them was Kellen, so he didn't worry about being jumped.

Donovan repeated the whistle to gain access, then waited as Deltra had before. But nothing happened. He whistled again and waited. "I get it, my whistling isn't the best. But the king sent me."

That worked. A whistle rang out in response, Donovan gave the final whistle, and the interchange was complete. The passage to the stone steps opened. Before he could go in, a feynar emerged from the brush. His golden yellow skin blended well with the trees and foliage, and a blue *sarta* wrapped around his right hand.

"You gave Altera a hard time."

"Only a little more than she gave me."

A hint of a smile was on the feynar's face. "I know Kadin reamed you for it, but I thought it was hilarious."

"You do not call him general?"

The feynar stepped aside and waved Donovan in. The opening began to close back up, and he thought he wasn't going to get an answer, but just before the way closed, the feynar's voice came through. "Not when he is your brother."

Donovan descended the stone steps into the ruined courtyard. He was hoping Altera wouldn't be there and he could avoid the awkwardness, but there she was. She was already unarmored this time and practicing the quarterstaff with another feyla. She was making some kind of joke and the two were laughing while mechanically going through different stances and taking turns defending and striking.

Donovan suddenly realized he did not know where to start. He still didn't want to face General Kadin, either, but he would have to eventually, if he stayed too long. Kellen and the other guards had stayed outside, so it was just him to face everything alone.

He wandered around a bit aimlessly. Fey were sneaking glances at him but saying nothing. He leaned his sword and shield against a wall and grabbed one of the quarterstaffs. He checked the height, then practiced a few motions Alexis had taught him.

"That would be more fun with a partner," Altera's voice sounded from behind.

Donovan looked over to see her standing a few paces from him, with a quarterstaff in her hand, resting one end on the ground. Her yellow hair was messy from practice, but looked fierce, like a lion's mane.

"Are you offering?"

"Of course. No one else in here can beat me, and I am tired of practicing stances. I want to see what you got."

Donovan nodded and shifted into position. Altera mirrored his stance, and they both gave each other a slight bow.

Altera immediately shifted to mid-guard and went for a jab, but Donovan stepped out of it. He was not quite quick enough to counter, so he settled for the dodge as Altera reset her defenses. She waited for a moment, expecting an attack, but Donovan remained defensive. She got impatient and feinted with a step to the right, then shifted to a low guard and came in for a hew. Donovan brought his staff around to block, then stepped away again.

Altera returned to defending, but Donovan kept his eyes on her and did not move forward. He could go on the offensive, but he did not know what would happen if things got out of hand again.

"What are you doing?" she asked.

Donovan did not respond. Altera let out blast of wind through her nose and stepped forward into a flurry of blows. Donovan blocked again and again and again, shifting through a rudder-guard repeatedly to block her attacks while he stepped away.

"*Ekuken!*" she grunted out the strong fey curse. "Why do you not strike back?"

"You will never win that way, lad," General Kadin's voice boomed through the room. His light green arms were crossed, and he watched the practicing with eagle eyes. "Good moves, but nothing gained from them."

"Just biding my time, General," Donovan replied.

"She is not made of glass, Donovan. Fight!"

Donovan wasn't sure what to do. He could at least throw a few attacks, even if he didn't bring his hips to bear into the strike. That would at least keep Altera on her toes. He shifted to a high guard. Altera matched him. He brought it around for a left hew, but Altera was quicker. She stepped to her left and brought her staff to low guard, batting Donovan's to the side and leaving him open. She jabbed him in the chest and he staggered back.

"Again," the general ordered.

Donovan and Altera re-engaged in a flurry of quick steps and stance changes. Bringing her staff into rudder guard, Altera blocked his move and then pounded him some more.

"Again," the general ordered a second time. This continued until Altera had beaten Donovan a dozen times. His chest was bruised in multiple places and hurt like gol when Altera struck the same place more than once. Both were breathing heavy, and Donovan could tell Adrenicka was pumping though Altera's veins. She was getting hits on him faster and faster.

"I can't win, not without Technique," he breathed out.

"Weakling," Altera spat out. Her voice had an echo. Fey magic. Donovan felt the sting of the insult.

"You can use magic, I cannot. Not a fair fight."

"Excuses!" Altera shouted at him.

Donovan's anger rose, and the vision hit him again. King Santos—Toby—Kaldar—he wasn't sure what he was seeing. But it was the same serpent-eyed man as before.

"Again," the general called out. By now, everyone else had stopped practicing and was watching the two of them battle.

"A moment," Donovan breathed out, still trying to control the vision. The serpent man laughed at him. He knew it wasn't Altera. He just had to regain control of his mind.

"I said again!" the general commanded.

Donovan went on the defensive, barely keeping up with Altera while he tried to sort out what to do.

"I am in your mind, mortal," the serpent man said. "You cannot escape me. I know you are in Fallavon, hiding from me. Come back to Nightingale and face me like a man."

Donovan did not know if this was all an illusion, or if somehow King Santos was speaking to him. He certainly wasn't going to take the chance and tell him the plan was to do exactly that. He kept evading and blocking Altera as much as he could. Her eyes began to glow with the power of Adrenicka and Donovan felt the strength of it in every attack. The vision was overpowering. He could not surrender to it like he had done before.

There had to be a way. If he could not face this vision, could he really face King Santos in person? Could he really stand against the might of Kaldar?

Altera came in for a mid-guard jab. Donovan blocked it, but he wasn't fast enough. She had the power position and pressed for a jab to his chest. Donovan stepped clear and brought his staff around and landed a strong hew down on her shoulder. Altera collapsed to a knee. The vision started to fade. When it did, Donovan saw Altera looking up at him with surprise and perhaps a hint of a smile.

"*Haln*, human," she said. It was another fey curse, but it was not an insult. "That was pretty good. I am going to need a mending after that blow."

"Sorry," Donovan said.

"Sorry?" Altera threw back at him. "I was complimenting you."

Donovan just smiled. She smiled back.

General Kadin walked over and put a firm hand on Donovan's shoulder. "The king probably would not want me to tell you this, but you have earned it. You are ready now."

"For what?" he said in between heavy breaths.

"For Nightingale."

General Kadin had not been exaggerating when he said the time had come. Donovan, Rohawk, and a hundred fey soldiers rode down the Folly-Fey road. Most of them were made up of King Beldon's secret army. The general had packed enough supplies to get them to Nightingale. There was talk of restocking in Boroshard's Folly. That made Donovan nervous. But the general insisted that the Folly wasn't safe. He suspected that Kaldaran had gone through there at some point, and Lady Renna was known for taking bribes if armies wanted to pass through.

The king and queen had to stay behind, but Altera was there, and of course, Rohawk. Both of them were spoiling for a fight.

The Folly-Fey road was worse off than when Donovan and Rohawk had come. A snowstorm had blown through and left a thick blanket across it and the nearby hills. But at least the sun was shining.

"What do you think we will find near Nightingale?" Altera asked Donovan. "My clan resides far from Kaldaran, but General Kadin told me some wild tales about them. Is it true that they use prisoners in ritual sacrifice?"

Donovan knew the answer all too well. "Yes. They draw it out too, and cause as much pain and agony as possible."

"One of many reasons it was so outrageous when the Gledalai stepped in on their behalf in that war," Rohawk said. "I wasn't even a part of it and I knew it was teching ridiculous."

"Hear, hear!" General Kadin called out.

Altera furrowed her brow. "That one still puzzles me."

"The Gledalai do not understand the importance of life the way we do," General Kadin answered. "To them, Kaldaran's ritual sacrifices are just a form of worship like any other. When we brought this up at the peace talks, I listened as one of them said to King Beldon, 'It's their culture—you must respect it.'"

Altera huffed. "Cold-blooded torture is 'cultural differences'?"

"Cold-blooded is both figuratively and literally an accurate description of the Gledalai," Rohawk said.

The General laughed. "I do not care what anyone says about you, Rohawk, I like you!"

Rohawk furrowed his brow and leaned over closer to Donovan. "What have they been saying about me?"

The army of Fallavon made camp north of the Folly-Fey road at the bottom of a rise called Sana Hill. It was the second night of camping, and it was as bitterly cold as the first. It was only half a day's walk from Boroshard's Folly, but they didn't plan to go through there. Sana Hill was large enough to hide them in case any Kaldarans used the road, and the Fallavon scouts set an all-night watch.

Tent flaps fluttered in the cold winter wind and the smell of fresh fire permeated the air. Donovan and his new friends sat around it, enjoying venison from a deer he had tracked and killed while everyone else set up the camp. It was a lucky break to find a deer so quickly, and a welcome treat that boosted the morale of the soldiers.

Rohawk licked the venison juices from his fingers, then turned to Donovan. "Are you going to tell them about our little problem?"

Altera raised a yellow brow. "Problem?"

Donovan shrugged. "We aren't planning to go through there, so what's the problem?"

"We will be close, though," Rohawk explained. "Lady Renna won't like us passing through any part of the forest. Especially since I might have killed someone."

"Lady Renna," Altera said, brows furrowed as though trying to think of where she heard the name before. "Wait, who did you kill?"

Donovan sighed. "I was invited to see the seer of Boroshard's Folly, and I brought Rohawk with me. She gave him some mysterious reading about taking a kingdom. Then she turned to me, thought for a moment, and started screeching like a wounded rabbit. She said something about how when I remember, everything will end. It seemed like nonsense, but it riled her up enough that she called out for her guards to kill us. We had to fight and run for our lives."

"I would not take what she says too seriously," Altera noted. "There used to be a feyla in my village who said she could see the future. As it turned out, she had a source in the Great Tree and was being fed all the letters the king sent and received. She used the knowledge in those letters to 'tell the future.'"

Donovan took in a breath. "Even if she is a fraud, she believes whatever she thinks she saw. That means she might cause trouble if I show my face again."

"The Lady barely ever leaves her house," Rohawk said. "Chances are she won't even notice us."

"Maybe, or maybe not," General Kadin answered. "Lady Renna does not like a group as big as ours passing through her home unannounced. That is part of the reason I stopped us here. I do not want to be announced."

"But earlier you said we were going around," Donovan pointed out.

"I plan to, but Leatherleaf forest is thick in the areas surrounding the Folly. Your horses will have trouble getting through, and our wolves, as skilled as they are moving through trees, still move faster in a straight line. The king told me to return soon, and I do not plan to waste a whole day giving the Folly a wide birth. We will pass on the outskirts and that should be enough."

"Fine with me," Rohawk agreed.

Donovan tossed his wooden skewer, now empty of meat, into the fire. "I hope you're right. That lady scares me."

Rohawk took off his boots and socks and put them near the fire. Everyone watched him with confused looks on their faces.

"Already soaked through," he said. "Need a new pair."

"To be honest, I am more worried about King Santos than Lady Renna," Donovan said.

"The Crowned of Kaldaran?" The general asked. "Do you believe he has truly accessed divine power?"

Donovan considered the question. "After what I saw, I would be more insane to disbelieve it. I am not speculating, General. King Santos took blow after blow and did not go down."

The general shrugged. "Cutting off the head always seemed to work for me."

Donovan did not respond. The general clearly didn't understand what was happening. *To be fair, I don't understand it either.*

Chapter Twenty-four

Donovan pulled his hood down further as the group rode into Leatherleaf Forest. The air was cold in the shade of the trees, and being one of only two people on horseback, he stood out like a green leaf in winter. The pace felt agonizingly slow as they navigated through the trees.

"Worried?" Altera asked Donovan. "Lady Renna will think twice about messing with a small army."

Donovan looked at her. "You underestimate her royal craziness."

"She can be remarkably petty," General Kadin agreed. "Stay alert. If we have to fight our way out of here, we will."

Altera furrowed her brow. "Then how will we get back to Fallavon?"

"One thing at a time," the general answered.

"Yes, first the Queen of Madness, then the King," Rohawk bellowed over the sound of crunching leaves.

"Could you talk a little louder?" Donovan asked. "Do you really have to keep making yourself so noticeable?"

Rohawk smirked and said nothing. Donovan caught the man sneaking glances at Altera. *Rohawk has chosen his beautiful feyla to try and woo.*

The forest went on and on for what seemed like forever. Donovan's horse seemed tired of navigating around the trees, turning this way and that. At one point they all dismounted to give the animals a break, since they weren't going much faster than walking speed anyway.

A sound of a trumpet report turned everyone's heads to the north, toward Boroshard's Folly. Out of the trees, a small group of soldiers approached. With them were Lady Renna and her daughter.

"Bag of bones," Rohawk muttered. "She came all the way out here just for us?"

"Who is it that leads this army so arrogantly through my forest?" the lady called out.

"It is not arrogance that compels me to be here, my Lady," the general answered as he walked over to her. He and all the Fallavon soldiers were still dismounted, but the fey looked ready to mount in an instant, either to run or to fight. General Kadin gave a half bow, then explained, "We are off to fight Kaldaran."

Lady Renna snarled. "In the name of that mangy cat? King Beldon?"

The General stiffened but kept his composure. "Yes, and in the name of Nightingale."

The Lady's eyes glazed over for a second, the same way they looked when she had her visions. "Ha!" she suddenly spat out. "Just as well I let you be off to it, then."

"She is letting us go?" Donovan asked Rohawk.

"Thank you," General Kadin said with another half bow.

"I will warn you," she hissed. "King Santos is Crowned. If you think mortal weapons can harm a Crowned, you are riding into your deaths."

That caused a stir amongst the soldiers. Her words added credibility to what Donovan had already told them.

"We will take our chances, my Lady," General Kadin said in a tight voice.

"You have been taking your chances this whole time, traveling with the Shadow Walker, and his friend, the soulburned."

"Bag of bones," Donovan whispered.

"You know that when Donovan remembers, the world will end, do you not, *General* Kadin?" She said his title with a mocking tone. "I should do everyone a favor and end you all here and now."

The general gave Lady Renna a glare so icy the winter wind felt warm. "Is that right, my Lady?"

Lady Renna suddenly looked unsure. Unless she had more soldiers hiding in the trees, she was outnumbered three to one. Her eyes glazed over for a moment, then she seemed to give a start like she was coming back to reality. She scowled again and opened her mouth, but her daughter stepped in, gently grabbing her arm.

"Mother, let these soldiers go. It will only bring trouble to fight with them."

Lady Renna glared at her daughter for a few seconds, then let out a huff. "Fine. I suppose I do not need to bother you. Besides," her scowl turned to a wicked smile, "I will simply let King Santos do the job for me."

"When we return, we expect hospitality," the general said, a hint of warning in his voice. "A visit from you will not be required."

Lady Renna's face twisted into rage. "You will regret this! You will all die!"

The general smiled, then waved for everyone to keep moving.

"Ha!" Rohawk said, loudly enough for Lady Renna to hear.

"I know who you are, Shadow Walker!" she rounded on him. "And I know you will betray your friends!"

The group of soldiers was already moving, ignoring Lady Renna's warning. Donovan caught Rohawk giving her a rather rude gesture with his hand before he turned back to focus on riding.

"Was that really necessary?" Donovan asked.

Rohawk shrugged. "You're not a fan of her predictions, either. Why do you care?'

Donovan thought for a moment. "Now is not the time to be making more enemies."

"Yes, but you have a friend like me. And Altera."

Altera looked over at him. "I agree with Donovan on this one."

Rohawk looked a bit deflated for a split second, but he was quick to hide it. "Nothing to do about it now but press on."

Another full day and a half of hard travel, and Nightingale was coming close. The group had no encounters with Kaldaran yet, but the signs that Kaldarans had been moving in the area were clear.

The plan was to meet up with the scouts from Fallavon. King Beldon had sent them the day Donovan arrived in the fey city, and by now they would have a much better handle on what was going on than anyone else. Donovan hoped introductions between the scouts and Nightingale had gone smoothly, and that their presence gave his city some hope.

The general led the army to the designated rendezvous point, but when they arrived, the Fallavon scouts were nowhere to be seen. A battle had obviously taken place. There was black and red blood in the snow, but only Kaldaran bodies. Everyone hoped that meant Fallavon had won. The alternative was that they were taken prisoner.

From there, Donovan stepped in to track the battle survivors. Paw prints indicated that Fallavon had won. He led the army through the snow-covered lands, and when they crested a snowy hill, Altera spotted the Fallavon scouts and got their attention.

Meeting up with those Fallavon faithful was like good friends reuniting after being apart for years. They gladly welcomed the secret army and exchanged short bows and hugs before settling down around a campfire together. It was just before sundown.

The leader of the scouts, Paval, started to go over all they had seen. "There was a band of about fifteen Kaldaran bastards that tried to ambush us yesterday. Had we not been caught off guard, we would have suffered no casualties. As it stands, Reena and Jonna are dead, but we killed all of them in answer. Our wolves do much better in the snow than their horses, but things are worse around here than we thought."

"Worse?" Donovan asked.

"Kaldaran occupies Nightingale," Paval answered.

Donovan felt his stomach drop.

"They are all inside?" the general asked.

"Yes. When King Beldon sent us, the last we heard was that Nightingale was struggling, but still under control of the City Guard. That has changed, but with your help, we are prepared to retake the city."

The general shook his head. "Not sure if we can do that. If they took Nightingale, they are probably strong enough to hold it against a hundred troops."

Paval was tying his long purple hair up into a bun so it would be out of his face for eating the pork that was almost done cooking. The scouts had captured a couple wild boars and were about to cook them when General Kadin's forces arrived. "What did you have in mind, friend?" he asked.

Donovan had hardly heard the last minute of conversation. Alexis was dead. She would never leave Nightingale—she would fight 'til the last. He stood, frozen in a cold far harsher than the winter around him. Frozen all the way to his soul. How long had he been gone? It wasn't right. He wasn't gone long enough for this to happen. That's what he kept telling himself. He stood up and walked several paces away from the fire, the conversation fading out as he stared out into the cold horizon.

After a moment, Altera was at his side. "Are you alright?"

Donovan shook his head. "Someone I love…she is dead. She was part of the City Guard of Nightingale."

"You…you had a mate?"

Donovan shook his head again. "Not a mate. But…I loved her, and we were…hoping to become mates."

"I understand this pain. I had a mate once. He was a strong feynar, a dragon warrior. An elite feynar soldier assigned to protect my father, the alpha of our clan. He died a good death in battle against the humans of Driggon." Altera paused, her eyes dropping before she continued. "The armor I wear was his, as is the weapon."

Donovan was overwhelmed with his own grief, but he forced out the words, "I'm sorry to hear that." He didn't know why Altera was telling him this. Maybe she considered him a friend.

"We do not want to wait that long," Paval's voice sounded from the camp. "They have prisoners, and we want to get them back."

Donovan snapped to attention and quickly walked back. "There are prisoners in Nightingale?"

"For now. We got one of the Kaldarans to squeal like a pig." Paval took a big bite of pork and devoured it quickly. "He said they would be offering sacrifices to Kaldar every night for the next two weeks and that Kaldar would come down with his wrath and kill all of us. I decided I'd rather not have to spend another minute with that Kaldaran murderer. So I killed him. Problem solved!"

"If they are offering sacrifices every night for two weeks," Donovan said, "that means at least fourteen prisoners."

"Not necessarily—Kaldarans sometimes sacrifice each other," Rohawk said. When Donovan glared at him, he added, "But yes, most likely."

Altera nudged Donovan, and whispered, "Tell them!"

Donovan took in a breath, then said, "Someone I care deeply about is in the city."

"How do you know?" Paval asked. "We only know they have prisoners, not who they are."

"She wouldn't abandon her duty," Donovan explained. "She's there, and if there is even a small chance she is alive, I want to try and retake Nightingale right away."

Paval looked up at Kadin. "General? What do you say?"

The general nodded. "The sooner the better."

"I still think it's smarter to wait for raiding parties to come out and ambush them," Rohawk put in. When Donovan shot him a glare, he added, "I want to see Alexis alive too, but we need to think about what we can do to defeat Kaldaran so we don't all die in the process."

General Kadin shook his head. "We do not have that kind of time. The king wants us back as soon as possible. There may not be a Fallavon we are welcome back to if we take too long."

"We're not exactly welcome in Fallavon as is," Altera joked.

"But what about King Santos?" Rohawk asked, ignoring her comment. "I'm not saying we pay any attention to Lady Renna's warning, but Donovan spoke true about him. I saw the man survive wounds that would kill any other. I have no doubt in my mind of that."

Donovan shifted nervously. If King Santos was Crowned, truly Crowned, they couldn't kill him.

"If this is true, why not capture him alive?" Paval suggested.

Donovan's eyes were lost in the fire, but he heard Paval and answered, "That's a possibility, but it will be difficult. I saw his strength—it's far beyond that of any normal man."

"It's something, though," Rohawk said. "Maybe he can still die if the wound is bad enough."

"Like I said, a clean cut to the neck and the head comes right off!" General Kadin mimed the action.

It can't be that easy. Donovan thought. *King Santos was far too confident in the battle at Crandell's farm. He knew he couldn't die.*

The conversation continued, but Donovan was checked out, his eyes focused on the fire, enjoying its warmth, admiring its beauty, and wondering what would happen if he came face to face with King Santos again.

Something in the fire stirred. The flames danced in unnatural ways. Donovan looked around the camp to see if anyone else noticed, but they were all gathered around Rohawk as he drew them a map of the city. He looked back into the fire, and the flames slowly shifted. A moment later, they looked vaguely like that bronze king.

King Santos is too strong for you to defeat on your own. Donovan heard the voice inside his head. **Lady Renna's prediction was correct.**

What do I do, then?

Lady Renna can only see what her god tells her. Wise, her god is, but also foolish. It is time we make a play of our own.

But who exactly is we *in this scenario? Who are you, bronze king?*

Someone you can trust. I told you that you are my champion. I do not intend to lose you again.

Donovan nodded. *Again, I ask, what do I do?*

Find the book. The one you left in the Chapel of K'var. King Santos has not found it, because I have hidden it from him. But you must hurry.

Is Alexis alive?

Find the book.

"Is Alexis alive?" Donovan said, aloud, to the fire.

"We have no way of knowing that," Paval answered. "But we are trying, Donovan. Please, come over here and look over our plans."

The image in the fire had disappeared. Donovan sighed and walked over to see what Rohawk and the others had come up with.

"We have wolves, I would like to get those into the city," the general said plainly.

"I will sneak in and kill the gate guards and open the gate," Rohawk suggested.

Donovan shook his head. "Those gates are loud and take two people to open."

Rohawk took a bite of the steaming hot pork one of the others handed to him. "Then you will come with me, Donovan," he said through a mouthful. Donovan was not much of a burglar, but he did know the city pretty well, and if Alexis was alive, he was going to get her.

"Alright, I will go with you. I recommend the City Gate, to the north." Donovan pointed to the crude drawing of the gate. "It's a little bit lighter, so it will be easier to open fast. Once we start turning the crank, it's going to raise gol in there."

"Gol is my specialty," Rohawk said, then turned to Paval. "Once the gate is open, all of you rush in and kill anything with a Kaldaran tabard."

The general smiled, then clapped his hands together. "I like it! Finally a chance to kill some Kaldarans again!"

Shouts of agreement rose from the group.

Donovan smiled a little. He was worried to death for Alexis, but there was a chance she was alive.

"I propose we do not wait," Paval said. "My soldiers are ready. We should go in the middle of the night."

The general nodded. "That will give a few hours of rest for my soldiers before we attack. I suggest you all take it. Tonight, we strike back against Kaldaran."

"What about King Santos?" Rohawk asked.

There was an awkward pause in the camp as everyone looked around, expecting someone else to say something.

"I will deal with him," Donovan said, breaking the silence. Rohawk raised his eyebrows at that. The general smiled and clapped Donovan on the back.

"Not if I get to him first, yes?" The general laughed.

"We have a plan, then," Paval said. "Everyone prepare as he or she sees fit."

The fey followed those orders. Some were looking over their weapons, tending to their wolves, or getting a couple extra hours of sleep. Those who chose to sleep would be ordered to do exercises before the attack to get their adrenicka flowing again.

Donovan considered all those options—minus the exercise—but couldn't decide on anything. He couldn't sleep. Checking over his gear took him all of a few minutes. He ended up pacing nervously near the campfire.

Altera came over, armor in hand, and took a seat. She pulled out a rag and started polishing it. "Do you really think this King Santos fellow is Crowned?"

Donovan stopped his pacing. "I do. I can't think of any other explanation, and if you knew me, you would know how skeptical I am."

"Not sure about that."

"What do you mean?"

"You said that you believe he can take mortal blows and live. And you are still willing to try and take him down? One of those things has to be false."

Donovan did not respond.

Altera looked back to her polishing. "As you know, my father is alpha of the wolf clan in the east. I have four brothers and three sisters. All my brothers are soldiers, and my three sisters are all married off to what you would call nobles. But not me. I was widowed, so I chose to fight. Father has never approved. We had an argument before I left home. He would not allow his pack leaders to teach me fighting, so I came to Fallavon to find someone who would."

"What will your father think when you return home?"

Altera paused her work. "He may disown me, and I will be a lone wolf."

Donovan nodded slowly. "I'm sorry to hear that."

Altera finished the piece of armor she was working on. It shone brilliantly in the light of the fire as the flames reflected off radiant metal. "We both know that sometimes it takes more courage to return home than to leave." With that, she rose, armor in hand, and walked over to her tent, disappearing inside.

"Women, am I right?" Rohawk was suddenly there, a couple steps away.

Donovan glared at him. "Don't do that. It's a bit unnerving."

Rohawk chuckled. "On a more serious note, I'm counting on you tonight, Donovan. This won't be easy, and if we fail, you are probably dead. I will be escaping for my life."

"How reassuring that you are counting on me to be the distraction while you get away."

Rohawk put a firm hand on Donovan's shoulder. "We're not the smoothest bunch…"

Donovan laughed, remembering the words shared at the Thirsty Horse with the Thirteenth Division. "But we're the best Nightingale's got."

It felt very strange for Donovan to be coming back to Nightingale unwelcome. The ratty trade town he loved didn't look that much different, but the banners of the Eye of Kaldar waved wickedly in the breeze atop the posts of the City Gate, proclaiming that the god of chaos and blood sacrifice had taken claim of the town. Before, Kaldaran had always been a distant evil. Donovan knew there was wickedness in the world—he witnessed it daily. But pure evil had never visited home before. Now, his home belonged to it.

Rohawk had advised ditching the cloaks, as they were too easily caught on something, or grabbed by an opponent during a fight. He insisted that, with all they had to do, Donovan would be wanting to shed layers before long. He also had to ditch the chainmail, which he was less happy about. Paval made a comment about how real feynars fought shirtless, but Donovan noticed he remained clothed.

Under the cover of night, Donovan and Rohawk were brought to just outside the city by riding double with Paval and one of his feylas, Brandwyn. Their horses were to be brought in with the rest of the army once the gate was open. When they were close, Rohawk and Donovan dismounted. Then they went to work. Rohawk had taught Donovan a few easy hand signals, and he gave the signal to follow. The two were off into the bitter cold, trudging through snow up to mid-calf.

"Please be alive, Alexis," Donovan said to himself in barely a whisper.

The cold stones that made the wall of Nightingale were getting closer. Torchlight in the watchtowers illuminated four men, two for each tower. That would be the security of the City Gate they would have to silence.

"Alright, here is where we split up," Rohawk said. "Take your time and go wide of the watchtower, then make your way back to it without being seen. Watch for me and make sure I am there and ready, then I will give you the signal to go. You must kill those men in the tower as fast as you possibly can. It isn't ideal, but everyone is counting on us. Ready?"

No, was the truth, but Donovan said, "Yes," and they split up.

Donovan followed Rohawk's instructions and went wide of the tower. They were lucky for cloud cover—a full moon reflecting off the snow would have been like attempting this during the day. He made it to the wall, and now came the first hard part.

Donovan was a damn good climber—he had done quite a bit out on hunts with Ramon and Lionel. There was a spot that he knew would be the best for getting in without being spotted by the tower. He had watched someone get in that way once when he returned late from a hunt. He never knew who it was, but he now realized that the person was about the right size to have been Banner. He hoped that she was safe somewhere with her grandfather.

Upon close inspection of that spot, Donovan saw that Banner had shoved metal pegs into the mortar in several spots. Small enough to not be noticed, but sticking out just enough to provide footholds. Barely. She was lighter and nimbler than he, and it took all his effort to make it up and over the wall. On the last part of the climb, he pulled himself up and over with all his might. He hung down at arm's length from the top of the other side before dropping, cushioning his fall as best he could. There was no response from inside the town—the snow had covered the sound of his entry.

The silence was maddening. It felt as if one little noise would be like a trumpet blast alerting all Kaldarans to his location. He crossed in between houses and toward the watchtower, taking care not to breathe too loudly. A faint orange glow stopped him cold, and he made himself as small as possible as he watched two Kaldaran guards walk past, torches in hands. They went by without looking at Donovan's hiding spot between two houses.

When the light from their torches had faded, Donovan moved and found the ladder for the watchtower. This was it. A torch near the bottom made him uneasy, but the other tower had one, and it was how he was able to see Rohawk. The man looked like he had been waiting. He held up his hand in a fist, then opened it and waved it forward. That meant go.

Donovan skipped several rungs as he vaulted up the ladder. The two watchmen turned to him, and both muttered something in surprise, but did not process what was happening in time. Donovan shoved a dagger in the throat of one, then moved immediately to grab the neck of the other. It was a grim way to end a life, but he had no choice other than to cut the airway of the other Kaldaran with his bare hands.

"You didn't have to come here," Donovan whispered as the last of the Kaldaran's life slipped away.

When both were dead, Donovan put his hands on the wheel used to lift the gate. He looked over and saw Rohawk was successful and was doing the same. He gave the same signal as before, and the two put all their might behind cranking the wheels. The chains rattled and groaned against their spindles, and before long, voices were sounding from the town. Donovan quietly prayed to any god who might chance to give a damn, asking for time as he cranked the wheel harder and harder. The voices coming from Nightingale grew louder. They would soon sound the alarm, and once they came to investigate the towers, it was over.

"Come on," Donovan grunted to himself. It seemed like an eternity, each turn of the wheel being painfully slow. He heard the padding of great wolf paws in the snow from outside. They were almost there. Donovan pushed with all his might.

"Hey, you!" a voice shouted from below. "Who authorized the openin' of the gate?"

Donovan did not respond. He pressed with all of his might, his muscles aching.

"Hey! Stop that!" the voice said, now from the bottom of the ladder. Donovan stifled a roar as he turned the wheel one more time and heard the rush of wolves coming into Nightingale. He pulled down the bar that would lock the gate in place, then turned just in time to see a Kaldaran cresting the ladder, sword in hand. Donovan kicked with all his might and broke the man's nose, sending him back down the ladder and into the snow. He then drew his arming sword and hurried after, jumping from about halfway down to land a downward thrust and kill the Kaldaran.

It was chaos at the bottom. King Beldon's faithful cracked bones with their wooden blades, and their *ferlons* shredded through chain mail with their claws and ripped out throats with their teeth. Fresh, red blood sprayed onto the streets. Donovan looked around for Altera and saw her coming in with two horses in tow.

Donovan mounted and looked at the Fallavon soldiers. Some of them seemed to be awaiting his command. "This way!" he shouted and led them down Broken Street. It was a mess of a road with random twists and turns and was crowded by buildings, but it would hide them and confuse the Kaldarans, who were still shaking the sleep out of their eyes.

Donovan felt a twinge of dread. *King Santos?* He swallowed hard and tried to ignore it. The Chapel of K'var was first, then he would face King Santos head on.

Further down Broken Street, Donovan called for a sudden turn, and the Fallavon wolves exploded out of an alleyway and into a group of Kaldaran soldiers who were looking toward the City Gate, wondering where their enemies had gone. Altera was at Donovan's side, using the reach of her large axe to kill the attacking Kaldarans before they could reach her. It was a clumsy weapon to be using mounted, but she made it look clean. Someone in Fallavon had been teaching her well.

Donovan shuddered at each flashing orange blade he saw coming from the Kaldaran soldiers. He was surprised to see how well the fey dealt with it. When the Kaldarans tried to use magic against them, the fey would step out of measure and let the magic go to waste as the Kaldarans swung wildly through the air, missing their targets.

Of course, that wasn't aways the case. Donovan watched a feynar get cut clean in two by a *Sunder* technique. He moved swiftly to avenge him.

The fighting had exploded now into an all-out blood bath. The advantage the fey had was spent and the Kaldarans were striking back in full force. The curious mix of black and red blood colored the untouched snow on the sides of the streets and ran down the stones and siding of homes.

Paval was possibly as much of an animal as his great wolf was. He swung those wooden blades with such speed the cracking of the weapons sounded like the beat of an enthusiastic drummer.

Donovan had been locked in the battle long enough that he did not realize where he was, until he saw the front door of his old home. There was a break in the fighting; he decided to go inside.

All of his once-precious furs were gone—looted by the Kaldarans. The place smelled something awful. Dirty cots were strewn about where the furs once were, and even the back room had been gone through. Most of his tools were still there, scattered about, deemed useless by a Kingdom that stole from others instead of make anything themselves.

Donovan thought about going upstairs to where Martha had died. But he knew he couldn't stay here. Not when others were outside spilling blood for his cause. Not when there was a chance Alexis was still alive. He had to find her. He had to find the book.

One thing at a time, he thought. He turned around to the entrance and froze.

"There you are," King Santos said. He stood inside the door, sword drawn, black blood on it. "I see you brought an army with you. Kaldar is pleased by the bloodshed, but he will be more pleased when we throw you on the altar and offer you to him."

"That's not going to happen," Donovan said. He felt a wave of dread hit him, but he pushed back against it as he had done before.

"You are far stronger than all the others, but you cannot defeat a Crowned." King Santos sheathed his sword bloody and pulled out a small, wicked looking knife. The bottom of the hilt was a serpent's eye, and the blade had a slight curve to it.

Donovan thought back to the bronze king. He had told him to get the book; did he stand a chance without it? Before he could decide, King Santos was on him. The man moved like lighting, and it was all Donovan could do to bring his sword to bear. King Santos walked into the blade, taking a stab to the gut. It didn't slow him one bit. He brought that wicked dagger down and landed a shallow cut on Donovan's chest.

The cut burned with pain unlike anything Donovan had felt before. He grunted in agony, but did not give up. He brought his sword around and cut King Santos straight to the bone of his left leg.

"It's useless!" King Santos taunted. "Give up and die!"

"That doesn't sound half bad right now, but I've got other plans." Donovan slammed his shield into King Santos and knocked him aside, then he bolted for the door. A knife thudded into the door frame just above his head, and he didn't stick around to see how close he had been to death. He jumped atop his horse and raced out of there, toward the Chapel of K'var.

He's going to the chapel! Kill him!

Donovan heard the voice in his head. It was like with the bronze king, but this was another king, King Santos. It sent a shiver down his spine. He raced down an alleyway but was quickly cut off by Kaldarans. He stopped and brought his horse around to turn back, but was cut off again.

"Gol!" he spat. "King of bronze, you have guided me before. Is this what you have led me to?"

No response.

"Get off your horse, now!" sounded Rohawk's voice right next to him.

Donovan's eyes bulged. "How did you get here?" Rohawk answered by pulling Donovan down off his horse. The Kaldarans rushed them, and just before they were on them, Donovan felt magic flowing through his veins. But it was not coming from him, it was coming from Rohawk's hand, tightly on his wrist.

"Shadows take us," Rohawk said. The words hummed with the power of Technique, and the world around them shifted.

It looked like they were still in Nightingale, but it wasn't the same. Some of the houses didn't look right. Some were bright and clear as the day, in the same condition as they were when just built. But others were covered in vines, or moss, or reduced to rubble. One house had blood slowly running out from the bottom of the door.

"Rohawk, where the gol are we?" Donovan asked. When he turned to look at Rohawk, he saw a man dressed in black armor, from head to toe. On his chest plate was a heart that was painted half white and half red. "Who...who are you?"

"It's me, Donovan," the black knight said in Rohawk's voice. "We don't have much time. Come with me. If we get separated, you will die."

The two broke into a run through the city, and Donovan saw more strange things that looked like Nightingale but not quite. When they passed his house, it was gone, replaced only by a fountain of blood.

"What is this place?" he asked Rohawk.

"*Harm-Ta*," he answered. "The place of shadows."

"Is this why everyone called you Shadow Walker?"

"Yes."

"Why does everything here look familiar and yet...nightmarish?"

"In *Harm-Ta*, what you see is what the deepest parts of your soul sees."

"Is that why I see you as a black knight? Noble and fallen all at the same time?"

Rohawk stopped at that, and looked at Donovan, though all Donovan could see was eyes behind a helmet. "I suppose I've gotten worse."

"How long can we stay here?"

"Not long. The longer we stay, the greater the risk. There are monsters in here unlike anything you will ever see in your life. No sign of them yet, but they will become more aware of our presence the longer we are here. We need to find somewhere safe to exit."

Donovan did not know if it was safe, but he knew where he needed to get to. "The Chapel of K'var."

"I guess that is as good as any, and far enough inside the city that the Kaldarans might not be there. You will have to help me find it. *Harm-Ta* is a place that you can navigate only once you know the deepest, darkest parts of your soul."

"Could it teach me about things I've forgotten?"

"I don't know, and we don't have time to—" Rohawk froze when an ear-piercing shriek ripped through the air. It sounded like the whine of a rabbit being eaten alive, only magnified a hundredfold and more…guttural. "As I said, no time. Come on."

They broke into a sprint this time. Donovan did not feel that running was wearing him out any. It was like running in a dream. He had to focus his mind to keep running, and when his mind drifted to look at something, he found himself slowing down.

"Keep up, Donovan!" Rohawk called out. "Focus on the task ahead, nothing else." The shriek rang out again. "Not even that, ignore that!"

The houses they ran past were a blur to Donovan unless he focused on them, and when he did, he would slow down. So he kept following Rohawk, and let everything rush past until the Shadow Walker suddenly stopped.

"Is that it?" he pointed. "What do you see?"

Donovan focused where Rohawk was pointing. He saw a giant, hundred-pace tall statue of a woman with two faces. She was holding a scale and weighing out the price of goods. But even at a distance, he could see the scale was weighted.

"A statue of a two-faced woman selling something, but she's cheating the scales in her favor."

"A lying goddess deceiving people?" Rohawk asked. "Sounds like a god-haters description of K'var, especially for everyone from Nightingale right now."

"But it's not a building, it's just a statue," Donovan explained. The shriek rang out a third time, and it sounded much, much closer. Donovan covered his ears, but that did nothing.

Rohawk clapped his hands in front of Donovan's face to get his attention, then made a hand gesture pointing to Donovan's eyes, then to him.

"Right, focus," Donovan said, his words being drowned out by the shriek.

Rohawk took off in another sprint; Donovan followed. He didn't bother looking at anything else besides Rohawk. Staying focused took effort; he felt drained by it. It was all he could do to keep his eyes on the Shadow Walker and hope that Rohawk knew where to go.

A fourth shriek rang out. Donovan looked behind this time and immediately regretted it. They were being chased by a creature that looked vaguely like a dragon, but instead of scales, it had rotting flesh that was sewn together to cover its bones. It was the size of a house, four wings, but one of them was mostly bone and looked useless. It had strangely human eyes, and the flesh that was sewn across it looked like human bodies as if they had been skinned and used for coverings.

"Bag of bloody bones! Is this some kind of punishment for skinning animals?" Donovan shouted. "What the gol is that thing?"

"Don't think about it, just run!" Rohawk shouted back. "Nearly there!"

Donovan focused harder, keeping his eyes on Rohawk, ignoring whatever it was that was chasing them. He chanced a glance at the statue, and saw they were now very close. He looked back at Rohawk and saw with just that glance, he had fallen behind.

There was another shriek, and Donovan heard something whip through the air. He suddenly tripped and fell to the ground, hard. He looked around and saw the flesh dragon had shot out its tongue like a whip and grabbed him.

"Rohawk!" he screamed out. The creature started dragging him towards its mouth.

"Damn it, Donovan!" Rohawk roared back. He hesitated to come help. His helmet disappeared, and Donovan saw his eyes beaming with a fear Donovan had not see before in the man.

Donovan knew he had less than a second to live. He instinctively reached for his sword, and it was there. He pulled it out of its scabbard and wrenched his body into a swing with all he could muster. It was enough. He cut the tongue and freed himself. The flesh monster screeched in agony and stumbled back a few paces.

Donovan hurried to get up, and felt Rohawk's hands on him, pulling him up quickly.

"Not going to tempt fate twice in one go," he said. Donovan felt the hum of Technique, and Rohawk spoke the words, "Shadow walk," again. The world around them shifted, and they were back in the cold evening air of Nightingale, the Chapel of K'var a mere fifty paces away.

The cold air stung—hard. Donovan's body had cooled off in the place of shadows. The sounds of battle clamored somewhere in the city, further north.

"How long were we gone?" Donovan asked.

"Less than a second," Rohawk answered. "At least, I think so. That's how it's always worked for me." The Shadow Walker tugged at his furs. He had cooled off quite a bit too.

"What was that thing? I'm getting chills just thinking about it."

"It has an ancient name I won't get into, but it translates to 'what men fear the most.'"

"Well said." Donovan looked over at the Chapel of K'var. "I need to go inside there and get something." He looked back at Rohawk who was staring off to the north.

"Do you feel it? He is coming our way. The Crowned of Kaldaran."

Donovan paused for a quick moment. He felt a twinge of dread, a similar feeling he always had when it came to King Santos.

"I...I can't. This is as far as I go. I'm sorry, Donovan. Best of luck."

"Rohawk, wait!" Donovan called out, but Rohawk had dipped into an alleyway. Donovan ran over and looked down it—no sign of him. "I better hurry, then." He turned to the Chapel of K'var and closed the distance.

Donovan considered what had just happened. He hadn't even heard of this power, though he had wondered why people called Rohawk the Shadow Walker or talked about the shadow in his soul. He had the power to go to another world. That seemed incredibly strong, but that flesh creature...Donovan shuddered. He didn't want to face that thing again for any reason. Next time, he might just take his chances against the dozen or so Kaldarans.

The chapel's stone steps were right in front of him now. Donovan took in a stinging, cold breath and exhaled vapor. The giant, wooden double doors had always looked imposing, but now they loomed like the gateway to gol itself. Dried blood stained the door in a splatter pattern, and someone had painted a crude eye of Kaldar on it.

He walked up the steps, placed his hand on the wooden door, and hesitated only a moment before pushing it open.

The temple was ransacked. The pew benches were splintered, the banners that once held the symbol of the Kingdom of K'var laid on the floor, shredded, covered in blood. But oddly enough, the torches were lit, casting orange light that grew faint near the center of the large room.

At the end of the chapel, the idol of K'var had been beheaded, her head replaced with that of the former King Santos, decayed but still frozen in the scream that was his last breath. Below that was a stone altar, upon which rested a woman. That's why the torches were lit; the Kaldarans were interrupted in the middle of a sacrifice.

Donovan's heart pounded. He took several quick steps to get a better look. "Alexis!" he called out. He saw her turn her head slightly toward him.

"Donovan!" she breathed out. "It's you! You came for me."

Donovan ran the rest of the way and took a good look at her. Her hair was a bit matted and dirty, her arms bruised with rope burns underneath her wrists, partially covered by iron shackles that held her in place now. She had smatterings of blood here and there, and wounds that were partially healed on her legs and chest. Her clothes were torn, but still intact.

"When they all rushed out to the sound of the alarm, I hoped and prayed that it was you," she said. "But how did you get them so riled up?"

"I'm here with an army from Fallavon. King Beldon accepted our deal."

Alexis smiled, her bottom lip reddened by a split. Her eyes were twinged with a little pain, but she smiled wider. "I just kept hoping you would come rescue me."

"You're not exactly rescued yet. Do you know where the key to these chains is?"

"No idea. Just give me your sword."

Donovan handed it over, and Alexis spoke, "*sunder.*" The bright orange glow of human magic illuminated the altar, and she cut the chains holding her hands, then the ones on her feet. "Donovan, we must get out of here. I feel a growing sense of dread that I think is from the Crowned of Kaldaran."

"I think Rohawk felt the same thing, but it's barely there for me. First, I have to find the key to the chest, then we can be on our way."

"The chest? Do you mean the sacred box of K'var?"

Donovan was already looking around for—grimly enough—the body of the priestess. Chances were, she would have the key on her. "Yes, the same one. Do you know if the priestess is around here?"

"They…sacrificed her a few days ago. I don't know what they did with her body."

"Wait, what am I doing? You can sunder the chest open, can't you?"

Alexis grimaced. "That would go against a significant part of what I believe in. I still would, but I don't think we have that kind of time. The chest has a binding enchanted with elementium. It will resist sundering. I could do it given enough time and energy, but I don't think I have either."

Donovan continued searching for the key, then took a moment to examine the chest itself. He had not seen it the first time, but Alexis was right. A blue elementium crystal was embedded in the back of the chest, enchanting the binding. Even if they tried to sunder through the wood parts, the binding was thick and intricate. They wouldn't be able to get the book out or access the lock.

"Donovan, we need to go. He's near," Alexis warned.

"We can't run forever. I need what's inside this chest to defeat him."

"What do you mean?"

Donovan thought about trying to explain it to her, but time was very short. "I had a vision, and I think I can trust it. The chapel has a back way out, doesn't it?"

Alexis nodded. "If you're about to suggest—"

"Go. I will try to find a way to get this open."

"I can't abandon you."

"You're not abandoning me. I just want you to be safe."

Suddenly, the doors to the chapel flung all the way open and Toby, King Santos of Kaldaran, walked in.

"I knew ya would come back," he said, his sword drawn as he slowly approached Donovan.

"Run!" he screamed to Alexis. She hesitated, but suddenly a knowing look crept into her eyes. She was scheming something, but turned and ran out the back door anyway.

"She won't make it out of the city," King Santos said as he stepped closer. "But good on you for tryin'. Takes a lot of courage to stand up to me. I just had the pleasure of seeing Fallavon soldiers soil themselves as they attempted to put up a fight against me."

"That's actually a form of a battle cry to them," Donovan shot back. He was trying to buy time, trying to open the chest by getting his knife under the lid, wiggling the lock. "And I'm not sure you're one to talk courage; you betrayed all of Nightingale and murdered the people who treated you and your crew well."

"And Fallavon murdered many of my people and forced us into a treaty instead of settlin' matters like true warriors."

Donovan couldn't resist standing up and pointing his knife at King Santos. "Your people were the ones who brought outsiders into that conflict."

"Of course ya believe everything King Beldon said to ya. Ya have guts, Donovan, I'll give ya that. But it's over."

Donovan turned back to the chest, and gave it one more try, but it wouldn't open.

"Nothin' in there can save ya. Turn and face yer death like a man."

Donovan did that and also drew his sword and readied his shield. He did not charge. He needed to buy more time until he thought of a way to get to the book.

"Kaldar told me ya wouldn't go down without a fight. He also told me who ya were before ya soulburned yerself. I can't believe I bought furs from you and shared ale with you this whole time without knowing who you were."

"Funny, I feel the same way about you."

"But I was a mere mortal back then," Toby continued. "Now, I am Crowned, but you," he raised a finger, "are still mortal."

King Santos roared and Donovan fell back as if he was hit by a moving wall of bricks. He stood up just in time to raise his shield to King Santos's falling sword. The sword was deep black, and whatever magic was affecting it, he did not want to find out the hard way.

"Impenetrable!" he said, reaching out for Technique the way he had seen so many others do time and time again.

Nothing but emptiness.

King Santos's blade felt like a large hammer as it slammed the shield. A crack broke through the air and Donovan screamed in agony as his arm went limp, the shield of Nightingale slipping off and falling to the ground with a clank. He gathered just enough strength to react and thrust his sword into Toby's gut. The King of Kaldaran smiled and pulled the sword the rest of the way in, all the way up to the guard.

"What made you think such an attack would work this time?" he said with a wicked smile. He kicked Donovan in the chest and sent him staggering back.

Donovan tried to stay standing and fumbled halfway across the chapel. He was putting a little distance between himself and King Santos, but pain was exploding in his ribs and back. He gained his balance and took steps back towards the front doors, with King Santos following slowly, savoring the moment. Donovan's vision was blurry but clearing, and when it did, he saw Alexis near the altar, stepping lightly toward the chest. A key was in her hand. *She found it. She must have found where they tossed the body of the priestess.*

King Santos laughed. "Such a stupid mortal! Is this what the gods are afraid of? A broken man crawling away in retreat? What a perfect champion you are, Donovan! Mortals have forgotten the gods, and you are like them, having forgotten yourself! Did you really think a man without a soul could ever stand against the power of a Crowned?"

A spirit shaped like a serpent appeared just above King Santos, coiling its body around his head. The eyes of the serpent were unmistakable. They were the eyes of Kaldar.

Donovan shook his head, trying to dispel the vision, but it was no use. The serpent hissed at him, and he groaned in pain as the feeling of dread finally hit him, going from light, steady pressure to complete agony. He looked over at Alexis. She was fumbling with the key, trying to stay quiet, trying to get the chest to open.

"Even if you kill me, Fallavon will fight you. They will find a way to kill you."

King Santos's cackling laughter echoed through the broken Chapel. "It will be my pleasure to take my vengeance upon the Lion Clan. This is the rebirth of the new Kingdom of Kaldaran, a strong one, with a strong king. I will finish what I started with Fallavon years ago."

Donovan wondered at that. Toby did not start the war with the Lion Clan. Was…Kaldar speaking?

"You will make a good sacrifice, even without your memory," King Santos continued. "Almost a shame, really. You were once a worthy foe. Now just a shadow of your true self. You don't even remember enough to understand a fragment of what I'm telling you."

Donovan shifted to look back at Alexis. She was pulling the book from the chest, her eyes wide. She looked over at Donovan, and he held out a hand and waved it toward him. She nodded and wound up, then threw the book with all her might, grunting with the effort.

King Santos's head snapped to her, then to the book, just as Donovan clutched it from the air. His eyes flared with fury. "What is this? Where did you get that? That book does not have the words of K'var!"

Donovan held the book out toward King Santos. This was his final moment. He had nothing to lose.

King Santos roared and charged forward, Donovan's sword still stuck in his belly, the blade swinging through the air back and forth with the movements of his body. The Crowned raised his dark blade to strike Donovan. In those last few seconds, Donovan's heart and soul called out.

King of my visions, whatever your name may be, if this is your book, if you can hear me, please, honor your servant, Lionel. Avenge your servant, Martha. Give me the strength to fight the god of chaos!

"Impenetrable!" he grunted through his broken ribs.

King Santos's blade came down.

There was a bright flash of light. Donovan felt power rushing through his veins. His back, chest, and shield arm exploded in pain for a moment. Something was wrong. Or maybe, something was right. The pain was similar to mending, and Donovan felt power flowing into him, coursing through his veins. The binding of the book was glowing with a bright white light. When King Santos's dark blade struck it, the blade shattered.

"What?!" King Santos roared. The serpent on his head had disappeared. "This cannot be! I am Crowned!" He dropped the hilt of the dark blade and reached out with his hands to strangle Donovan, but Donovan fought back. He roared a battle cry and brought the book around, slamming it into King

Santos's face. The King of Kaldaran reeled from the blow, tumbling backwards and tripping over a broken pew.

Donovan charged forward, his body whole and singing with life. With both hands he took hold of the book and slammed it into King Santos's face again. Bones cracked, the Crowned's face disfigured and twisted from the force of the blow. But he cried out, still alive.

"You have not won!" Kaldar roared. "You know what will happen if you kill this body! I will find another, a stronger one! Then I will hunt you down and kill you!"

With one hand still clutching the book tightly, Donovan used his other and grabbed his own sword from the king's stomach pulling it free with all his might. "Sunder!" he shouted. He felt the energy flow out from his heart, the sacrifice made, as human magic soared into the blade with orange light. He brought it around, cutting off King Santos's head. The head tumbled to the ground.

Donovan paused for a moment to take it all in. He had done it. He had killed a Crowned. The Crowned were real and he had killed one.

Suddenly, the head of King Santos screamed, and a spirit serpent, the same one as before, flew out from the mouth and into the air before disappearing in the ceiling. Then the scream died out. Toby, the King Santos of Kaldaran, was dead, his mouth frozen open in a silent scream.

Donovan turned and ran for Alexis.

"Donovan!" she said, tears streaming down the sides of her face. "You saved us!"

Donovan set his sword and book aside. "Martha and Lionel deserve the real thanks. They showed me the way. We should visit their graves later. Not to mention your act of bravery there, finding that key. Where was it?"

"I just guessed that they hadn't taken the bodies all that far after the sacrifices. I found a hole dug out back. Thank the gods for the cold or it would have smelled worse, but the poor priestess was near the top. The key was clutched in her grasp…she had died protecting it."

"She played her part protecting this city. It's the least K'var could do for us…"

Alexis nodded, then chuckled with joy.

Donovan put his hand to her face and smiled, tears streaming down his eyes. "It's not quite over yet," he explained. "The soldiers of Fallavon are still outside fighting. Are you well enough to wield a sword?"

"I can try, but I don't know," she answered. "How bad is it out—"

The doors to the Chapel suddenly flew open; General Kadin, Paval, and a few fey soldiers with them rushed in. Their eyes all shone with the power of Adrenicka.

The general took one look at King Santos's decapitated head, then laughed. "I told you cutting off the head always works!"

"General Kadin!" Donovan called back. "How goes the fighting? Where can we help?"

"The battle is won!" Paval roared out. "We are sweeping through the city now to make sure we round up any remaining Kaldaran bastards."

The general turned and gave a hand signal. Paval nodded and took the rest of the soldiers with him back out into the night.

"You did it, Donovan!" the General said, then laughed. "I saw King Santos fighting with some of my feynars. I think the man really was Crowned. How did you best him?"

Donovan looked over at Alexis. She seemed as at a loss of words as he was. "Honestly, General Kadin, I'm not sure I can explain it just yet."

The General gave him a firm pat on the back. "Makes no difference to me. Come! Let's build a bonfire and celebrate!"

Chapter Twenty-five

The fire crackled as Donovan sat in his new home in Nightingale, Captain Gerald's former home, and wrote a letter to King Beldon of Fallavon with an update on Nightingale's progress of rebuilding. Night had already settled in and he was eager to write the letter and be finished with his day.

There was a lot of work to be done, most of it in the dead of winter. The Kaldarans had done a great deal of damage in their short stay. A small section of the city had been burned out, possibly by accident, but nobody knew. All of the alehouses has been raided, which wasn't great for morale. Many of the homes had been ransacked as well.

After Donovan killed King Santos, most of the remaining Kaldarans surrendered. That wasn't like Kaldaran at all, but when Donovan talked to some of them, he immediately knew why. They had lost spirit for the fight, most of them seemed mindless, often unaware of where they were and why. *It was almost like a...soulburn.* Perhaps the Crowned had some influence on them, and when the spirit of Kaldar fled, some of their insanity cleared.

Donovan paused at that thought and considered how much of that detail he should include in his letter to the king. Before he could decide, a knock on the door grabbed his attention.

"Hello," Alexis said from the entry. "May I come in?"

Donovan smiled wide. "Of course."

Alexis walked in and removed her heavy outer cloak, setting it on a hook near the fire. "General Kadin is leaving tomorrow. He says everything here is secure for now, K'var forbid an attack from...well, K'var."

Donovan chuckled. "How ironic would that be."

"No kidding. How are you doing? How is your arm?"

Donovan put his hands on her arms and held her there lightly. "It's fine. I'm fine. Whatever King Santos did to me is gone."

"And...that book..."

Donovan walked over to a chest and produced a key from his pocket. He turned the lock and opened it, pulling the book out.

"I can't use Technique without it," Donovan said. "But as long as I have it with me, I can."

Alexis smiled. "You are the first soulburned to ever use Technique again! Book or no, that's a good start."

"Yes," Donovan said, his eyes drifting to the fire. He picked up another log and set it in, then sighed.

"What's wrong?"

"Still no memory of...my memories."

Alexis shifted a bit. "Maybe it needs time. This is just the first step; the rest is sure to follow."

Donovan smiled a little. "Thanks."

"Any word from King Beldon?"

"I'm writing him now, but now that I know General Kadin is leaving, it might not be necessary. He can fill the king in on everything I would be writing anyway."

Alexis took a seat at Donovan's table, and he joined her. "No sign of Captain Gerald."

"You must be happy," Donovan said with a smile.

"I don't know about that. He was my political adversary, but he still tried hard. When he fled, it killed the morale of everyone who had stayed. It put me in charge, which is what I had always wanted, but...well, let's just say it made me question my own loyalties, and if I should stay."

"But you did."

Alexis looked him in the eyes. "I believed you would return, and I wanted to be here for that. Looks like I was right."

Donovan took her hand. "If the captain comes back, will I have to give up the house?"

Alexis chuckled. "Well first of all, the captain is here, because that's you. And second, I think there would be a riot if that happened. All the survivors hate him, and I don't blame them one bit."

"Good," Donovan said. He and Alexis looked into each other's eyes for a moment. "Can we finally continue our conversation? The one we had before I left?"

Alexis leaned in, her lips meeting Donovan's. He pulled her in closer and deepened the kiss. A primal desire stirred within him, exploding to life. They were safe. They were safe and in love.

They parted the kiss, but Donovan held on to her hands. "Good talk."

She chuckled, her face turning red. "I did not think this would happen. At first I thought there was a good chance you would die, then I was nearly certain I would die."

A sudden knock at the door made Alexis jump a little. She had been like that since King Santos took her prisoner.

"You alright?" Donovan asked.

"I will be."

"You sure?"

She shook her head. "Just answer the door, please?"

Donovan chuckled and did just that. Standing on the other side was Rohawk. He mumbled a greeting and pushed his way past Donovan, nodding at Alexis as he sat down near the fire.

"Come on in," Donovan said with thick sarcasm. "Make yourself at home."

"Can you and I talk?" he asked Donovan.

"Sounds serious," Alexis said as she stood. "I should be going anyway. Rumor has it a shipment of ale came in, and I want to make sure people don't kill each other getting their hands on it." Donovan frowned, but as Alexis passed by him, she whispered, "We will pick up where we left off later. I promise."

He nodded, and she squeezed his arm before going back outside.

"Rohawk, your timing is perfect. For the wrong reasons."

"You're welcome," Rohawk joked, but his heart wasn't in it. "I owe you an apology."

"For saving my life with your shadow thing? I can't be mad about that."

"I didn't save your life. In the end, you saved it yourself. I almost let you get eaten by the Fear, then I left you to face King Santos on your own."

"I suppose," Donovan drew out the words. "But I'm not sure how I would have made it to the chapel without you. Honestly, not to sound ungrateful, but it still baffles me that you've come this far at all. Nightingale can pay you, but it's not what you deserve. Most of the reserves were drained paying mercenaries during the war."

Rohawk seemed to be thinking hard about what he was about to say next. "Someone has a hit out on you."

"I'm sure all of Kaldaran."

"No, this wasn't related to them. Someone put out a hit on you through the cult. The Dark Hand assassins."

Donovan blinked. "What in gol are you talking about?"

"Old, old assassin cult. If my research is correct, they go back tens of thousands of years. If someone contacts them to kill someone, then whoever gets assigned the job has to do it. If that person doesn't, they send someone to kill him."

"And you know all of this how?"

Rohawk gave him a sideways glance.

"Because you were the first one they asked to do the job," Donovan finished the thought.

"Before you ask me why I didn't warn you, I thought they would come for me first and I would take care of it then and there. That's usually how it works. But I guess not always. I'm sorry for what happened to Martha. You cleaned it up good, though. That must have been one gol of a lucky shot, killing that Dark Hand."

"He mentioned something about the vampire. Is that you?"

Rohawk chuckled. "A lot of Dark Hands have their cult names. That one's mine. It has more than one meaning, but I don't want to get into all of them."

Donovan shook his head slowly. He was stunned. "Why would someone put a target on me? Obviously, Vinson tried, but this was before that."

"I don't have the answer to that."

"But you said they asked you to do the job. Didn't they tell you anything about me?"

"It doesn't quite work that way. I don't want to go into details; the less you know the better."

"Are they going to keep trying?"

"I don't have the answer to that either, but that's another reason I've been keeping an eye on you."

Donovan felt a bit nervous at that. *Maybe the Grand Magistrate didn't hire an assassin after all. But that doesn't quite fit. That feynar seemed pushed by ideology. He didn't seem like a contract killer.* "So why didn't you do it?" As soon as he had said the words, Donovan realized how cold it sounded.

Rohawk grinned at first, then laughed. "You still catch me off guard now and then. Would you believe me if I said I don't kill good people? This isn't the first contract I've denied."

"I can believe that, but you've gone above and beyond denying a contract. You've fought for Nightingale. Why?"

Rohawk paused again. The rogue was certainly doing a lot of thinking. "There's something about you, Donovan. I've spent most of my life a rogue, a thief, a mercenary. I have a connection to the world of shadows I can't get rid of, and if Lady Renna is to believed, it will prevent me from getting the thing I want most. Before you ask, no, I'm still not going to answer questions about that."

Donovan shrugged. "That's fine, but I still don't understand the rest of your answer."

Rohawk stood and walked to the door. He put his hand on the latch, but did not open it. "You're soulburned, but you're still trying to remember who you are. I've never met someone so completely teched over who decided to just keep trying anyway. That's impressive. I want to learn how to do that." With that, he gave a nod and was out the door, into the cold of the night.

Donovan stood for a moment soaking in that conversation. He didn't like the idea that cult assassins could still be after him, but he had Rohawk on his side. He hoped they would cancel each other out and he wouldn't have to worry about it.

There was another knock at the door.

"Popular tonight," Donovan mumbled as he went to open it. Alexis was standing on the other side.

"Thought I was going to abandon you?"

Donovan grinned. "Honestly? Yes."

She smiled back. "I have good news. There's plenty of ale to go around, so we're opening the Thirsty Horse for the night. Want to join me?"

"About time! Let's go!"

Donovan woke with a splitting headache. It had been a good night, but a bit too much for his taste. A lot of ale had been brought in, and no one was going to deny the Captain of Nightingale as much as he wanted. Donovan reached that much only two hours in, and then things got really out of hand when people kept pushing more and more drink on him. But everyone had been happy. That meant a lot to Donovan. Things had not been happy in Nightingale for a long time. Even before the Kaldaran invasion, the city was decaying. Now it was bursting back to life.

Donovan bundled up in some furs and got on his feet. First thing was to get a fire going. Out on the dining table, a note had been left with a satchel of herbs on it.

Eodius's special blend. For a rough night of drinking. – Alexis.

Donovan managed a slight smile, which was about all he could do at the moment. Eodius had been one of the survivors from the war. The Kaldarans had kept him around to force him to mend. He started the fire and got some water boiling, then tossed the herbs in and had a cup of tea in no time. He felt his throbbing head starting to soothe.

A knock at the door interrupted his temporary reprieve.

"Too early," he groaned, then went to the door and opened it. There stood a yellow-skinned feynar with orange hair. He gave Donovan a half bow.

"Good morning. I hope I am not too early."

"Not at all," Donovan muttered.

"Pardon?"

"Skot, you're tall, I said."

The feynar blinked. "My name is Ivan, I am a royal messenger in service to his majesty, King Beldon. My instructions were to deliver this message to you. You are Donovan, yes?"

"Yes."

Ivan nodded and held out a letter.

"This couldn't wait until the afternoon?" Donovan said as he took the letter and started to open it.

"I…" Ivan stammered. "I am sorry. I do not know the contents of the letter, so it could be urgent. I arrived in the middle of the night and waited until now to deliver it, so I did try to wake you at a decent hour."

"It's alright. I apologize for being rude. Thank you."

"I will be in town for the night to rest my *ferlon* and gather provisions. King Beldon said he was expecting a response. I will come by tomorrow for it." Ivan gave a half bow and was off.

Donovan shut the door and sat down with the letter. No sooner had he taken a seat, the door opened and Alexis came in.

"Good morning! How are you?"

Donovan managed a weak smile. "Pretty hung over, but alright."

"I am not surprised; they pushed drinks on you pretty hard last night."

"I am taking it as the compliment it is, rather than the splitting headache it…also is."

"Important letter?" Alexis asked as she latched the door tightly.

"Official message from the king. He said he is very happy to hear about the progress we've made rebuilding Nightingale, and expects proper tribute once we are ready."

"When will that be?" Alexis asked. "That seems a bit soon to be asking. I hope he doesn't have high expectations—Kaldaran did a lot of damage around here."

"I think it's his sense of humor."

"Is that all?"

"No, there's more. He wants me back in Fallavon, and Rohawk, if he will come."

"Oh…" Alexis said, her face crestfallen.

Donovan stood and pulled her close to him. "He also extends the invitation to you."

"Oh!" Alexis said with a bit of excitement. "Our first trip together! That could be fun."

"Perhaps…"

She eyed him up and down carefully. "Donovan, what haven't you told me about your time there?"

He sighed. "It's not exactly a safe place for anyone with human blood. But the King mentions that in his letter and is offering an armed escort to make sure we arrive safely."

"Something in your voice tells me you want to go."

Donovan set the letter down and looked back at her. "King Beldon taught me a lot about myself in my short stay there. Not only that, but he took a risk sending so many of his soldiers here to fight for us. He is asking in return that we strengthen the bond between Nightingale and Fallavon by going back and showing his people that humans can be good. The fey live a lot longer than we do, and they hold on to mistrust a lot longer, as well. Considering what we have both been through with Kaldaran, you can imagine how that feels."

Alexis nodded. "I think a visit is a splendid idea."

"This would be longer than a simple visit," Donovan gently warned. "He wants us to stay at least a month, and he is requesting that I learn wolf riding, of all things."

Alexis laughed. "That sounds amazing, honestly. But do you think Nightingale will be alright with us gone?"

Donovan shrugged. "Well, it's been through a lot worse."

"True, but we are more or less running things around here."

"I have an idea for that."

Alexis raised a brow.

"I received a different letter yesterday. Word has reached Ramon and Tybalt about our victory, and they are coming back after they finish a long hunt. It sounds like they will be here within the week. Let's get them set up to help run things around here while we are gone."

"That's a great idea!" she smiled. "Does this mean we aren't leaving right away?"

"The king says he can wait another month. I think that timing should work well."

"Perfect! Anything else in the letter?"

"Queen Philantha asked how I was doing. That is very nice of her. I did not get a lot of time with her apart from the dancing."

Alexis pulled back. "Dancing? Donovan, you went dancing in Fallavon? I heard the dances there are incredible."

"I guess now we *have* to go." Donovan laughed and wrapped his arms around her. "Only if you will be my partner next time."

"Of course," she said as she buried her head in his chest. They stood there for a moment, enjoying each other's company.

Alexis looked up at him. "But first, one more month here in Nightingale."

Inside the Chapel of K'var, Donovan worked on reglazing a broken window. He wasn't skilled enough to come anywhere near the stained glass that was there before, but it was better than nothing.

He sat down on one of the only good remaining pews and took a break. He still had a little way to go on the window, but it was progress.

The book was at his side, as he never left it anywhere. Martha had died for it, and it had pained him to leave it behind on his trip to Fallavon. But now, it was the only way to use human magic. He wasn't going to lose it.

"I like what you've done so far," sounded a voice from behind.

Donovan turned, and the bronze king was there in the Chapel.

"No one here to help you?"

"No one wants to. K'var abandoned us and couldn't even do us the decency of letting us know we were on our own."

"And you don't feel the same way?"

"I do. But the Priestess of K'var kept the book safe, and in the end, that helped save Nightingale. This is the best thing I can do to repay her."

The king came over and took a seat next to Donovan. "That's a kind gesture."

Donovan eyed him up and down. He looked real. Not real in the sense that he looked human. The actual bronze skin and fiery eyes were far too unusual. But he didn't look like only a vision. Donovan slowly reached out to try and touch the king's shoulder, only to freeze when the king's head snapped over to him.

"We have more work to do. A lot more. You've made great progress, but Kaldar is not completely dealt with. I know you're going to Fallavon next. Take the book with you."

"I wasn't planning to leave it. Never again, I hope. I need it to use magic. Do you know why that is?"

The bronze king's eyes gleamed. "You still have a long way to go. I cannot stay, but I wanted to at least let you know that you did a wonderful thing here in Nightingale, and I am proud of you."

Donovan wasn't sure how he felt about that. It felt...good...but also strange.

The king gave him a firm pat on the shoulder, and disappeared the moment he did.

Donovan stood up. "Wait, was that real?" He looked around to see if anyone else had seen what happened, but no one was there. He sighed, and went to pick up his glass knife. When he did, he noticed a single drop of what looked like bronze had dripped onto the pew.

End of Book 1 of the Crowned Series

About the Author

Joseph Wolfe writes primarily for an adult audience interested in clean(ish) books with action, adventure and strong male leads, For more information, blog posts, and upcoming releases, visit merrywolf.com

www.ingramcontent.com/pod-product-compliance
Lightning Source LLC
Chambersburg PA
CBHW031204020726
47499CB00002B/484